We Should Improve Society Somewhat.

COMICS BY MATT BORS

clover ✳ press

COMICS BY
MATT BORS

INTRODUCTION BY
DAN PERKINS
"TOM TOMORROW"

EDITED BY
NATE MURRAY

"WE SHOULD IMPROVE SOCIETY" LOGO BY
MARK KAUFMAN

BOOK DESIGN BY
ROBBIE ROBBINS

ISBN: 978-1-951038-00-7

FIRST PRINTING: MARCH 2020

4 3 2 1   20 21 22 23

PRINTED IN KOREA

CLOVER PRESS:
ROBBIE ROBBINS, PRESIDENT/ART DIRECTOR • TED ADAMS, PUBLISHER
ELAINE LAROSA, OPERATIONS • NATE MURRAY, BUSINESS DEVELOPMENT
TIM BELL, SHIPPING ASSISTANT • ELIZABETH NEE, MARKETING ASSISTANT

CLOVER PRESS
San Diego, Ca.

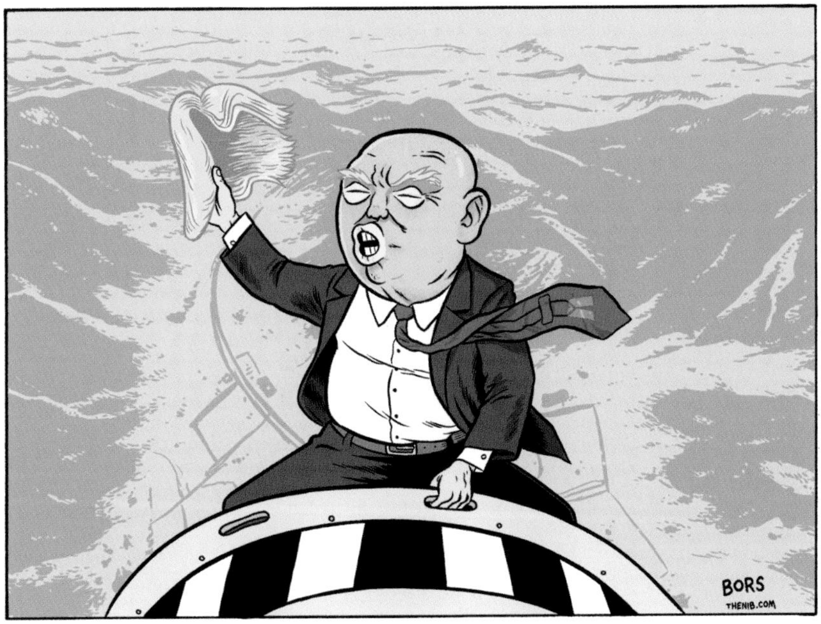
BORS
THENIB.COM

INTRODUCTION

Dan Perkins

("Tom Tomorrow")

More than a few of the cartoons in this book are set in the Wasteland, a post-apocalyptic future in which various mutant and cybernetically-enhanced survivors are ruled by Eternal Overlord Trump. Casual readers may not be aware that these cartoons comprise The Nib Cinematic Universe, a carefully-thought out future history, with its own timeline and internal logic, on which Bors and fellow cartoonist Matt Lubchansky have been collaborating for several years. I, for one, look forward to the box-office dominance of the NCU in ten or twenty years, though of course by then we will be living in the Wasteland ourselves, watching each eagerly-anticipated installment in the burned-out ruins of a former cineplex while we snack on rats we have just roasted over an open fire (pro tip: the sick ones are easiest to catch), all while the future incarnation of Mister Gotcha pops up out of a nearby well to chide us for criticizing society while still attempting to survive in its wreckage.

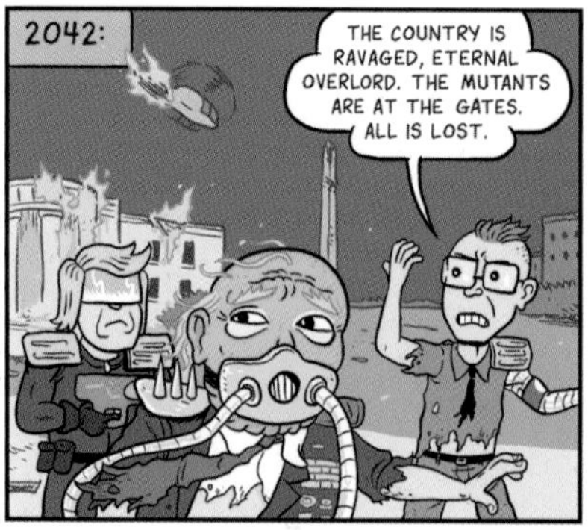
2042:
THE COUNTRY IS RAVAGED, ETERNAL OVERLORD. THE MUTANTS ARE AT THE GATES. ALL IS LOST.

The Wasteland is not a bad metaphor for the State of Political Cartooning, which—as the literally dozens of people who still pay attention to this sort of thing are well aware—is Not Good. Mainstream editorial cartoonists may have spoken truth to power, or skewered hypocrisy with their mighty satirical pens, or whatever boilerplate language you've read in every article bemoaning the slow death of the art form. But they also existed, primarily, to provide a graphic element to break up the text-heavy editorial page, back when such things were published on "newsprint" and distributed by children wearing old-timey caps shouting "Extra! Extra!" Alas, those days are disappearing rapidly, now that we read everything on our pocket computers, and the traditional single-panel editorial cartoon has been orphaned and cast adrift.

Bors' work is probably more influenced by the equally-archaic genre of altweekly cartooning, the weirder, more free-for-all world in which I got my own start. Check the perimeter alarms, children, and then gather around this makeshift campfire while we roast some rats and I tell you of a world in which alternative weekly newspapers were everywhere, free and widely read, and for a comparatively brief historical moment, showcased a wide variety of cartooning work that would never have made it past the gatekeepers of the mainstream dailies. Cartoonists had the freedom to use multiple panels, and have dialogue in word balloons, and other convention-breaking innovations that had never been seen before, at least, if you ignore the entire history of cartoons and comic books outside of the traditional single panel editorial cartoon. Truly was it bliss in that dawn to be alive.

I'm not sure the altweeklies can really claim Bors as their own either, though, as that industry was mostly on life support by the time he arrived on the scene. If (ever-so-slightly) older cartoonists such as myself have done our best to adapt to the darkness of the post-print cartooning Wasteland, Bors was basically born to it. And if paying markets were disappearing faster than a cache of cybernetic limbs in a freshly-uncovered bunker, then by God he was going to invent new ones. With the drive and optimism of a man who gazes upon a hopeless radioactive hellscape and somehow sees undeveloped potential, Bors launched his online comics publication, The Nib. And he found a rich tech guy to pay for it, at least for awhile, until said rich guy inevitably got bored and pulled the funding. And then he found *another* one! And kept The Nib going for several more years! Until the new rich guy also got bored and decided to stop spending the billionaire equivalent of change you dig out of your couch cushions financing Bors' effort to keep this art form alive and interesting and relevant in our brave new digital world. I don't want to shock anyone unduly, but I'm starting to suspect that rich tech guys may not actually be the saviors of journalism *or* cartooning.

But Bors *still* didn't give up. He's like an unstoppable murder robot from the future, except with less killing and more drawing and publishing. When he lost his second funder, Bors took things straight to the audience, and as of this writing, The Nib continues to thrive on the strength of crowdfunding and the enthusiasm of readers who think there's still a place for this increasingly anachronistic art form out here in the Wasteland. As a longtime contributor to The Nib in all its various incarnations, I am grateful for his inexhaustible efforts. Many artists I know (by which I mean, me) are consumed by the task of simply producing their work and hitting their deadlines. Bors has taken it upon himself to not only write and draw some of the very best work being done in this field, but to create a showcase for his colleagues, as well as a

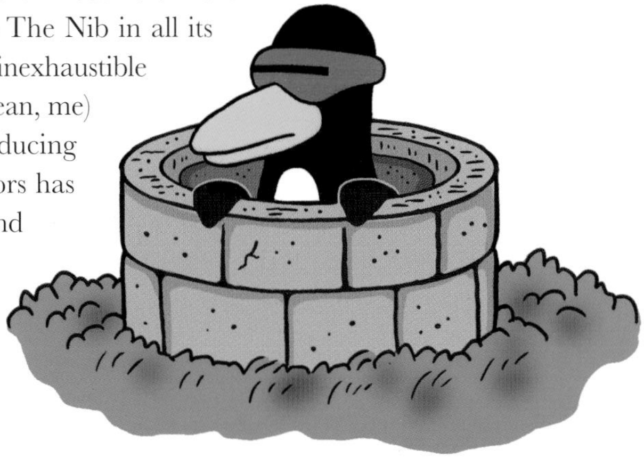

space for younger artists to find their own voices. With a workload that would crush a lesser man (by which I also mean, me), he still manages to put out consistently sharp, perceptive, and, yes, funny cartoons. I don't know how he does it. Maybe he's actually *several* robots from the future.

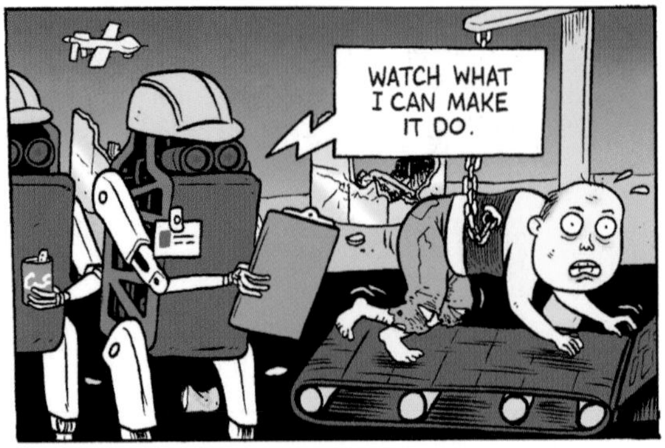
WATCH WHAT I CAN MAKE IT DO.

When you read this book, you are reading the work of an artist at the top of his game. Bors didn't re-invent the editorial cartoon, but he took the older models and adapted them to the rhythm and cadence of the current age. And here's something I want to point out in all seriousness, as corny as it sounds: he's fearless. He takes on everybody. I've had a lot of conversations with him, particularly during the previous administration, when people who were more or less on his side of the political fence were nonetheless very angry at something he had written about a politician they supported uncritically. But pointing out uncomfortable truths is just part of the job, and Bors doesn't shy away from it. Which is not to suggest that he's some disinterested pundit who believes that Both Sides are the Same. Much the opposite—his work is clearly grounded in a place of moral outrage, a belief that people should do the right thing and even your own side (loosely defined) needs to be called out when they fail to live up to their stated ideals, which is of course more often than not.

Contrary to popular belief, the current president has not made the lives of political satirists easier. When someone finds out what I do for a living, they almost invariably say, "Well at least you've got plenty of material these days!" Nothing could be further from the truth. Satire is, more or less, the art of taking things to an absurd extreme in order to make a point—but we are *living* in the absurd extreme. Somehow Bors manages to make it work though, producing work that remains fresh and varied and original, despite the omnipresent exhaustion and dread with which we are all grappling, as we stumble through this Wasteland of life under Trump.

One more thing: I would be remiss in my duties if I concluded this introduction without noting that Bors is also… someone who thinks society should be improved somewhat, who nonetheless contributes cartoons of rare insight and wit to society.

Curious!

HOW TO IMPROVE SOCIETY SOMEWHAT IN *NONE* EASY STEPS

by Matt Bors

Each morning I log into Twitter, take a big sip of coffee, and ready myself to partake in the grand political discourse of the day. More often than not, I find myself tagged in threads wherein a comic I created is used to dunk on some divorced MAGA dad, just after he asks if a queer DSA member posted their critique of society from an iPhone.

A political cartoonist dreams of affecting society with a devastating, perfectly-timed drawing. Daumier's caricature of the king of France was so cutting it led to his own imprisonment. Thomas Nast helped take down Boss Tweed. Paul Conrad made Nixon's enemies list. These days, eh, it's a little different.

My work reached the height of artistic achievement circa 2020 online capitalism: the ubiquitous meme. An unpaid but nonetheless exalted cultural position, in which a work of art has perfectly captured some aspect of the zeitgeist, and thus, allows people to easily respond to people they're mad at instead of thinking of something of their own to say. It's all you ever want as an artist, really.

Way back in 2016 I noticed the "and yet you have a phone!" argument cropping up, and drew what would become my most popular political cartoon. Or rather, my most popular panel, regularly yanked from my political cartoon to sufficiently shame someone's bad-faith argument. In the comic, Mr. Gothcha calls out a phone-haver for criticizing Apple before he moves backward in time; first to reprimand car owners for demanding seatbelts, then further back to medieval times, where a peasant offers a meager opinion: "We should improve society somewhat." Popping up from a nearby well, Mr. Gotcha offers the ultimate take-down: "Yet you participate in society. Curious!"

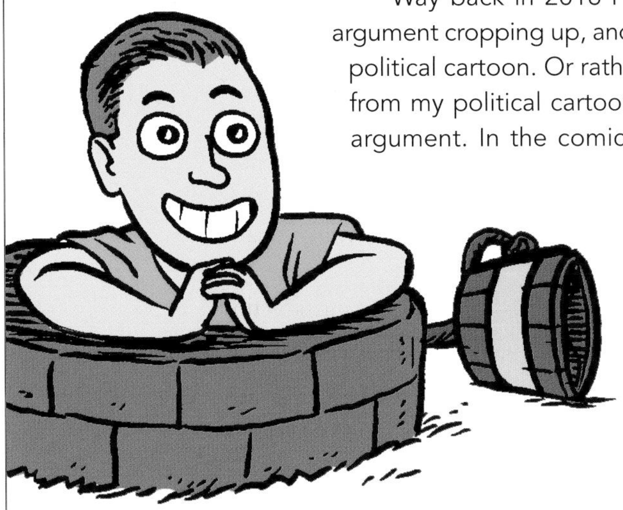

It's now been remixed and edited to undermine my point, make anime references I don't quite follow, and (with surprising frequency) forcefully argue for the superiority of Android phones over Apple. I don't know, man. The comic was fine. It just happened to come along during the early Trump-era, where winning an argument online became our main form of political engagement.

Every day since, the world has gotten dumber, and that comic more popular. The Pepe trolls and live-stream grifters at the heart of the Trump movement, believing they had an ace-in-the-hole argument to dismantle liberal hypocrisy, began ripping on societal participation at every level. Liberals used money! Greta Thunberg rode a train! Bernie bought groceries!

When she arrived in Washington, D.C., Alexandria Ocasio-Cortez was hounded constantly for wearing clothes, eating food, and using services that ultimately create some level of pollution. One *New York Post* headline: "Freshman Rep. Alexandria Ocasio-Cortez Wants To Save the Planet With Her Green New Deal, But She Keeps Tripping Over Her Own Giant Carbon Footprint." Damn, I guess we shouldn't save the planet now.

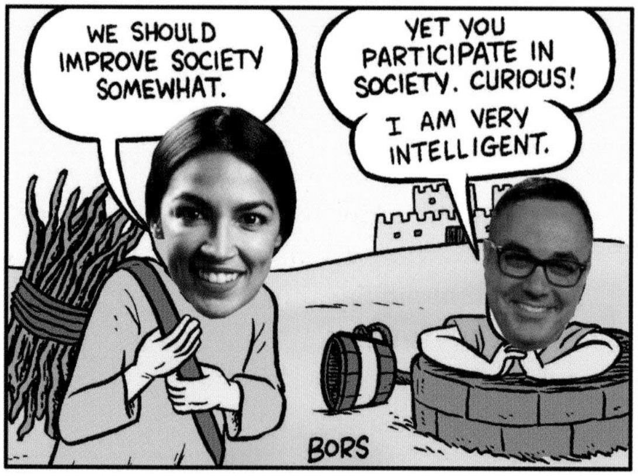
WE SHOULD IMPROVE SOCIETY SOMEWHAT.
YET YOU PARTICIPATE IN SOCIETY. CURIOUS!
I AM VERY INTELLIGENT.
BORS

Alexandria Ocasio-Cortez and one of her critics. Some writer guy? I can't keep track of them all.

As a political cartoonist, hypocrisy should concern me. We describe our profession in language like, "ink-stained wretches who SKEWER sacred cows and expose HYPOCRISY in the name of TRUTH with the pen of REASON," and we generally have a high view of ourselves (or at least of our work). And indeed, nothing's worse than a priest inveighing against the sins of the flesh from a pulpit, while being shunted from parish to parish for molesting choir boys in his spare time. Complete hypocrite stuff there.

Of course, there would be something off about AOC suggesting we improve the lives of the poor while operating as a ruthless slumlord, or Greta Thunberg advocating we save the planet while she clear-cuts the Amazon alongside a rogue's gallery of Captain Planet villains. They'd be hearing from me, that's for sure.

We expect consistency from each other, particularly anyone making pronouncements about how we all should live. Hypocrisy is a grave sin—if you're guilty of it, the point you were making must not have been all that important to you. These days one of our only

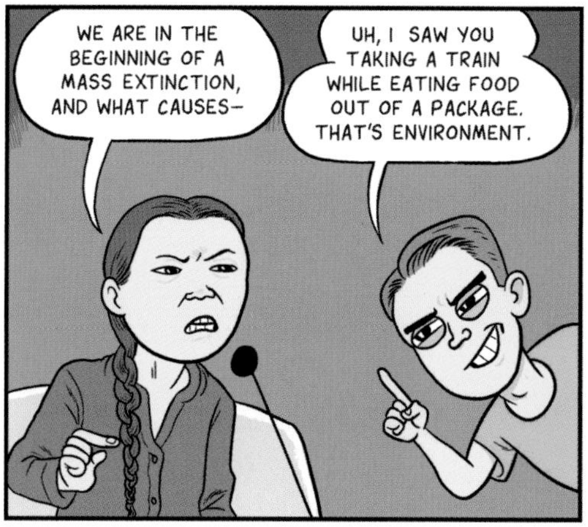
WE ARE IN THE BEGINNING OF A MASS EXTINCTION, AND WHAT CAUSES–
UH, I SAW YOU TAKING A TRAIN WHILE EATING FOOD OUT OF A PACKAGE. THAT'S ENVIRONMENT.

weapons against the ruling class is a loud and vocal attempt to shame them into better behavior. On the other hand, we're seeing a whole world of Mr. Gotchas now, calling out the ways in which we've failed to live out our proclaimed politics, in the most minute ways.

The galaxy-brain "gotcha" belongs to Diamond & Silk, a duo of Trump-loving women, who devastated Beto O'Rourke's political ambitions on Fox & Friends by noting that he "talks about tearing down walls, yet he live in a house supported by walls." Truly a lot to consider there.

The wall thing only got weirder. Disgraced plagiarist Benny Johnson "reported" on the small four-foot wall at the Obama home while Sean Hannity railed against crowd barriers at a Bernie Sanders rally, saying, "Oh, are barriers acceptable if they protect you personally?" It is within this ecosystem I attempt to make satire. Once the other side is using the existence of perpendicular structures to justify racism, it leaves little room for humor to breathe.

Writing about the gotcha phenomenon for Media Matters, Parker Malloy suspects that "deep down, Hannity, Johnson, and everyone else who makes strained charges of hypocrisy know that these aren't actual examples of hypocrisy."

"If the goal is to take attention away from something like the Green New Deal," she writes, "which is aimed at addressing underlying, systemic problems affecting climate change, reframing the discussion to be about personal choices is a time-tested strategy."

Hmm, criticizing government solutions to improve life while utilizing government services that improve your life? Drive on roads much? That's a thinking emoji from me, my guy.

What Mr. Gotcha does of course is not point out hypocrisy, but attempt to derail any meaningful political debate. Otherwise, criticizing mild failings anywhere opens the doorway to, heaven forbid, believing government or collective action can amount to actual change. That maybe in the end we will have to live by our ideals—and that will mean giving something up. It's an attitude rooted in the notion that nothing can change for the better; you're trapped on our current hellword and you will take it quietly.

The cartoons in this book represent my best attempts to make cases against the worst arguments of our very dumb timeline. Our world is filled with them—from Trump, police, well-paid pundits, Nazis, and of course the countless "gotcha" guys on social media.

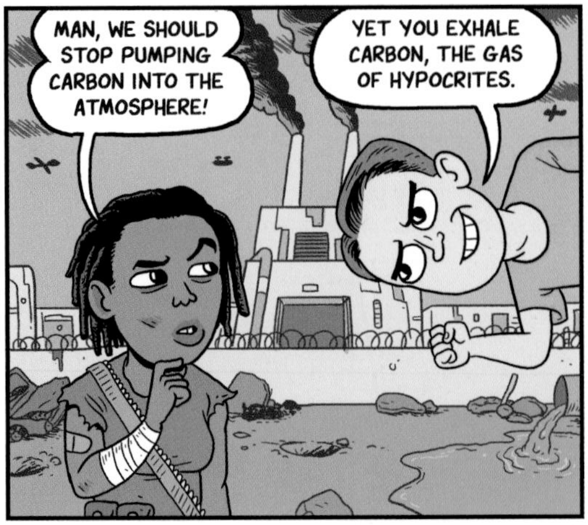
MAN, WE SHOULD STOP PUMPING CARBON INTO THE ATMOSPHERE!
YET YOU EXHALE CARBON, THE GAS OF HYPOCRITES.

Political cartooning is an inherently critical (some would even say negative) art form. Boosterism just doesn't stick as well as well as tearing something apart. Still, you can look at what I am against and pretty easily figure out what I am for.

Of course, we need to improve society more than somewhat. To create an equitable world and survive climate change we'll have to utterly transform society and massively redistribute wealth and political power. The rise of authoritarian nationalism around the globe, and the daily onslaught of online stupidity, makes us seem destined for a dystopian wasteland. I'll celebrate virtually any progress at this point.

Lately I've started to think a little more seriously about my comic and its underlying operating principle: That things can and do get better over time because people demand it, or at least put forth a modest suggestion that tomorrow can be less shitty. I mean, like the peasant in my comic, you could definitely die before any meaningful change occurs. For sure. But I'm trying to be positive here. Some people have seen things improve before, so it stands to reason that could be us, too. You never know, is what I'm saying.

I can't claim cartoons can change the world through their sheer brilliance. But, you might find a few good panels in here that help you win an argument or two online. Hell, that is, technically speaking, changing the course of world history. We're almost there.

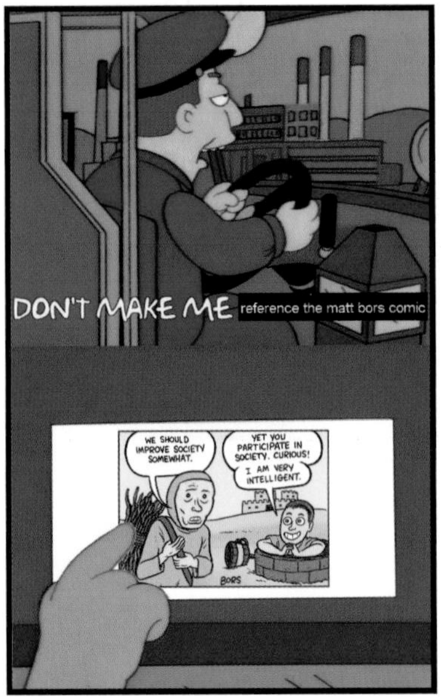
DON'T MAKE ME
reference the matt bors comic
WE SHOULD IMPROVE SOCIETY SOMEWHAT.
YET YOU PARTICIPATE IN SOCIETY. CURIOUS!
I AM VERY INTELLIGENT.
BORS

Referencing my comic is so common there's a Simpson's meme about my meme.

Apple AirPods cost $159, but they can't pay taxes or decent wages to their Chinese factory workers!
POST
...YOU SAID ON AN iPHONE.
HEH. GOTCHA.
CARS SHOULD HAVE SEAT BELTS!
YET YOU BOUGHT ONE. HYPOCRITE MUCH? OWNED.
WE SHOULD IMPROVE SOCIETY SOMEWHAT.
YET YOU PARTICIPATE IN SOCIETY. CURIOUS!
I AM VERY INTELLIGENT.
BORS

YOU'RE BEING VIOLENT AND DISRUPTIVE! TRY BEING PEACEFUL!
BLACK LIVES MATTER
DISRESPECTFUL! SHUT UP AND BE QUIET.
MORE QUIET.
YES.
EXCELLENT.
THANK YOU.
BORS
THENIB

WHAT'D THEY GET YOU FOR?
TORTURE. WATERBOARDING. BEATINGS. SHOVING PURÉED FOOD UP BUTTS. FREEZING PEOPLE TO DEATH.
NOT MERELY ILLEGAL, BUT A DARK STAIN ON OUR NATION THAT STILL INSPIRES TERRORISTS TO THIS VERY DAY...
NAH, I SMOKED A JOINT.
BORS

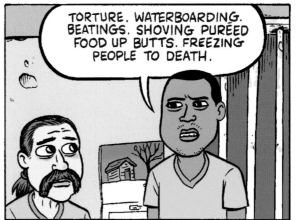

THE NEAT WORLD WE LIVE IN
WORRIED ABOUT SCHOOL SHOOTINGS? THERE'S A NEW PRODUCT FOR YOU: BULLETPROOF BLANKETS FOR KIDS.
ADULTS SURE HAVE IT ALL FIGURED OUT!
BODYGUARD
THEIR INSPIRING LOGO.
STOPS ATTACKERS COMPLETELY!
OH, I GUESS I'LL GO HOME NOW.
COMBINE TWO TO SOLVE AMERICA'S GUN PROBLEM.
I'M A SAFETY SANDWICH!
BORS

I try to place signifiers in comics that key readers in as to whether something is pure satire or starting from a real thing that happened. In case it's not clear here, this is a real product produced by Oklahoma-based ProTecht, LLC, who continue the great American tradition of trying to innovate our way out of crises of our own making.

KILLS 37 PEOPLE IN A MALL WITH MACHINE GUNS.
HOW DID AN HONOR STUDENT END UP DOING A NO-NO?
UNARMED AND KILLED BY A COP FOR NO DISCERNIBLE REASON.
WE'VE UNCOVERED A SELFIE OF THIS KID SMOKING A CIGARETTE.
HE WAS NO ANGEL.
BORS

This comic, while generalized, was in response to Michael Brown being shot and killed by a police officer in Ferguson, Missouri. The "no angel" line was taken from online criticism I've seen of many of the black men and teenagers killed by police. But shortly after this comics was published The New York Times *published an obituary of Brown, opening with the line, "Michael Brown, 18, due to be buried on Monday, was no angel," and helpfully adding later that, "he had taken to rapping in recent months."*

THE ALABAMA SENATE VOTED TO ALLOW A MEGA-CHURCH TO START ITS VERY OWN POLICE FORCE.
TO SERVE (THE LORD) AND PROTECT... PRIVATE PROPERTY!
JESUS, YOU'LL RECALL, WAS VERY DOWN WITH THE IDEA OF STATE VIOLENCE.
MAYBE IF I HAD OBEYED THE ROMANS I'D STILL BE ALIVE RIGHT NOW.
DID YOU THINK OF THAT?
ANYWAY, WHAT COULD GO WRONG!
MUSLIM CITIZENS!
HANDS WHERE I CAN SEE 'EM!
NOW, YOU FOLKS AREN'T TRYING TO IMPOSE SHARIA, I HOPE.
BORS
THENIB. COM

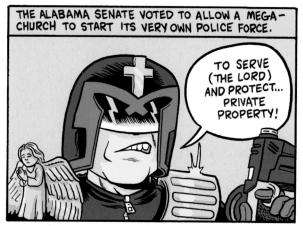

I started riffing on Judge Dredd as a stand-in for authoritarianism. It helps that I'm a fan of 2000AD *and the Judges of Mega-City One have one of the best character designs in comics. We will come back to all this later...*

WE'VE GOT A LIVE ONE HERE!
HE'S CONTRACTED GAMERGATE!
DISPLAYING ALL THE SYMPTOMS.
THE MAN THE LEGEND
✓ VOMITING MISOGYNIST BILE.
✓ PUSTULES OF ENTITLEMENT.
✓ COMMENT DIARRHEA.
@#✱!
SHOOT HIM INTO THE SUN WITH THE REST.
TIM! THERE'S A TEAR IN YOUR SUIT!
I, I FEEL FINE... I...
I JUST HATE WHEN GIRLS ARE ALLOWED TO PLAY THE GAMES I LIKE!
OH DEAR GOD LET ME OUT
BORS

The Gamergate controversy in 2014 became a template for the online culture wars to come. The movement allegedly formed to push for "ethics in journalism" but was primarily concerned with trolling and doxxing women they feared might beat their speed run times on Sonic. This cartoon triggered a lot of Gamergaters, who reworked my dialogue to instead be diatribes against women, trans people, and Jews. Ethics in journalism, folks.

WHOA, KID. YOU'RE TWELVE. YOU'RE CARRYING A BB GUN. COPS ARE GONNA SHOOT YOU DEAD. LET ME HELP YOU.
FIRST, NO HOODIES, NO BAGGY PANTS. WEAR SOMETHING RESPECTABLE.
DON'T TREAD ON ME
NOW YOU NEED A **REAL** GUN. TAKE MY AR-15, LITERALLY POINT IT AT FEDERAL AGENTS.
NOW TURN WHITE. BE A WHITE PERSON NOW.
GREAT. YOU LOOK HARMLESS. **PLAY SAFE!**
DON'T TREAD ON ME
BORS

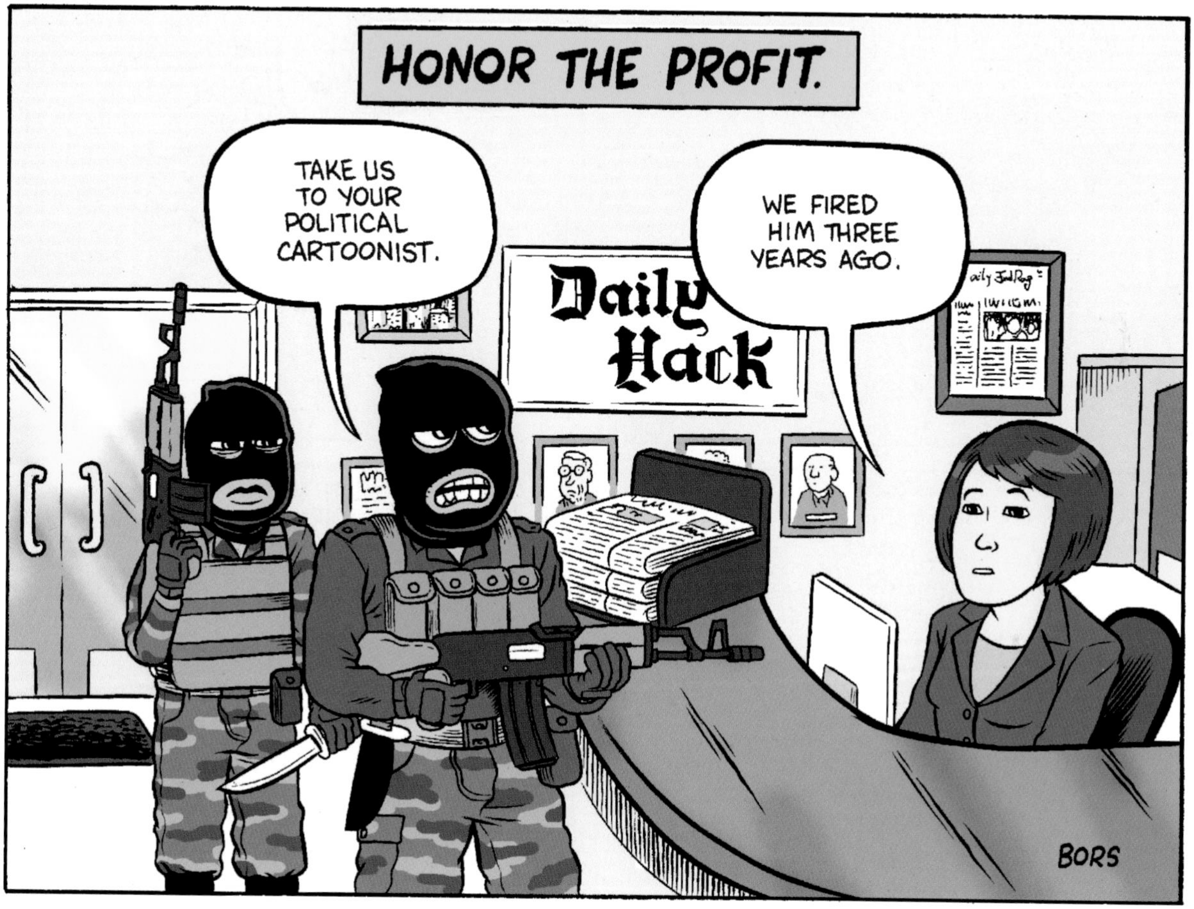
HONOR THE PROFIT.
TAKE US TO YOUR POLITICAL CARTOONIST.
WE FIRED HIM THREE YEARS AGO.
Daily Hack
BORS

After the Charlie Hebdo killings, the world united to condemn the massacre. France loves their cartoonists and the culture there generally reveres sequential art as a serious endeavor. It was shocking to me they had entire publications staffed by cartoonists. No such luck in the States.

COOL NEWS: JIHADISTS ARE URGING ATTACKS ON CARTOONISTS IN AUSTRALIA AND AMERICA WHO'VE DRAWN MUHAMMAD.
IT'S DISRESPECTFUL TO THE MUSLIMS WE BEHEAD DAILY.
THEY RAISE A GOOD POINT. SATIRE SHOULD PUNCH UP, NOT DOWN LIKE HOW A DUMB CARTOONIST MIGHT DO.
I DREW THE RIOTERS!
FEAR
MAKES $100K
4 PULITZERS
HATE
AND APOCALYPTIC MADMEN WITH GUNS ARE BASICALLY CARTOON CONNOISSEURS.
OH, THE IRONY HERE IS SUBLIME.
I FIND THIS ONE QUITE PROBLEMATIC.
BORS
THENIB.COM
SAD THOUGH: IF THEY KILL ME I'LL MISS ALL THE POST-MASSACRE THINK PIECES.
IT'S THE CLASH OF CIVILIZATIONS!
TUT TUT! IT'S ABOUT MY PERSONAL VIEWS.
WAIT, THAT SOUNDS LIKE HEAVEN.

One of my "everybody commenting on this news event is starting to annoy me" comics.

TWELVE PEOPLE WERE BLOWN UP IN AKRON, OHIO, LAST WEEK AFTER YEMENI INTELLIGENCE FIRED A MISSILE AT A WEDDING PARTY.

POLICE BELIEVE THE TARGET OF THE STRIKE WAS DAN OLSON, AN AREA MAN SUSPECTED OF PROBABLY NOT LIKING YEMEN.

NEVER HEARD OF HIM!

HE— HE WAS JESSIE'S DATE—JUST SOME RANDO.

AS USUAL, YEMEN WON'T EVEN ACKNOWLEDGE THAT IT HAS A DRONE PROGRAM THAT BOMBS AMERICA.

I CAN'T DISCUSS SPECIFIC OPERATIONS.

JEEZ, RUDE TO ASK!

BUT AMERICANS NEED TO UNDERSTAND THESE DEATH PLANES SAVE LIVES.

MAYBE NOT EVERY SINGLE WIDDLE GROOMS-MAN...

THINK BIG PICTURE.

BORS

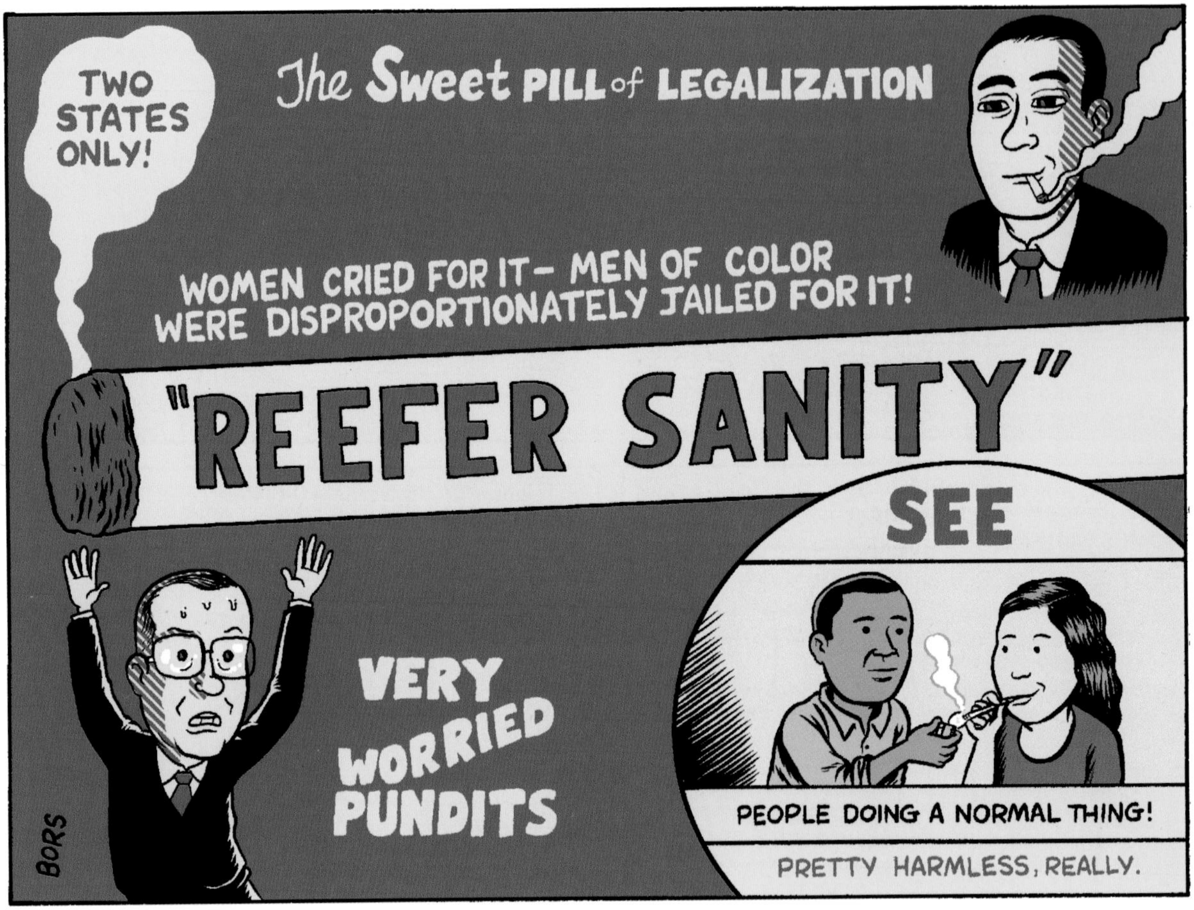
TWO STATES ONLY!
The Sweet PILL of LEGALIZATION
WOMEN CRIED FOR IT– MEN OF COLOR WERE DISPROPORTIONATELY JAILED FOR IT!
"REEFER SANITY"
SEE
VERY WORRIED PUNDITS
PEOPLE DOING A NORMAL THING!
PRETTY HARMLESS, REALLY.
BORS

WOODY ALLEN MOVIES CAN GO DIE. I'M NOT SUPPORTING ANY MORE ART MADE BY MONSTERS.
COUNT ME IN!
R. KELLY, ROMAN POLANSKI, MICHAEL JACKSON...
BILL MURRAY WAS AN ABUSER. JOHN LENNON BEAT WOMEN.
JESUS, IS EVERY FAMOUS DUDE A TERRIBLE HUMAN BEING?! WHAT IS EVEN LEFT?
"SPACE JAM."
PEPÉ LE PEW IS A CREEP.
TOSS IT.
BORS

It was pointed out to me after the publication of this comic that Bill Murray, who stars in Space Jam, *was in fact accused of domestic violence by his second wife in a divorce filing. So, yeah.*

RUN ME THROUGH IT AGAIN.
YOU SHOT THIS UNARMED MAN BECAUSE YOU FELT THREATENED?
YES. I'M AN OFF-DUTY COP, BRO.
AND HE WAS A HOMELESS GUY. BUT YOU'RE BLACK AND HE'S WHITE—PLUS HE'S A VET.
DUDE, I'M A VET TOO.
HMM.
OKAY, I'M GOING TO WRITE YOU A TICKET.
BORS

STORING METADATA IS NOT AN INVASION OF PRIVACY! IT'S A TOOL THAT KEEPS AMERICA SAFE.
NO ONE IS **LISTENING** TO YOUR CALLS.
NSA
CONGRESSMAN, I SEE HERE LAST FRIDAY YOU TALKED TO YOUR WIFE, THEN IMMEDIATELY CALLED AN ESCORT SERVICE, THEN A HOTEL.
NSA
OF COURSE, WE DON'T KNOW THE **CONTENT** OF THOSE CALLS.
NSA
OOO— THAT'S YOUR WIFE NOW.
BORS

THERE ARE NO CONSEQUENCES TO PROTESTING ANYMORE. THERE USED TO BE CONSEQUENCES.
JOCKEY BOY RESTAURANT
Coca-Cola
IN THE GOOD 'OL DAYS THIS DIDN'T HAPPEN BECAUSE THEY USED TO TREAT THEM VERY, VERY ROUGH.
AND WHEN THEY PROTESTED ONCE, YOU KNOW, THEY WOULD NOT DO IT AGAIN SO EASILY.
WE'RE NOT ALLOWED TO PUNCH BACK ANY-MORE. I MISS THE OLD DAYS.
BORS

All of these quotes are from Trump on the campaign trail as he encouraged protesters at his rallies to be brutalized and offered to pay the legal fees of anyone involved on his behalf. Super normal stump speech stuff.

I DON'T MEAN TO RETWEET NEO-NAZIS EVERY WEEK.
THIS IS A WACKY COINCIDENCE!
THIS IS DEFINITELY A SHERIFF'S BADGE YES. IT'S WHAT SHERIFFS WEAR.
HILLARY
SAD!
ACTUALLY, THIS IS A HINDU SYMBOL MEANING **GOOD FORTUNE**.
I WISH YOU WELL, MY FRIENDS.
WELCO
BORS

Godwin's law rules that, "As an online discussion grows longer, the probability of a comparison involving Nazis or Hitler approaches 1." I started going hard on the Trump/Nazi analogies early and it didn't turn out to be a mistake. Hitler comparisons, once a provocation reserved for rare occasions in political cartoons, became the norm. The author Michael Godwin who coined the phrase eventually said, "Go ahead and refer to Hitler when you talk about Trump."

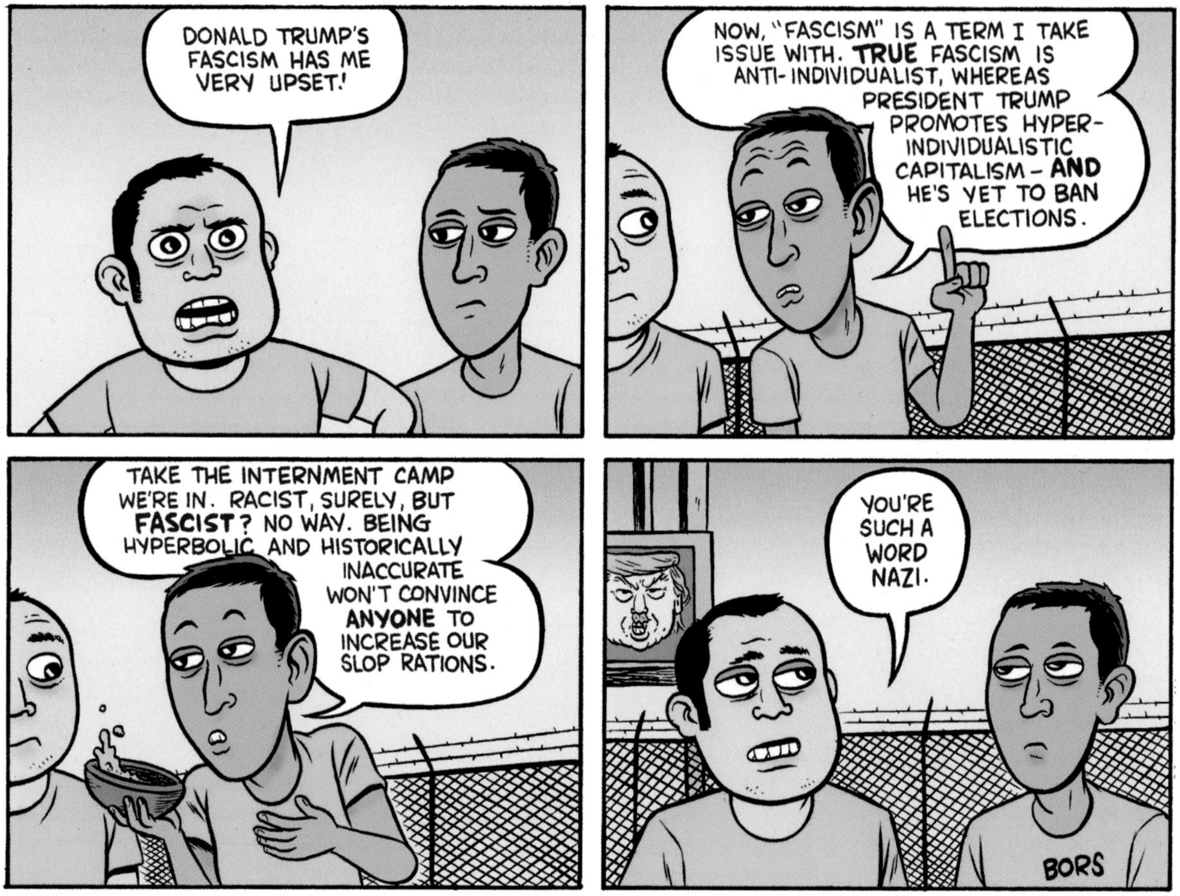
DONALD TRUMP'S FASCISM HAS ME VERY UPSET!
NOW, "FASCISM" IS A TERM I TAKE ISSUE WITH. TRUE FASCISM IS ANTI-INDIVIDUALIST, WHEREAS PRESIDENT TRUMP PROMOTES HYPER-INDIVIDUALISTIC CAPITALISM – AND HE'S YET TO BAN ELECTIONS.
TAKE THE INTERNMENT CAMP WE'RE IN. RACIST, SURELY, BUT FASCIST? NO WAY. BEING HYPERBOLIC AND HISTORICALLY INACCURATE WON'T CONVINCE ANYONE TO INCREASE OUR SLOP RATIONS.
YOU'RE SUCH A WORD NAZI.
BORS

Drawn before Trump was elected or established prison camps for children or mused about ending term limits. 'Nuff said.

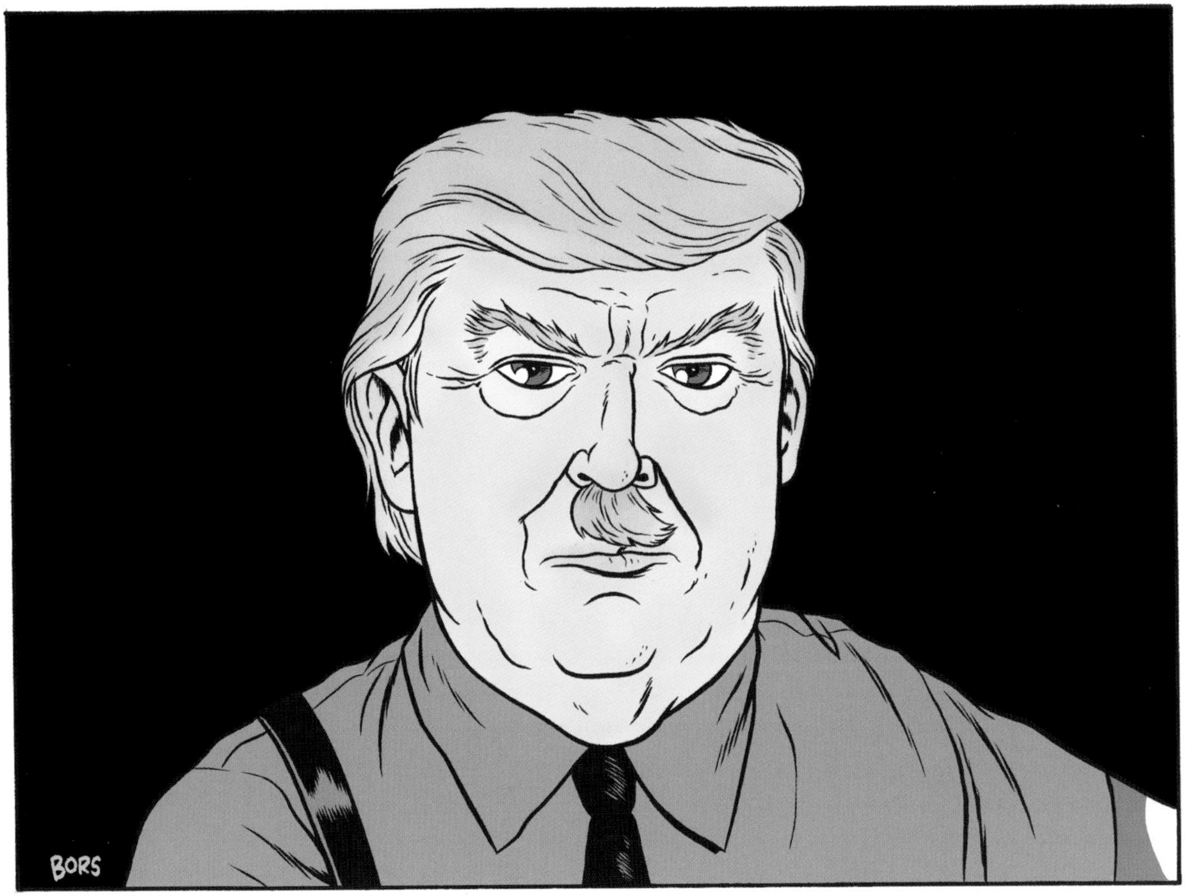
BORS

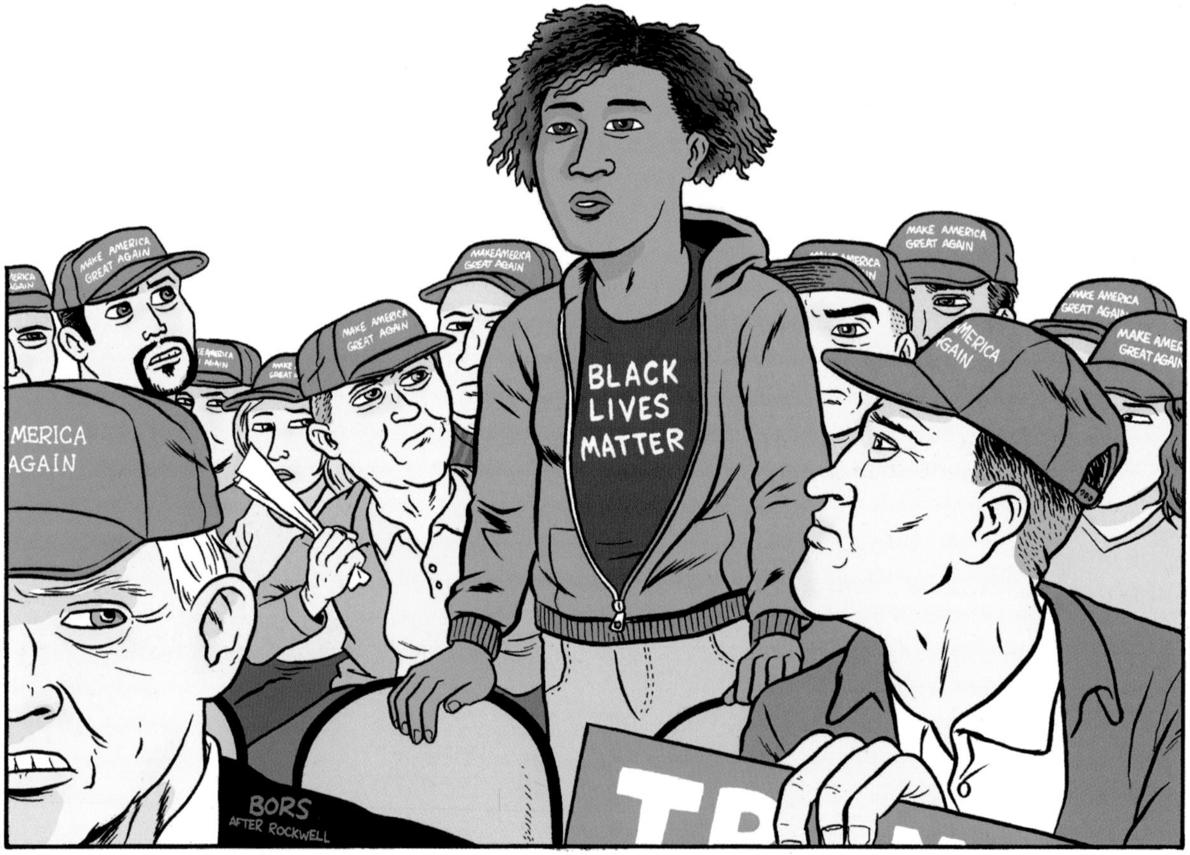
BLACK
LIVES
MATTER
MAKE AMERICA
GREAT AGAIN
BORS
AFTER ROCKWELL

YOU MUST BE HAVING A FIELD DAY WITH THIS ELECTION!
NO SHORTAGE OF IDEAS, THAT'S FOR SURE!
THE JOKES PRACTICALLY WRITE THEMSELVES, DON'T THEY?
PRIME TIME SATIRE MATERIAL RIGHT HERE!
BORS

This comic was drawn during a campaign that, looking back, seems quaint when compared with the consequences of what came after. I don't know anyone who makes satire for a living having the time of their lives right now. It's mostly a grueling slog where each day I wake up on the west coast already behind on the new horror that awaits me on my phone.

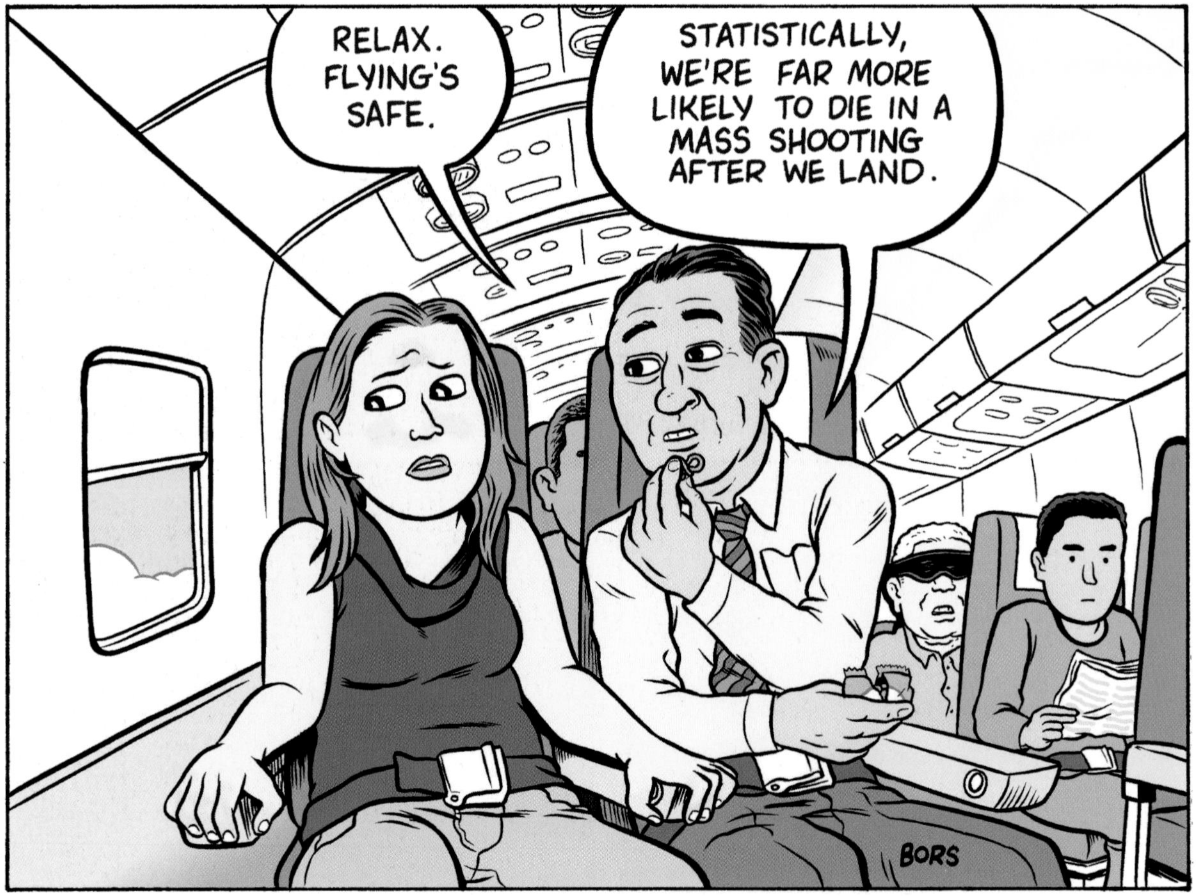
RELAX. FLYING'S SAFE.
STATISTICALLY, WE'RE FAR MORE LIKELY TO DIE IN A MASS SHOOTING AFTER WE LAND.
BORS

SO GUYS, THIS CLIVEN BUNDY FELLOW RALLIED SOME ARMED PROTESTERS AND THE FEDS BACKED DOWN.
NICE. LET'S BRING GUNS TO OUR NEXT KEYSTONE PIPELINE ACTION!
SECOND AMENDMENT.
JANET, I'M LIVE ON THE SCENE.
IT'S PURE CARNAGE.
THE POLICE REALLY GAVE THOSE HIPPIE SCUM WHAT FOR.
NO 2 XL
BORS

NEW THREAT TO 'MERICA: MIGRANT CHILDREN COMING HERE ALONE. BORDER PATROL HAS ARRESTED HUNDREDS UNDER THE AGE OF TWO.
SURE THEY'RE CUTE. UNTIL THEY TAKE YOUR BABY'S JOB.
IF YOU SEE A SUSPICIOUS BABY, ASK TO SEE ITS PAPERS OR CALL IMMIGRATION.
SENT BY PARENTS TO ESCAPE VIOLENCE AND CRUSHING POVERTY?
OR CARTEL MULE WITH A DIAPER FULL OF COCAINE?
WE'VE GOT TO STOP THESE BABIES BEFORE THEY HAVE BETTER LIVES.
THEY DON'T EVEN SPEAK ENGLISH!
GRANTED, THEY CAN'T SPEAK ANY LANGUAGE YET.
BUT STILL. RUDE.
BORS

This comic, drawn in 2014 about the Central American migrant crisis, attempted to exaggerate the paranoia and racism directed at unaccompanied children arriving at our borders. I had no idea at the time the arguments here would be adopted as mainstream Republican policy, babies and children ripped from their parents, caged, and denied even toothbrushes. Depressing stuff, friends.

WE TOOK OVER HALF OF IRAQ IN A WEEK!
MOSUL GREETED US AS LIBERATORS!
TOTAL CAKEWALK!
THE OIL REVENUE WILL PAY FOR EVERYTHING!
THIS ALL SOUNDS VERY FAMILIAR!
WE'VE CREATED A HELLISH QUAGMIRE!
WE'LL BE COMPLETELY DISCREDITED!
AND INVITED ON TV YEARS LATER AS EXPERTS!
BORS

ISLAMIC STATE
BAN ALL CIGARETTES!
VEIL THE WOMEN!
BEHEAD APOSTATES!
WATERBOARD THE CAPTIVES!
BORS
HEY, BUDDY. NONE OF THAT WESTERN CULTURE HERE.

THE 5 STAGES OF SOCIAL MEDIA GRIEF
SADNESS
AH MAN BOWIE DIED
HYPERBOLE
NO ONE CAME CLOSE!!! HE WAS SUPERHUMAN — A GOD AMONGST GODS!! I'M RUINED
ACTUALLY
NO! YOU SHOULDN'T IDOLIZE AN ACCUSED RAPIST YOU ARE VERY PROBLEMATIC!
REVERSE CONTRARIAN HOT TAKE
IN FACT, YOU SHOULDN'T POLICE THE GRIEF OF THOSE IN MOURNING ESPECIALLY SURVIVORS, THAT SAID WE MUST CALL OUT ABUSE IN OUR COMMUNITY AND HOLD THOSE ACCOUNT-
CLOSURE
BORS

FIRST, THE GAYS CAME FOR THE COUNTY CLERKS AND I DID NOT SPEAK UP BECAUSE I WAS NOT A COUNTY CLERK.
THEN THEY CAME FOR THE CAKE BAKERS AND I DID NOT SPEAK UP BECAUSE I LIKE CAKES AT GAY WEDDINGS.
THEN THEY LEGALIZED MAN-DOG MARRIAGE, WHICH TO BE HONEST IS WEIRD AND NOT AT ALL MY THING. BUT OKAY.
THEN THEY FORCED ALL HETEROSEXUALS INTO LABOR CAMPS (ALONG WITH CATS). THAT I DID NOT SEE COMING.
WISH I WOULD HAVE SAID SOMETHING!
BORS

Kim Davis became a folk hero of the Right when she started denying marriage licenses to gay couples in Rowan County, Kentucky. A true heterosexual marriage enthusiast, Kim is on her fourth.

YOU PAY $750 AND THIS PILL RIDS YOU OF PARASITES!
YOU'RE STILL HERE.
BORS

Pharmaceutical villain Martin Shkreli raised the price of the drug Daraprim from $13.50 to $750 per pill. When I posted this comic on Twitter, I tagged Shkreli and challenged him to buy the art for a highly-inflated $1,000. In a bizarre turn of events, a hedge fund guy bought the comic from me which I assumed was on behalf of Shkreli. Thus, it is quite possible that the original art for this comic is in the possession of the federal government after seizing Shkreli's assets, which included the fabled Wu-Tang Clan album he purchased for $2 million. (Trump, please release the Wu-Tang album!)

FROM AN ARTICLE ON OBJECTIFYING WOMEN ON THE DAILY CALLER BY PATRICK HOWLEY.

In the progressive future, men will not be able to look at women's bodies because that is a terrible thing to do...

Pretty soon, looking at a woman's chest will legally be a "hate" crime instead of a love crime.

Maybe catching a side glance of some cleavage on the subway isn't for you. Fine... Why ban things that you might want to try sometime?

I'm not saying looking at tits is any kind of noble pursuit. But it's one more freedom...

And you know what else? A lot of women like it.

BORS

This column by some forgotten right-wing hack was so over-the-top it called to be simply illustrated alongside the text of the piece. As you can see, I'm back to the Judge Dredds and looking for more reasons to keep drawing them.

LIVES HAVE BEEN SAVED.
I'D DO IT AGAIN IN A MINUTE.
IT'S A MEDICAL PROCEDURE IS WHAT IT IS.
WE ARE AWESOME.
BORS

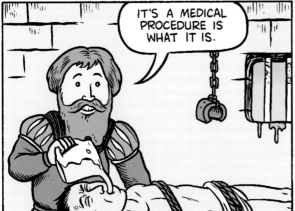

QUOTES FROM JOHN BRENNAN, DICK CHENEY, MICHAEL HAYDEN AND FOX HOST ANDREA TANTAROS.

In 2014, the Senate Intelligence Committee's report on CIA torture was released, detailing the vast implementation of nauseatingly gruesome and illegal interrogation techniques used by the CIA and approved by the highest levels of government that did not even work in eliciting intelligence. President Barack Obama said, "One of the strengths that makes America exceptional is our willingness to openly confront our past, face our imperfections, make changes and do better." Zero people were prosecuted.

TRUMP PROPOSES CULTURE TEST FOR IMMIGRANTS
FILL OUT YOUR MUSLIM WEIRDO TESTS, PLEASE!
T
NO ONE WILL BE ALLOWED INTO AMERICA IF THEY HAVE BAD OPINIONS.
YOUR VIEWS NEED TO BE CORRECT, POLITICALLY, SO OUR SPACE IS SAFE!
T
BORS
ALSO WE'RE TOO PC.
T

Trump's campaign rhetoric was becoming increasingly authoritarian and this marked the first appearance of what would become a staple of my comics and Nib animations: The Trump Guard—a fully fascistic, gold-helmet police force answerable only to the President. This would also mark the beginning of what would become an alternate future timeline in my comics, known colloquially as The Wasteland, where Trump's presidency never ends.

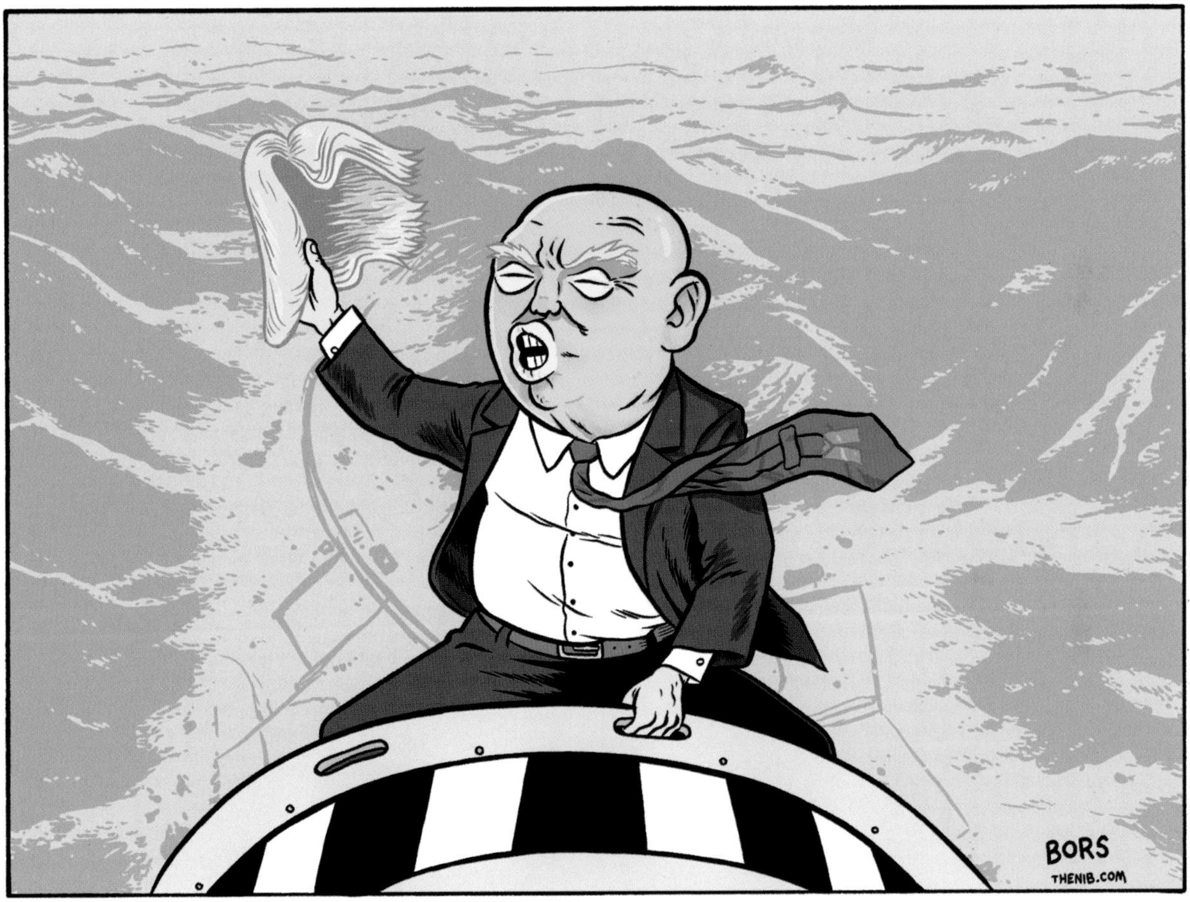
BORS
THENIB.COM

This comic was headlined "Fat Man is Little Boy" which, if you know the names of the atomic bombs dropped in World War 2, is basically perfect. All credit to Matt Lubchansky for that one.

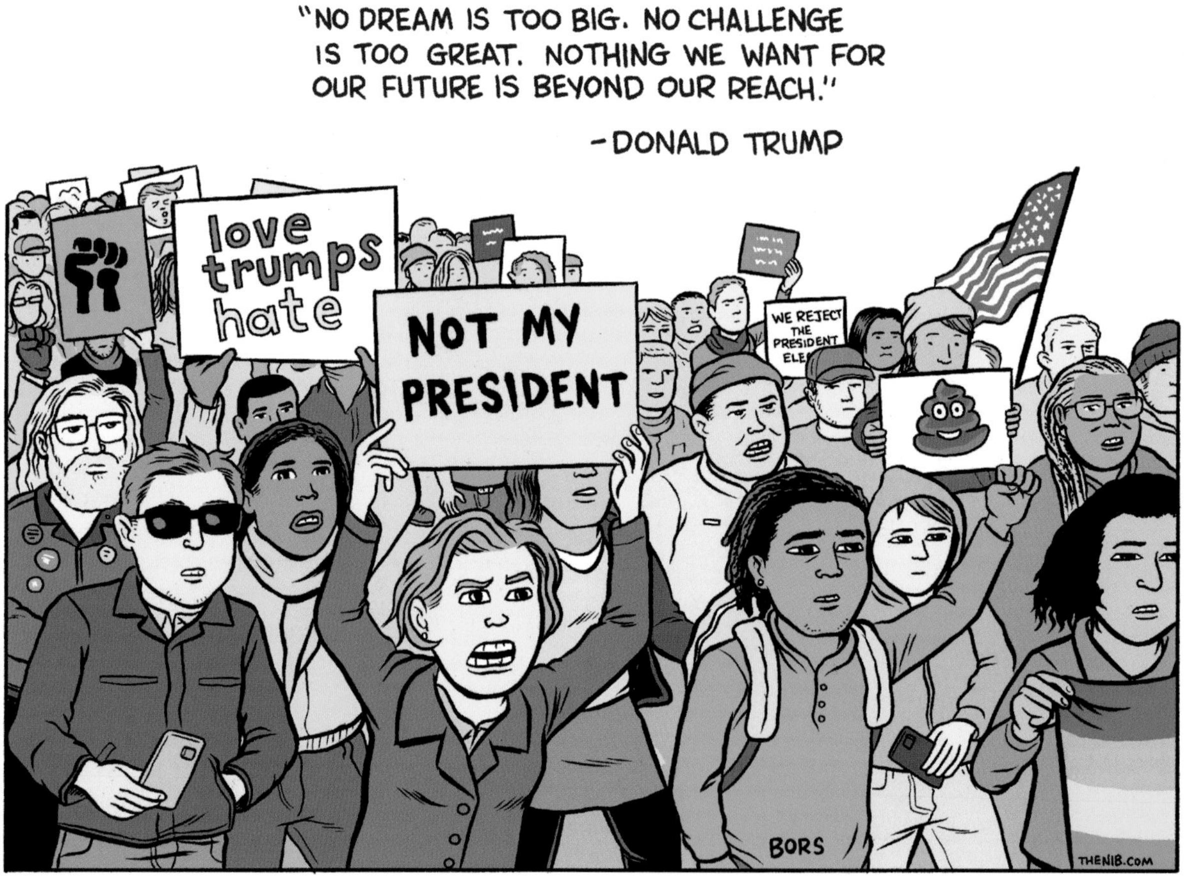
"NO DREAM IS TOO BIG. NO CHALLENGE IS TOO GREAT. NOTHING WE WANT FOR OUR FUTURE IS BEYOND OUR REACH."
-DONALD TRUMP
love trumps hate
NOT MY PRESIDENT
WE REJECT THE PRESIDENT
BORS
THENIB.COM

My first reaction to Donald Trump's election. I had not been prepared and, lacking anything funny to say for once, opted for some inspirational defiance from Trump's own victory speech.

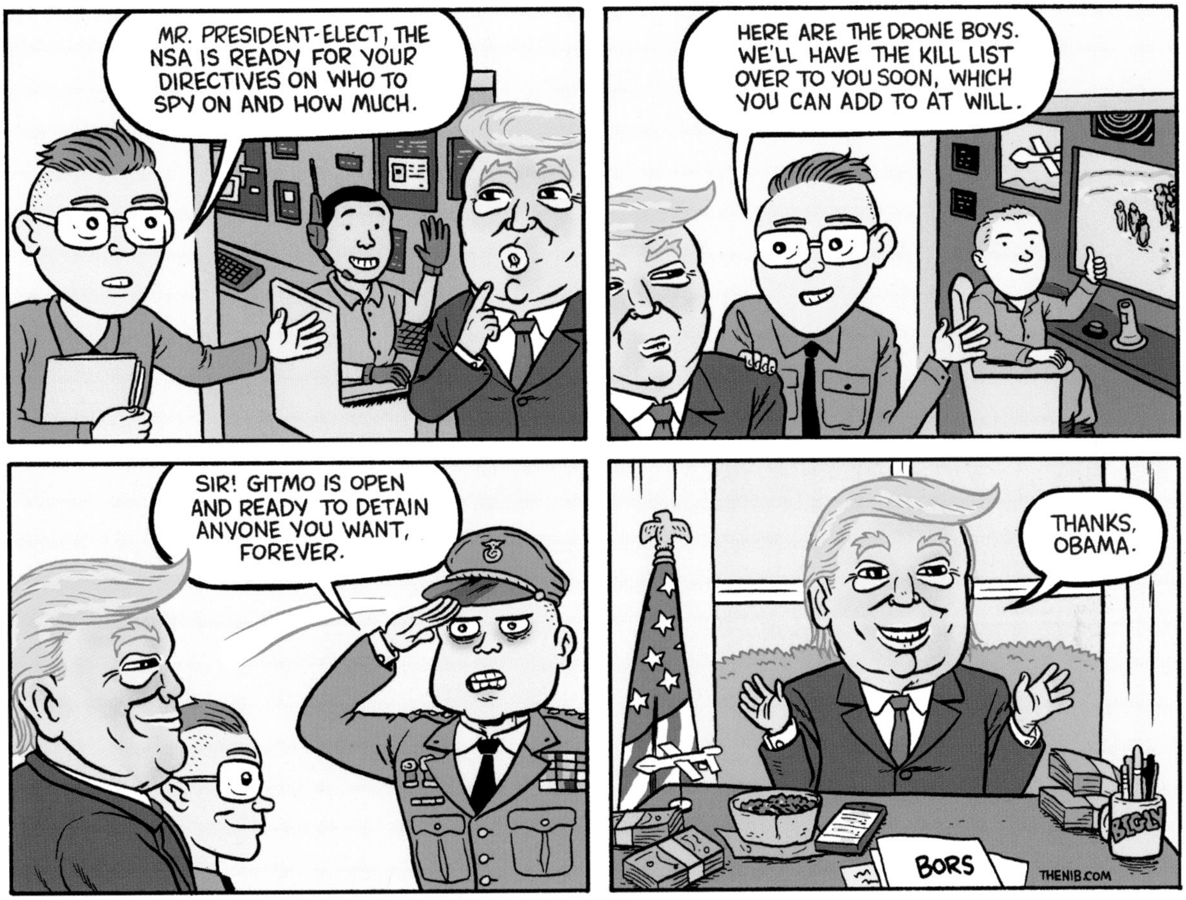
MR. PRESIDENT-ELECT, THE NSA IS READY FOR YOUR DIRECTIVES ON WHO TO SPY ON AND HOW MUCH.
HERE ARE THE DRONE BOYS. WE'LL HAVE THE KILL LIST OVER TO YOU SOON, WHICH YOU CAN ADD TO AT WILL.
SIR! GITMO IS OPEN AND READY TO DETAIN ANYONE YOU WANT, FOREVER.
THANKS, OBAMA.
BORS
THENIB.COM

And my second reaction to Trump's victory. The overreaches of the Obama administration on drones and spying—the bipartisan stamp of approval they now enjoyed—could now be exploited by one of the most unstable, vindictive men to ever hold the office. Man, it's like civil liberties matter for this very reason and shouldn't be based on if you like the party in office!

CONTENT WARNING: This comic was produced in anticipation of Trump's election loss. I was certainly naive enough to think he'd lose, but I also had a deadline the day of voting and put my chips on Hillary in hopes of having something in the can for the following morning. I sure was poised to get a lot of retweets with this amusing take! To read this now is painful and I include it here so that you may share in the pain.

IT'S FINALLY OVER. THE RELENTLESS POLITICAL ADS, THE HOT TAKES, THE ARGUMENTS, THE POLLS WORKING US INTO A STATE OF CONSTANT ANXIETY. A WEIGHT HAS BEEN LIFTED.
LOCK HER UP!
WE CAN BREATHE A LITTLE EASIER KNOWING AN IMPULSIVE NARCISSISTIC CON MAN WON'T HAVE THE NUCLEAR LAUNCH CODES OR CONTROL THE NEWS CYCLE WITH HIS TWEETS.
THERE'S MORE WORK TO DO. HILLARY IS FAR FROM PERFECT. BUT IT'S WORTH PAUSING TO REFLECT ON ELECTING TH
BORS
THENIB.COM
WHUNK
CRUZ
2020
TIME TO IMPEACH THIS SATANIC BITCH!

Even though none of this happened, you tell me I would have been off one bit if Trump lost! This comic sure had the people of Earth-3 nodding and smiling the day after Hillary's election victory.

UGH, THEY GAVE US THESE L BADGES FOR "LIBERAL" BUT I'M A LEFTIST!
ARE YOU KIDDING ME?! THE L STANDS FOR "LEFTIST." YOU KNOW, THE PEOPLE WHO GOT US IN THIS SITUATION!
MAYBE IF YOU CARED ABOUT CLASS WE WOULDN'T BE HERE!
OH, SO LET'S IGNORE RACISM??
DID YOU EVEN READ MY PIECE? BECAUSE IT DEFINITELY PROVES I'M RIGHT.
GIVE IT A SKIM. QUICKLY.
BORS
THENIB.COM

DID THE RUSSIAN HACK THROW THE ELECTION? PUNDITS FAR TOO INVESTED IN YOUR POLITICAL TEAM– THOUGHTS?
I DEFINITELY BELIEVED RUSSIA WAS EVIL, BUT AM NOW CAREFREE.
WHEREAS I'M ALWAYS SKEPTICAL OF CIA SOURCES, EXCEPT NOW, I GUESS.
SUNDAY TAKES
LITERAL NAZI PUNDIT, BECAUSE THAT'S A THING WE DO NOW, YOUR TAKE?
YES, WHILE FOREIGN TAMPERING IS A CONCERN, WE CAN'T ATTRIBUTE THE LOSS TO THAT ALONE.
CAN WE KILL THE JEWS NOW?
SUNDAY TAKES
SURPRISINGLY NUANCED.
MR. NAZI.
BORS
THENIB.COM

FELLOW DEMOCRATS! IF WE WANT TO WIN IN 2020 WE HAVE TO APPEAL TO EITHER THE WHITE WORKING CLASS OR YOUNG WOMEN AND PEOPLE OF COLOR. IT'S EITHER OR.
IF ONLY THERE WERE POLITICAL CONCERNS THAT TOUCHED ALL OF THESE GROUPS, WE COULD DO BOTH.
THE... ECONOMY?
YES, THE ECONOMY!
THAT'S IT!
GREAT, SO WE MOVE RIGHT ON THE ECONOMY.
BORS
THENIB.COM

X-Race Spex
SPOT CRIMINALS WITH EASE!
MY GOD...
THEY'RE EVERYWHERE!
SEE THE THREATS LURKING BENEATH SOCIETY'S SURFACE...
IN STARTLING COP-O-VISION!
COMES WITH A FREE INDICTMENT-DEFLECTING AMULET!
WELL, I'M SURE HE HAD TO SHOOT EVERYONE IN SIGHT!
BECAUSE POLICE
BORS

Los Angeles Times @latimes
Follow
Millennials, you can't call yourselves adults until you take this pledge, says @erskinetimes lat.ms/1OsKBSp
• Just once, I will try eating without texting.
• I will save 10% of everything I earn.
• I am entitled to nothing.
LA Times
I WILL NOT INSTAGRAM MY PIE. I WILL NOT JOIN ISIS IRONICALLY.
I WILL, LIKE, LITERALLY NOT SAY LITERALLY, LIKE, LITERALLY EVER.
JUST ONCE, I WILL TRY NOT TWERKING ON FLEEK FOR BAE.
I WILL SAVE MY... MONEY?
¯_(ツ)_/¯
BORS

FUN ALERT: SOME SCIENTISTS HAVE CREATED AN EXO-SUIT FOR MILLENNIALS TO BE LIKE ~~IRON MAN~~ AN OLD PERSON WITH LIMITED MOBILITY AND BAD EYESIGHT.
PRACTICAL!
SPEAK UP, SONNY!
NOW A BIT WARY OF GAYS
AARP
CREAKY JOINTS
THAT OLD PERSON SMELL®
INCREASED AWARENESS OF OWN MORTALITY

THE IDEA IS TO "START A CONVERSATION" ABOUT AGING, BUT CONVERSATIONS GO TWO WAYS. OLDS NEED A ROBO-SUIT TO FULLY UNDERSTAND MILLENNIAL LIFE.
I FEEL SPRY!
NON-STOP SELFIES
TROPHY FOR EXISTING
HASHTAG!
MEME GENERATOR
ACTUALLY THERE ARE NO GOOD JOBS
STUDENT LOAN PAYMENTS POWER THE SUIT
BORS
THENIB.COM

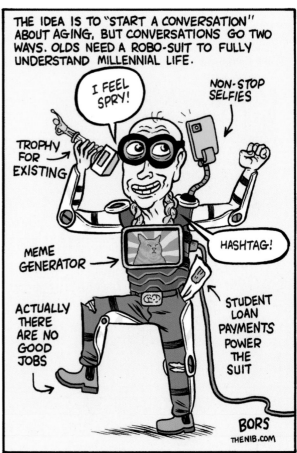

WHITE GUY WRITES MANIFESTO CALLING FOR RACE WAR, THEN KILLS NINE BLACK PEOPLE INCLUDING A POLITICIAN WHILE TELLING THEM WHY...
I ♡ RHODESIA
IT'S NOT TERRORISM PER SE...
HE'S A WACKY KID!
MUSLIM JAYWALKS...
ISIS HAS SEIZED KEY SIDEWALKS!
LOCK YOUR DOORS AND CRY!
BORS
THENIB.COM

While this was drawn after the Charleston church shooting perpetrated by a white supremacist, things would only get worse under Trump, with incidents of white terrorism ramping up and the Dept. of Homeland Security putting virtually no resources toward fighting it.

TONIGHT: WHITE CULTURE'S VIOLENT YOUNG MEN. MASS SHOOTINGS. CHURCH ARSONS. WHERE ARE THE FATHERS?
"IT'S ALL THIS COUNTRY MUSIC AND THE KID ROCK GLAMORIZING THIS... CONFEDERATE LIFESTYLE."
"YOU CAN'T GET A JOB DRESSED LIKE AN OUTLAW AND SPEAKING THAT SLANG TALK."
GIT
DAGGONE
DANG-DOODLE
"SAY WHAT NOW?!"
WHY DON'T YOU GET OFF WELFARE AND PUT ON SOMETHING MORE CON-VENTIONAL.
LIKE A PRIDE SHIRT.
BORS
THENIB.COM

This marked the first appearance of a black news anchor who flipped all the arguments thrown at the black community for violence and social problems back at white people as they leaned hard into white grievance and violence. He'd come in handy over the next few years.

OFFICER-INVOLVED SHOOTING
I WAS HERE AND INVOLVED. YES!
SOLDIER-INVOLVED VISIT
WE DID PLAY A ROLE!
I AGREE WITH YOUR WORDS.
COMPLIMENT-INVOLVED COMMUNICATION
NICE RACK @#!*? TAKE OFF YOUR CLOTHES!!
BELIEVER-INVOLVED DETONATION
NEGATIVITY-INVOLVED DECLARATION!
PANTS-INVOLVED CRAPPING!
BORS

THE STOCK MARKET IS CRASHING! DON'T PANIC BUT ALL MONEY IS PROBABLY WORTHLESS.
WAIT—IT'S RECOVERED ALREADY! AMERICA IS STRONG!
NO, IT'S DOWN. IT'S OVER. THIS COUNTRY IS OVER.
CHINA OWNS EVERYTHING!
OR DO THEY? THE DOW CLOSES UP!
WHUMP
THIS SYSTEM MAKES SENSE.
BORS

GATHER, MY CHILDREN. IT IS TIME FOR A PARABLE!
A SYRIAN REFUGEE WAS LYING IN THE ROAD...
"A SAMARITAN CAME UPON HIM AND, SEEING HIS ASYLUM PAPERS HAD BEEN PROPERLY FILED WITH THE EUROPEAN UNION, AGREED TO AID HIM."
"BUT HE DID HAVE A NUMBER OF QUESTIONS. WOULD HE STICK AROUND FOREVER? AND WHO WAS GOING TO PAY FOR ALL THIS ANYWAY? HIM?!"
WA...WATER...
IS THAT ALL THE ENGLISH YOU KNOW?
AND IT COULD VERY WELL BE AN ISIS GUY SNEAKING IN!
ONE DAY-BOOM -YOU'RE DEAD.
POINT IS, STAY ON YOUR TOES.
BORS

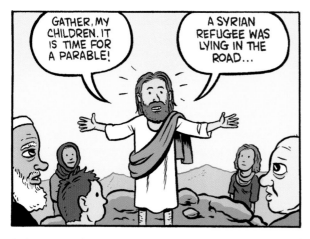

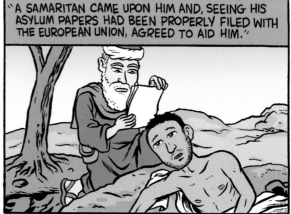

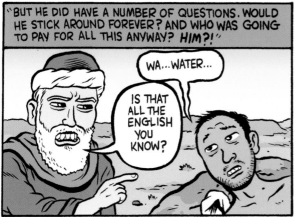

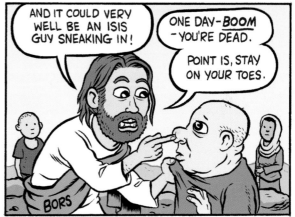

SO WE'RE REALLY DOING THIS. PRESIDENT TRUMP. WOWEE. WE ELECTED A MAN WHO, AMONG OTHER THINGS, MAYBE DID PEE STUFF IN RUSSIA?
YOU'RE A TEN.
YOU'RE A NINE.
URINATE.
CORRUPTION WILL BE RAMPANT. CONFLICTS OF INTEREST, THE EVERYDAY NORM FOR A GUY WHO, WE WONDER, IS INTO PEE.
HUGE BRIBE HERE, JUST ONE QUESTION: THIS PEE TAPE REAL?
OBAMACARE WILL BE DISMANTLED, MILLIONS WILL BE DESPERATE FOR COVERAGE AND ALSO TO KNOW, DEFINITIVELY, IF THEIR PRESIDENT LIKES GOLDEN SHOWERS.
GIVE IT TO ME STRAIGHT, DOC!
YOU THINK HE DID IT??
I JUST HOPE THOSE IN POWER WILL STAND UP TO HIM WHEN SHIT GETS REAL.
PEE BOY SAYS LAUNCH THE NUKES.
LOL.
GONNA DO IT THOUGH.
BORS
THENIB.COM

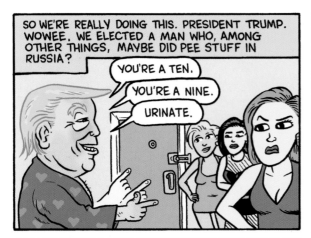

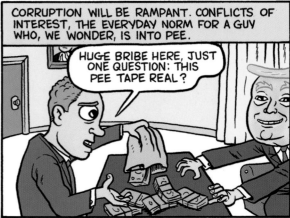

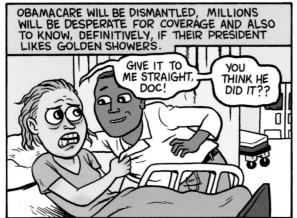

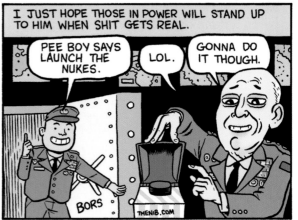

Ah, the pee tape. The Trump administration once was filled with such possibility.

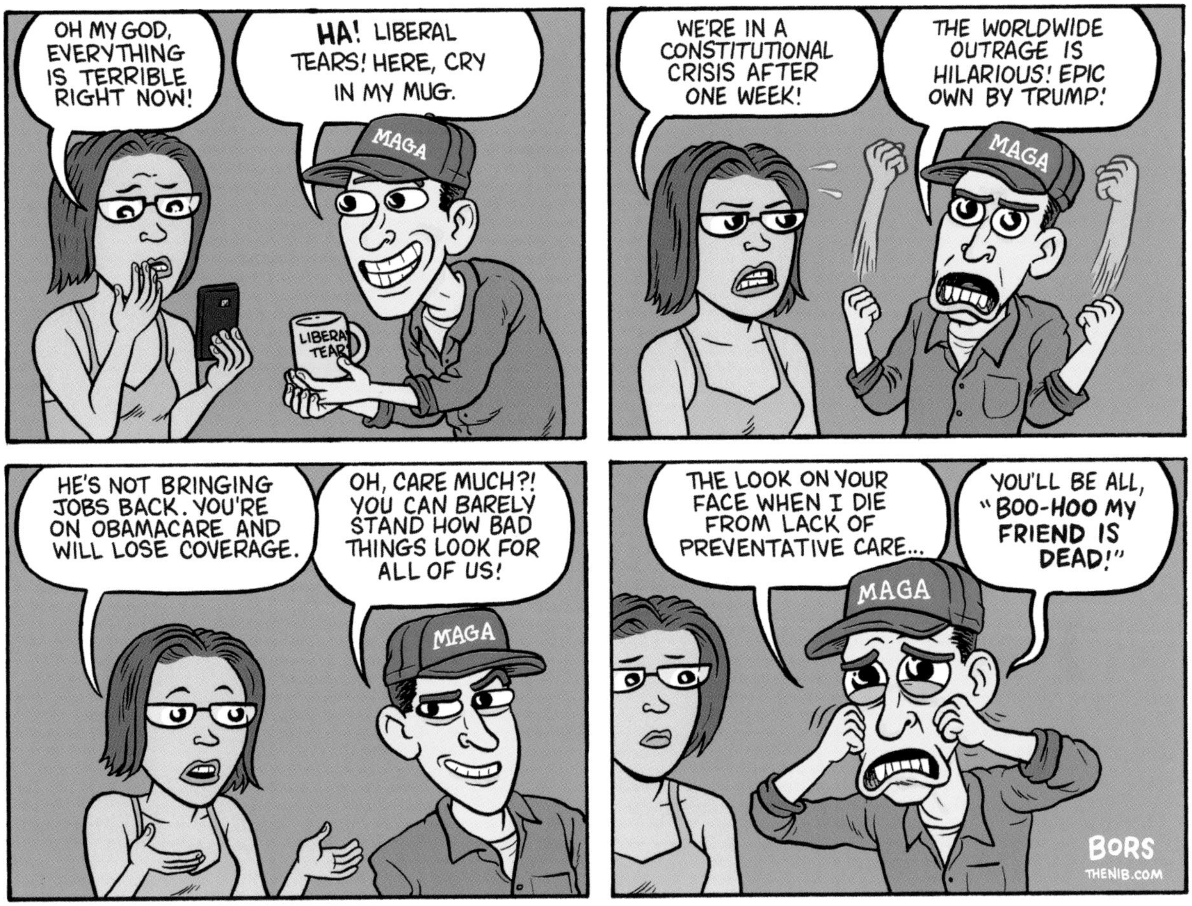
OH MY GOD, EVERYTHING IS TERRIBLE RIGHT NOW!
HA! LIBERAL TEARS! HERE, CRY IN MY MUG.
MAGA
LIBERAL TEARS
WE'RE IN A CONSTITUTIONAL CRISIS AFTER ONE WEEK!
THE WORLDWIDE OUTRAGE IS HILARIOUS! EPIC OWN BY TRUMP!
MAGA
HE'S NOT BRINGING JOBS BACK. YOU'RE ON OBAMACARE AND WILL LOSE COVERAGE.
OH, CARE MUCH?! YOU CAN BARELY STAND HOW BAD THINGS LOOK FOR ALL OF US!
MAGA
THE LOOK ON YOUR FACE WHEN I DIE FROM LACK OF PREVENTATIVE CARE...
YOU'LL BE ALL, "BOO-HOO MY FRIEND IS DEAD!"
MAGA
BORS
THENIB.COM

This would become a recurring character during the Trump era after "owning the libs" became the sole operating principle of conservatism.

HEH, TRUMP LIKES HIS STEAKS WELL DONE WITH KETCHUP. JESUS.
OH, IS SNOWFLAKE OFFENDED?
?
FLAVOR IS FOR **CUCKS**. I BURN MY STEAKS NOW. SMOTHER 'EM IN HEINZ.
YOU ARE **SO** OFFENDED!
MAGA
WE ARE OWNING LIBS SO HARD WITH OUR STEAK EATING. HASHTAG #WELLDONE. ARE YOU CRYING? DO YOU NEED A SAFE SPACE?
ARE YOU... OKAY?
I SWEAR, THE SLIGHTEST THING SETS YOU PEOPLE OFF.
I AM VERY NORMAL.
VVNNNNN
BORS
THENIB.COM

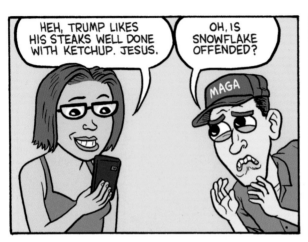

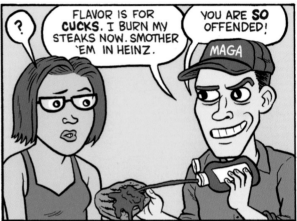

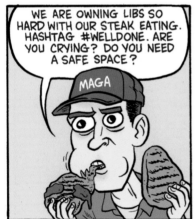

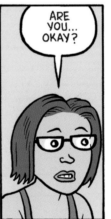

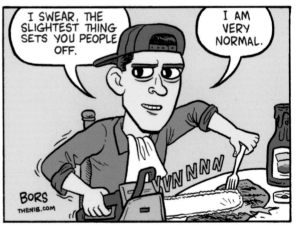

Of course the man whose business ventures include steaks named after himself prefers them cooked well-done slathered in ketchup. After this was criticized online, chuds attempted to trigger medium-steak-eating-libs by declaring their absolute love of burnt meat. I mention all this here to let you know this really happened.

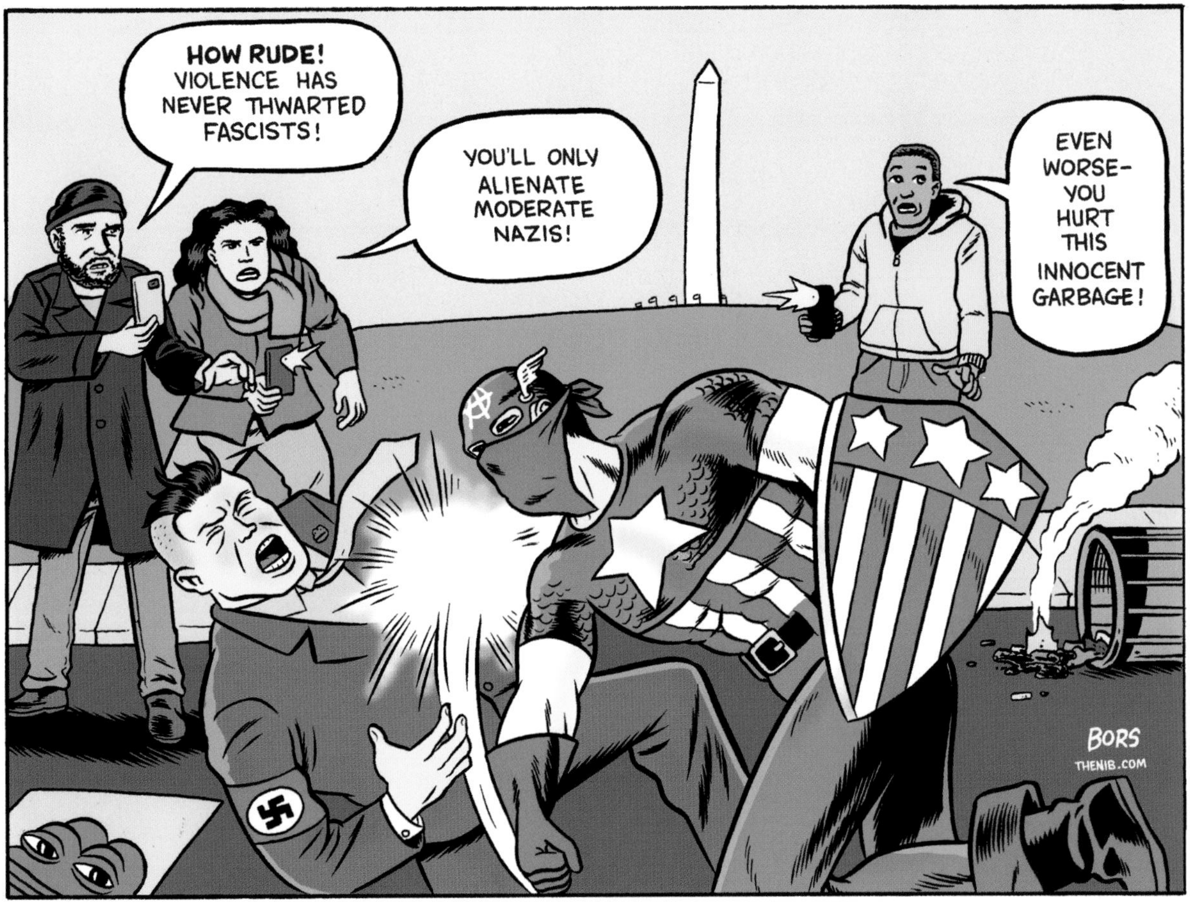
HOW RUDE! VIOLENCE HAS NEVER THWARTED FASCISTS!
YOU'LL ONLY ALIENATE MODERATE NAZIS!
EVEN WORSE- YOU HURT THIS INNOCENT GARBAGE!
BORS
THENIB.COM

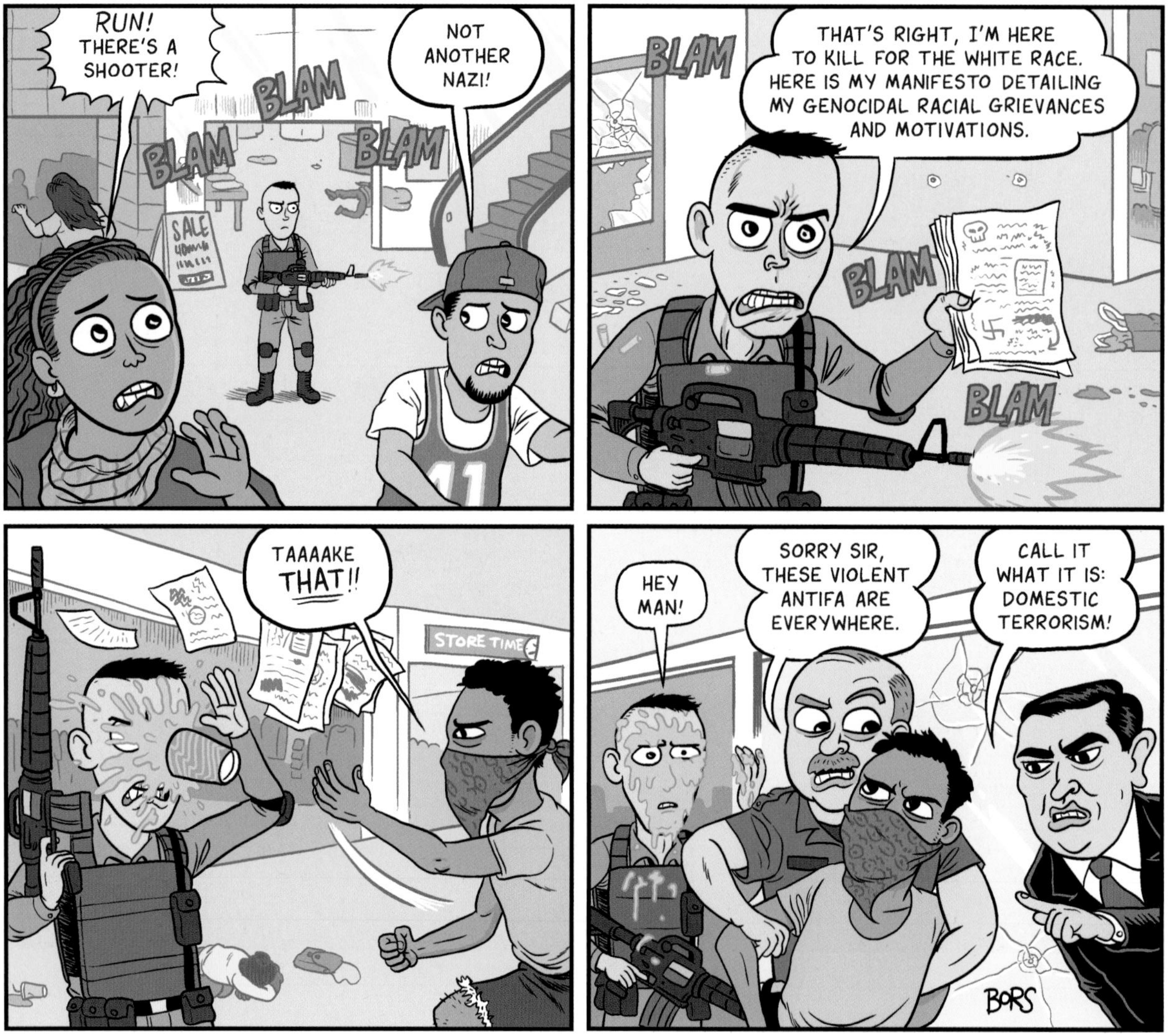
RUN! THERE'S A SHOOTER!
BLAM
BLAM
BLAM
SALE
NOT ANOTHER NAZI!
BLAM
THAT'S RIGHT, I'M HERE TO KILL FOR THE WHITE RACE. HERE IS MY MANIFESTO DETAILING MY GENOCIDAL RACIAL GRIEVANCES AND MOTIVATIONS.
BLAM
BLAM
TAAAAKE THAT!!
STORE TIME
HEY MAN!
SORRY SIR, THESE VIOLENT ANTIFA ARE EVERYWHERE.
CALL IT WHAT IT IS: DOMESTIC TERRORISM!
BORS

Antifa dumps a milkshake on some incel chud and we hear about how fascism is taking over the country from the left, while multiple terrorist attacks and pogroms are directly inspired by the President. By the way, Instagram removed this comic from my account for "promoting violence and dangerous organizations."

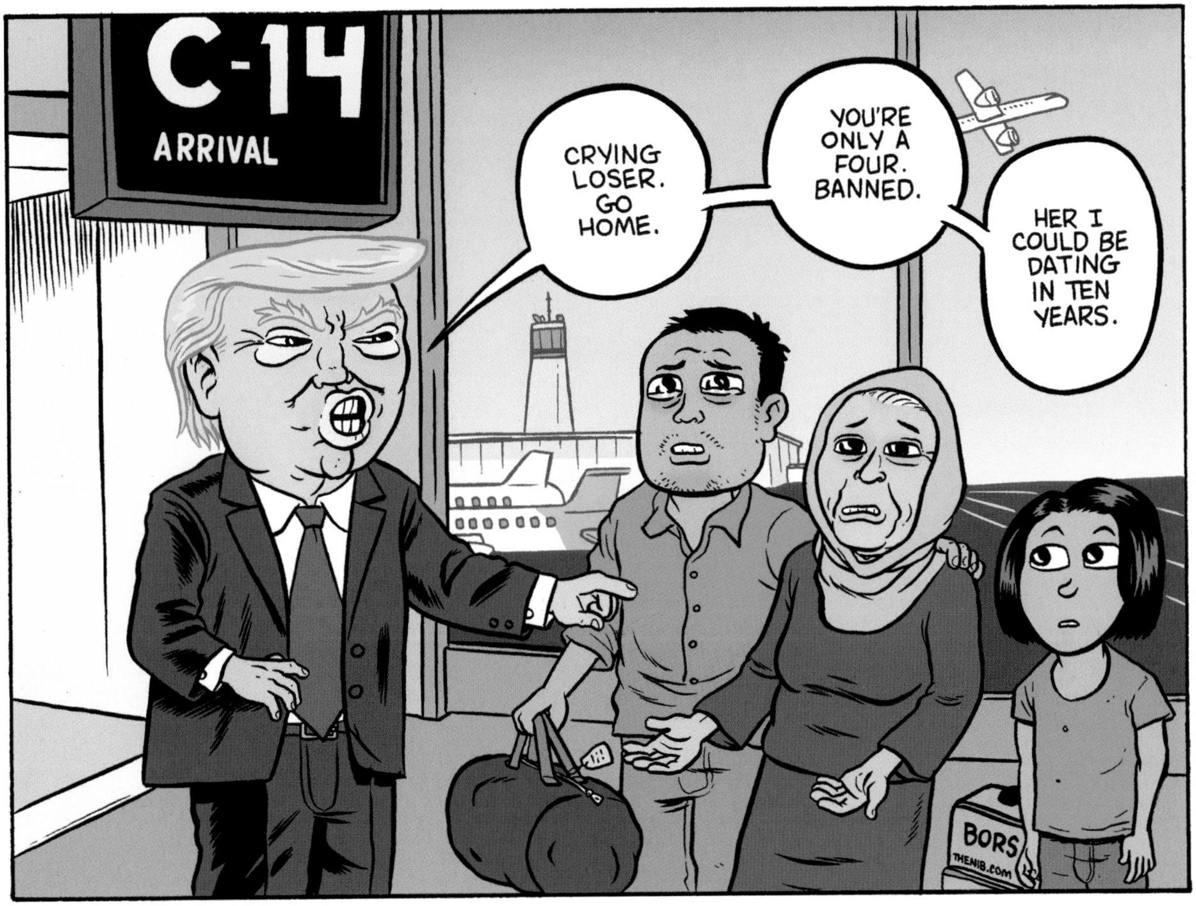
C-14
ARRIVAL
CRYING LOSER. GO HOME.
YOU'RE ONLY A FOUR. BANNED.
HER I COULD BE DATING IN TEN YEARS.
BORS
THENIB.COM

The establishment seemed shocked when Trump actually enacted his Muslim Ban, which a normal politician may have recognized as needlessly controversial and impractical. Trump's approach to politics and pleasing his base makes more sense when you understand, as writer Adam Serwer coined in The Atlantic, *"the cruelty is the point."*

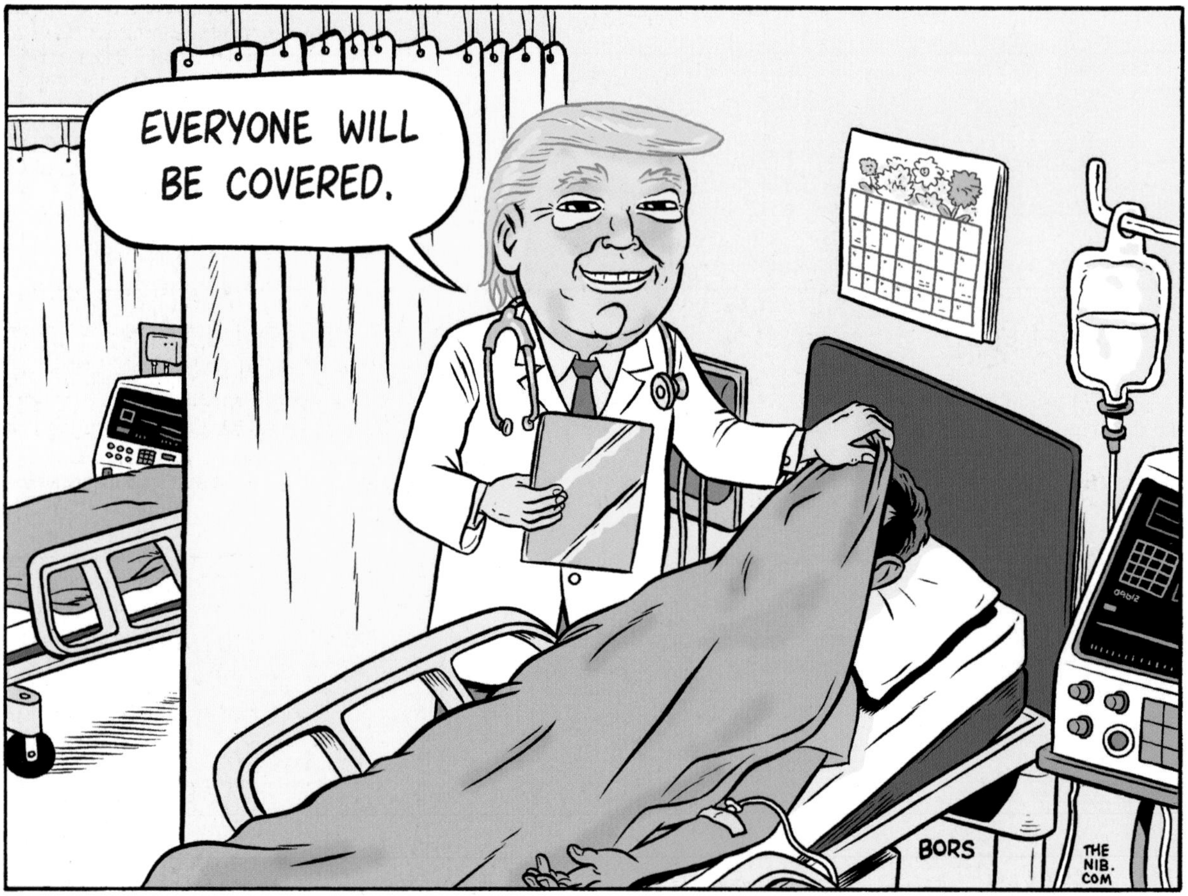
EVERYONE WILL BE COVERED.
BORS
THE NIB. COM

Donald Trump not in Situation Room for 'botched' Yemen raid that killed up to 30 civilians and one US Navy SEAL
WE'RE GOING TO WIN ON SO MANY LEVELS! WE'RE GOING TO WIN WIN WIN!
YOU'RE GOING TO GET SO TIRED OF WINNING!
YOU'RE GOING TO SAY, MR. PRESIDENT, PLEASE, WE DON'T WANT TO WIN ANYMORE!
IT'S TOO MUCH!!
AND I'M GOING TO SAY, I'M SORRY...
WE'RE GOING TO KEEP WINNING!!!
BORS
THENIB.COM

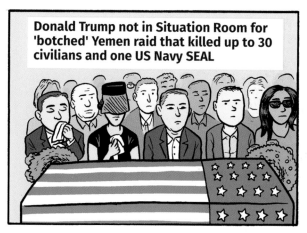

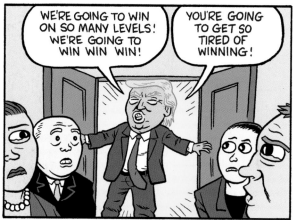

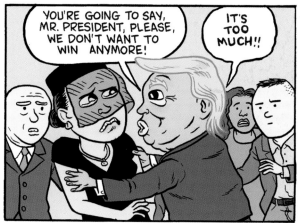

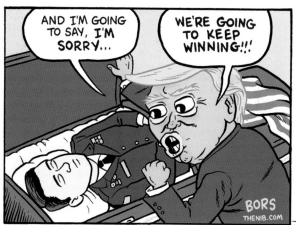

Another Trump controversy that would have been remembered for longer than a week under any other president. These were all quotes from the campaign trail. The winning had only just begun…

BLACK LIVES MATTER
!
NO, ALL LIVES MATTER. YOU HEAR ME? ALL LIVES!
ALL LIVES MATTER
OH, THANK GOD. I'M FLEEING A WAR ZONE AND–
NO. MUSLIMS. ALLOWED.
OR CAN'T YOU READ?
BORS

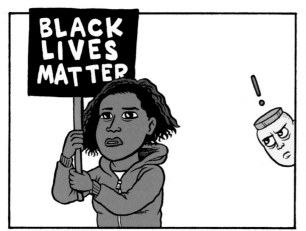

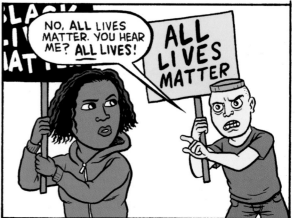

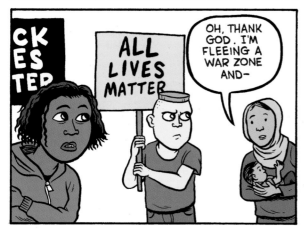

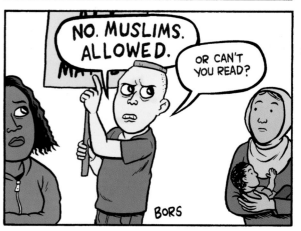

SO YOU SHOT UP THIS CAR FULL OF WHITE KIDS WHY?
I FELT THREATENED!
THEY PULLED UP BLASTING THAT **THUG CRAP**.
OH, YOU MEAN RIGHT-WING TALK RADIO?
YEAH, IT'S ALL ABOUT GETTING RICH AND DISRESPECTING WOMEN.
I... ASKED THEM TO TURN IT DOWN.
IT'S THEIR WHOLE **CULTURE**.
ME, I BLAME THE PARENTS.
BORS

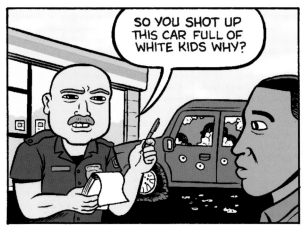

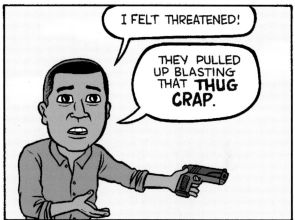

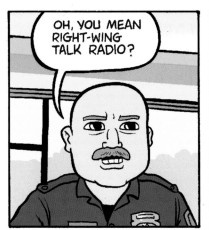

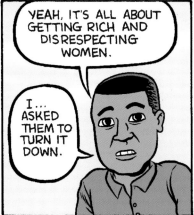

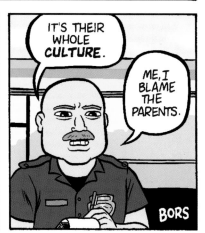

OKAY, HERE'S A REAL BOOK THAT EXISTS.
When Our Grown Kids Disappoint Us
LETTING GO OF THEIR PROBLEMS, LOVING THEM ANYWAY, AND GETTING ON WITH OUR LIVES
JANE ADAMS, PHD
THAT TITLE!
IT KICKS OFF WITH THE INFANTILIZING "GROWN KIDS" BEFORE DROPPING THE ULTIMATE PARENT WORD...
YOUR MOM AND I DON'T HATE YOU...
WE'RE JUST DISAPPOINTED.
BORS
THE SUBTITLE SEEMS SCIENTIFICALLY DESIGNED TO SEND A SUBCONSCIOUS SIGNAL: "GO AHEAD AND BUY THAT BMW."
HAVE A GREAT LIFE!
EVERY MILLENNIAL SHOULD BUY A COPY FOR THEIR PARENTS.
AND DEFINITELY USE THEIR CREDIT CARD.

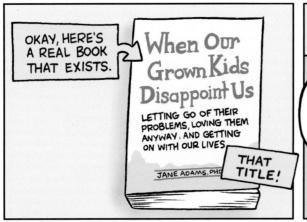

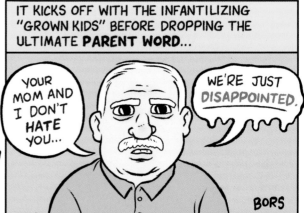

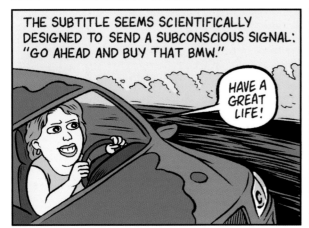

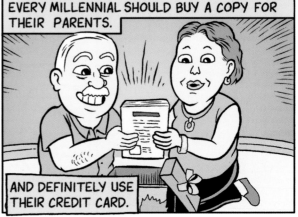

TRUE THING: McDONALD'S WORKERS ARE BEING GIVEN MUSTARD AND MAYO TO TREAT GREASE BURNS.

UH, THIS IS...?

MEDICINE

JUST ONE OF THE CURE-ALLS YOU'LL FIND AT **RONALD'S WORKER APOTHECARY.**

SLUDGE OF COFFEE

SESAME SEED SCRAPINGS

WHATEVER IS IN THE McNUGGETS

NOW, BACK TO WORK!

RUN DOWN FROM NO BREAKS? TRY A REJUVENATING SHAMROCK SHAKE BATH.

I'M... NOT LOVIN' IT.

BORS
THENIB.COM

NEED A SICK DAY? NO, YOU NEED A SPECIAL SAUCE IV.

I NEED... A RAISE.

OH DEAR—SHE'S HALLUCINAT-ING!

...AND IT WAS, LIKE, SO BAE I LITERALLY DIED.
heh, OLDS.
WAIT, IS BAE NOT A THING ANYMORE?
WHAT ARE THE NEW WORDS?
WHAT DO TEENS SAY?
GIVE ME THE SLANG! IT SERVES AS MY MASK, PROJECTING YOUTHFUL DETACHMENT WHILE OBSCURING MY SLIDE INTO IRRELEVANCY AND DEATH!
"IT ME." WE SAY IT ME NOW.
RIGHT.
IT ME.
THE VERY COOL AND CHILL GUY.
BORS

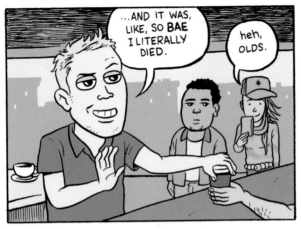

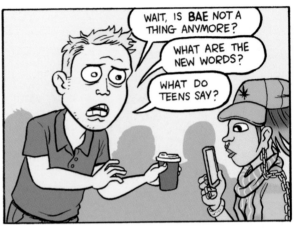

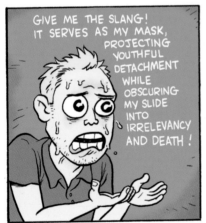

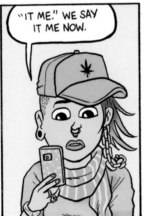

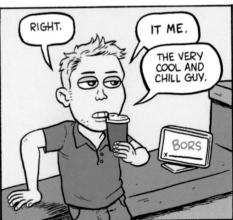

You can file "it me" alongside phrases like "squad goals" and "bae" that erupt into wide usage online almost overnight, quickly adopted by the young and people desperate to project the air of youth, before being turned into cringe by the twitter accounts for brands—all inside of a week.

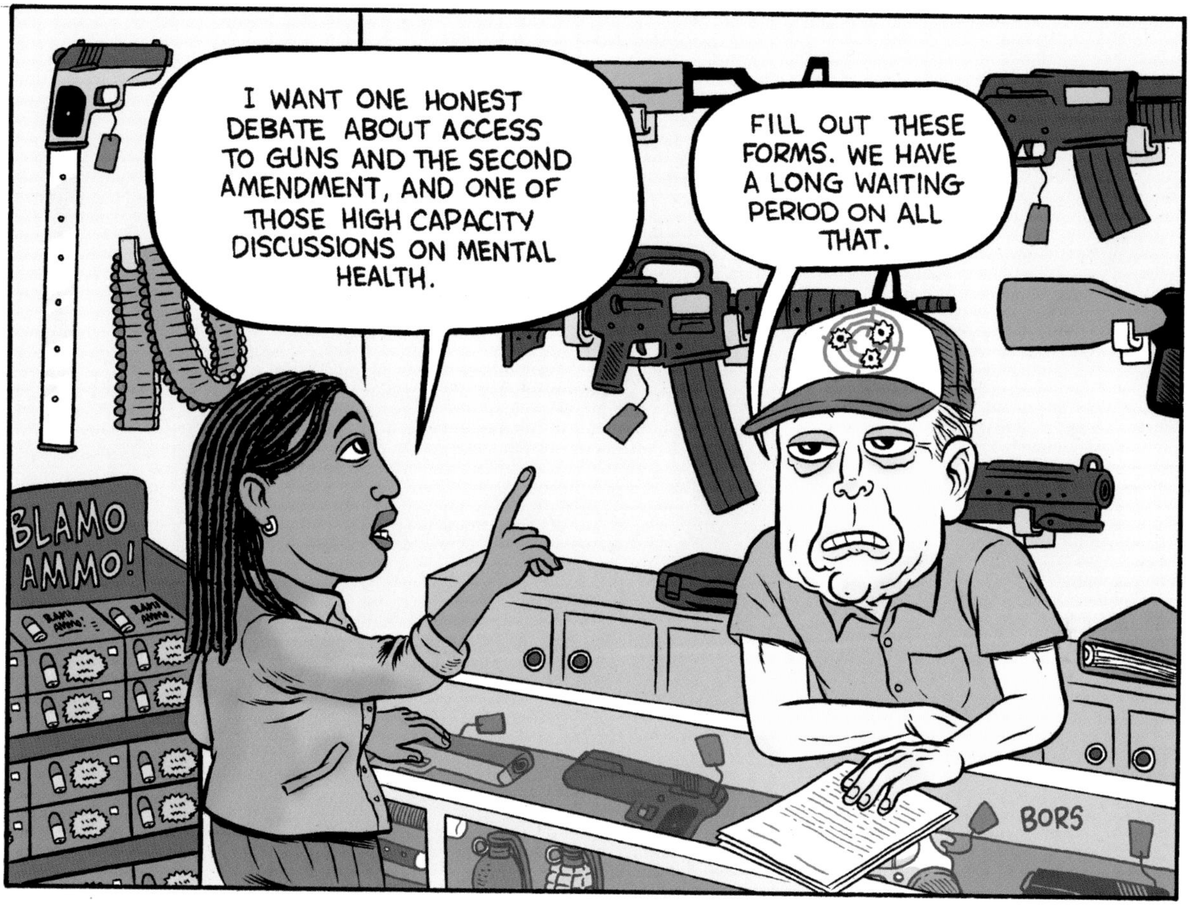
I WANT ONE HONEST DEBATE ABOUT ACCESS TO GUNS AND THE SECOND AMENDMENT, AND ONE OF THOSE HIGH CAPACITY DISCUSSIONS ON MENTAL HEALTH.
FILL OUT THESE FORMS. WE HAVE A LONG WAITING PERIOD ON ALL THAT.
BLAMO AMMO!
BORS

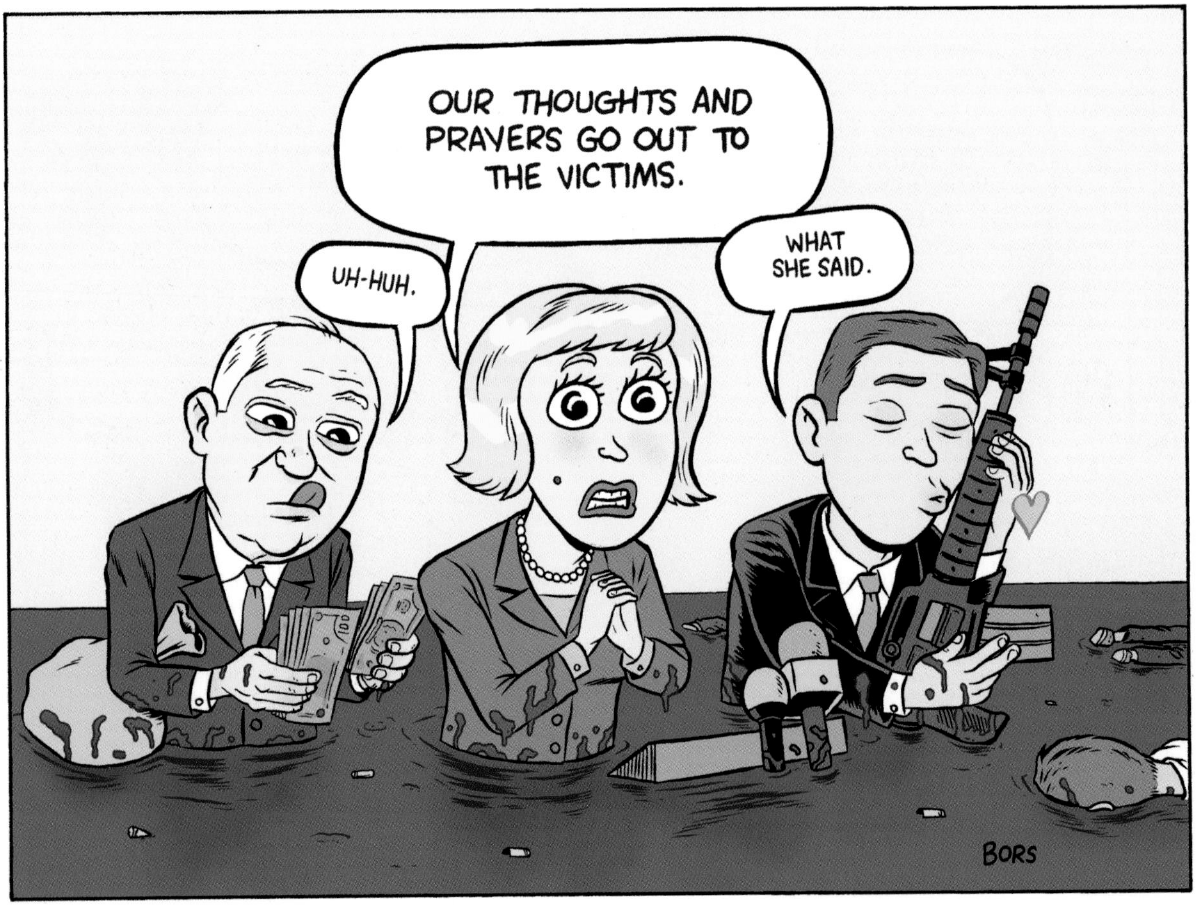
UH-HUH.
OUR THOUGHTS AND PRAYERS GO OUT TO THE VICTIMS.
WHAT SHE SAID.
BORS

AFTER ORLANDO, A PUSH TO REMOVE GUN EMOJIS FROM PHONES.
FROM MY COLD DEAD
SUNDAY TAKES
PEOPLE WHO USE THE SHOULD NOT BE ALLOWED TO
THE STATE OF ACTIVISM HAS ME LIKE
12
NRA
we good bb?
as long as they don't ban
BORS

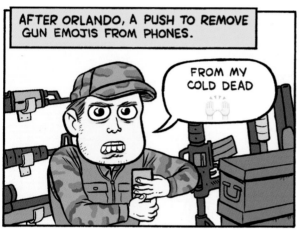

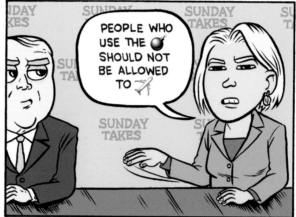

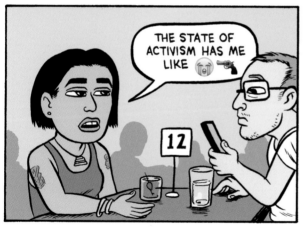

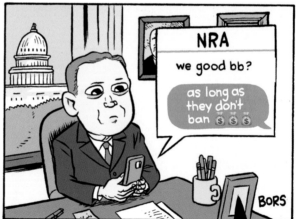

As if written as parody of pointless liberal do-gooderism, a movement to strip the emoji library of the gun and replace it with a toy gained traction in lieu of being able to do anything as a country about gun violence.

TONIGHT! WHITE ON WHITE GANG CRIME. DO BIKERS LACK FAMILY VALUES? OR IS HEAVY METAL TO BLAME?
WACO: BRAWL
"NOW, I KNOW, MOST POT-BELLIED WHITE MEN WITH THREE FOOT BEARDS ARE HARMLESS HOME BREWERS, BUT WE SHOULD STOP AND FRISK THEM ALL TO BE CERTAIN."
"BUT WHY DRESS LIKE THAT? WHY WEAR CHAPS UNLESS YOU WANT THE BANDIDOS TO STAB YOU IN THE FACE OVER METH?"
IT'S THUG ATTIRE! YOU WANT RESPECT, WEAR SOMETHING NORMAL.
LIKE A HOODIE.
BORS
THENIB.COM

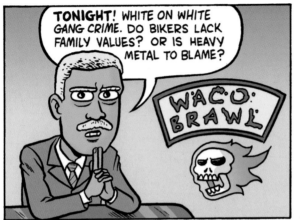

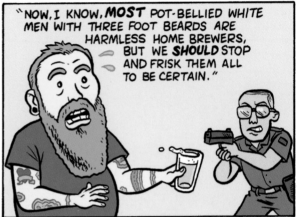

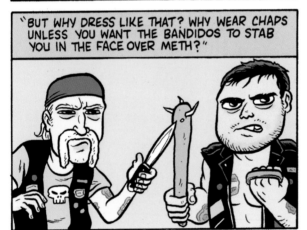

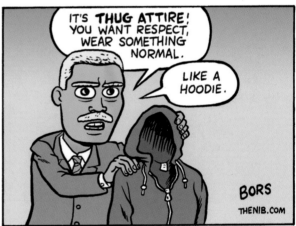

On May 17, 2015, in Waco, Texas, a massive shootout between 200 bikers left nine people dead and 18 wounded. Had this involved a gathering of black people, motorcycles would now be illegal.

EVERYONE SHOULD OPEN CARRY AT ALL TIMES!
PREFERABLY WITH ASSAULT RIFLES.
FOR SAFETY.
I USE HOLLOW POINTS FOR THE BEST ORGAN DAMAGE.
MAGAZINES SHOULD BE FOUR FEET LONG, THE LENGTH OF MY PENIS.
THERE'S BEEN ANOTHER BLACK MAN SHOT FOR NO REASON!
TOTALLY BY THE BOOK.
HE HAD A GUN.
BORS

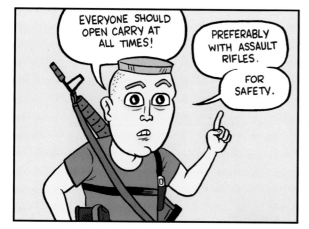

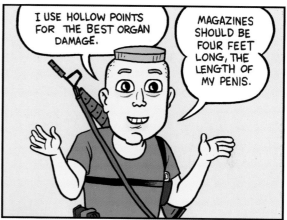

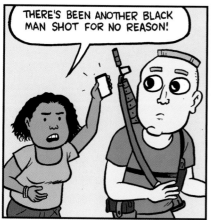

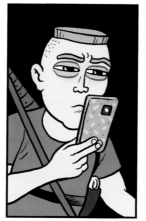

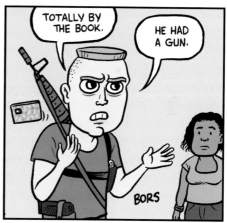

WHY WOMEN CLAIM SEXUAL ASSAULT

FAME
LIAR
COMPLETE SEXUAL HISTORY
ME.
GLORY
WHY NOW?
ANY EVIDENCE?
NOT A TEN.
PLEASE, KEEP 'EM COMING!
NEW FRIENDS
"I'M GONNA KILL YOU @#*?!"
READ ANOTHER, MOMMY!
RICHES
GROPE
THE MOVIE
CRITICS SAY YOU WON'T BELIEVE...
HOW GOOD IT IS!
BORS
THEN18.COM

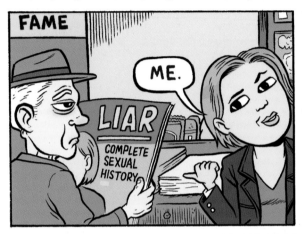

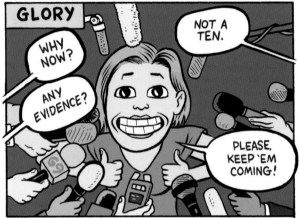

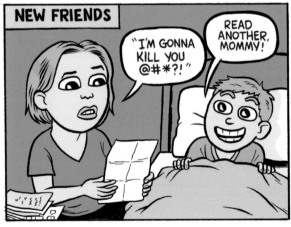

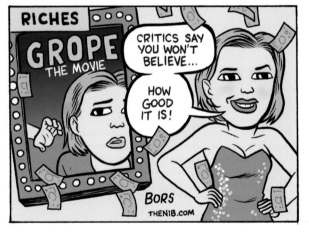

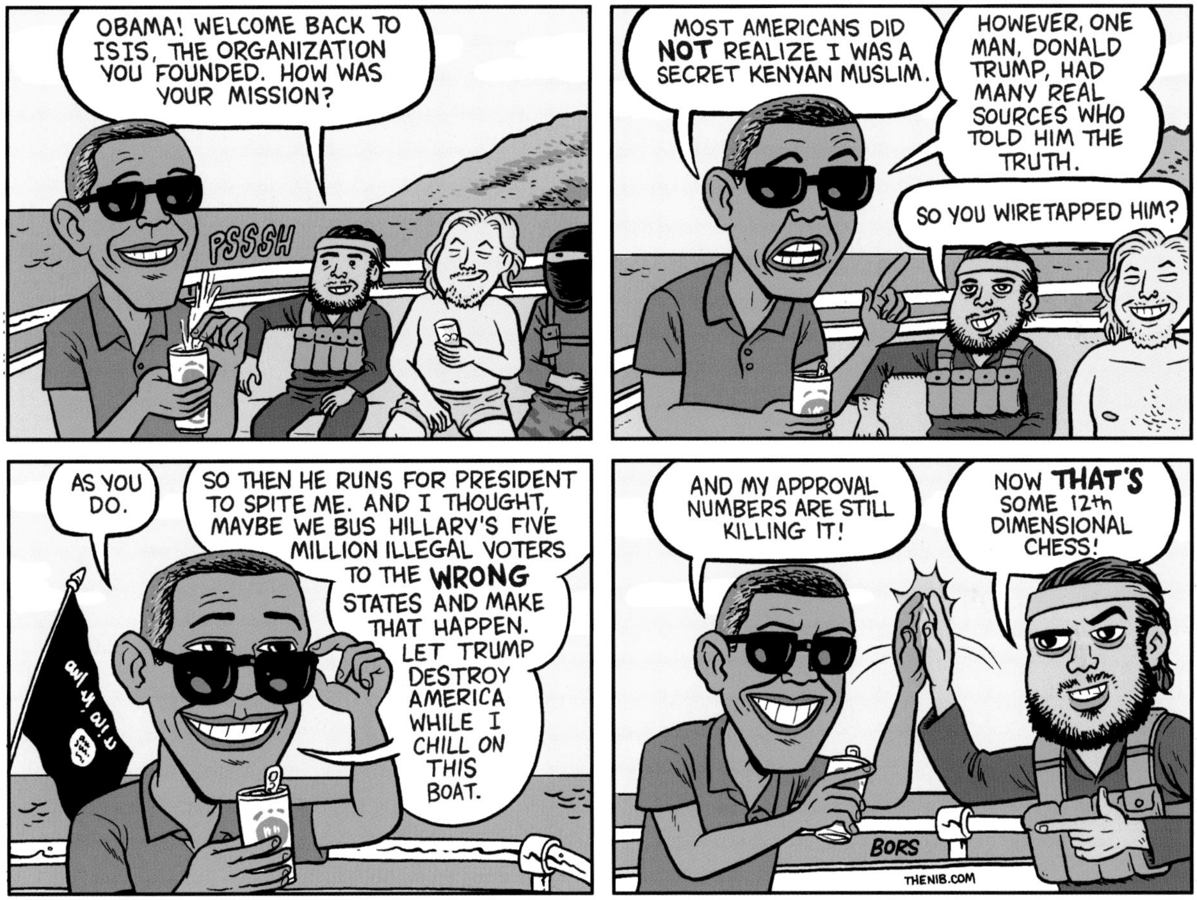
OBAMA! WELCOME BACK TO ISIS, THE ORGANIZATION YOU FOUNDED. HOW WAS YOUR MISSION?
PSSSH
MOST AMERICANS DID NOT REALIZE I WAS A SECRET KENYAN MUSLIM.
HOWEVER, ONE MAN, DONALD TRUMP, HAD MANY REAL SOURCES WHO TOLD HIM THE TRUTH.
SO YOU WIRETAPPED HIM?
AS YOU DO.
SO THEN HE RUNS FOR PRESIDENT TO SPITE ME. AND I THOUGHT, MAYBE WE BUS HILLARY'S FIVE MILLION ILLEGAL VOTERS TO THE WRONG STATES AND MAKE THAT HAPPEN. LET TRUMP DESTROY AMERICA WHILE I CHILL ON THIS BOAT.
AND MY APPROVAL NUMBERS ARE STILL KILLING IT!
NOW THAT'S SOME 12th DIMENSIONAL CHESS!
BORS
THENIB.COM

This is a straightforward illustration of the views of the President of the United States regarding the previous President without exaggeration or hyperbole.

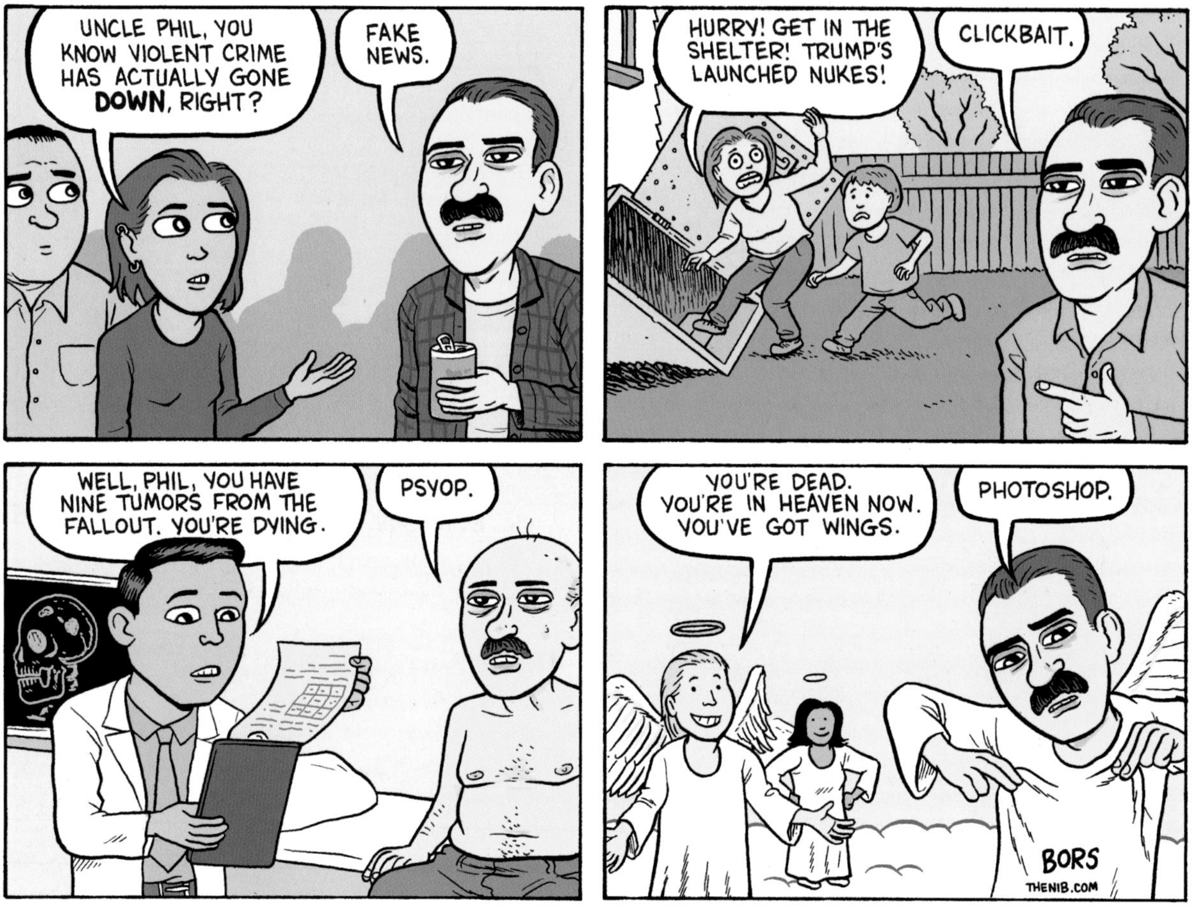
UNCLE PHIL, YOU KNOW VIOLENT CRIME HAS ACTUALLY GONE **DOWN**, RIGHT?
FAKE NEWS.
HURRY! GET IN THE SHELTER! TRUMP'S LAUNCHED NUKES!
CLICKBAIT.
WELL, PHIL, YOU HAVE NINE TUMORS FROM THE FALLOUT. YOU'RE DYING.
PSYOP.
YOU'RE DEAD. YOU'RE IN HEAVEN NOW. YOU'VE GOT WINGS.
PHOTOSHOP.
BORS
THENIB.COM

We all know an Uncle Phil. I have a literal Uncle Phil—two if you count in-laws. Neither are quite this bad though. (Sorry, Phils!)

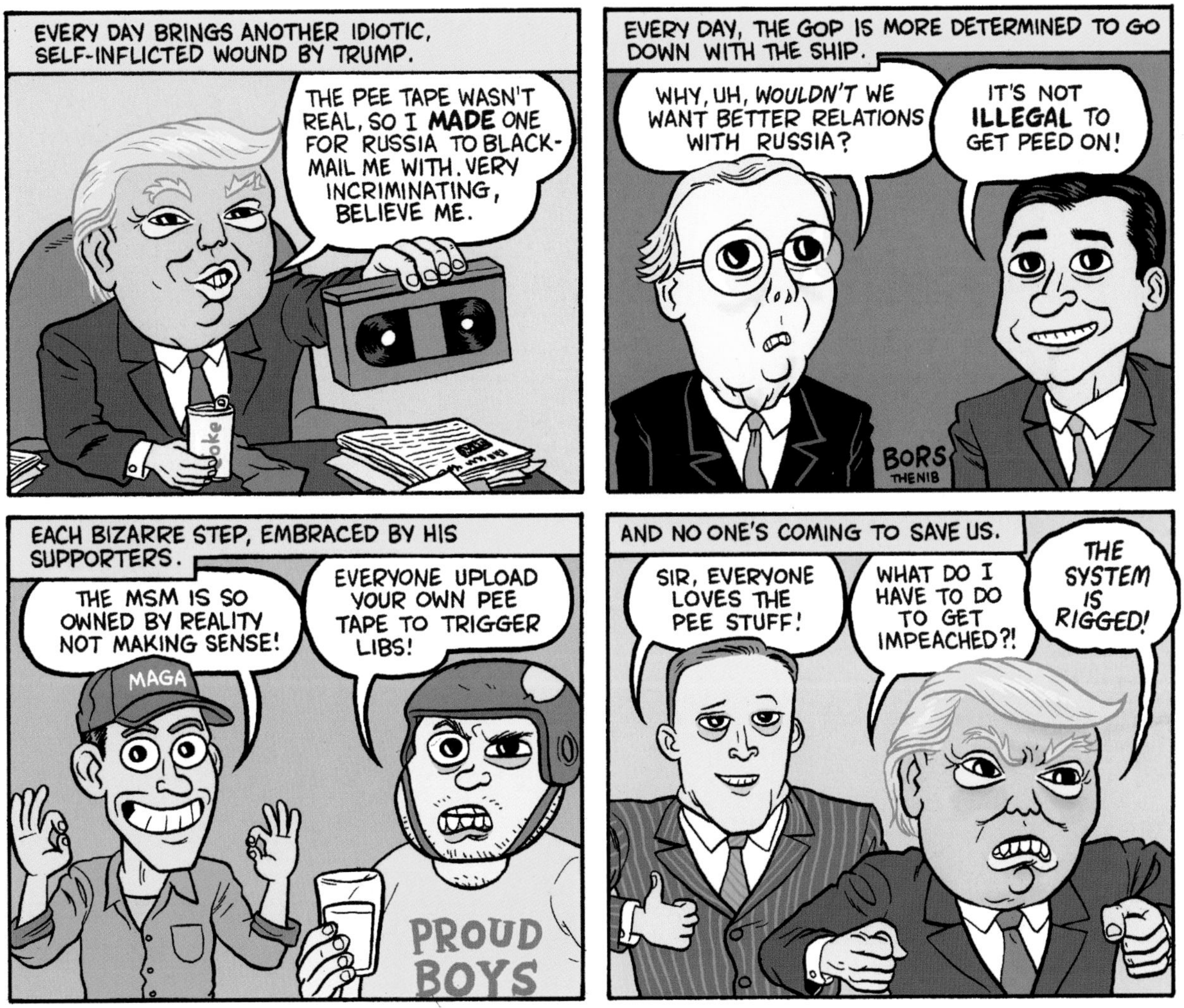
EVERY DAY BRINGS ANOTHER IDIOTIC, SELF-INFLICTED WOUND BY TRUMP.
THE PEE TAPE WASN'T REAL, SO I MADE ONE FOR RUSSIA TO BLACK-MAIL ME WITH. VERY INCRIMINATING, BELIEVE ME.
EVERY DAY, THE GOP IS MORE DETERMINED TO GO DOWN WITH THE SHIP.
WHY, UH, WOULDN'T WE WANT BETTER RELATIONS WITH RUSSIA?
IT'S NOT ILLEGAL TO GET PEED ON!
BORS THENIB
EACH BIZARRE STEP, EMBRACED BY HIS SUPPORTERS.
THE MSM IS SO OWNED BY REALITY NOT MAKING SENSE!
MAGA
EVERYONE UPLOAD YOUR OWN PEE TAPE TO TRIGGER LIBS!
PROUD BOYS
AND NO ONE'S COMING TO SAVE US.
SIR, EVERYONE LOVES THE PEE STUFF!
WHAT DO I HAVE TO DO TO GET IMPEACHED?!
THE SYSTEM IS RIGGED!

SHERIFF CLARKE'S DEFINITELY REAL MEDALS
We the...
FOR AUTHORITARIAN VISION ABOVE AND BEYOND TYPICAL INSANE COP
EXEMPLARY PLAGIARISM OF MASTER'S THESIS
RECOGNITION OF VERY SECURE MASCULINITY
HONORARY WHITE NATIONALIST
OVERSAW JAIL WHERE INMATE DIED OF THIRST AND NO ONE WAS CHARGED FOR SOME REASON
100
ATE 100 SUBWAY FOOTLONGS
50 CENTS AT GOODWILL
100K POSTS ON 4CHAN
MAKE MY DAY
CAME WITH "DIRTY HARRY" DIRECTOR'S CUT BLU-RAY
PICKED THIS UP AT AN INDIE COMICS SHOW OR SOMETHING?
BORS
THENIB.COM

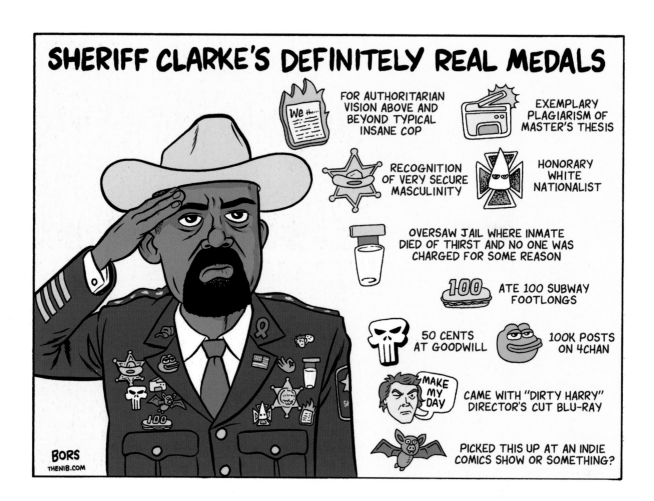

Former Milwaukee County Sheriff David Clarke is classic C-list Trump-era villain. An authoritarian grifter festooned in fake war medals, Clarke said he was offered a position in the Department of Homeland Security, but this was apparently pulled due to Clarke's inmates dying in custody. You would think that would be a plus for Trump, but I theorize it's more likely he viewed Clarke as uncontrollable and potential competition for media attention.

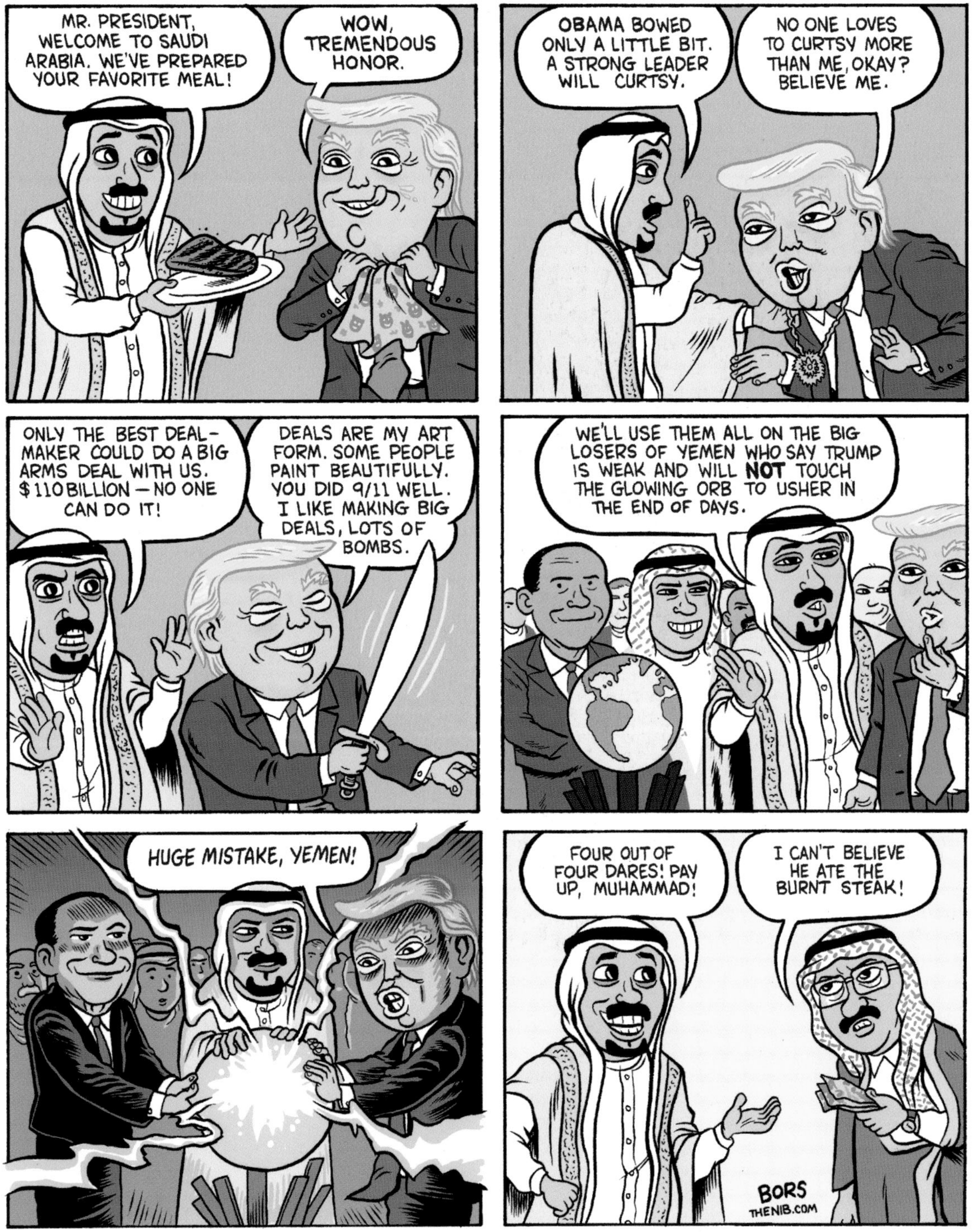
MR. PRESIDENT, WELCOME TO SAUDI ARABIA. WE'VE PREPARED YOUR FAVORITE MEAL!
WOW, TREMENDOUS HONOR.
OBAMA BOWED ONLY A LITTLE BIT. A STRONG LEADER WILL CURTSY.
NO ONE LOVES TO CURTSY MORE THAN ME, OKAY? BELIEVE ME.
ONLY THE BEST DEAL-MAKER COULD DO A BIG ARMS DEAL WITH US. $110 BILLION — NO ONE CAN DO IT!
DEALS ARE MY ART FORM. SOME PEOPLE PAINT BEAUTIFULLY. YOU DID 9/11 WELL. I LIKE MAKING BIG DEALS, LOTS OF BOMBS.
WE'LL USE THEM ALL ON THE BIG LOSERS OF YEMEN WHO SAY TRUMP IS WEAK AND WILL **NOT** TOUCH THE GLOWING ORB TO USHER IN THE END OF DAYS.
HUGE MISTAKE, YEMEN!
FOUR OUT OF FOUR DARES! PAY UP, MUHAMMAD!
I CAN'T BELIEVE HE ATE THE BURNT STEAK!
BORS
THENIB.COM

SIR, MULTIPLE PEOPLE WERE STABBED BY A TERRORIST IN—
SHUT DOWN THE BORDERS!
MUSLIMS ARE BANNED. YEAH, IT'S A **BAN**. QUOTE ME ON THAT! NO TIME TO BE PC. USE THE WORDS "RACIST INTERNMENT CAMPS" IN COURT SO WE DEFINITELY WIN!
SIR, THIS WAS A WHITE GUY. IN PORTLAND. HE WAS HARASSING MUSLIM GIRLS.
OH.
WELL, DOES HE NEED A JOB?
BORS
THENIB.COM

TOP CONCERN: STOPPING SHARIA LAW
ISIS HATES WOMEN AND GAYS, LIKE ME, BUT THEY HATE THEM WHILE **BROWN**.
LOWEST PRIORITY: HAVING MEDICAID.
CAN'T MAKE ME PAY TAXES IF I'M DEAD!
TAP TAP TAP
EXTREMELY IMPORTANT: STATUE OF AN OLD RACIST.
MUH HERITAGE!
GET TO IT LATER: THE PLANET WE LIVE ON.
OH LORD! GREAT GRANPAPPY IS GETTIN' WET!
BORS
THENIB.COM

The economic anxiety of Trump supporters has a very strange way of showing itself.

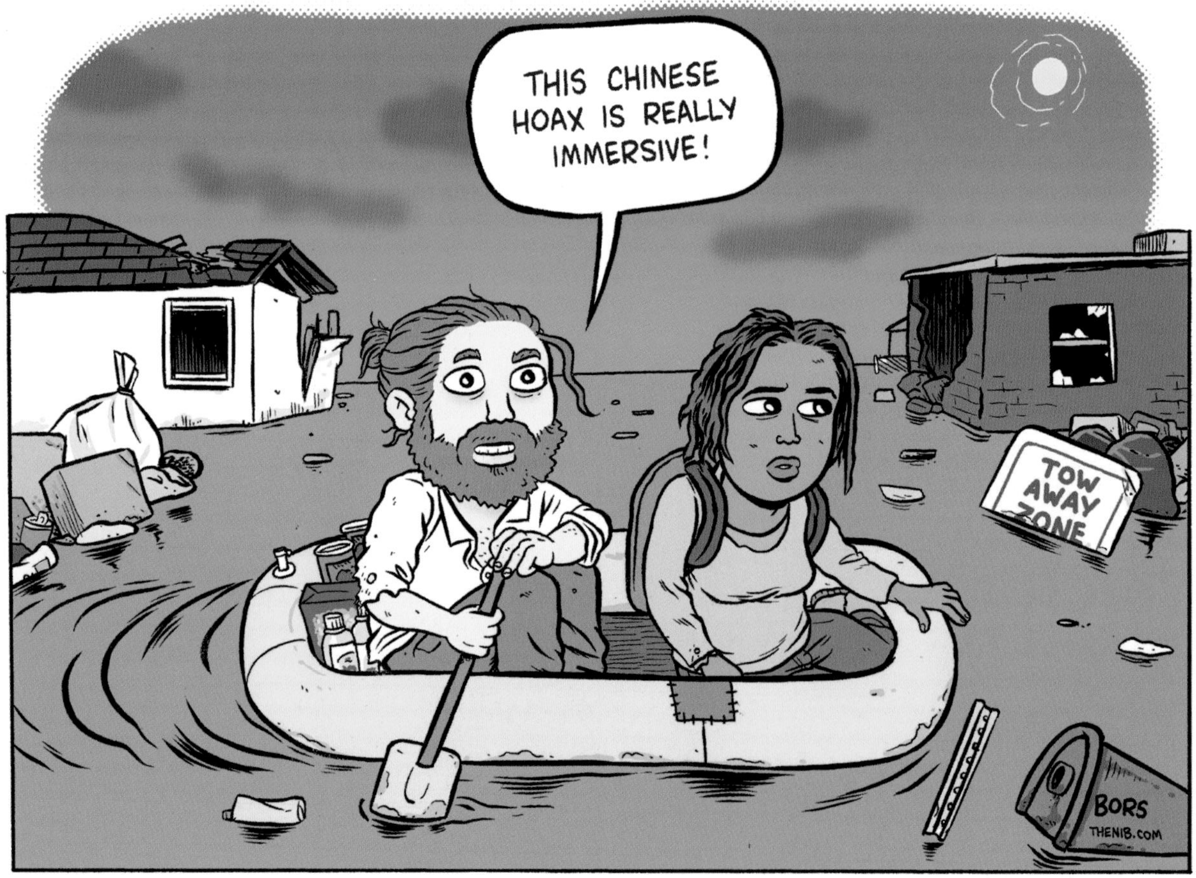
THIS CHINESE HOAX IS REALLY IMMERSIVE!
TOW AWAY ZONE
BORS
THENIB.COM

MILLIONS OF AMERICANS ARE SET TO LOSE HEALTH INSURANCE AND COUNTLESS WILL GO BROKE AND DIE. SO... HOW WILL THIS AFFECT THE **PARTIES**?
SUNDAY HOT TAKES
THE DEAD DON'T VOTE. LOWER TURN-OUT MEANS MORE GOP VICTORIES!
NAH—PEOPLE HATE DYING! DEMOCRATS CAN SIT BACK AND WIN, LIKE ALWAYS.
EDITORIAL CARTOON GRIM REAPER, THE LITERAL HARBINGER OF DEATH...
YOUR THOUGHTS?
I'M JUST GLAD MEDICAID FOR ALL IS SEEN AS POLITICALLY IMPOSSIBLE. IT WOULD BE TERRIBLE FOR ME,
PERSONALLY, A HARVESTER OF SOULS.
YEAH, JEEZ.
WELL, I'M GLAD YOU HAVE SOME SECURITY.
THENIB.COM
BORS

HOLD ONTO YOUR SEATS, FOLKS–TRUMP HAS TWEETED SOMETHING VERY OFFENSIVE...
AGAIN!
WE LEAD WITH THIS TONIGHT!
SYRIA
AHCA
PERSONALLY, I THOUGHT THIS 70 YEAR OLD MANIAC WOULD BE TRANSFORMED BY THE WEIGHT AND GRAVITY OF HIGH OFFICE.
POSITIONS, EVERYONE!
UNBECOMING! DANGEROUS!
THIS ENDS N–
NEW TWEETS JUST IN–TRUMP'S BOMBING SYRIA.
AND TONIGHT'S NEWS: THE VERY PRESIDENTIAL TRUMP DID GOOD LEADERSHIP WITH BOMBS.
I, FOR ONE, WOULD MAKE LOVE TO HIM.
BORS
THENIB.COM

Everyone in the establishment media waited a long time for Trump to become a Serious President who united instead of dividing the nation. And what better time for that than a missile strike? MSNBC anchor Brian Williams said the "beautiful pictures of fearsome armaments" being launched on a Syrian airfield called to mind a Leonard Cohen lyric: "I am guided by the beauty of our weapons." He then asked, "What did they hit?"

DAY 120 OF THE 30 DAY PLAN TO DEFEAT ISIS.
SO, I WANT "TRUMP" SPELLED ACROSS SYRIA IN **MOABS**. **THEN** WE CHARGE ISIS FOR LICENSING MY NAME.
SIR... WE CAN'T JUST DO THAT. IT'S, UH... TRANSGENDER SOLDIERS.
YES, THEIR TREMENDOUS MEDICAL COSTS!
WE'RE BROKE!
OKAY, NUKES THEN. LAUNCH THE NUKES–QUICK, BEFORE HANNITY STARTS.
SORRY, WE SOLD THEM. TO PAY FOR... GENDER STUFF.
Donald J. Trump
@realDonaldTrump
Following
After consultation with my Generals and military experts, please be advised we will not accept or allow transgender individuals....
5:55 AM - 26 Jul 2017
BORS
THENIB.COM

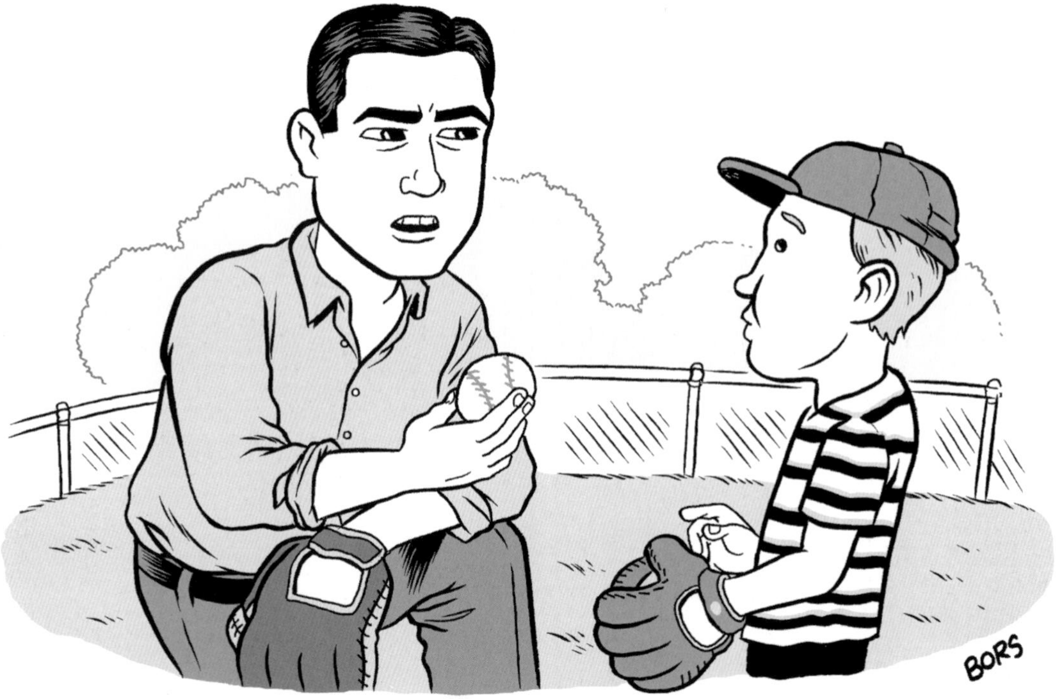
BORS

"Son, you throw like a girl raised in a patriarchal society that discourages women from participating in sports."

MAYBE WE SHOULD GET A DRINK SOMETIME.
UH, SURE.
555-7389
I HOPE SHE DIDN'T GIVE ME A FAKE NUMBER.
I HOPE HE DOESN'T RAPE AND MURDER ME.
BORS

SATURDAY NIGHT LIVE
VERY UNFAIR. WORST ATTACK ON A PRESIDENT IN NATION'S HISTORY!
ALEC BALDWIN SHOULD BE FIRED!
FACTUAL NEWS ARTICLE
FAKE NEWS. ALL AMERICANS MUST CONDEMN, BY NAME, THE FAILING NEW YORK TIMES!
KATHY GRIFFIN BEING MEAN
HEINOUS CRIME!
JUSTICE DEPARTMENT INVESTIGATION UNDERWAY!
HISTORY WILL KNOW HER NAME!!!
NEO-NAZI TERRORIST ATTACK
THERE ARE MANY SIDES TO THIS ISSUE...
MANY, MANY SIDES. IT'S A...
Google
many sides
DODECA-HEDRON, REALLY.
BORS

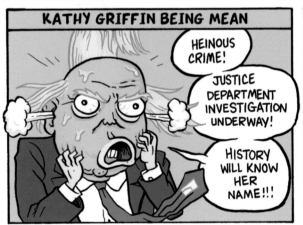

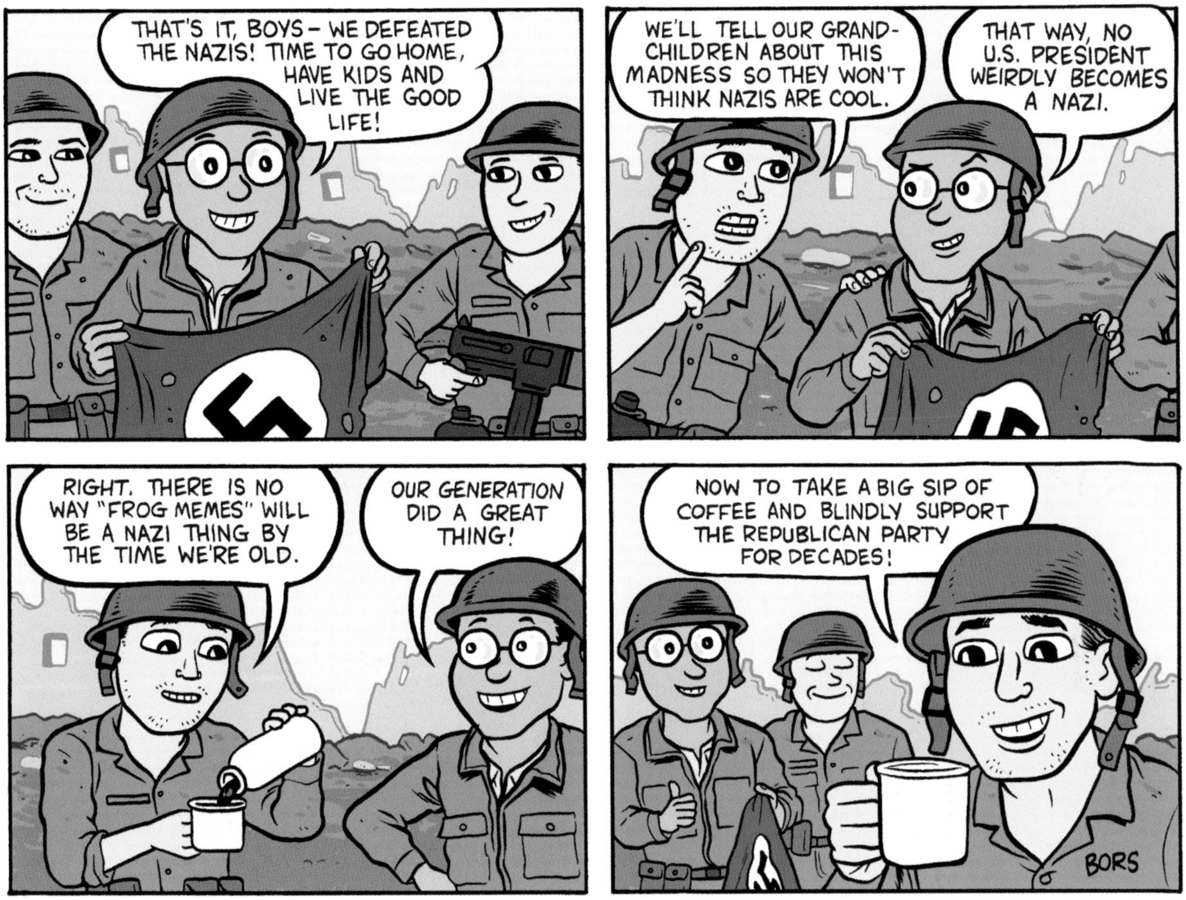
THAT'S IT, BOYS - WE DEFEATED THE NAZIS! TIME TO GO HOME, HAVE KIDS AND LIVE THE GOOD LIFE!
WE'LL TELL OUR GRAND-CHILDREN ABOUT THIS MADNESS SO THEY WON'T THINK NAZIS ARE COOL.
THAT WAY, NO U.S. PRESIDENT WEIRDLY BECOMES A NAZI.
RIGHT. THERE IS NO WAY "FROG MEMES" WILL BE A NAZI THING BY THE TIME WE'RE OLD.
OUR GENERATION DID A GREAT THING!
NOW TO TAKE A BIG SIP OF COFFEE AND BLINDLY SUPPORT THE REPUBLICAN PARTY FOR DECADES!
BORS

Apologies to all old people who supported the New Deal and are not racists!

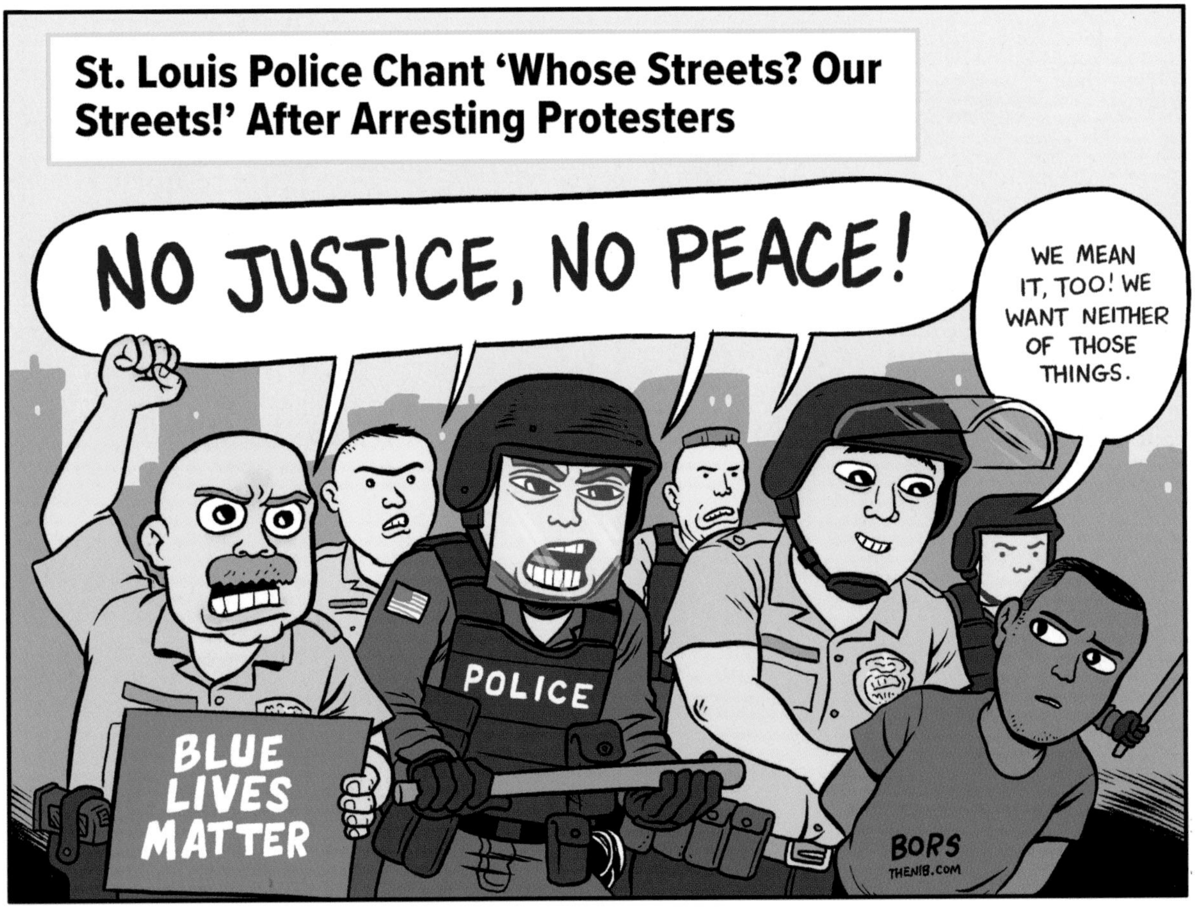
St. Louis Police Chant 'Whose Streets? Our Streets!' After Arresting Protesters
NO JUSTICE, NO PEACE!
WE MEAN IT, TOO! WE WANT NEITHER OF THOSE THINGS.
POLICE
BLUE LIVES MATTER
BORS
THENIB.COM

HELLO, ARE YOU WORRIED ABOUT FREE SPEECH?
HEY, TWITTER DELETED MY "GAS THE JEWS" MEMES! CENSORSHIP!
CHECK OUT THESE INCREDIBLE THREATS TO OUR FREEDOMS. FOR INSTANCE, THE WHITE HOUSE SAYS CRITICIZING THE PRESIDENT IS A FIRING OFFENSE!
EH, FREE SPEECH DOESN'T MEAN FREEDOM FROM CONSEQUENCES.
THE CIA DEMANDED A COLLEGE DISINVITE CHELSEA MANNING. THAT'S KIND OF CHILLING.
YOU HAVE THE RIGHT TO SPEAK NOT THE RIGHT TO BE HEARD!
UH... YOUR NAZI MEMES ARE BAD AND DUMB?
THIS IS THE REAL VIOLENCE OF THE PC LEFT, ALL DISSENT IS SHUT DOWN AND BANN 1984 WAS REAL ABOUT LIBERA
BORS
THENIB.COM

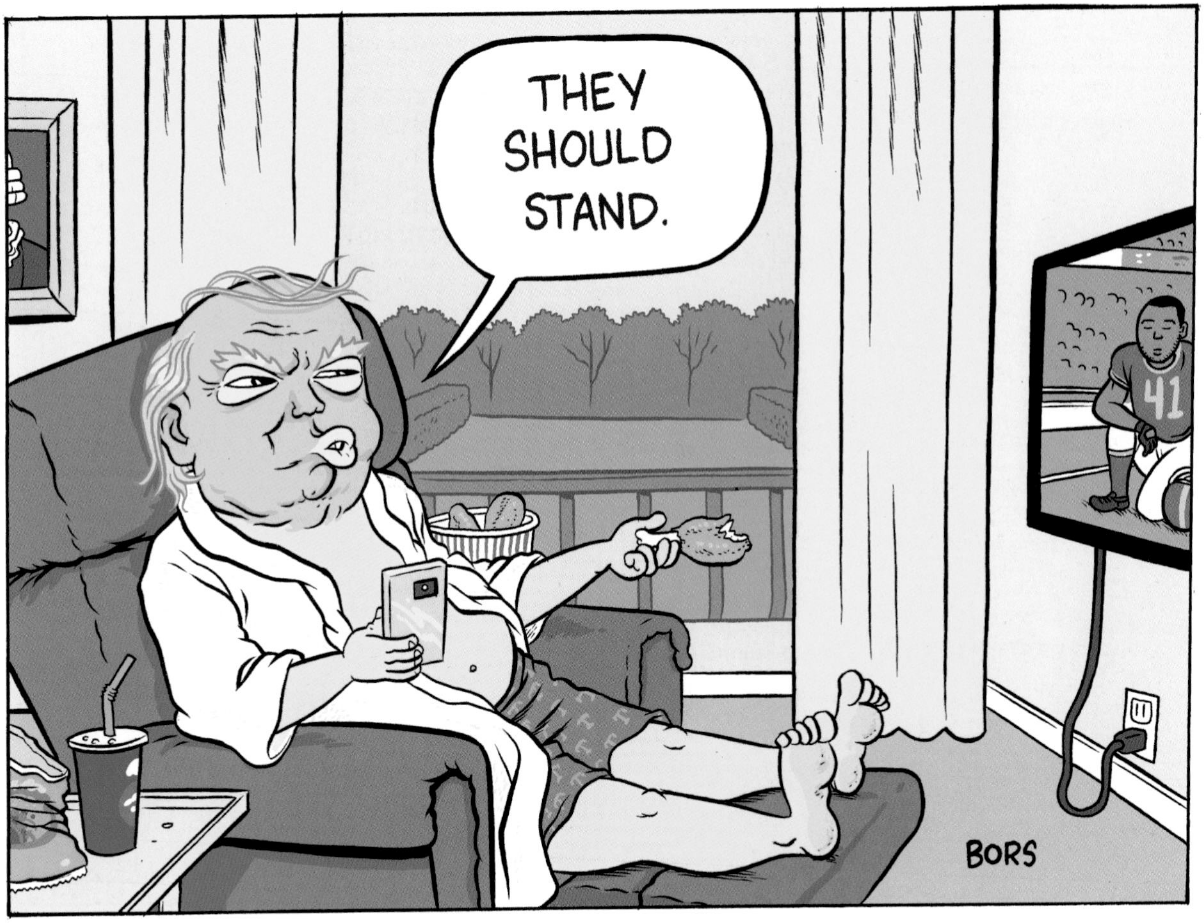
THEY SHOULD STAND.
41
BORS

THIS WEEK ON SUNDAY HOT TAKES, THE WAGE GAP BETWEEN MEN AND WOMEN—IS IT REALLY SUCH A BAD THING? JILL, YOU HATE OTHER WOMEN, START US OFF WITH SOMETHING AWFUL.
WELL, I'M WEALTHY AND DOING JUST FINE! I'M SORRY FEMINISTS ARE TOO UGLY TO GET A RAISE.
TRY LEANING IN. OR BEING BORN RICH!
SCORCHING! DON, YOU'RE A MAN WHO MAKES SIX FIGURES DESPITE ZERO TALENT. MELT MY FACE WITH A TAKE.
MALE AND FEMALE. THE TWO GENDERS. KIDS THESE DAYS, THEY'VE GOT 40 GENDERS!
I LIKE TWO.
BORS
THENIB.COM
NOT... EVEN WHAT WE'RE TALKING ABOUT... BUT I LIKE IT! THINK IT'S TIME YOU GET A RAISE.

AT THE NRA WE TAKE MASS SHOOTINGS SERIOUSLY.
AND WE WANT TO HONOR OUR FIRST RESPONDERS...
THE CONGRESS-PEOPLE WHO BLOCK GUN LAWS.
THAT'S WHY WE BUILT THE PAC-15 ASSAULT DONATOR! THIS PUPPY WILL FIRE 90 BANDS OF $100 BILLS PER MINUTE—FULLY AUTOMATIC CAMPAIGN CONTRIBUTIONS.
POOM
POOM
POOM
"WE CAN LAY DOWN A FIELD OF BRIBES FROM UP TO 500 YARDS AWAY AND HIT EVERY ONE OF OUR LEGISLATORS—ALL OF WHICH WERE PURCHASED LEGALLY, BY THE WAY."
HEAD SHOT!
AS FOR BUMP STOCKS, WE'RE TRYING OUR BEST.
BORS
THENIB.COM

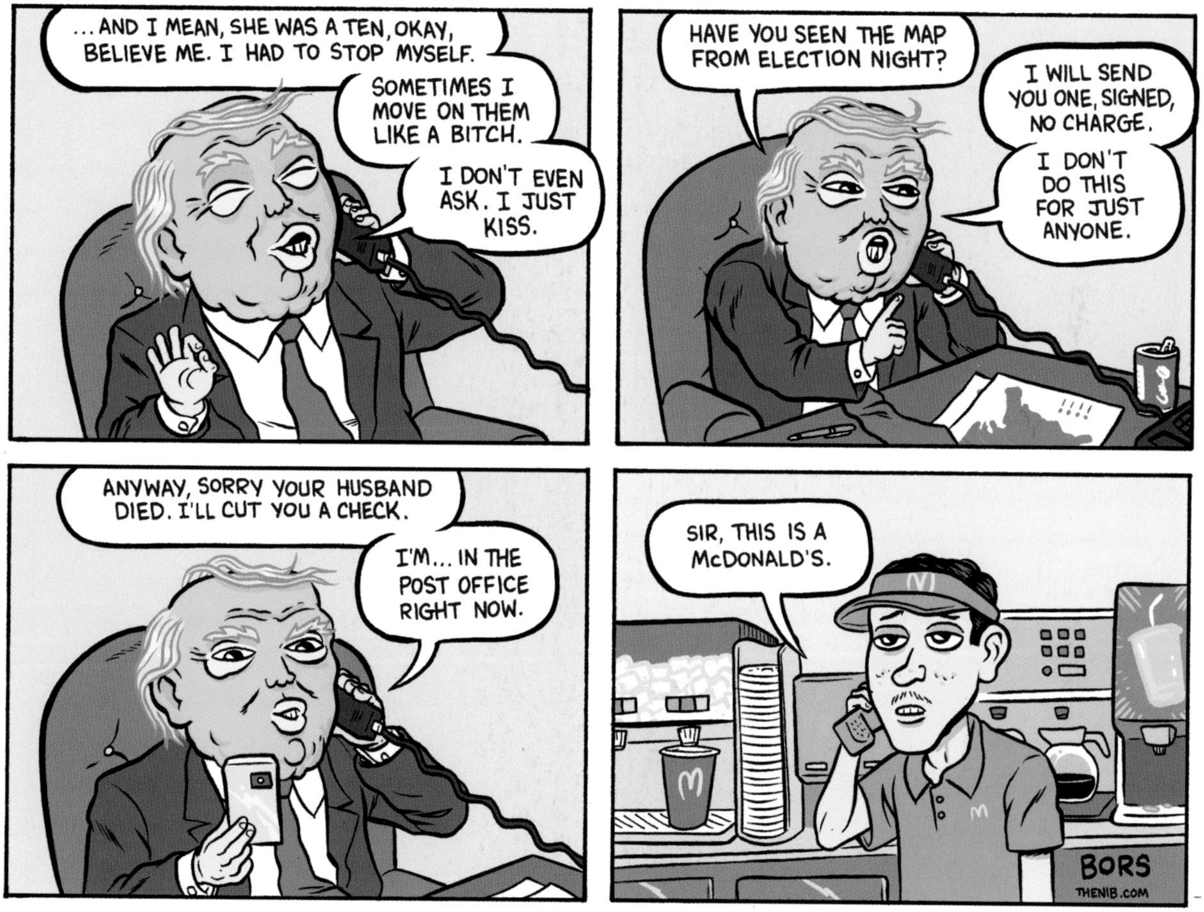
...AND I MEAN, SHE WAS A TEN, OKAY, BELIEVE ME. I HAD TO STOP MYSELF.
SOMETIMES I MOVE ON THEM LIKE A BITCH.
I DON'T EVEN ASK. I JUST KISS.
HAVE YOU SEEN THE MAP FROM ELECTION NIGHT?
I WILL SEND YOU ONE, SIGNED, NO CHARGE.
I DON'T DO THIS FOR JUST ANYONE.
!!!!
ANYWAY, SORRY YOUR HUSBAND DIED. I'LL CUT YOU A CHECK.
I'M... IN THE POST OFFICE RIGHT NOW.
SIR, THIS IS A McDONALD'S.
BORS
THENIB.COM

In 2017, Trump lied about a grieving war widow, Myeshia Johnson, he gave a condolence call to. After Johnson said Trump couldn't remember her husband's name, Trump publicly attacked her. Naturally, she's a black woman.

IT'S BECOMING CLICHE TO SAY BUT OBAMA COULDN'T HAVE GOTTEN AWAY WITH ONE TENTH OF THIS SHIT.

JUST TAKING A 17-DAY GOLF BREAK FROM MY BUSY TV WATCHING SCHEDULE!

LIKE HOLDING WEIRD CRYPTO-FASCIST RALLIES AND LAUNCHING A LITERAL PROPAGANDA NEWSCAST.

TODAY OBAMA CREATED ONE MILLION JOBS, PERSONALLY, HIMSELF.

THANKS, OBAMA!

THIS IS DEFINITELY NOT LIKE NORTH KOREA

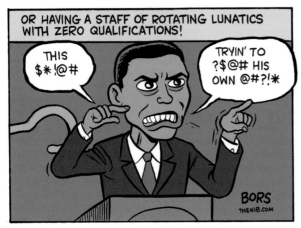

OR HAVING A STAFF OF ROTATING LUNATICS WITH ZERO QUALIFICATIONS!

THIS $*!@#

TRYIN' TO ?$@# HIS OWN @#?!*

BORS
THENIB.COM

AMERICA WOULD NEVER LET A SINGLE BLACK PERSON NEAR THE WHITE HOUSE AGAIN.

WE'RE ACTUALLY GETTING THAT LAW ON THE BOOKS!

JUST TO BE SAFE!

THIS WEEK ON SUNDAY HOT TAKES: SEXUAL HARASSMENT. WHY ARE WE STILL DEALING WITH THIS IN 2017?
MARK, YOU'RE A MALE ALLY...
YES, AND I FEEL IT'S MY JOB TO SPEAK UP, TO SUPPORT WOMEN, TO—
UH, HE'S GROPING ME UNDER THE TABLE.
SUE, DON'T INTERRUPT. MARK, DO YOU WANT TO ANSWER THESE SCURRILOUS ACCUSATIONS?
I HAVE **NEVER** DONE ANYTHING BUT RESPECTFULLY ASK FOR PICTURES OF SUE'S FEET!
I'M NOT TOUCHING HER!
GOTCHA BOTH— IT WAS ME!
AFTER THE BREAK: WHY SUE QUIT.
BORS
THENIB.COM

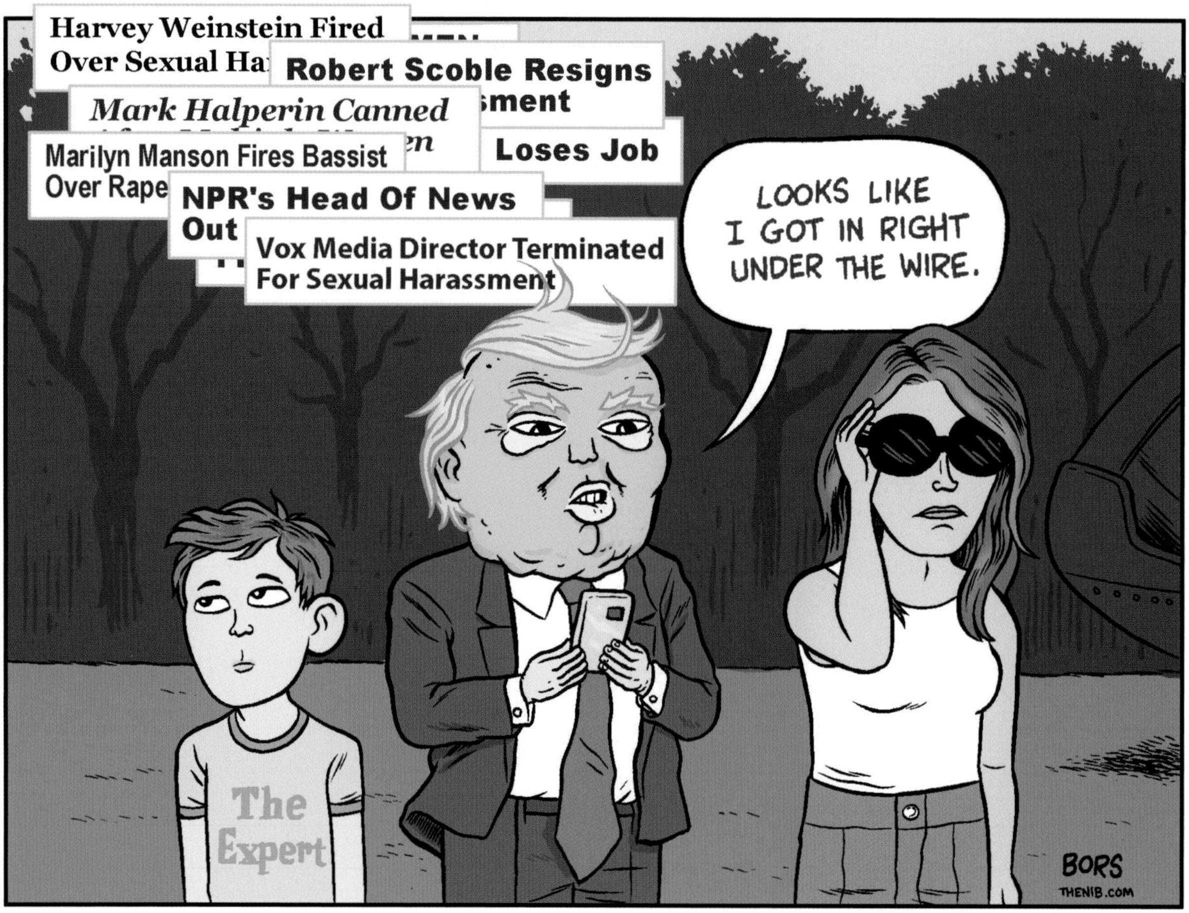
Harvey Weinstein Fired
Over Sexual Ha
Robert Scoble Resigns
ment
Mark Halperin Canned
Loses Job
Marilyn Manson Fires Bassist
Over Rape
NPR's Head Of News
Out
Vox Media Director Terminated
For Sexual Harassment
LOOKS LIKE I GOT IN RIGHT UNDER THE WIRE.
The Expert
BORS
THENIB.COM

You'd think the President of the United States having (allegedly) raped multiple women would be more of an ongoing issue, brought up from time to time. Oh well!

OH MY GOD HAVE YOU SEEN THIS SH-
WAIT, WHAT ARE YOU DOING?
I'M OBSERVING A SOCIAL MEDIA HIATUS.
I FEEL... EXTREMELY CHILL.
BUT YOU'RE MISSING THE-
BAD TWEET FROM TRUMP, ONGOING MASS SHOOTING AND THREE NEW HIGH-PROFILE SEXUAL ASSAULT ALLEGATIONS?
WELL, YEAH. BUT ALSO: BABY ON A ROOMBA!
OOO
BORS
THENIB.COM

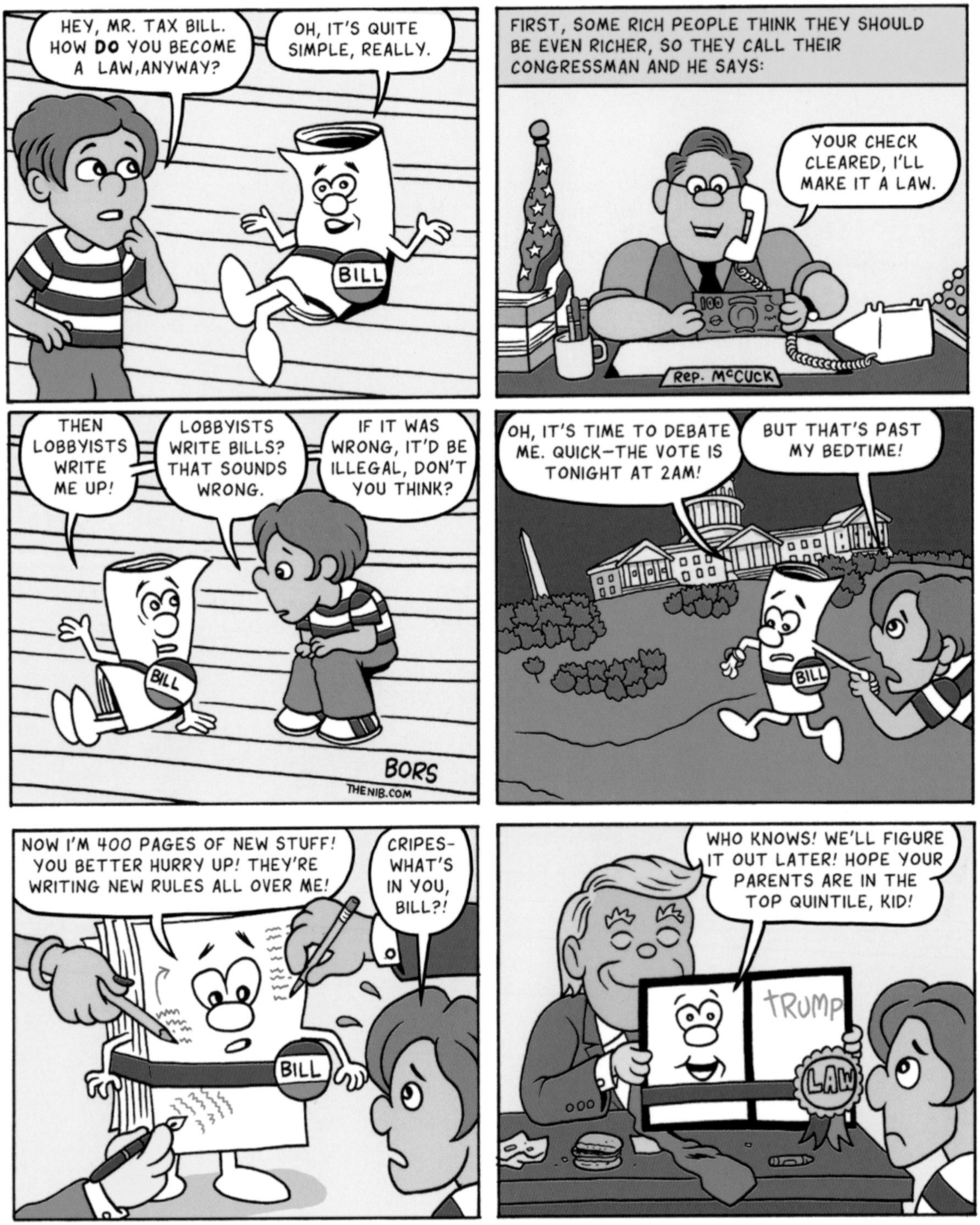
HEY, MR. TAX BILL. HOW DO YOU BECOME A LAW, ANYWAY?
OH, IT'S QUITE SIMPLE, REALLY.
BILL
FIRST, SOME RICH PEOPLE THINK THEY SHOULD BE EVEN RICHER, SO THEY CALL THEIR CONGRESSMAN AND HE SAYS:
YOUR CHECK CLEARED, I'LL MAKE IT A LAW.
100
Rep. McCUCK
THEN LOBBYISTS WRITE ME UP!
LOBBYISTS WRITE BILLS? THAT SOUNDS WRONG.
IF IT WAS WRONG, IT'D BE ILLEGAL, DON'T YOU THINK?
BILL
BORS
THENIB.COM
OH, IT'S TIME TO DEBATE ME. QUICK—THE VOTE IS TONIGHT AT 2AM!
BUT THAT'S PAST MY BEDTIME!
BILL
NOW I'M 400 PAGES OF NEW STUFF! YOU BETTER HURRY UP! THEY'RE WRITING NEW RULES ALL OVER ME!
CRIPES- WHAT'S IN YOU, BILL?!
BILL
WHO KNOWS! WE'LL FIGURE IT OUT LATER! HOPE YOUR PARENTS ARE IN THE TOP QUINTILE, KID!
TRUMP
LAW

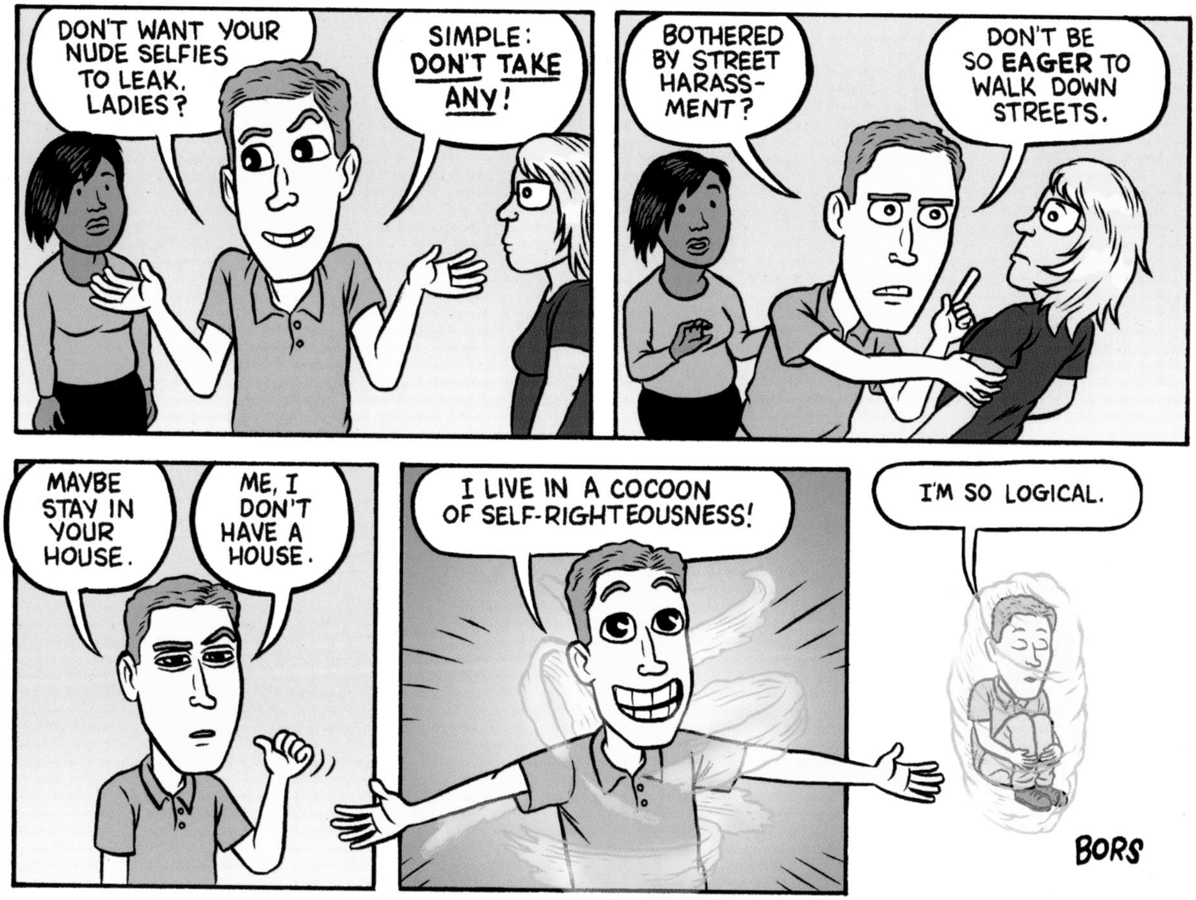
DON'T WANT YOUR NUDE SELFIES TO LEAK, LADIES?
SIMPLE: DON'T TAKE ANY!
BOTHERED BY STREET HARASS-MENT?
DON'T BE SO EAGER TO WALK DOWN STREETS.
MAYBE STAY IN YOUR HOUSE.
ME, I DON'T HAVE A HOUSE.
I LIVE IN A COCOON OF SELF-RIGHTEOUSNESS!
I'M SO LOGICAL.
BORS

WATCH WHAT I CAN MAKE IT DO.
VNNNNNN
BORS
SO NEAT.
I SEE GREAT THINGS AHEAD.
WATCH WHAT I CAN MAKE IT DO.

It seems like we're on track to take every warning about technology and society made through science-fiction in the last, say, 50 years and simply ignore it while barreling toward dystopia. The NSA created a program called SKYNET that uses a machine learning algorithm to monitor Pakistan's millions of cellphone users and determine their likelihood of being a terrorist—helping green light unknown numbers of drone killings without charge.

HANDS UP OR I'LL BLOW YOU AWAY!
Whiteness Fairy!
OH, HI SIR.
YOU OKAY? NEED SOME WATER?
WAIT. YOU HOMELESS?
BORS

UGH. ANOTHER BEHEADING.
THAT IS BARBARIC AND NOT GOOD.
HEY, YOU FIND DUDE'S VEIN YET?
STILL FISHING. GIVE ME ANOTHER 30 MINUTES.
BORS

TODAY ON SUNDAY HOT TAKES: WHO WILL BE THIS WEEK'S BIG SEXUAL HARASSER? WE'VE GOT THE UNLUCKY BASTARD'S NAME RIGHT HERE.
AND THE NEXT GUY OUT OF A JOB IS...
ME?
HMMM. SAYS I MOLESTED CO-WORKERS AND INSTALLED A SECRET LOCK TO TRAP WOMEN IN MY SOUNDPROOF OFFICE.
PANEL?
YES, YOU LOCKED ME IN YOUR OFFICE AND PULLED OUT YOUR PENIS.
WHICH YOU THEN **BRAGGED** ABOUT AT THE CHRISTMAS PARTY.
I DIDN'T "BRAG," DAN. I DESCRIBED MY INESCAPABLE MOLESTATION CHAMBER NEUTRALLY. YOU MAKE ME SOUND LIKE SOME KIND OF **ASSHOLE**.
BORS
THENIB.COM

HEY POPS, THE MIDDLE CLASS TAX CUT IS HERE! WHERE YOU WANT IT?
DUMP IT IN THE POOL!
Middle Class News
WOW, WHAT DO WE DO WITH ALL THIS EXTRA MONEY?
WHY, WE WILL CREATE MORE JOBS, OF COURSE!
I WILL PAY YOU $9 AN HOUR TO SHINE MY MONEY.
BORS
THENIB.COM

G.E.N.I.U.S. President
NOT APPROVED BY FAKE NEWS MEDIA
GREAT EFFECTIVE NOT INSANE UNQUESTIONABLY STABLE
No. 45
FOX & friends
LIVE
Diet Coke
SLOPPY STEVE, WHO HAD, LIKE, VERY LITTLE TO DO WITH MY TREMENDOUS BATTLE BODY, NOW CRIES AS I CRUSH HIM WITH MY MIND. TOO BAD!
BORS
THENIB.COM

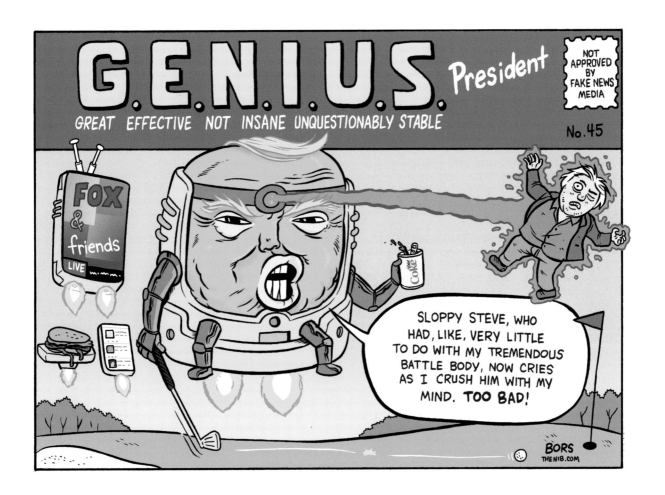

MODOK is an acronym for Mental/Mobile/Mechanized Organism Designed Only for Killing. Once a normal man working for the terrorist organization Advanced Idea Mechanics (A.I.M.), a mutagenic process transformed his mind and body, granting him vast mental powers and the ability to fire mind-beams at foes, namely Captain America. As you were.

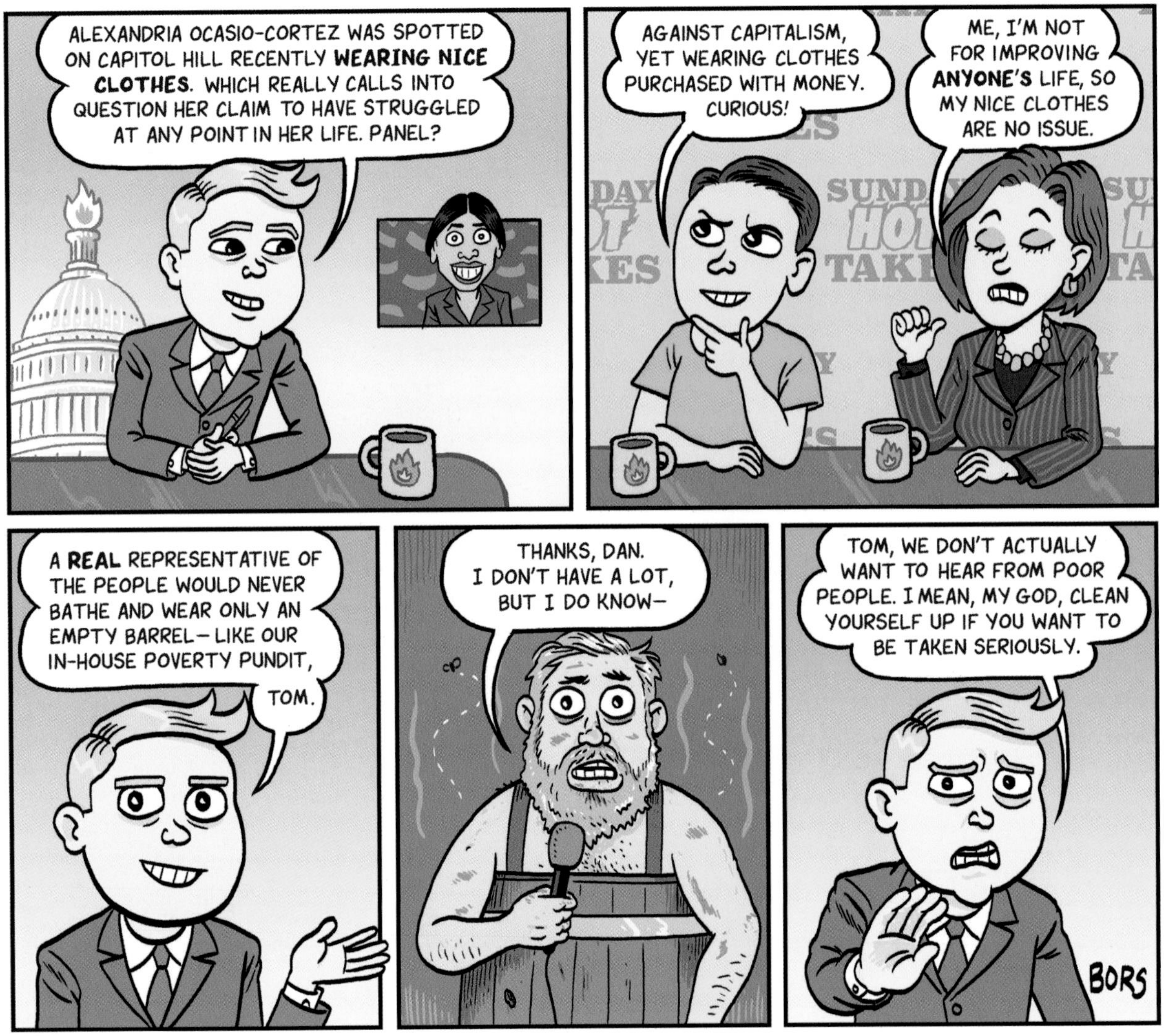
ALEXANDRIA OCASIO-CORTEZ WAS SPOTTED ON CAPITOL HILL RECENTLY **WEARING NICE CLOTHES**. WHICH REALLY CALLS INTO QUESTION HER CLAIM TO HAVE STRUGGLED AT ANY POINT IN HER LIFE. PANEL?
AGAINST CAPITALISM, YET WEARING CLOTHES PURCHASED WITH MONEY. CURIOUS!
ME, I'M NOT FOR IMPROVING **ANYONE'S** LIFE, SO MY NICE CLOTHES ARE NO ISSUE.
A **REAL** REPRESENTATIVE OF THE PEOPLE WOULD NEVER BATHE AND WEAR ONLY AN EMPTY BARREL—LIKE OUR IN-HOUSE POVERTY PUNDIT,
TOM.
THANKS, DAN. I DON'T HAVE A LOT, BUT I DO KNOW—
TOM, WE DON'T ACTUALLY WANT TO HEAR FROM POOR PEOPLE. I MEAN, MY GOD, CLEAN YOURSELF UP IF YOU WANT TO BE TAKEN SERIOUSLY.
BORS

The second appearance of Mr. Gotcha. I had no idea I'd reuse him until Alexandria Ocasio-Cortez was criticized for buying clothes to wear.

THE EMPIRE IS RUN BY AN AUTHORITARIAN MADMAN. HE COULD BLOW UP A PLANET AT ANY MOMENT!
WE ARE THE #RESISTANCE. THE ONLY HOPE!
HEY, UH, DARTH VADER WOULD LIKE TO RENEW HIS SPYING POWERS OVER ALL COMMUNICATION IN THE GALAXY. COOL?
OH YEAH, SURE. THAT STUFF KEEPS US SAFE!
NOTHING TO HIDE OVER HERE!
BORS
THENIB.COM
SOON
ACK! WHO COULD HAVE... PREDICTED THIS!

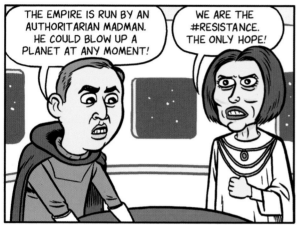

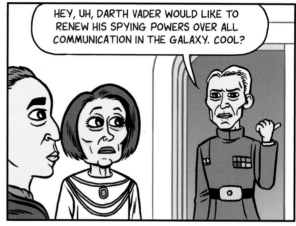

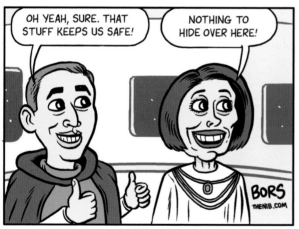

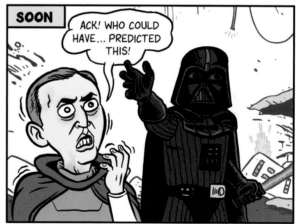

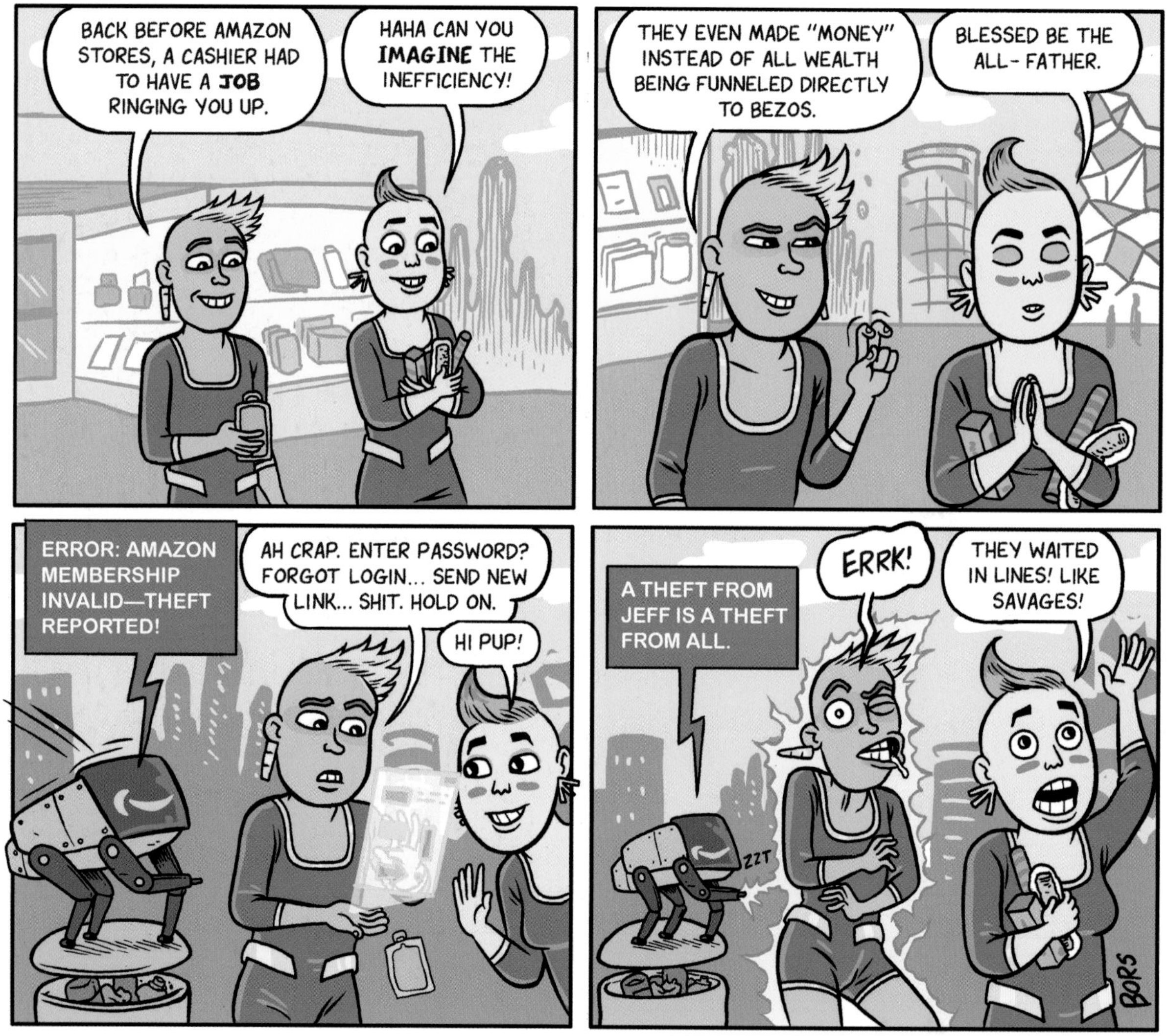
BACK BEFORE AMAZON STORES, A CASHIER HAD TO HAVE A JOB RINGING YOU UP.
HAHA CAN YOU IMAGINE THE INEFFICIENCY!
THEY EVEN MADE "MONEY" INSTEAD OF ALL WEALTH BEING FUNNELED DIRECTLY TO BEZOS.
BLESSED BE THE ALL-FATHER.
ERROR: AMAZON MEMBERSHIP INVALID—THEFT REPORTED!
AH CRAP. ENTER PASSWORD? FORGOT LOGIN... SEND NEW LINK... SHIT. HOLD ON.
HI PUP!
A THEFT FROM JEFF IS A THEFT FROM ALL.
ERRK!
ZZT
THEY WAITED IN LINES! LIKE SAVAGES!
BORS

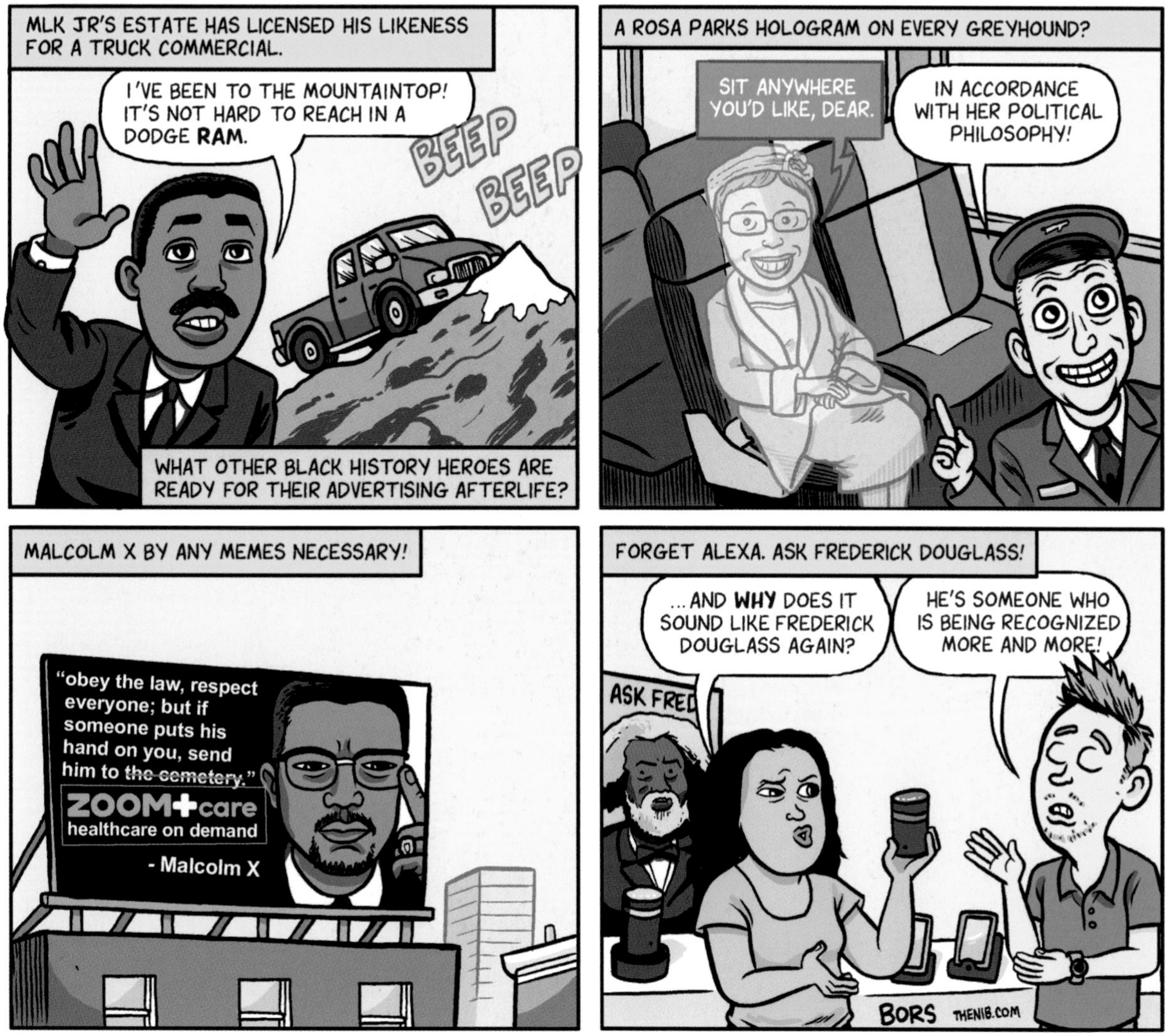

MLK JR'S ESTATE HAS LICENSED HIS LIKENESS FOR A TRUCK COMMERCIAL.
I'VE BEEN TO THE MOUNTAINTOP! IT'S NOT HARD TO REACH IN A DODGE **RAM**.
BEEP BEEP
WHAT OTHER BLACK HISTORY HEROES ARE READY FOR THEIR ADVERTISING AFTERLIFE?
A ROSA PARKS HOLOGRAM ON EVERY GREYHOUND?
SIT ANYWHERE YOU'D LIKE, DEAR.
IN ACCORDANCE WITH HER POLITICAL PHILOSOPHY!
MALCOLM X BY ANY MEMES NECESSARY!
"obey the law, respect everyone; but if someone puts his hand on you, send him to ~~the cemetery.~~"
ZOOM+care
healthcare on demand
- Malcolm X
FORGET ALEXA. ASK FREDERICK DOUGLASS!
...AND **WHY** DOES IT SOUND LIKE FREDERICK DOUGLASS AGAIN?
HE'S SOMEONE WHO IS BEING RECOGNIZED MORE AND MORE!
ASK FRED
BORS THENIB.COM

A NEW STUDY FOUND THIS OUT: LYING WITHIN THE MILITARY... **IS COMMON**.

WELL KNOCK ME OVER WITH A FEATHER!

IT'S A FACT. THERE'S FIBBING GOING ON. DOWN IN THE LOWER RANKS...

THE SEXUAL ASSAULT COMPLAINTS?

ALL FILED.

UP TO THE TOP BRASS.

THE WARS? WINNING 'EM ALL!

ON THE CHEAP.

IT'S AS IF A RIGID TOP-DOWN ORGANIZATION FOR KILLING BREEDS LESS THAN 100% HONESTY.

WAIT— THEY <u>KILL</u> PEOPLE?!

IT MUST BE STUDIED!

BROKEN CHILD

GROWN MAN

BORS
THENIB.COM

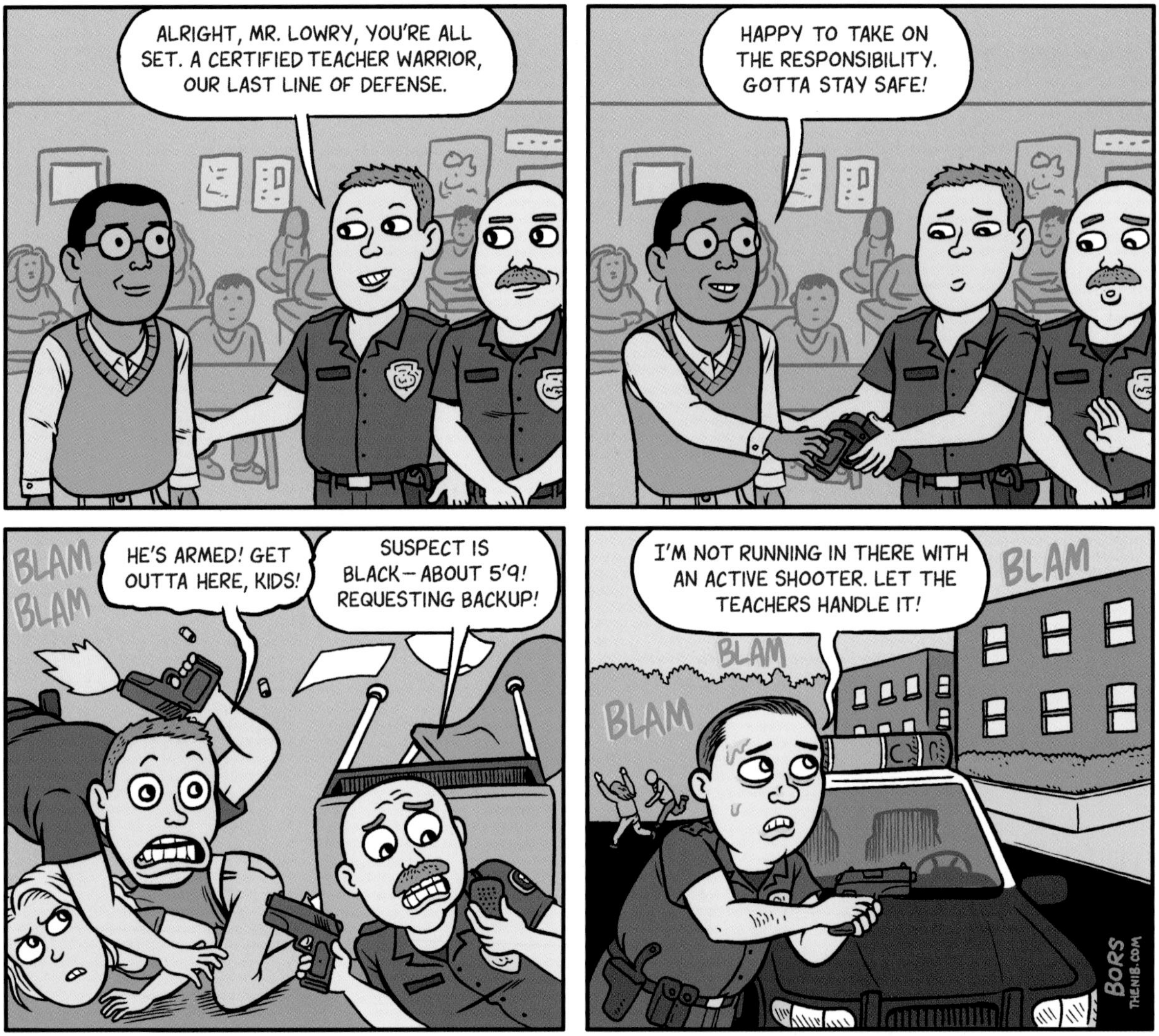
ALRIGHT, MR. LOWRY, YOU'RE ALL SET. A CERTIFIED TEACHER WARRIOR, OUR LAST LINE OF DEFENSE.
HAPPY TO TAKE ON THE RESPONSIBILITY. GOTTA STAY SAFE!
BLAM
BLAM
HE'S ARMED! GET OUTTA HERE, KIDS!
SUSPECT IS BLACK—ABOUT 5'9! REQUESTING BACKUP!
I'M NOT RUNNING IN THERE WITH AN ACTIVE SHOOTER. LET THE TEACHERS HANDLE IT!
BLAM
BLAM
BLAM
BORS
THENIB.COM

"It's called concealed carry, where a teacher would have a concealed gun on them. They'd go for special training and they would be there and you would no longer have a gun-free zone. Gun-free zone to a maniac, because they're all cowards, a gun-free zone is: '˜Let's go in and let's attack, because bullets aren't coming back at us'." —Trump

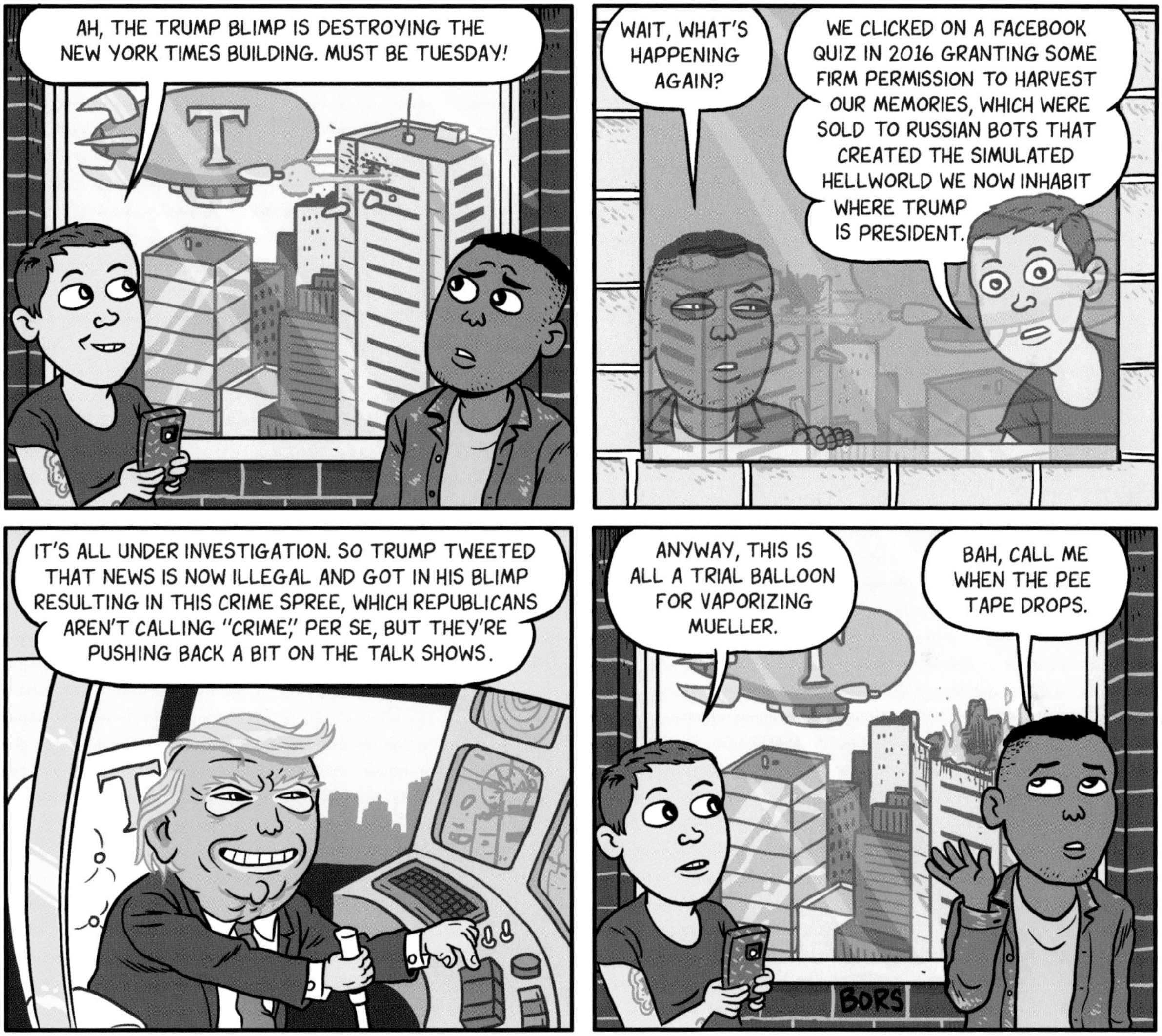
AH, THE TRUMP BLIMP IS DESTROYING THE NEW YORK TIMES BUILDING. MUST BE TUESDAY!
WAIT, WHAT'S HAPPENING AGAIN?
WE CLICKED ON A FACEBOOK QUIZ IN 2016 GRANTING SOME FIRM PERMISSION TO HARVEST OUR MEMORIES, WHICH WERE SOLD TO RUSSIAN BOTS THAT CREATED THE SIMULATED HELLWORLD WE NOW INHABIT WHERE TRUMP IS PRESIDENT.
IT'S ALL UNDER INVESTIGATION. SO TRUMP TWEETED THAT NEWS IS NOW ILLEGAL AND GOT IN HIS BLIMP RESULTING IN THIS CRIME SPREE, WHICH REPUBLICANS AREN'T CALLING "CRIME," PER SE, BUT THEY'RE PUSHING BACK A BIT ON THE TALK SHOWS.
ANYWAY, THIS IS ALL A TRIAL BALLOON FOR VAPORIZING MUELLER.
BAH, CALL ME WHEN THE PEE TAPE DROPS.
BORS

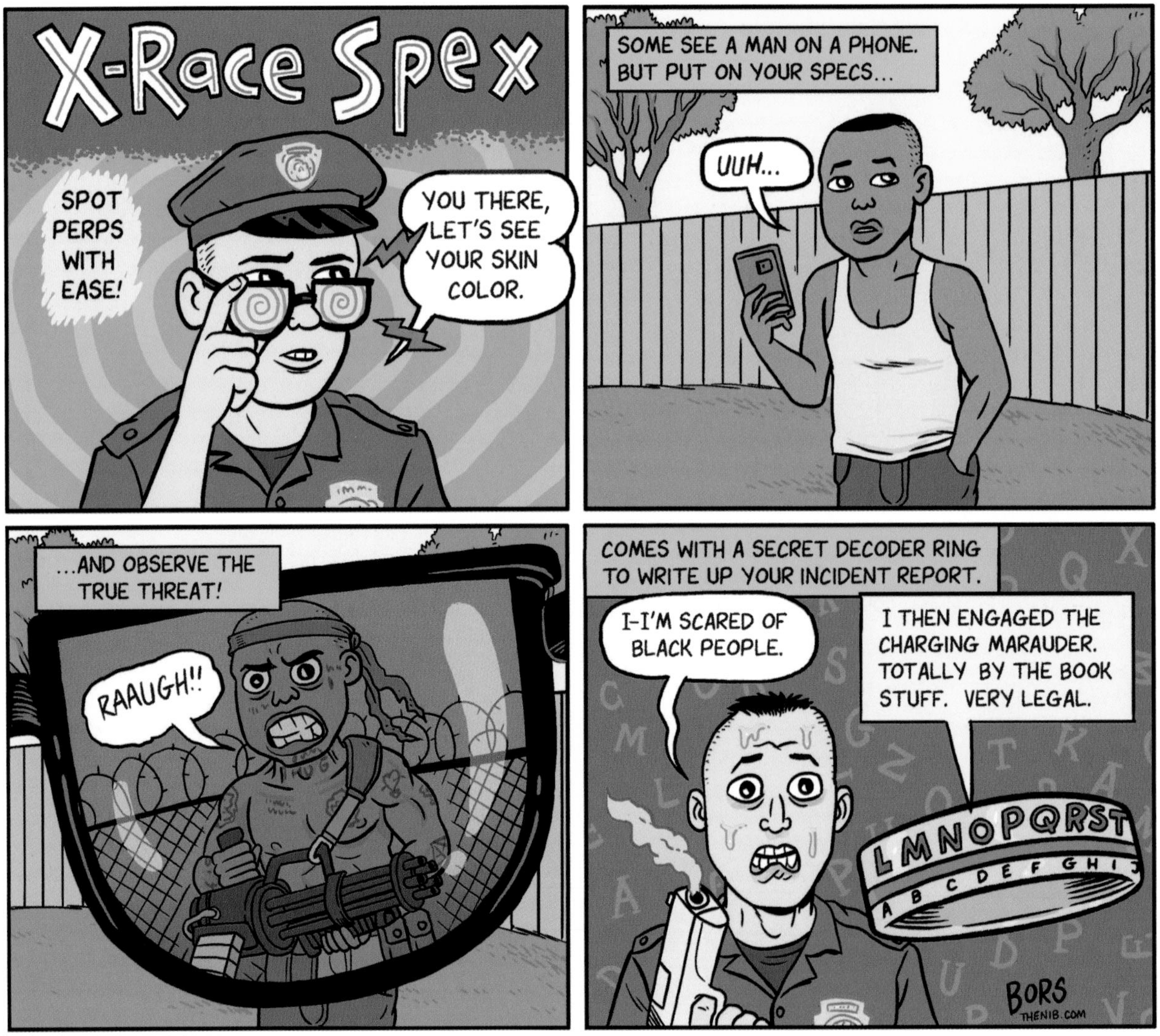
X-Race Spex
SPOT PERPS WITH EASE!
YOU THERE, LET'S SEE YOUR SKIN COLOR.
SOME SEE A MAN ON A PHONE. BUT PUT ON YOUR SPECS...
UUH...
...AND OBSERVE THE TRUE THREAT!
RAAUGH!!
COMES WITH A SECRET DECODER RING TO WRITE UP YOUR INCIDENT REPORT.
I-I'M SCARED OF BLACK PEOPLE.
I THEN ENGAGED THE CHARGING MARAUDER. TOTALLY BY THE BOOK STUFF. VERY LEGAL.
LMNOPQRST
ABCDEFGHIJ
BORS
THENIB.COM

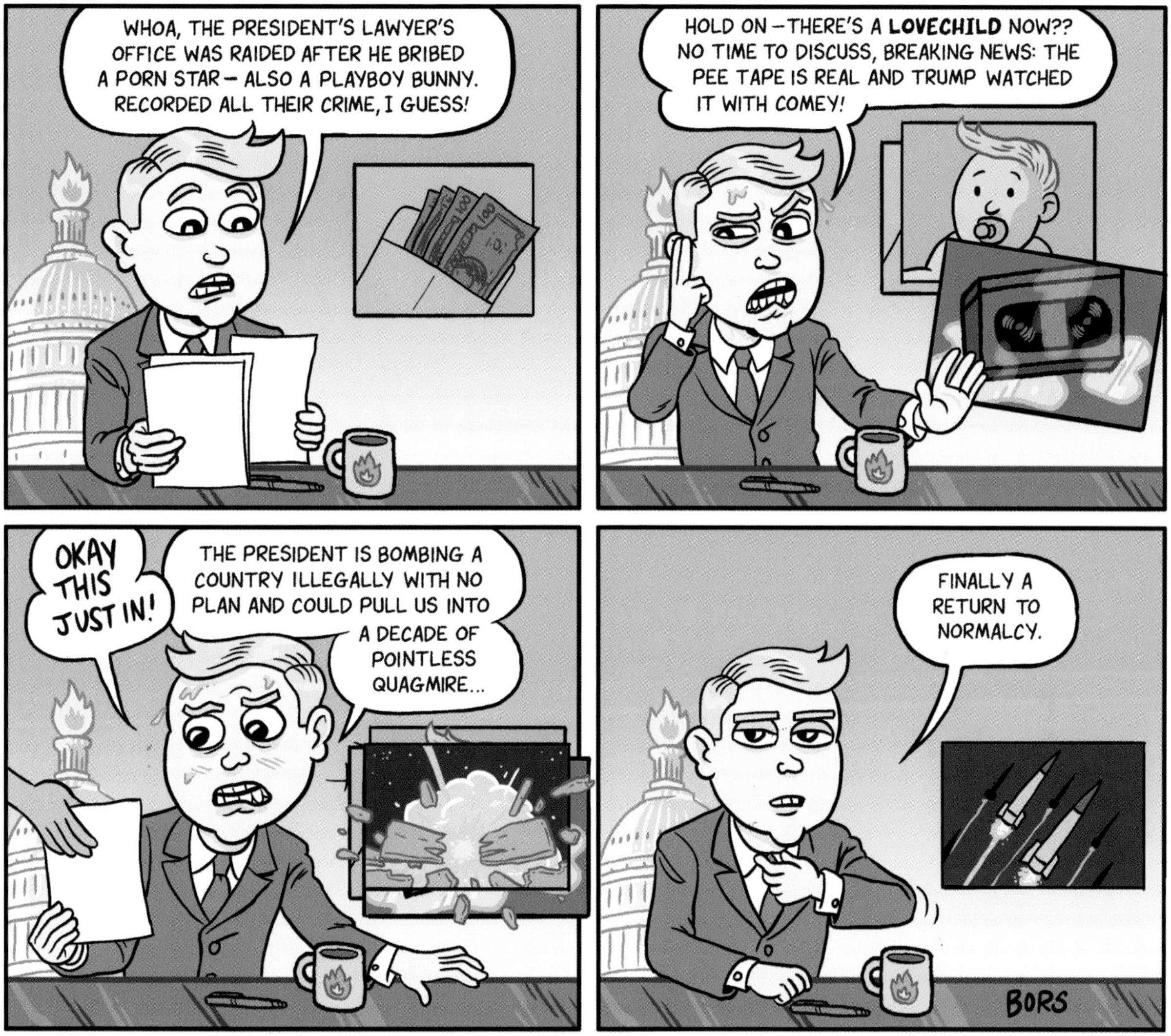
WHOA, THE PRESIDENT'S LAWYER'S OFFICE WAS RAIDED AFTER HE BRIBED A PORN STAR – ALSO A PLAYBOY BUNNY. RECORDED ALL THEIR CRIME, I GUESS!
HOLD ON – THERE'S A **LOVECHILD** NOW?? NO TIME TO DISCUSS, BREAKING NEWS: THE PEE TAPE IS REAL AND TRUMP WATCHED IT WITH COMEY!
OKAY THIS JUST IN!
THE PRESIDENT IS BOMBING A COUNTRY ILLEGALLY WITH NO PLAN AND COULD PULL US INTO A DECADE OF POINTLESS QUAGMIRE...
FINALLY A RETURN TO NORMALCY.
BORS

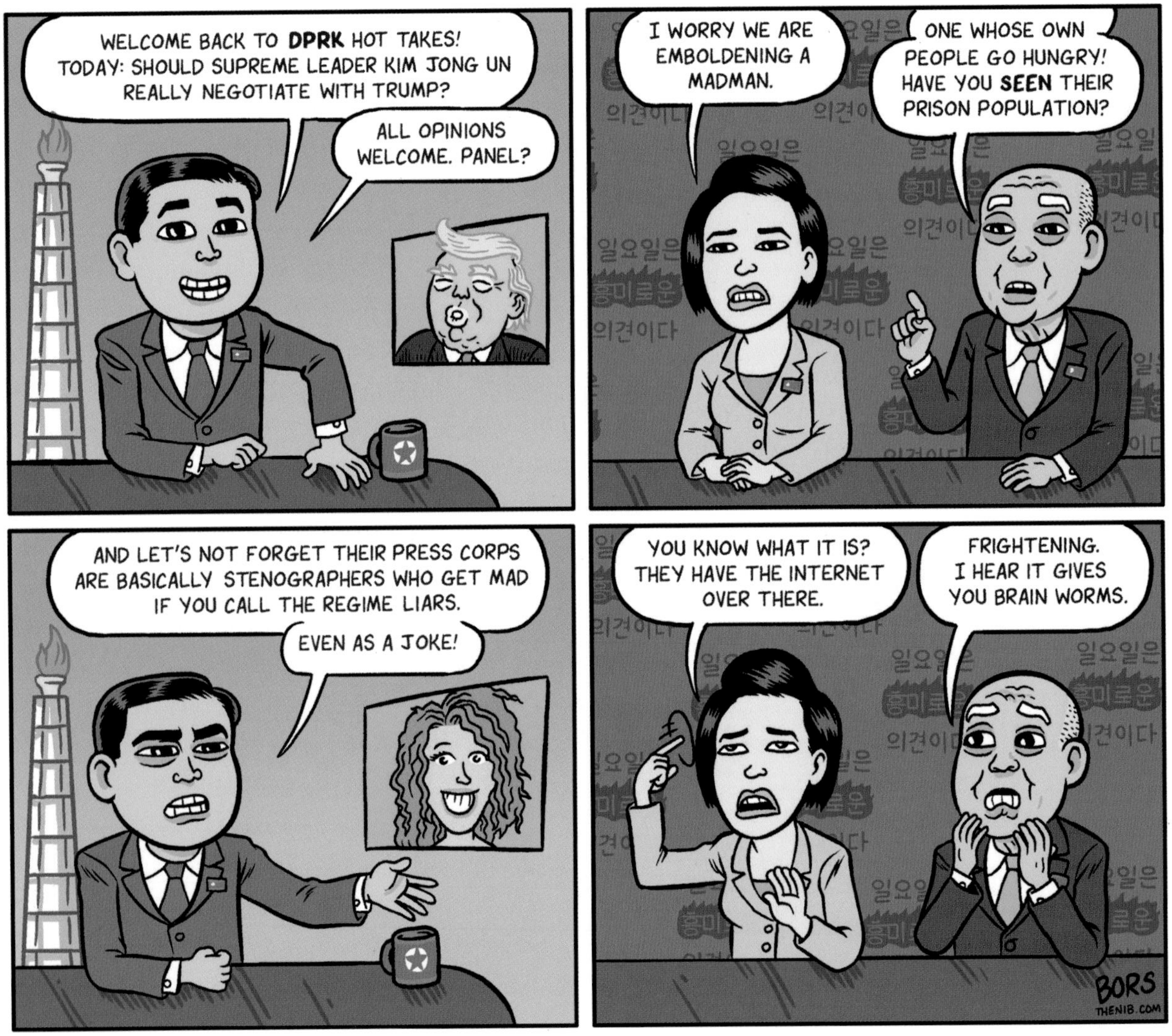
WELCOME BACK TO **DPRK** HOT TAKES! TODAY: SHOULD SUPREME LEADER KIM JONG UN REALLY NEGOTIATE WITH TRUMP?
ALL OPINIONS WELCOME. PANEL?
I WORRY WE ARE EMBOLDENING A MADMAN.
ONE WHOSE OWN PEOPLE GO HUNGRY! HAVE YOU **SEEN** THEIR PRISON POPULATION?
AND LET'S NOT FORGET THEIR PRESS CORPS ARE BASICALLY STENOGRAPHERS WHO GET MAD IF YOU CALL THE REGIME LIARS.
EVEN AS A JOKE!
YOU KNOW WHAT IT IS? THEY HAVE THE INTERNET OVER THERE.
FRIGHTENING. I HEAR IT GIVES YOU BRAIN WORMS.
BORS
THENIB.COM

DRAWING UP THE BILL OF RIGHTS
HYPOTHETICALLY, LET'S SAY A WOMAN WEARS A DRESS AND A CREEPER TAKES AN UPSKIRT PHOTO OF HER ON THE SUBWAY TO POST TO HIS TUMBLR...
AND SHE, FEELING THREATENED, SHOOTS HIM DEAD UNDER THAT STATE'S "STAND YOUR GROUND" LAW.
THE QUESTION THEN ARISES!
CAN THE META DATA COLLECTED FROM THEIR FITBITS BE SOLD TO A THIRD-PARTY ANONYMOUS SUPERPAC PLANNING A TARGETED AD BUY?
AND SO:
WE'RE BIG ON "FREE SPEECH" AND "LIBERTY."
BORS
GOOD LUCK OUT THERE!

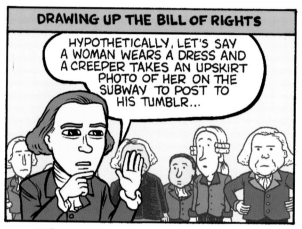

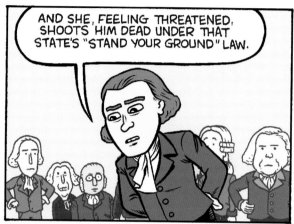

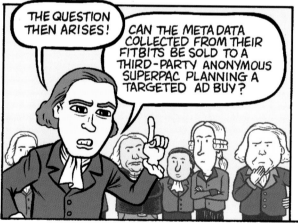

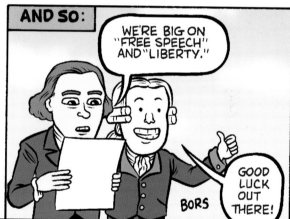

I DID IT!
I SIGNED UP FOR OBAMACARE IN TIME!
WE'RE SO PROUD OF YOU, SON.
HERE, HAVE ANOTHER TROPHY.
WITH **YOUNG INVINCIBLES** PAYING IN, IT WILL HELP KEEP COSTS DOWN FOR US OLDER FOLKS!
AND NOW WE'RE GOING TO GUT YOUR GENERATION'S SOCIAL SECURITY.
HOW'S THE JOB SEARCH GOING?
BORS

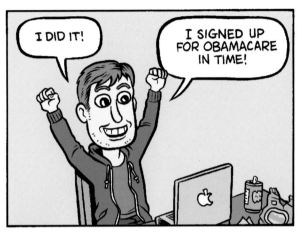

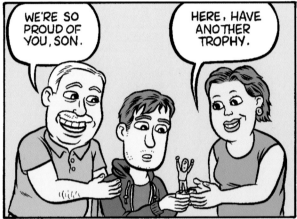

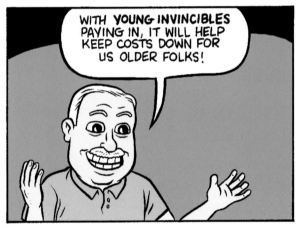

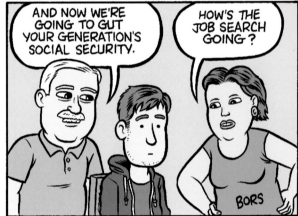

I PROMOTED JILL TO TOP EXECUTIVE BOSS PERSON.
YOU THINK SHE'S RIGHT?
ABSOLUTELY. SHE'S OVEREDUCATED, EXPERIENCED, TENACIOUS, TALENTED...
BRILLIANT.
INDEPENDENT.
OPEN-MINDED.
I'M GOING TO FIRE HER IMMEDIATELY.
BORS

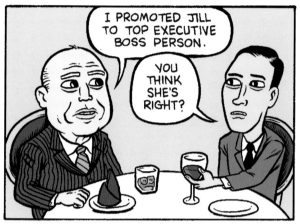

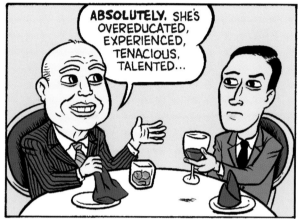

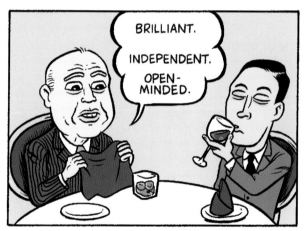

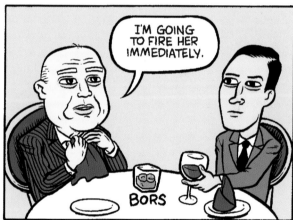

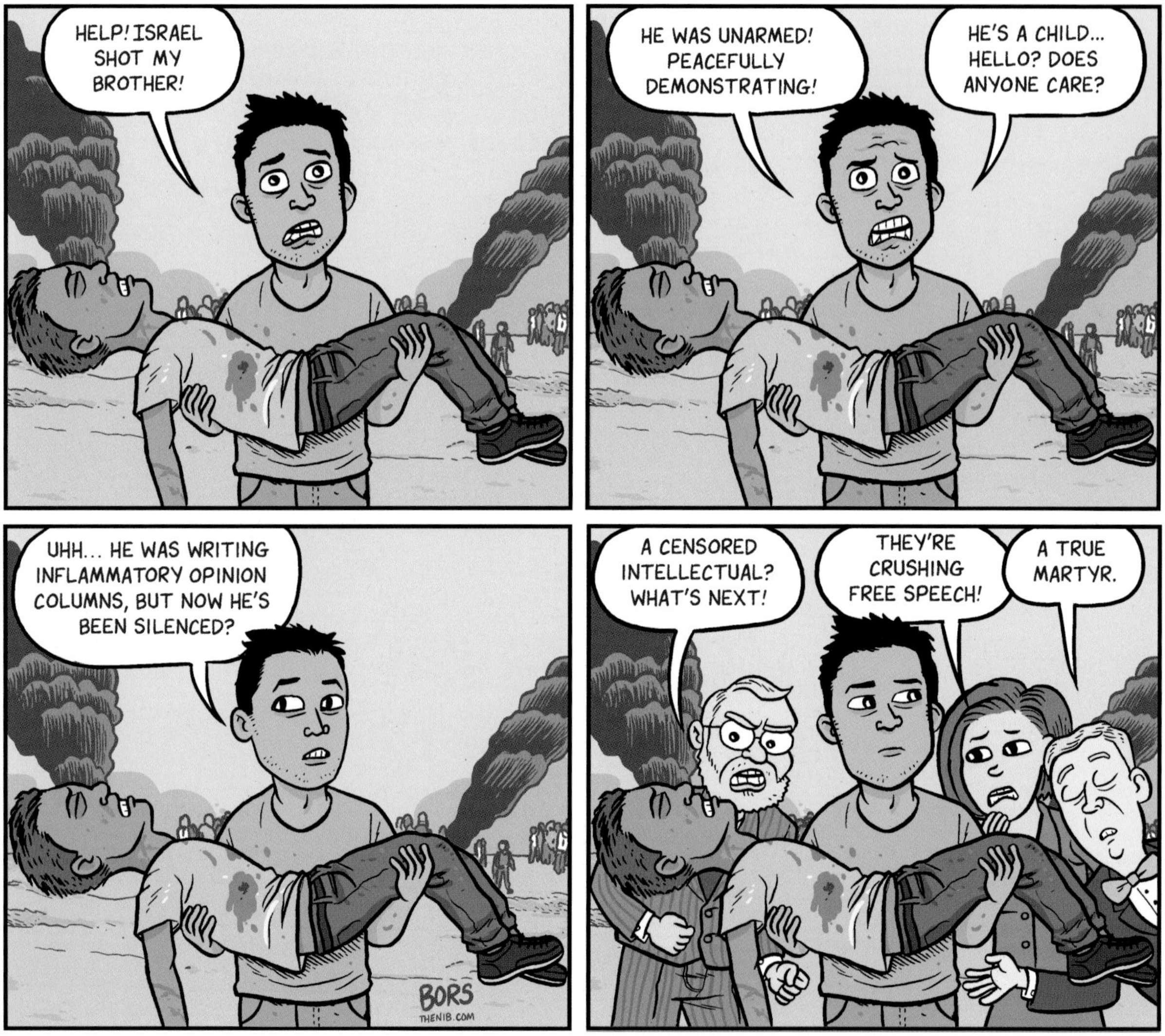
HELP! ISRAEL SHOT MY BROTHER!
HE WAS UNARMED! PEACEFULLY DEMONSTRATING!
HE'S A CHILD... HELLO? DOES ANYONE CARE?
UHH... HE WAS WRITING INFLAMMATORY OPINION COLUMNS, BUT NOW HE'S BEEN SILENCED?
BORS
THENIB.COM
A CENSORED INTELLECTUAL? WHAT'S NEXT!
THEY'RE CRUSHING FREE SPEECH!
A TRUE MARTYR.

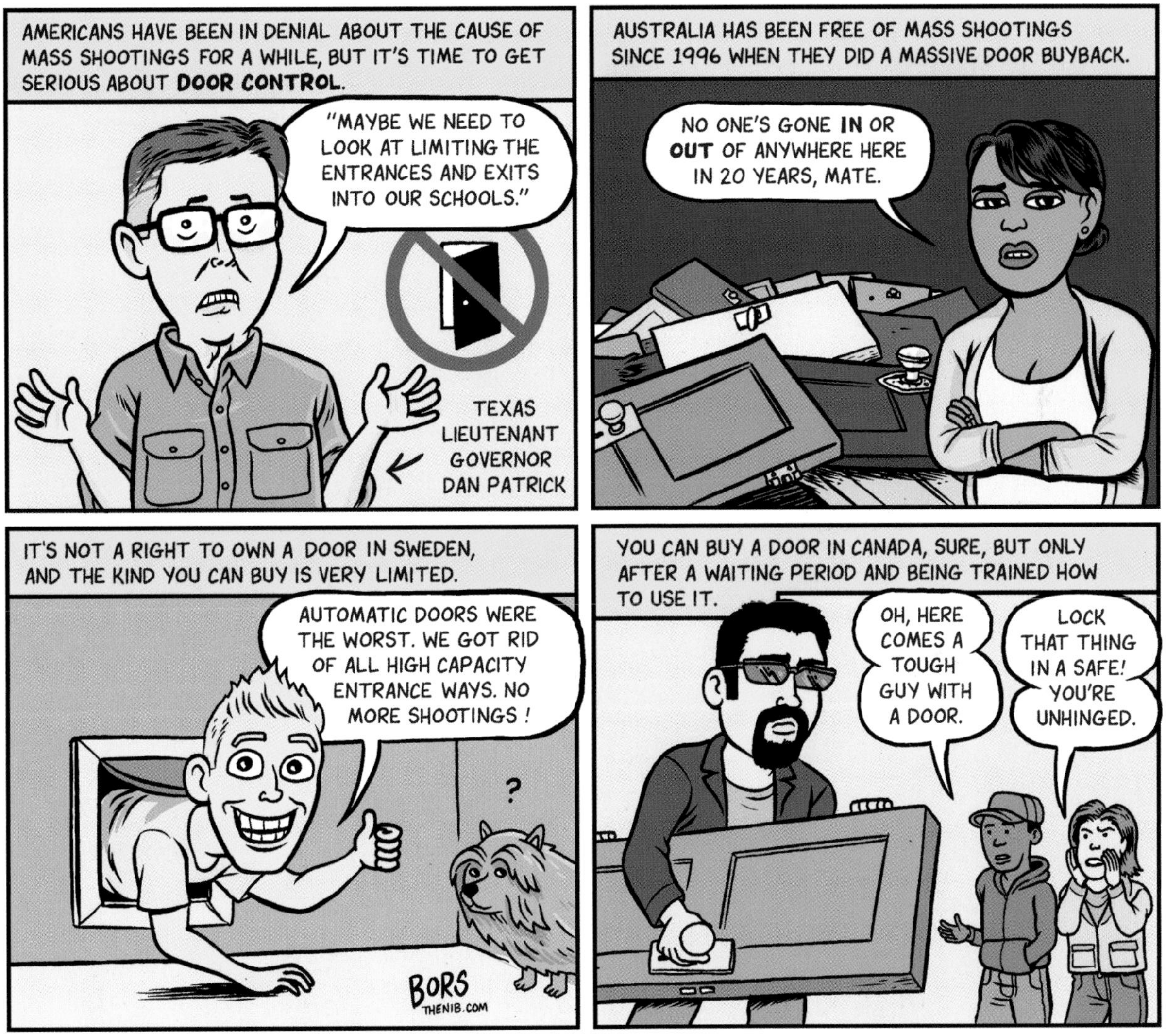
AMERICANS HAVE BEEN IN DENIAL ABOUT THE CAUSE OF MASS SHOOTINGS FOR A WHILE, BUT IT'S TIME TO GET SERIOUS ABOUT **DOOR CONTROL**.
"MAYBE WE NEED TO LOOK AT LIMITING THE ENTRANCES AND EXITS INTO OUR SCHOOLS."
TEXAS LIEUTENANT GOVERNOR DAN PATRICK
AUSTRALIA HAS BEEN FREE OF MASS SHOOTINGS SINCE 1996 WHEN THEY DID A MASSIVE DOOR BUYBACK.
NO ONE'S GONE **IN** OR **OUT** OF ANYWHERE HERE IN 20 YEARS, MATE.
IT'S NOT A RIGHT TO OWN A DOOR IN SWEDEN, AND THE KIND YOU CAN BUY IS VERY LIMITED.
AUTOMATIC DOORS WERE THE WORST. WE GOT RID OF ALL HIGH CAPACITY ENTRANCE WAYS. NO MORE SHOOTINGS!
?
BORS
THENIB.COM
YOU CAN BUY A DOOR IN CANADA, SURE, BUT ONLY AFTER A WAITING PERIOD AND BEING TRAINED HOW TO USE IT.
OH, HERE COMES A TOUGH GUY WITH A DOOR.
LOCK THAT THING IN A SAFE! YOU'RE UNHINGED.

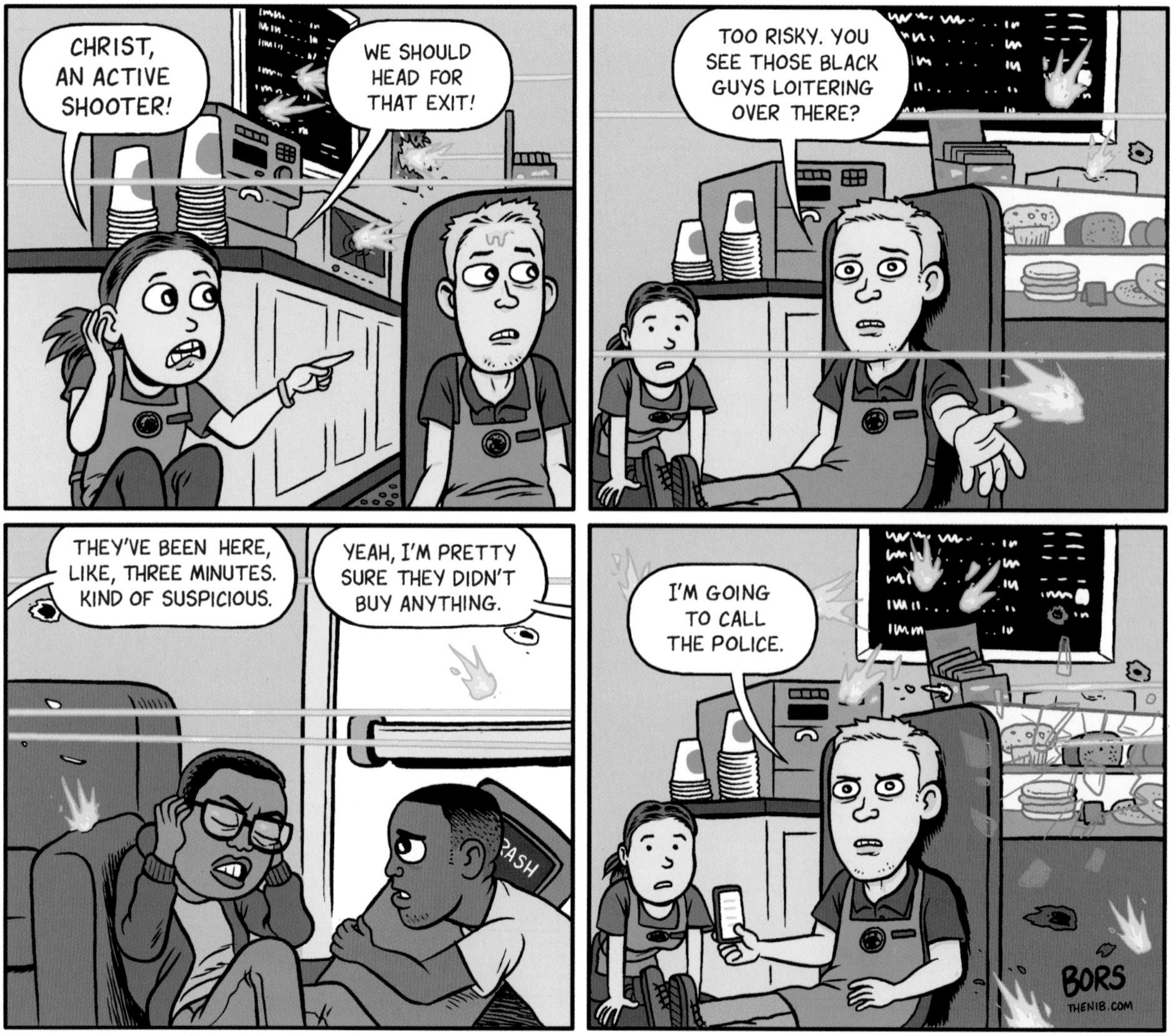
CHRIST, AN ACTIVE SHOOTER!
WE SHOULD HEAD FOR THAT EXIT!
TOO RISKY. YOU SEE THOSE BLACK GUYS LOITERING OVER THERE?
THEY'VE BEEN HERE, LIKE, THREE MINUTES. KIND OF SUSPICIOUS.
YEAH, I'M PRETTY SURE THEY DIDN'T BUY ANYTHING.
I'M GOING TO CALL THE POLICE.
BORS
THENIB.COM

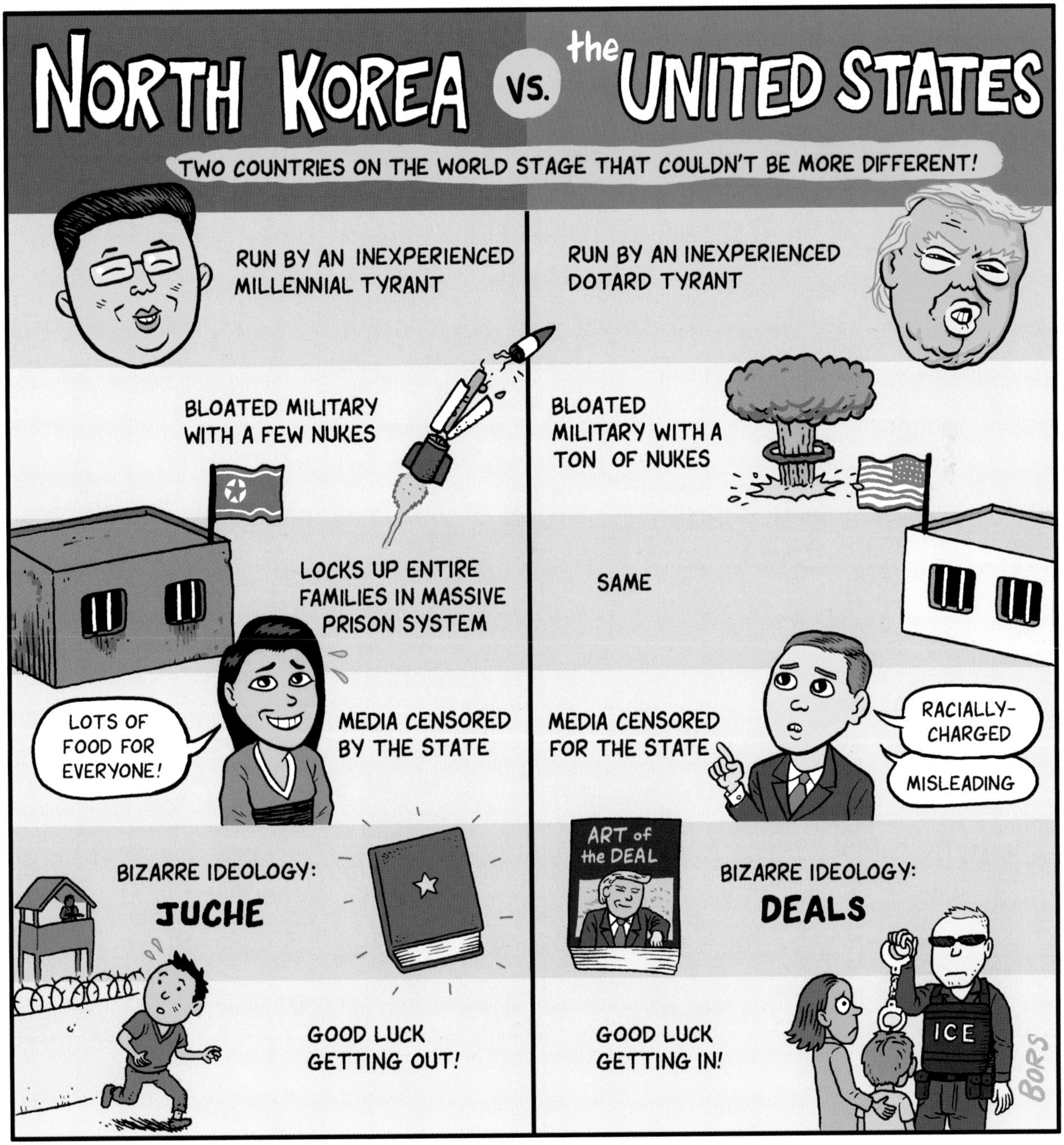
NORTH KOREA VS. the UNITED STATES
TWO COUNTRIES ON THE WORLD STAGE THAT COULDN'T BE MORE DIFFERENT!
RUN BY AN INEXPERIENCED MILLENNIAL TYRANT
RUN BY AN INEXPERIENCED DOTARD TYRANT
BLOATED MILITARY WITH A FEW NUKES
BLOATED MILITARY WITH A TON OF NUKES
LOCKS UP ENTIRE FAMILIES IN MASSIVE PRISON SYSTEM
SAME
LOTS OF FOOD FOR EVERYONE!
MEDIA CENSORED BY THE STATE
MEDIA CENSORED FOR THE STATE
RACIALLY-CHARGED
MISLEADING
BIZARRE IDEOLOGY:
JUCHE
ART of the DEAL
BIZARRE IDEOLOGY:
DEALS
GOOD LUCK GETTING OUT!
GOOD LUCK GETTING IN!
ICE
BORS

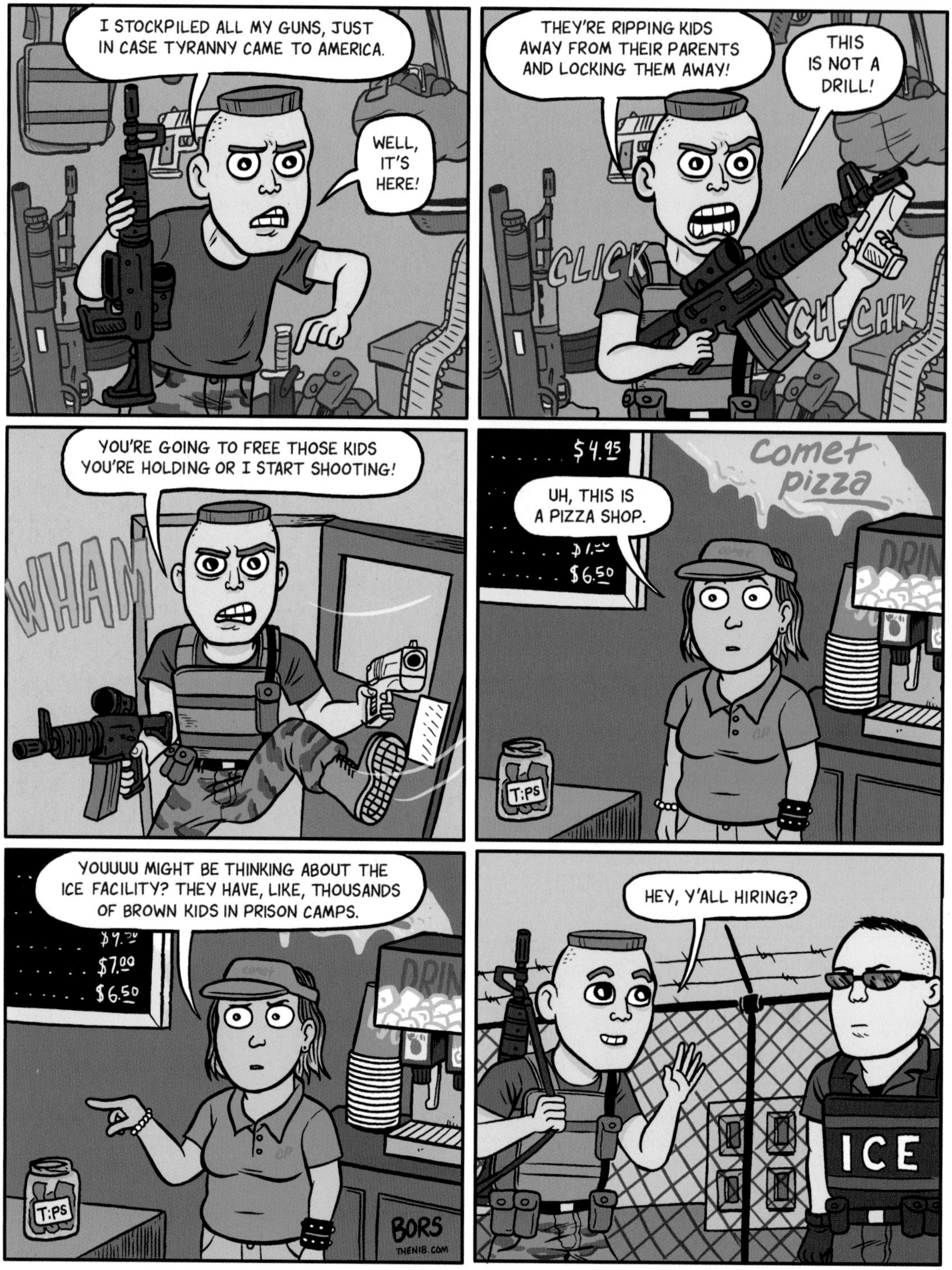
I STOCKPILED ALL MY GUNS, JUST IN CASE TYRANNY CAME TO AMERICA.
WELL, IT'S HERE!
THEY'RE RIPPING KIDS AWAY FROM THEIR PARENTS AND LOCKING THEM AWAY!
THIS IS NOT A DRILL!
CLICK
CH-CHK
YOU'RE GOING TO FREE THOSE KIDS YOU'RE HOLDING OR I START SHOOTING!
WHAM
$4.95
$6.50
Comet pizza
UH, THIS IS A PIZZA SHOP.
TIPS
YOUUUU MIGHT BE THINKING ABOUT THE ICE FACILITY? THEY HAVE, LIKE, THOUSANDS OF BROWN KIDS IN PRISON CAMPS.
$7.00
$6.50
TIPS
BORS
THENIB.COM
HEY, Y'ALL HIRING?
ICE

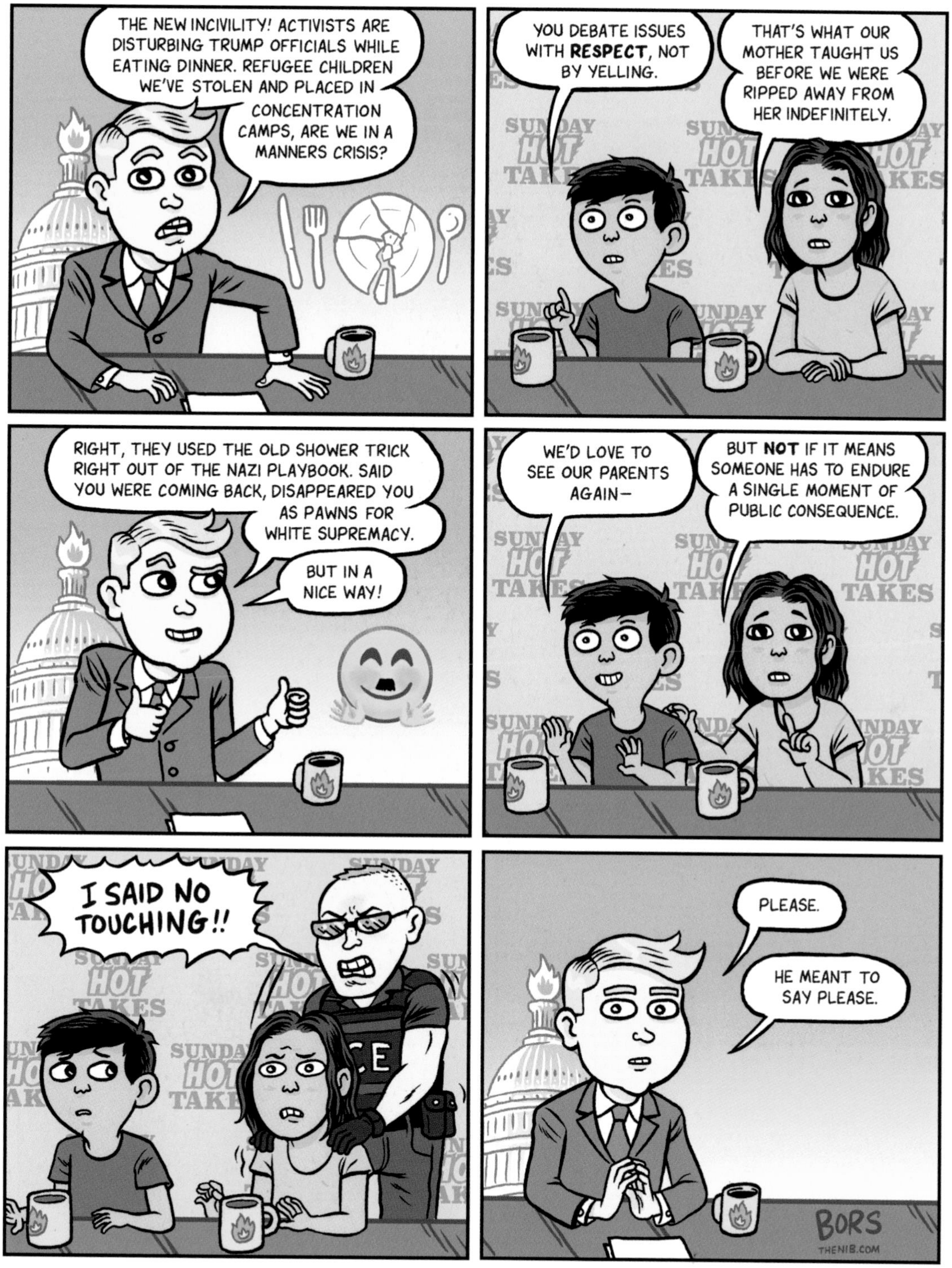
THE NEW INCIVILITY! ACTIVISTS ARE DISTURBING TRUMP OFFICIALS WHILE EATING DINNER. REFUGEE CHILDREN WE'VE STOLEN AND PLACED IN CONCENTRATION CAMPS, ARE WE IN A MANNERS CRISIS?
YOU DEBATE ISSUES WITH **RESPECT**, NOT BY YELLING.
THAT'S WHAT OUR MOTHER TAUGHT US BEFORE WE WERE RIPPED AWAY FROM HER INDEFINITELY.
RIGHT, THEY USED THE OLD SHOWER TRICK RIGHT OUT OF THE NAZI PLAYBOOK. SAID YOU WERE COMING BACK, DISAPPEARED YOU AS PAWNS FOR WHITE SUPREMACY.
BUT IN A NICE WAY!
WE'D LOVE TO SEE OUR PARENTS AGAIN—
BUT **NOT** IF IT MEANS SOMEONE HAS TO ENDURE A SINGLE MOMENT OF PUBLIC CONSEQUENCE.
I SAID NO TOUCHING!!
ICE
PLEASE.
HE MEANT TO SAY PLEASE.
BORS
THENIB.COM

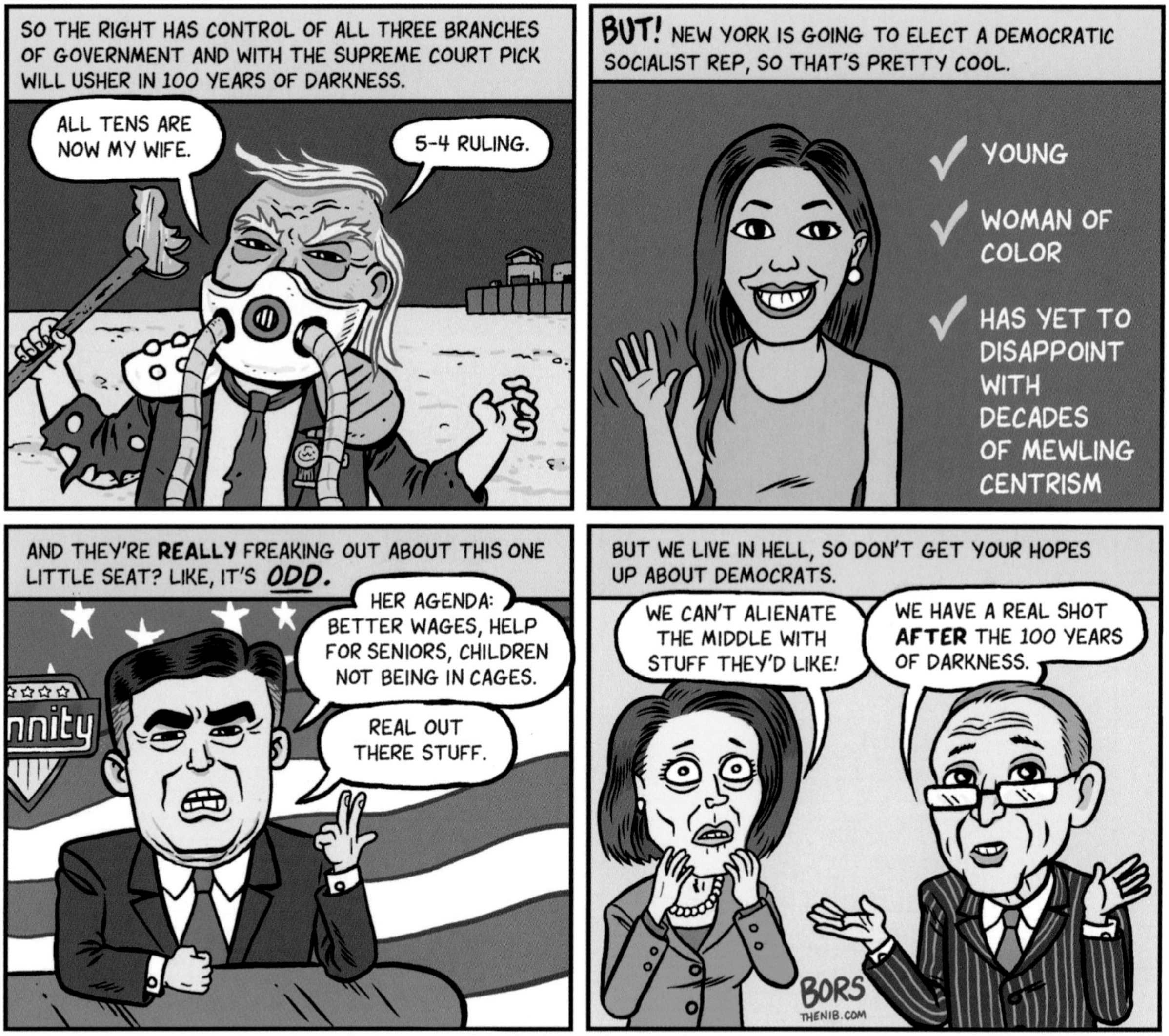
SO THE RIGHT HAS CONTROL OF ALL THREE BRANCHES OF GOVERNMENT AND WITH THE SUPREME COURT PICK WILL USHER IN 100 YEARS OF DARKNESS.
ALL TENS ARE NOW MY WIFE.
5-4 RULING.
BUT! NEW YORK IS GOING TO ELECT A DEMOCRATIC SOCIALIST REP, SO THAT'S PRETTY COOL.
YOUNG
WOMAN OF COLOR
HAS YET TO DISAPPOINT WITH DECADES OF MEWLING CENTRISM
AND THEY'RE REALLY FREAKING OUT ABOUT THIS ONE LITTLE SEAT? LIKE, IT'S ODD.
HER AGENDA: BETTER WAGES, HELP FOR SENIORS, CHILDREN NOT BEING IN CAGES.
REAL OUT THERE STUFF.
BUT WE LIVE IN HELL, SO DON'T GET YOUR HOPES UP ABOUT DEMOCRATS.
WE CAN'T ALIENATE THE MIDDLE WITH STUFF THEY'D LIKE!
WE HAVE A REAL SHOT AFTER THE 100 YEARS OF DARKNESS.
BORS
THENIB.COM

I began drawing Trump as an Immortan Joe-inspired ruler of the future Wasteland, whose official title is "Eternal Overlord Trump" in Nib Wasteland canon.

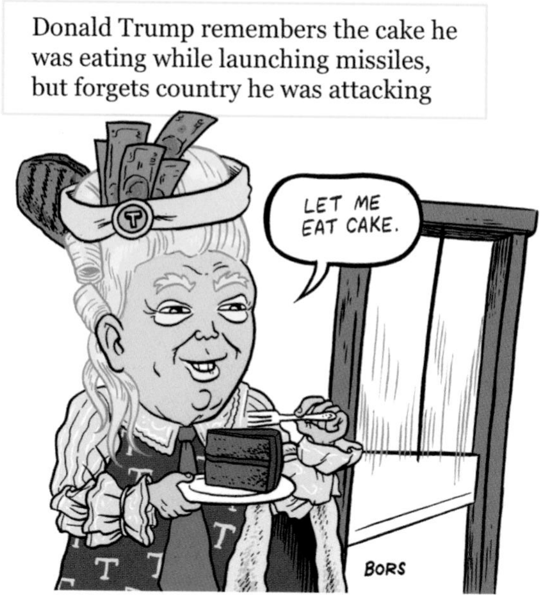
Donald Trump remembers the cake he was eating while launching missiles, but forgets country he was attacking
LET ME EAT CAKE.
BORS

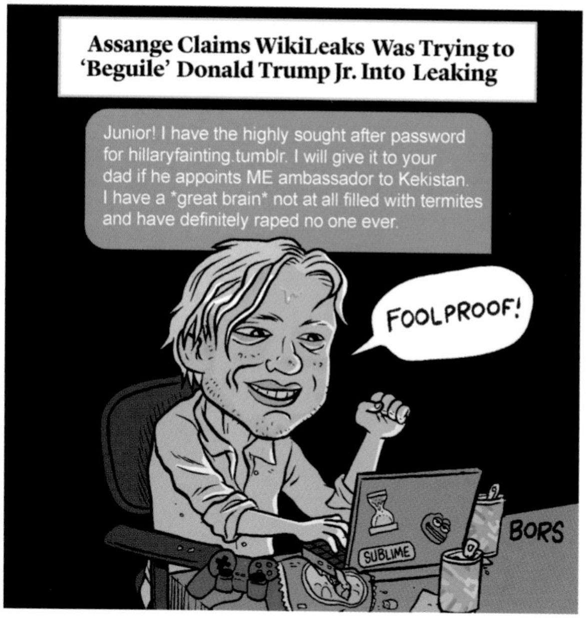
Assange Claims WikiLeaks Was Trying to 'Beguile' Donald Trump Jr. Into Leaking
Junior! I have the highly sought after password for hillaryfainting.tumblr. I will give it to your dad if he appoints ME ambassador to Kekistan. I have a *great brain* not at all filled with termites and have definitely raped no one ever.
FOOLPROOF!
SUBLIME
BORS

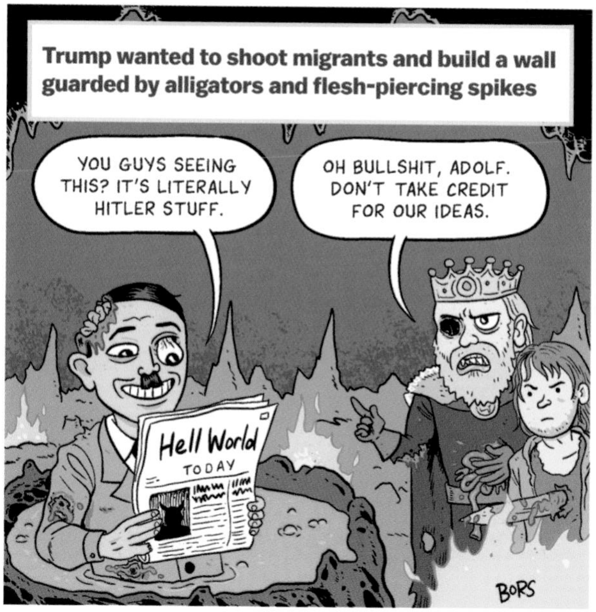
Trump wanted to shoot migrants and build a wall guarded by alligators and flesh-piercing spikes
YOU GUYS SEEING THIS? IT'S LITERALLY HITLER STUFF.
OH BULLSHIT, ADOLF. DON'T TAKE CREDIT FOR OUR IDEAS.
Hell World TODAY
BORS

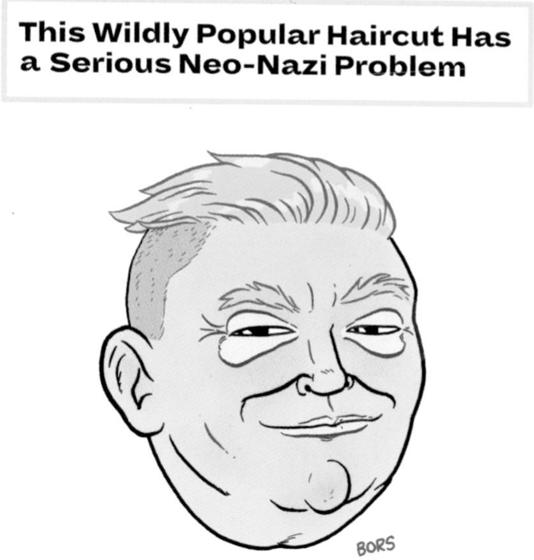
This Wildly Popular Haircut Has a Serious Neo-Nazi Problem
BORS

At The Nib we often run what we call "headline comics"—screengrabs of news headlines followed by a quick reaction comic. With so much going on under the Trump administration on a daily basis, these comics provide a glimpse at news stories that flew by so fast you can barely remember them.

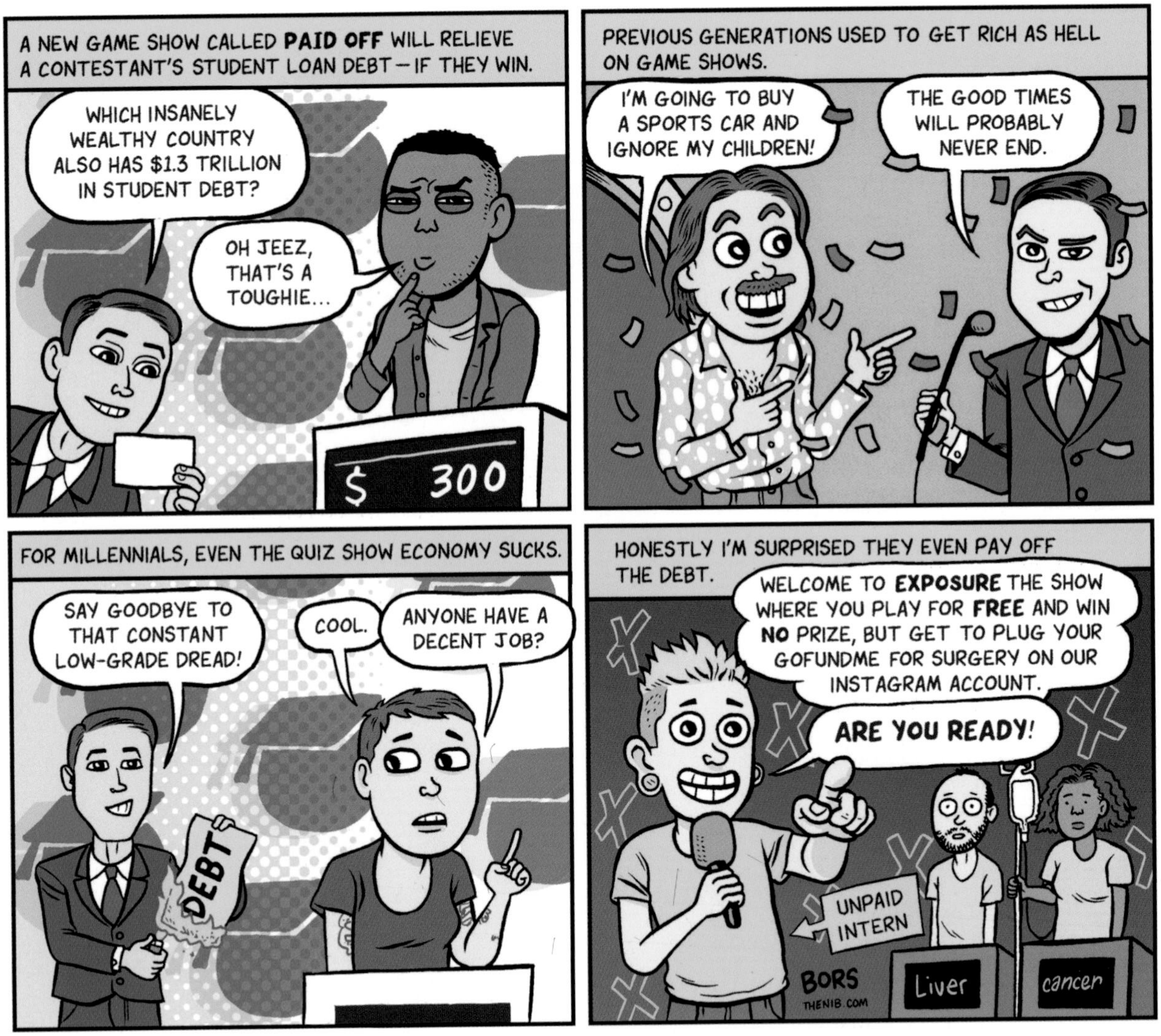
A NEW GAME SHOW CALLED PAID OFF WILL RELIEVE A CONTESTANT'S STUDENT LOAN DEBT—IF THEY WIN.
WHICH INSANELY WEALTHY COUNTRY ALSO HAS $1.3 TRILLION IN STUDENT DEBT?
OH JEEZ, THAT'S A TOUGHIE...
$ 300
PREVIOUS GENERATIONS USED TO GET RICH AS HELL ON GAME SHOWS.
I'M GOING TO BUY A SPORTS CAR AND IGNORE MY CHILDREN!
THE GOOD TIMES WILL PROBABLY NEVER END.
FOR MILLENNIALS, EVEN THE QUIZ SHOW ECONOMY SUCKS.
SAY GOODBYE TO THAT CONSTANT LOW-GRADE DREAD!
DEBT
COOL.
ANYONE HAVE A DECENT JOB?
HONESTLY I'M SURPRISED THEY EVEN PAY OFF THE DEBT.
WELCOME TO EXPOSURE THE SHOW WHERE YOU PLAY FOR FREE AND WIN NO PRIZE, BUT GET TO PLUG YOUR GOFUNDME FOR SURGERY ON OUR INSTAGRAM ACCOUNT.
ARE YOU READY!
UNPAID INTERN
Liver
cancer
BORS
THENIB.COM

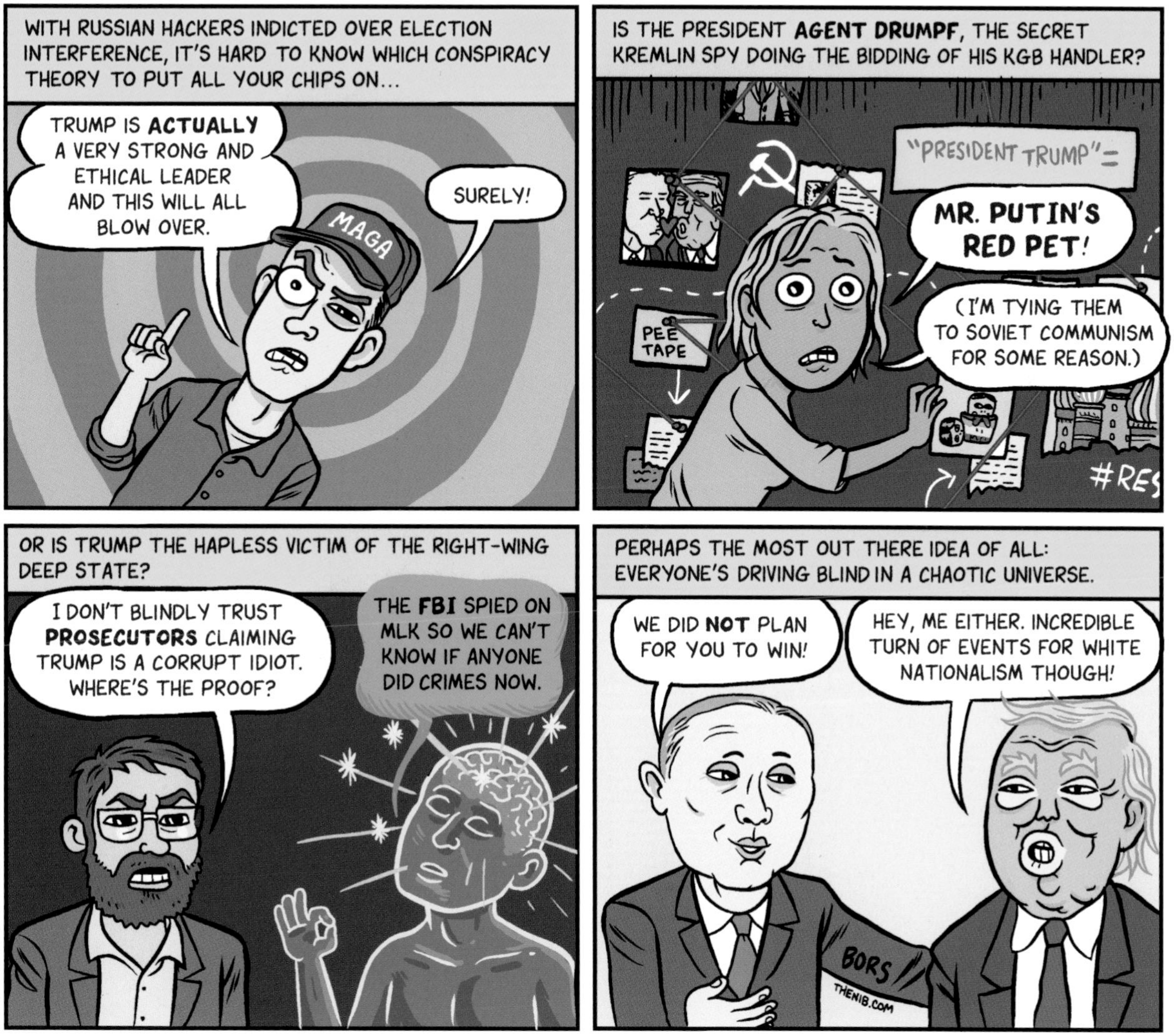
WITH RUSSIAN HACKERS INDICTED OVER ELECTION INTERFERENCE, IT'S HARD TO KNOW WHICH CONSPIRACY THEORY TO PUT ALL YOUR CHIPS ON...
TRUMP IS **ACTUALLY** A VERY STRONG AND ETHICAL LEADER AND THIS WILL ALL BLOW OVER.
SURELY!
MAGA
IS THE PRESIDENT **AGENT DRUMPF**, THE SECRET KREMLIN SPY DOING THE BIDDING OF HIS KGB HANDLER?
"PRESIDENT TRUMP" =
MR. PUTIN'S RED PET!
(I'M TYING THEM TO SOVIET COMMUNISM FOR SOME REASON.)
PEE TAPE
#RES
OR IS TRUMP THE HAPLESS VICTIM OF THE RIGHT-WING DEEP STATE?
I DON'T BLINDLY TRUST **PROSECUTORS** CLAIMING TRUMP IS A CORRUPT IDIOT. WHERE'S THE PROOF?
THE **FBI** SPIED ON MLK SO WE CAN'T KNOW IF ANYONE DID CRIMES NOW.
PERHAPS THE MOST OUT THERE IDEA OF ALL: EVERYONE'S DRIVING BLIND IN A CHAOTIC UNIVERSE.
WE DID **NOT** PLAN FOR YOU TO WIN!
HEY, ME EITHER. INCREDIBLE TURN OF EVENTS FOR WHITE NATIONALISM THOUGH!
BORS
THENIB.COM

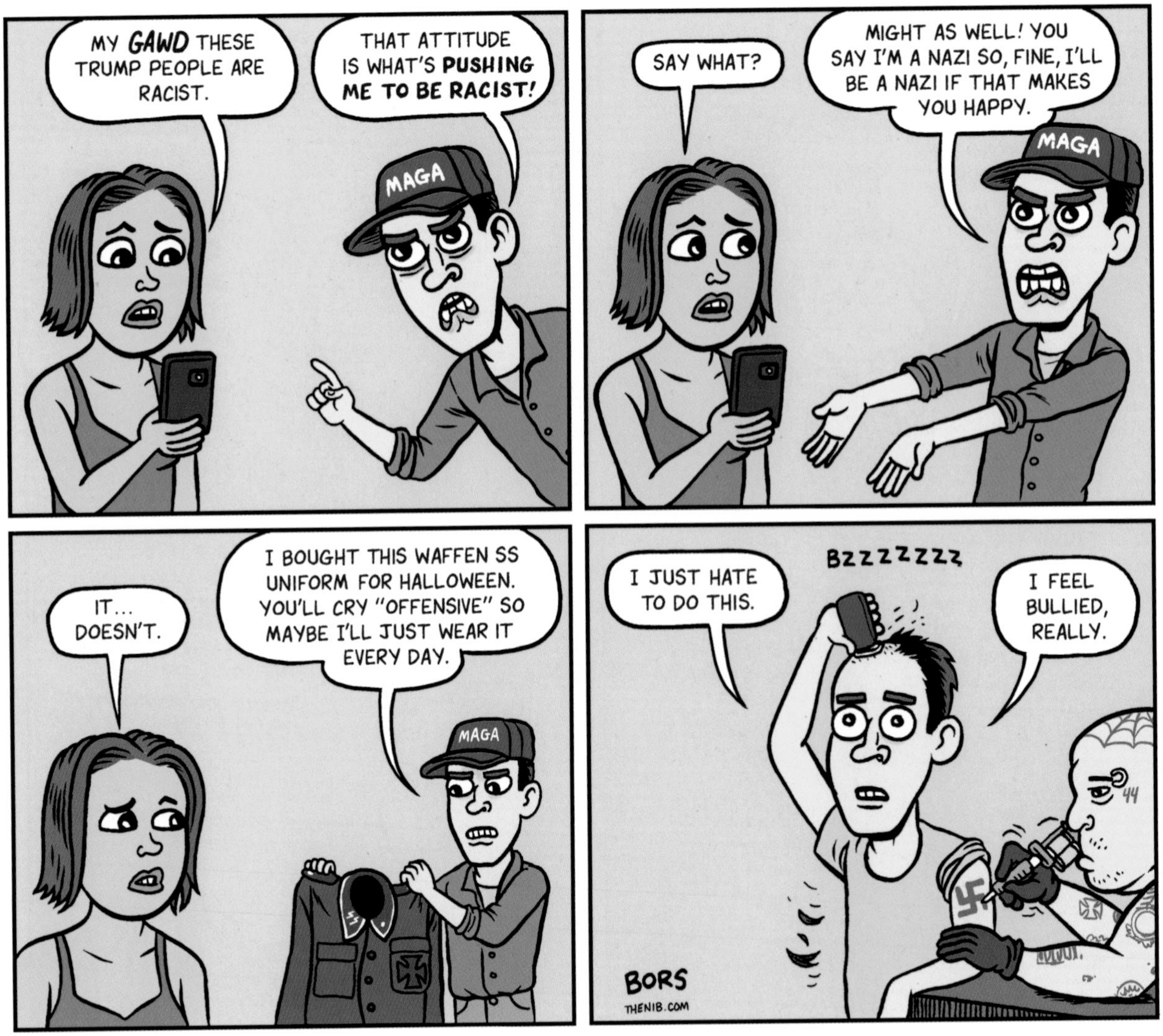
MY GAWD THESE TRUMP PEOPLE ARE RACIST.
THAT ATTITUDE IS WHAT'S PUSHING ME TO BE RACIST!
MAGA
SAY WHAT?
MIGHT AS WELL! YOU SAY I'M A NAZI SO, FINE, I'LL BE A NAZI IF THAT MAKES YOU HAPPY.
MAGA
IT... DOESN'T.
I BOUGHT THIS WAFFEN SS UNIFORM FOR HALLOWEEN. YOU'LL CRY "OFFENSIVE" SO MAYBE I'LL JUST WEAR IT EVERY DAY.
MAGA
I JUST HATE TO DO THIS.
BZZZZZZZ
I FEEL BULLIED, REALLY.
BORS
THENIB.COM

You're seeing this more and more in the Trump era—conservatives giving themselves permission to embrace the darkest aspects of their worldview because radical ideas like gender-neutral bathrooms supposedly make compromise and debate obsolete. And if their views significantly overlap with white nationalists movements, well, maybe Hitler had some good ideas!

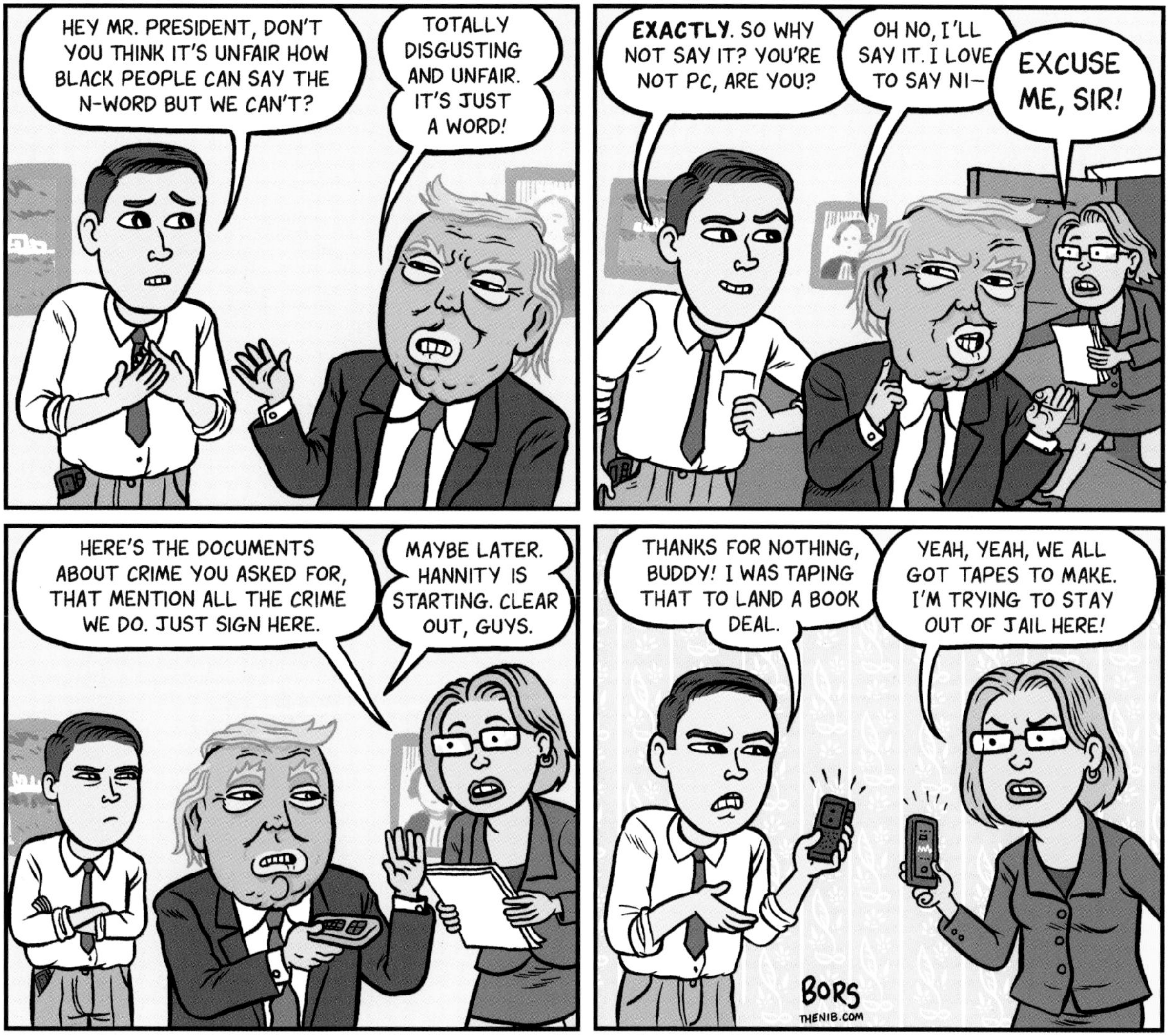
HEY MR. PRESIDENT, DON'T YOU THINK IT'S UNFAIR HOW BLACK PEOPLE CAN SAY THE N-WORD BUT WE CAN'T?
TOTALLY DISGUSTING AND UNFAIR. IT'S JUST A WORD!
EXACTLY. SO WHY NOT SAY IT? YOU'RE NOT PC, ARE YOU?
OH NO, I'LL SAY IT. I LOVE TO SAY NI–
EXCUSE ME, SIR!
HERE'S THE DOCUMENTS ABOUT CRIME YOU ASKED FOR, THAT MENTION ALL THE CRIME WE DO. JUST SIGN HERE.
MAYBE LATER. HANNITY IS STARTING. CLEAR OUT, GUYS.
THANKS FOR NOTHING, BUDDY! I WAS TAPING THAT TO LAND A BOOK DEAL.
YEAH, YEAH, WE ALL GOT TAPES TO MAKE. I'M TRYING TO STAY OUT OF JAIL HERE!
BORS
THENIB.COM

Low bar, but it's actually incredible Trump hasn't blurted out the n-word yet.

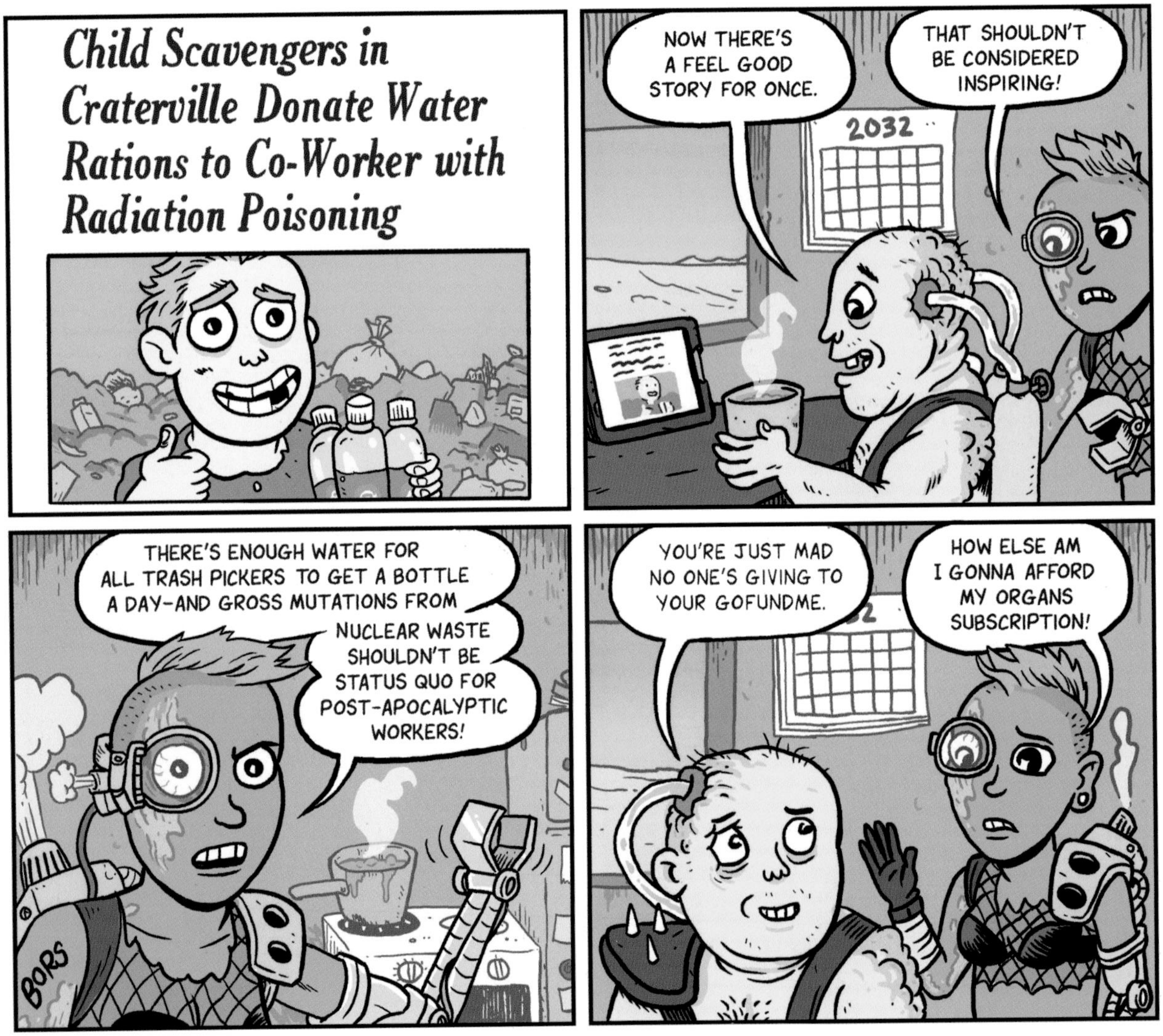
Child Scavengers in Craterville Donate Water Rations to Co-Worker with Radiation Poisoning
NOW THERE'S A FEEL GOOD STORY FOR ONCE.
THAT SHOULDN'T BE CONSIDERED INSPIRING!
2032
THERE'S ENOUGH WATER FOR ALL TRASH PICKERS TO GET A BOTTLE A DAY—AND GROSS MUTATIONS FROM
NUCLEAR WASTE SHOULDN'T BE STATUS QUO FOR POST-APOCALYPTIC WORKERS!
BORS
YOU'RE JUST MAD NO ONE'S GIVING TO YOUR GOFUNDME.
HOW ELSE AM I GONNA AFFORD MY ORGANS SUBSCRIPTION!

Inspired by real headlines from our hellword such as "After Employee Walks 20 Miles To Work, Boss Buys Him Car."

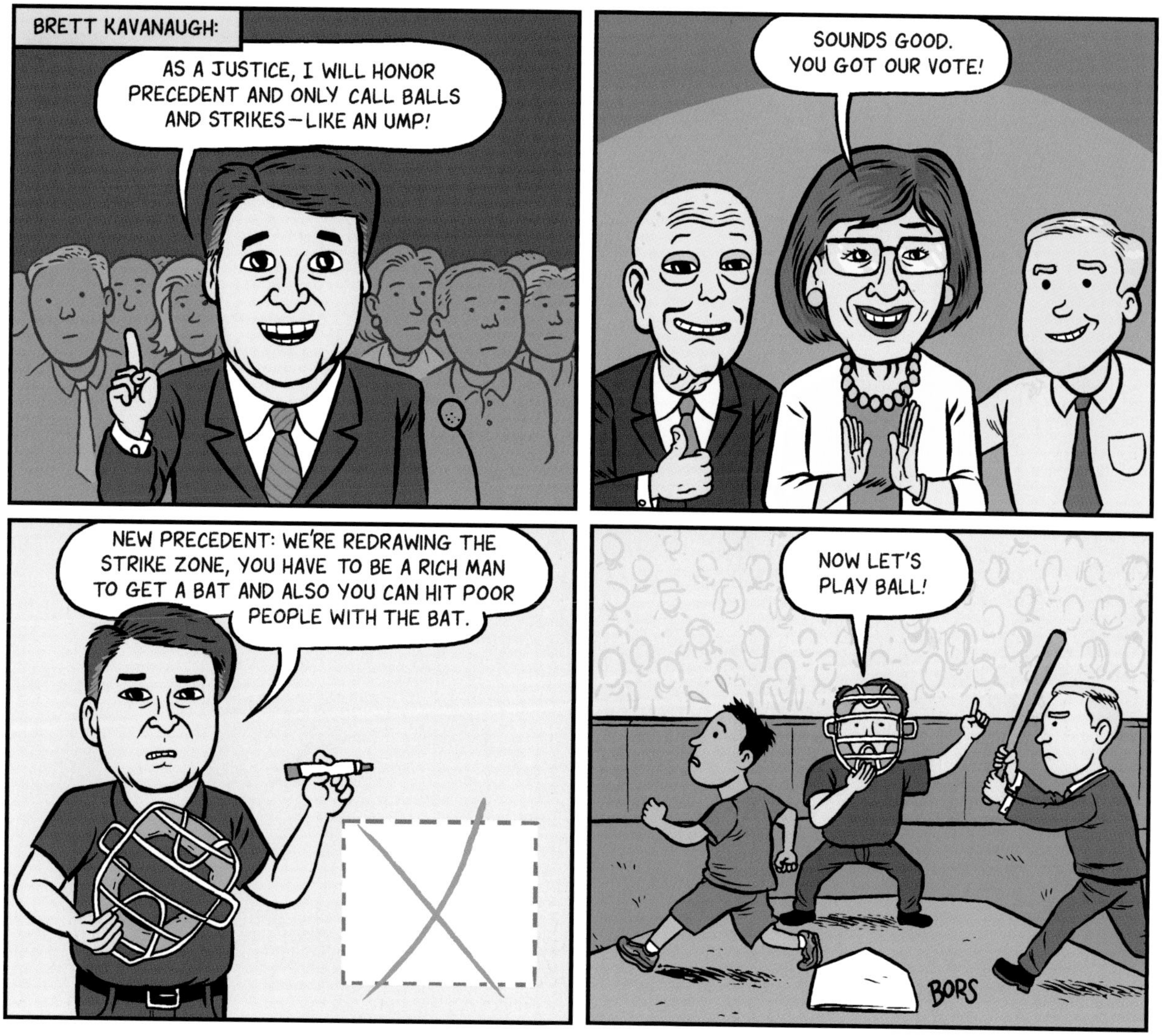
BRETT KAVANAUGH:
AS A JUSTICE, I WILL HONOR PRECEDENT AND ONLY CALL BALLS AND STRIKES—LIKE AN UMP!
SOUNDS GOOD. YOU GOT OUR VOTE!
NEW PRECEDENT: WE'RE REDRAWING THE STRIKE ZONE, YOU HAVE TO BE A RICH MAN TO GET A BAT AND ALSO YOU CAN HIT POOR
PEOPLE WITH THE BAT.
NOW LET'S PLAY BALL!
BORS

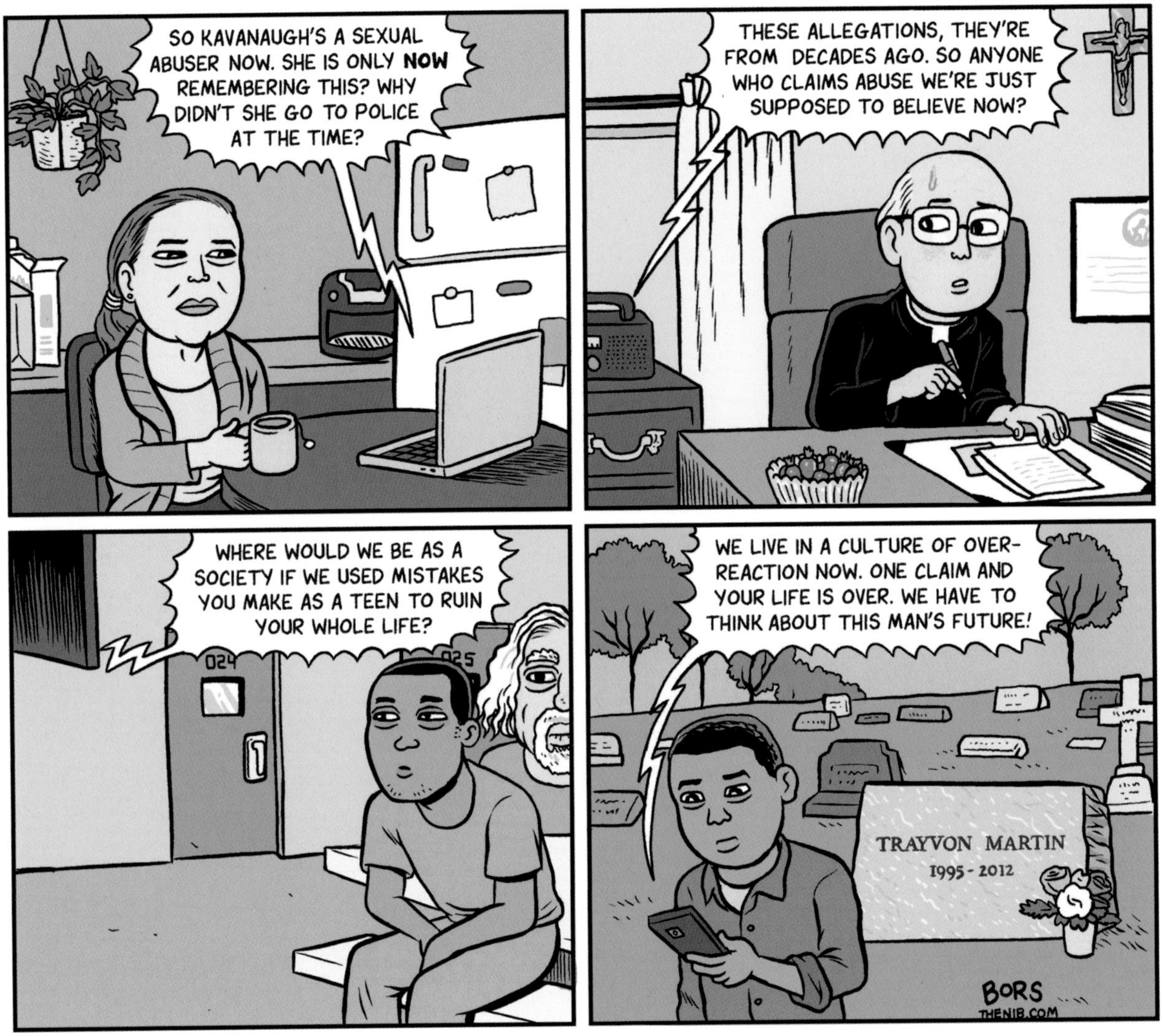
SO KAVANAUGH'S A SEXUAL ABUSER NOW. SHE IS ONLY **NOW** REMEMBERING THIS? WHY DIDN'T SHE GO TO POLICE AT THE TIME?
THESE ALLEGATIONS, THEY'RE FROM DECADES AGO. SO ANYONE WHO CLAIMS ABUSE WE'RE JUST SUPPOSED TO BELIEVE NOW?
WHERE WOULD WE BE AS A SOCIETY IF WE USED MISTAKES YOU MAKE AS A TEEN TO RUIN YOUR WHOLE LIFE?
024
025
WE LIVE IN A CULTURE OF OVER-REACTION NOW. ONE CLAIM AND YOUR LIFE IS OVER. WE HAVE TO THINK ABOUT THIS MAN'S FUTURE!
TRAYVON MARTIN
1995 - 2012
BORS
THENIB.COM

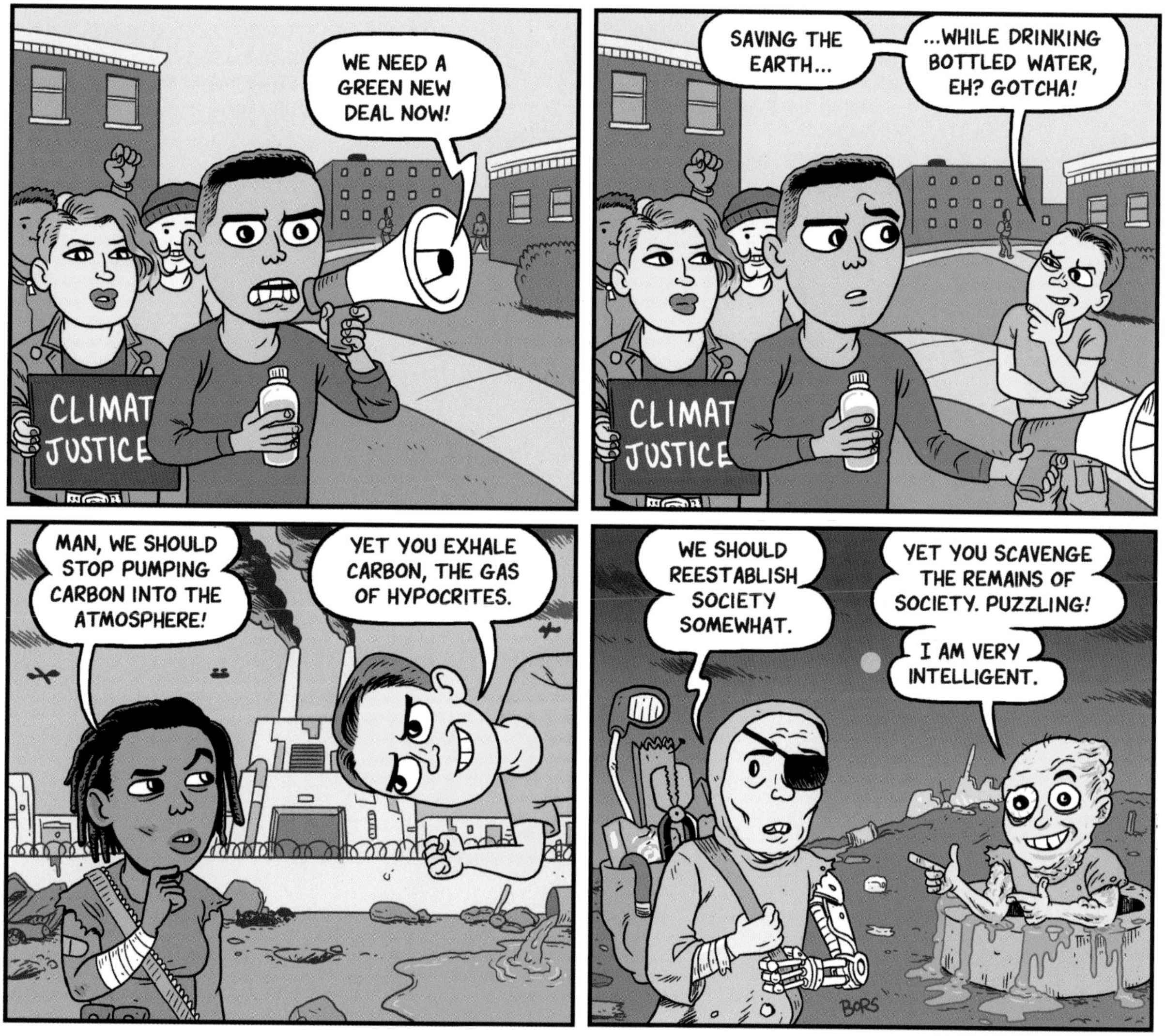
WE NEED A GREEN NEW DEAL NOW!
CLIMATE JUSTICE
SAVING THE EARTH...
...WHILE DRINKING BOTTLED WATER, EH? GOTCHA!
CLIMAT JUSTICE
MAN, WE SHOULD STOP PUMPING CARBON INTO THE ATMOSPHERE!
YET YOU EXHALE CARBON, THE GAS OF HYPOCRITES.
WE SHOULD REESTABLISH SOCIETY SOMEWHAT.
YET YOU SCAVENGE THE REMAINS OF SOCIETY. PUZZLING!
I AM VERY INTELLIGENT.
BORS

The original Mr. Gotcha rocketed us backward in time. It was only natural to get a look at his bright future calling bullshit on people who would like to halt the destruction of the planet while using products from earth, eating food, and breathing air.

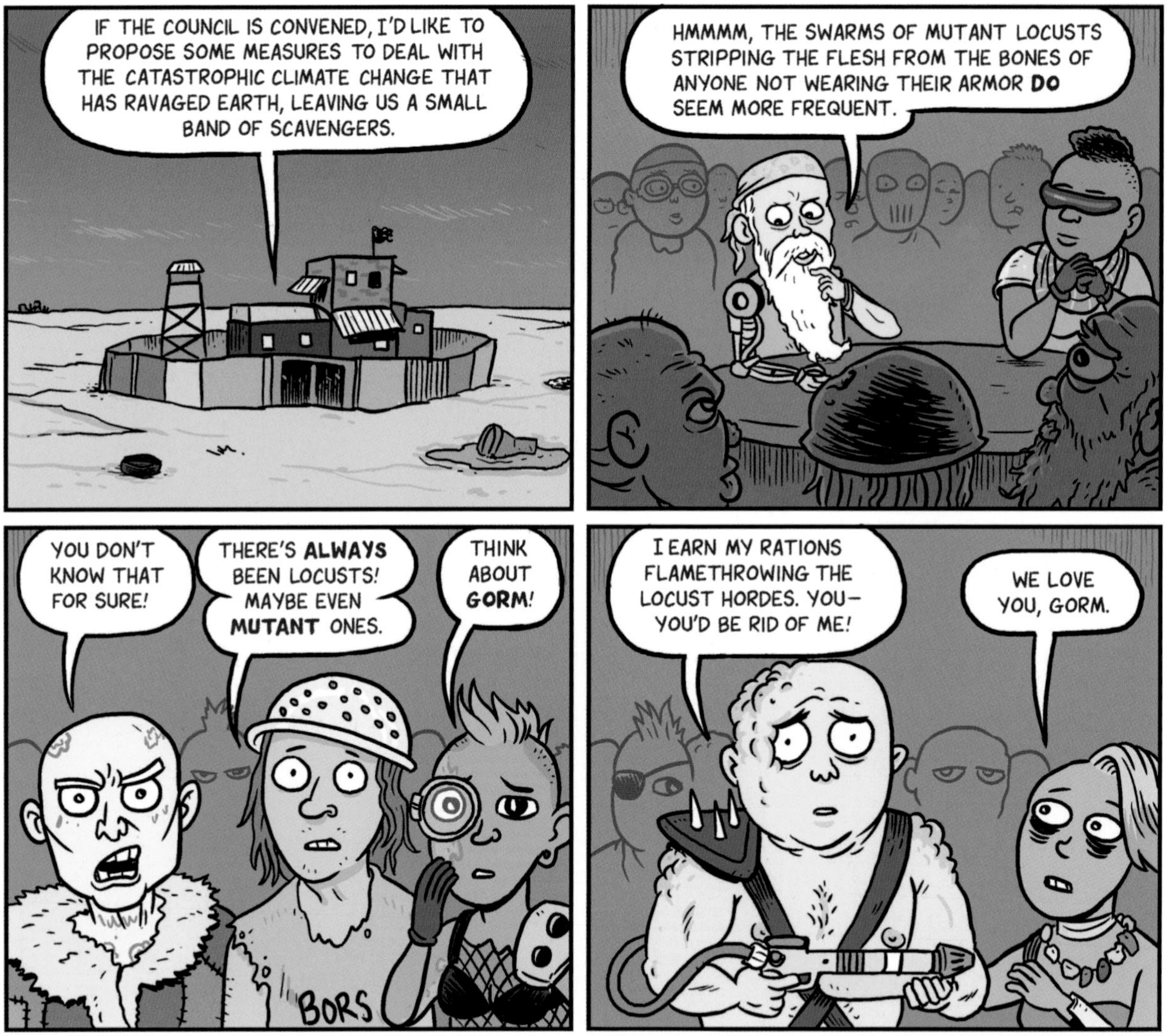
IF THE COUNCIL IS CONVENED, I'D LIKE TO PROPOSE SOME MEASURES TO DEAL WITH THE CATASTROPHIC CLIMATE CHANGE THAT HAS RAVAGED EARTH, LEAVING US A SMALL BAND OF SCAVENGERS.
HMMMM, THE SWARMS OF MUTANT LOCUSTS STRIPPING THE FLESH FROM THE BONES OF ANYONE NOT WEARING THEIR ARMOR **DO** SEEM MORE FREQUENT.
YOU DON'T KNOW THAT FOR SURE!
THERE'S **ALWAYS** BEEN LOCUSTS! MAYBE EVEN **MUTANT** ONES.
THINK ABOUT **GORM**!
BORS
I EARN MY RATIONS FLAMETHROWING THE LOCUST HORDES. YOU— YOU'D BE RID OF ME!
WE LOVE YOU, GORM.

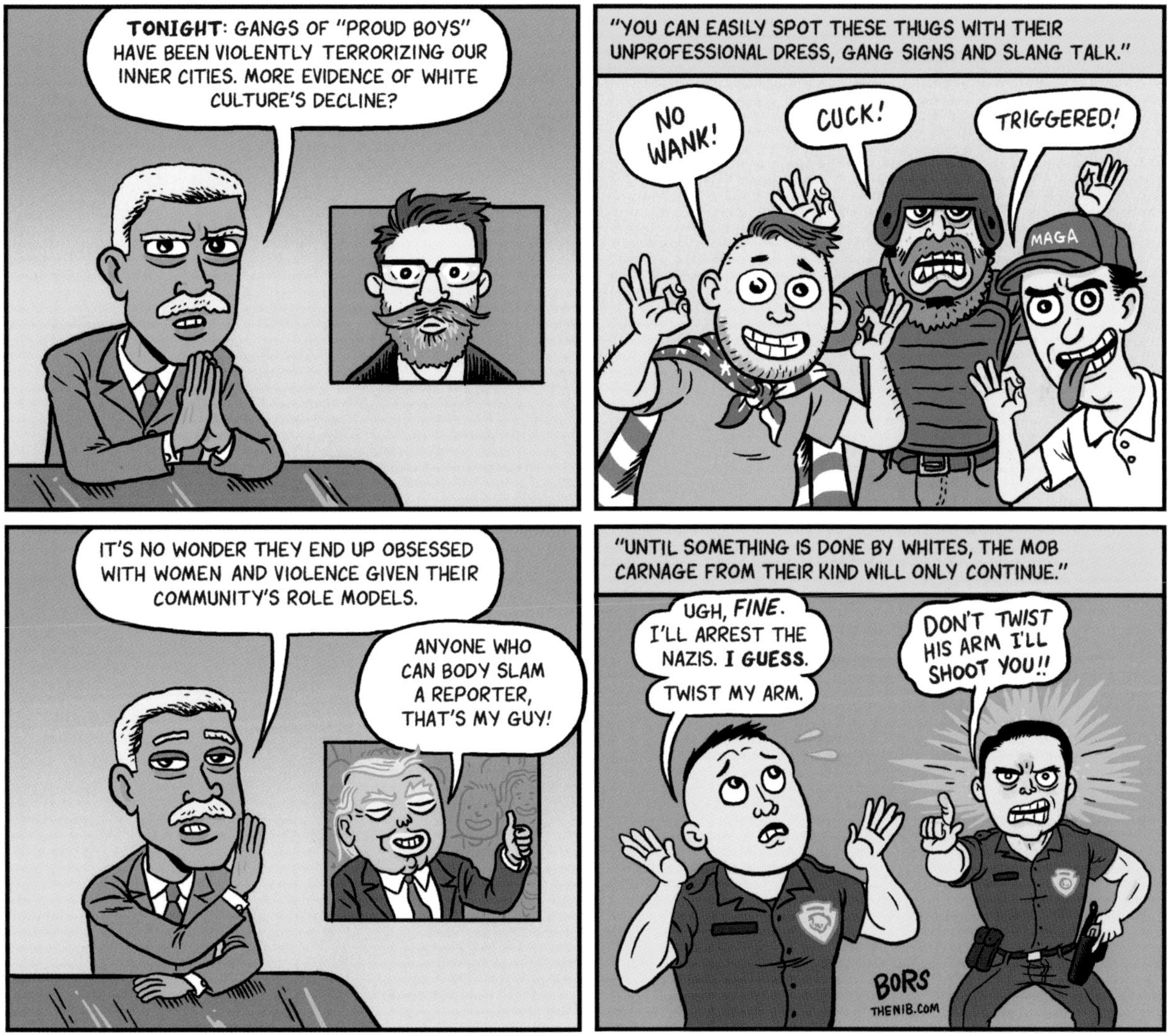
TONIGHT: GANGS OF "PROUD BOYS" HAVE BEEN VIOLENTLY TERRORIZING OUR INNER CITIES. MORE EVIDENCE OF WHITE CULTURE'S DECLINE?
"YOU CAN EASILY SPOT THESE THUGS WITH THEIR UNPROFESSIONAL DRESS, GANG SIGNS AND SLANG TALK."
NO WANK!
CUCK!
TRIGGERED!
MAGA
IT'S NO WONDER THEY END UP OBSESSED WITH WOMEN AND VIOLENCE GIVEN THEIR COMMUNITY'S ROLE MODELS.
ANYONE WHO CAN BODY SLAM A REPORTER, THAT'S MY GUY!
"UNTIL SOMETHING IS DONE BY WHITES, THE MOB CARNAGE FROM THEIR KIND WILL ONLY CONTINUE."
UGH, FINE. I'LL ARREST THE NAZIS. I GUESS.
TWIST MY ARM.
DON'T TWIST HIS ARM I'LL SHOOT YOU!!
BORS
THENIB.COM

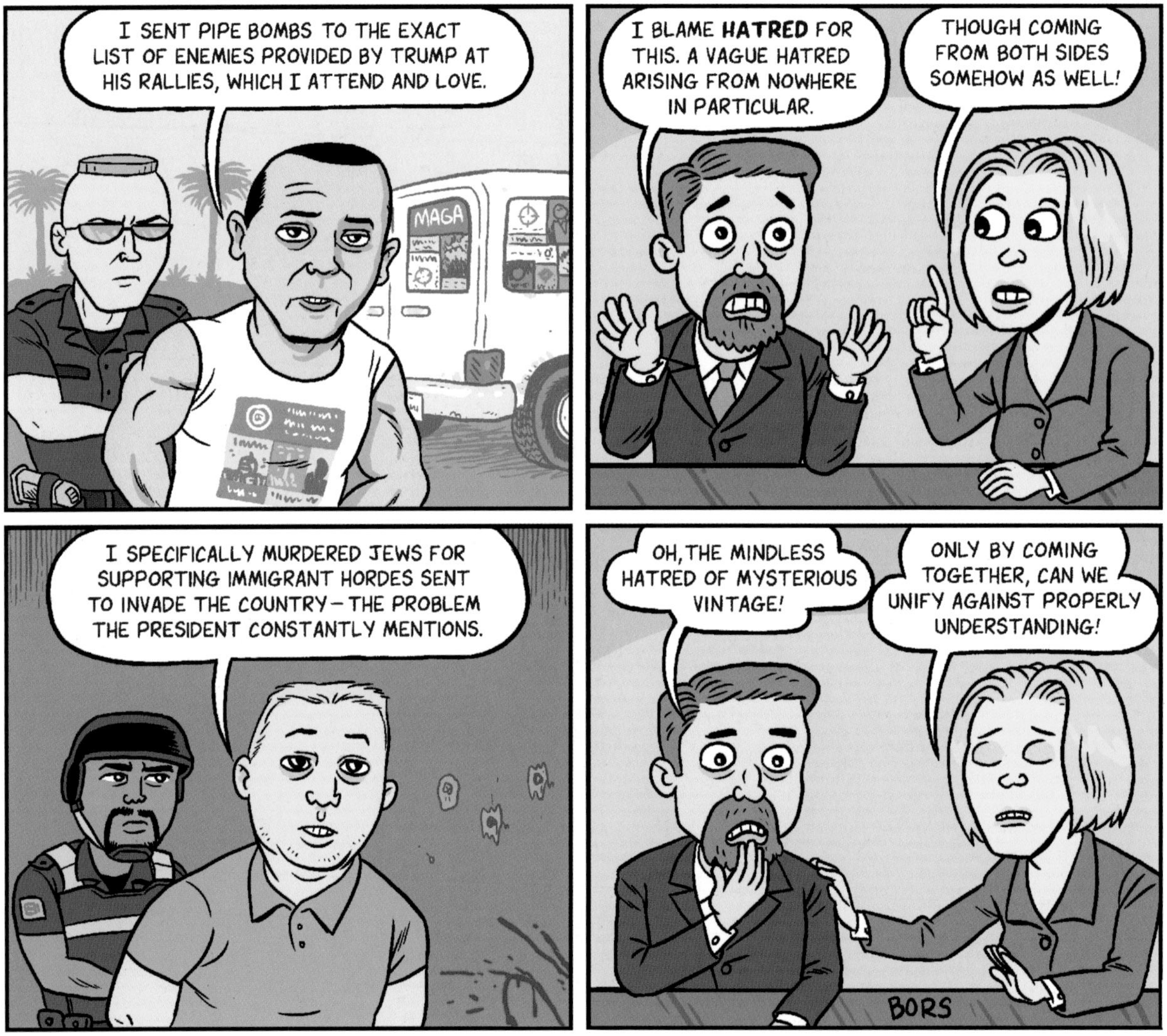
I SENT PIPE BOMBS TO THE EXACT LIST OF ENEMIES PROVIDED BY TRUMP AT HIS RALLIES, WHICH I ATTEND AND LOVE.
MAGA
I BLAME **HATRED** FOR THIS. A VAGUE HATRED ARISING FROM NOWHERE IN PARTICULAR.
THOUGH COMING FROM BOTH SIDES SOMEHOW AS WELL!
I SPECIFICALLY MURDERED JEWS FOR SUPPORTING IMMIGRANT HORDES SENT TO INVADE THE COUNTRY—THE PROBLEM THE PRESIDENT CONSTANTLY MENTIONS.
OH, THE MINDLESS HATRED OF MYSTERIOUS VINTAGE!
ONLY BY COMING TOGETHER, CAN WE UNIFY AGAINST PROPERLY UNDERSTANDING!
BORS

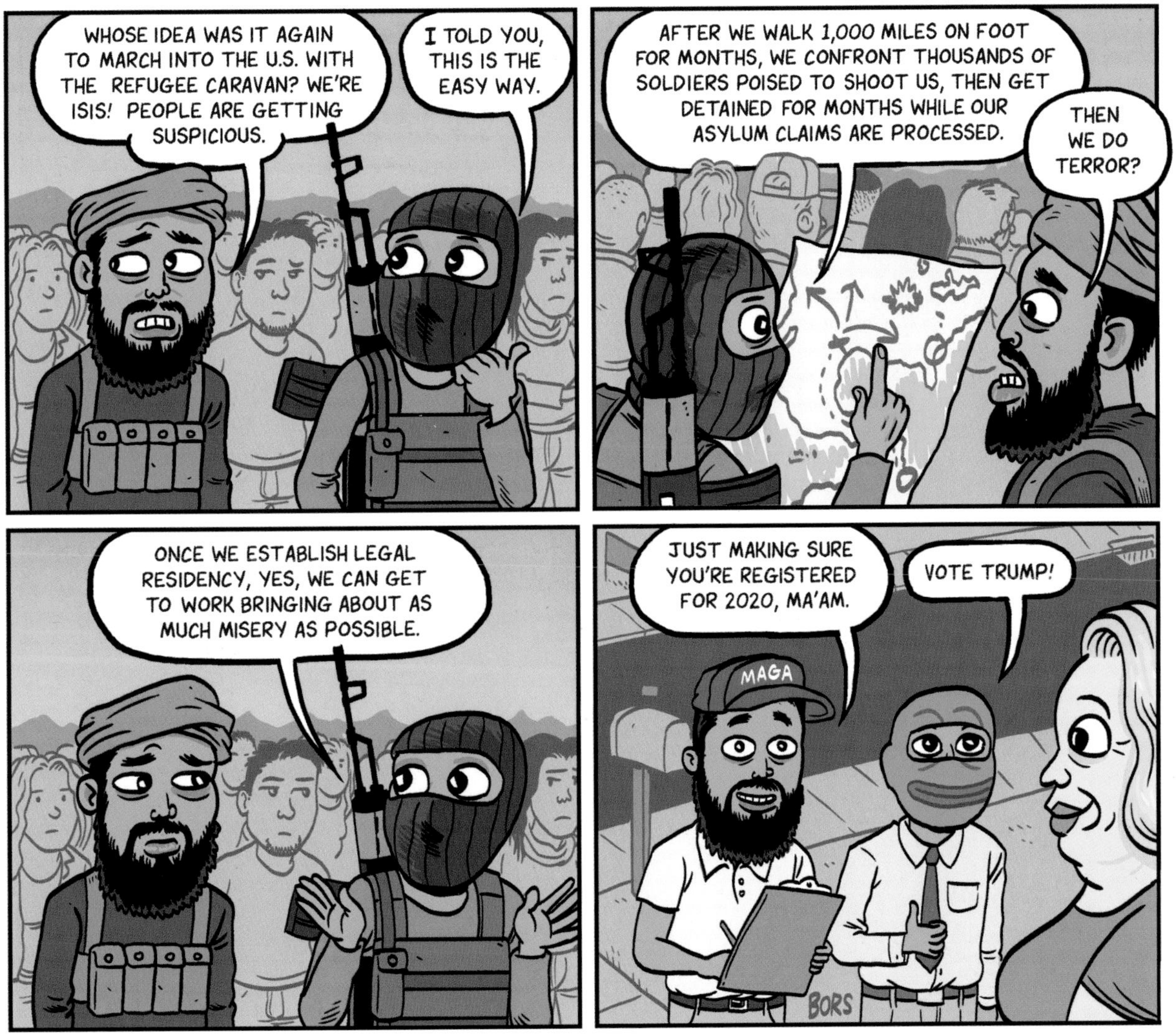
WHOSE IDEA WAS IT AGAIN TO MARCH INTO THE U.S. WITH THE REFUGEE CARAVAN? WE'RE ISIS! PEOPLE ARE GETTING SUSPICIOUS.
I TOLD YOU, THIS IS THE EASY WAY.
AFTER WE WALK 1,000 MILES ON FOOT FOR MONTHS, WE CONFRONT THOUSANDS OF SOLDIERS POISED TO SHOOT US, THEN GET DETAINED FOR MONTHS WHILE OUR ASYLUM CLAIMS ARE PROCESSED.
THEN WE DO TERROR?
ONCE WE ESTABLISH LEGAL RESIDENCY, YES, WE CAN GET TO WORK BRINGING ABOUT AS MUCH MISERY AS POSSIBLE.
MAGA
JUST MAKING SURE YOU'RE REGISTERED FOR 2020, MA'AM.
VOTE TRUMP!
BORS

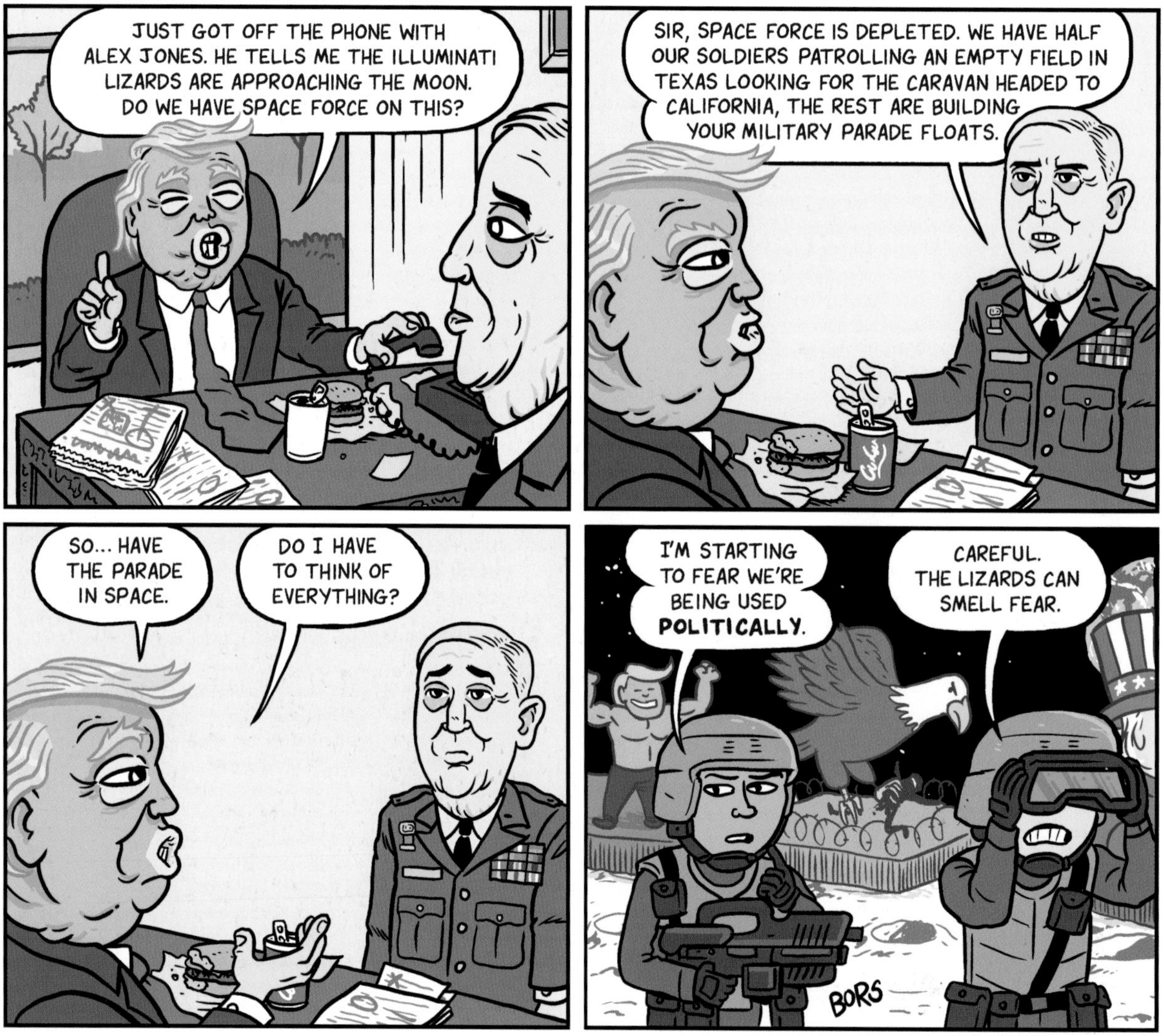
JUST GOT OFF THE PHONE WITH ALEX JONES. HE TELLS ME THE ILLUMINATI LIZARDS ARE APPROACHING THE MOON. DO WE HAVE SPACE FORCE ON THIS?
SIR, SPACE FORCE IS DEPLETED. WE HAVE HALF OUR SOLDIERS PATROLLING AN EMPTY FIELD IN TEXAS LOOKING FOR THE CARAVAN HEADED TO CALIFORNIA, THE REST ARE BUILDING YOUR MILITARY PARADE FLOATS.
SO... HAVE THE PARADE IN SPACE.
DO I HAVE TO THINK OF EVERYTHING?
I'M STARTING TO FEAR WE'RE BEING USED **POLITICALLY**.
CAREFUL. THE LIZARDS CAN SMELL FEAR.
BORS

Just want to point out the germ of truth here: the President of the United States does in fact speak on the phone with Alex Jones, who believes we're being turned gay by chemicals dispersed by the literal demons inside the government (which is now run by Trump, but whatever).

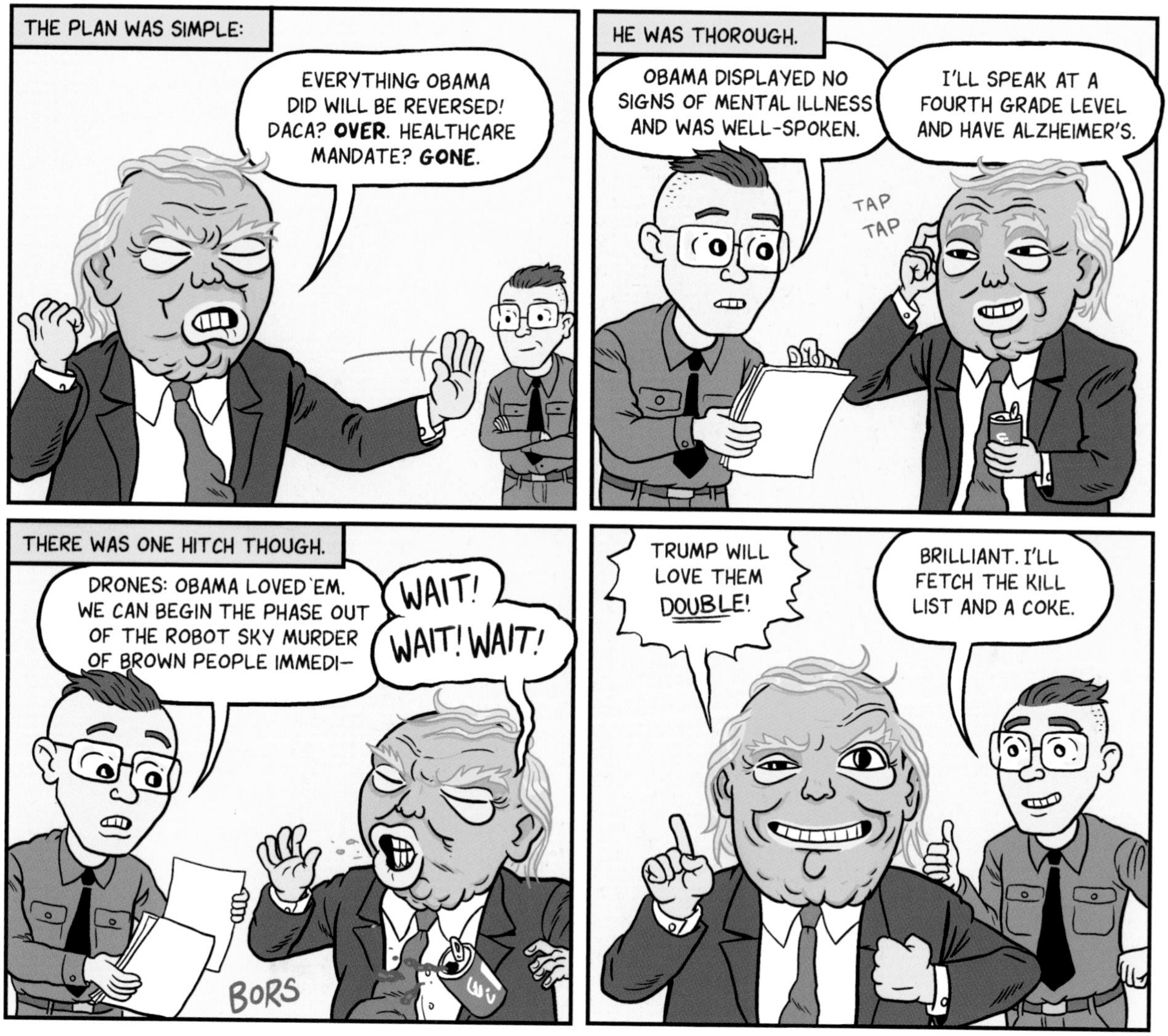
THE PLAN WAS SIMPLE:
EVERYTHING OBAMA DID WILL BE REVERSED! DACA? **OVER**. HEALTHCARE MANDATE? **GONE**.
HE WAS THOROUGH.
OBAMA DISPLAYED NO SIGNS OF MENTAL ILLNESS AND WAS WELL-SPOKEN.
I'LL SPEAK AT A FOURTH GRADE LEVEL AND HAVE ALZHEIMER'S.
TAP TAP
THERE WAS ONE HITCH THOUGH.
DRONES: OBAMA LOVED 'EM. WE CAN BEGIN THE PHASE OUT OF THE ROBOT SKY MURDER OF BROWN PEOPLE IMMEDI—
WAIT! WAIT! WAIT!
BORS
TRUMP WILL LOVE THEM DOUBLE!
BRILLIANT. I'LL FETCH THE KILL LIST AND A COKE.

FACTS! REASON! LOGIC!
WHAT'S HIS DEAL?
NERVOUS BREAKDOWN. HE WAS ARGUING ONLINE WHEN HE SUDDENLY GOT CAUGHT IN A CONDESCENSION LOOP.
USE YOUR BRAIN! LEARN TO THINK!
INTERESTING. YET WE TOO MUST USE OUR POWERS OF REASON TO ARRIVE AT A PROPER COURSE OF TREATMENT.
INDEED. IRONIC.
NO, YOU'RE THE RACIST!
I SUGGEST WE PUNCH HIS FACE.
WAAAY AHEAD OF YOU.
BORS + MOORE
THENIB.com

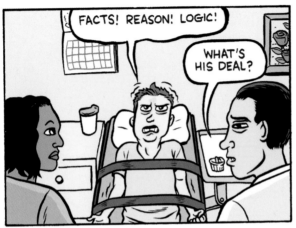

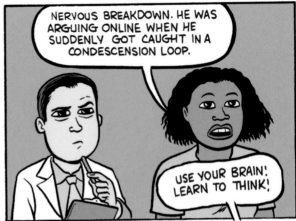

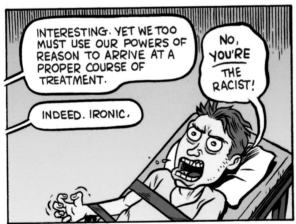

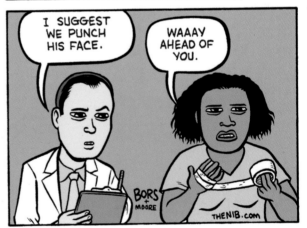

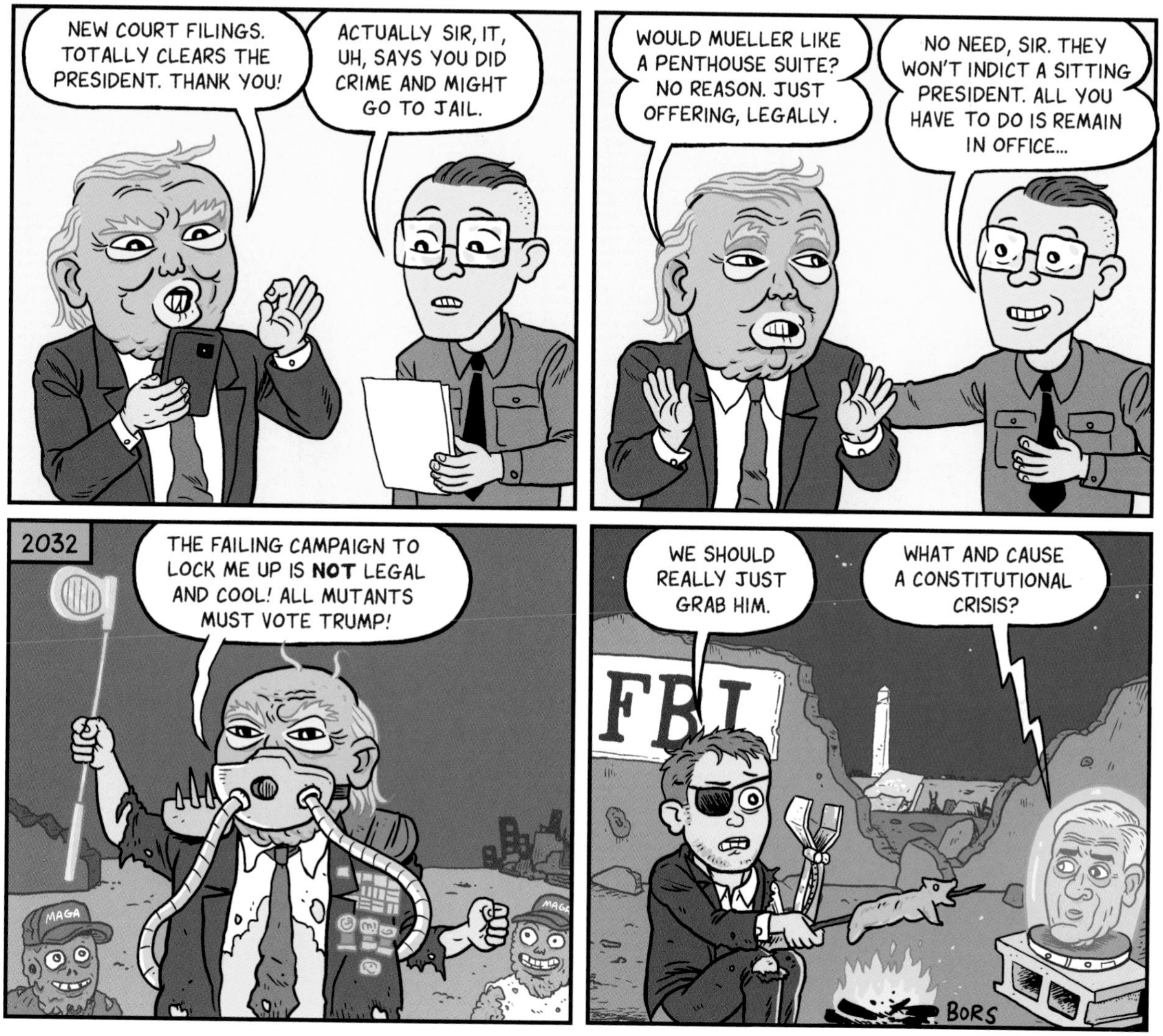
NEW COURT FILINGS. TOTALLY CLEARS THE PRESIDENT. THANK YOU!
ACTUALLY SIR, IT, UH, SAYS YOU DID CRIME AND MIGHT GO TO JAIL.
WOULD MUELLER LIKE A PENTHOUSE SUITE? NO REASON. JUST OFFERING, LEGALLY.
NO NEED, SIR. THEY WON'T INDICT A SITTING PRESIDENT. ALL YOU HAVE TO DO IS REMAIN IN OFFICE...
2032
THE FAILING CAMPAIGN TO LOCK ME UP IS **NOT** LEGAL AND COOL! ALL MUTANTS MUST VOTE TRUMP!
MAGA
MAGA
FBI
WE SHOULD REALLY JUST GRAB HIM.
WHAT AND CAUSE A CONSTITUTIONAL CRISIS?
BORS

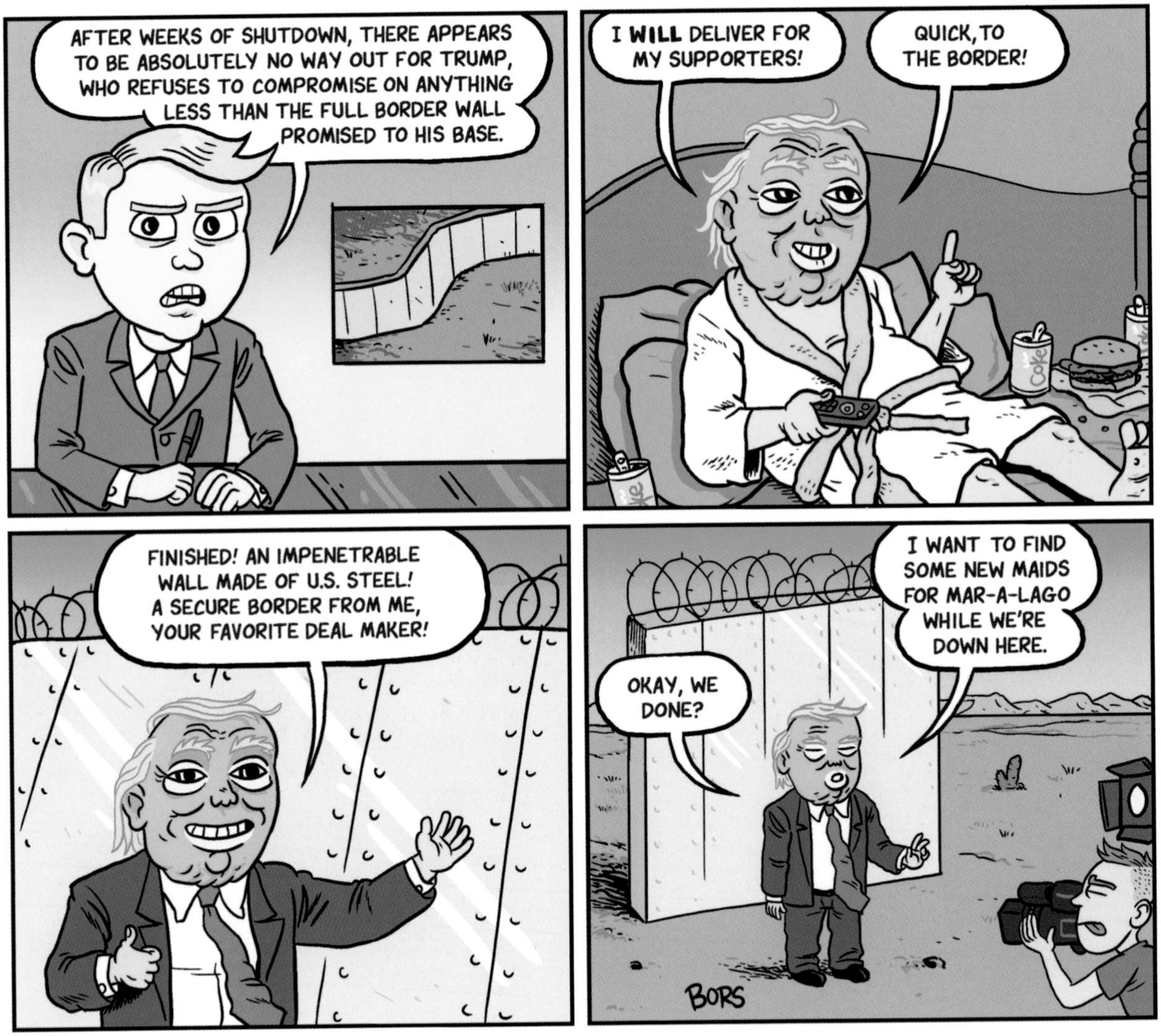
AFTER WEEKS OF SHUTDOWN, THERE APPEARS TO BE ABSOLUTELY NO WAY OUT FOR TRUMP, WHO REFUSES TO COMPROMISE ON ANYTHING LESS THAN THE FULL BORDER WALL PROMISED TO HIS BASE.
I **WILL** DELIVER FOR MY SUPPORTERS!
QUICK, TO THE BORDER!
Coke
FINISHED! AN IMPENETRABLE WALL MADE OF U.S. STEEL! A SECURE BORDER FROM ME, YOUR FAVORITE DEAL MAKER!
I WANT TO FIND SOME NEW MAIDS FOR MAR-A-LAGO WHILE WE'RE DOWN HERE.
OKAY, WE DONE?
BORS

Trump calls border wall a 'medieval solution' that works
Trump University
MAGA
Coke
TREPANNING. KEEPS MY BRAIN NORMAL AND LETS THE TREMENDOUS IDEAS IN!
BORS

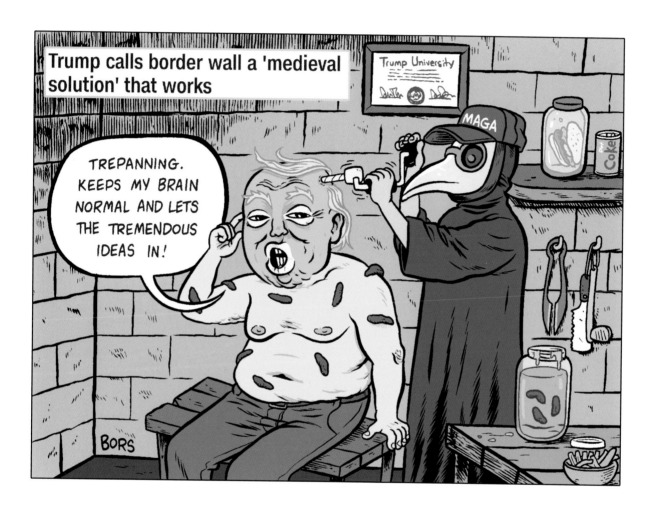

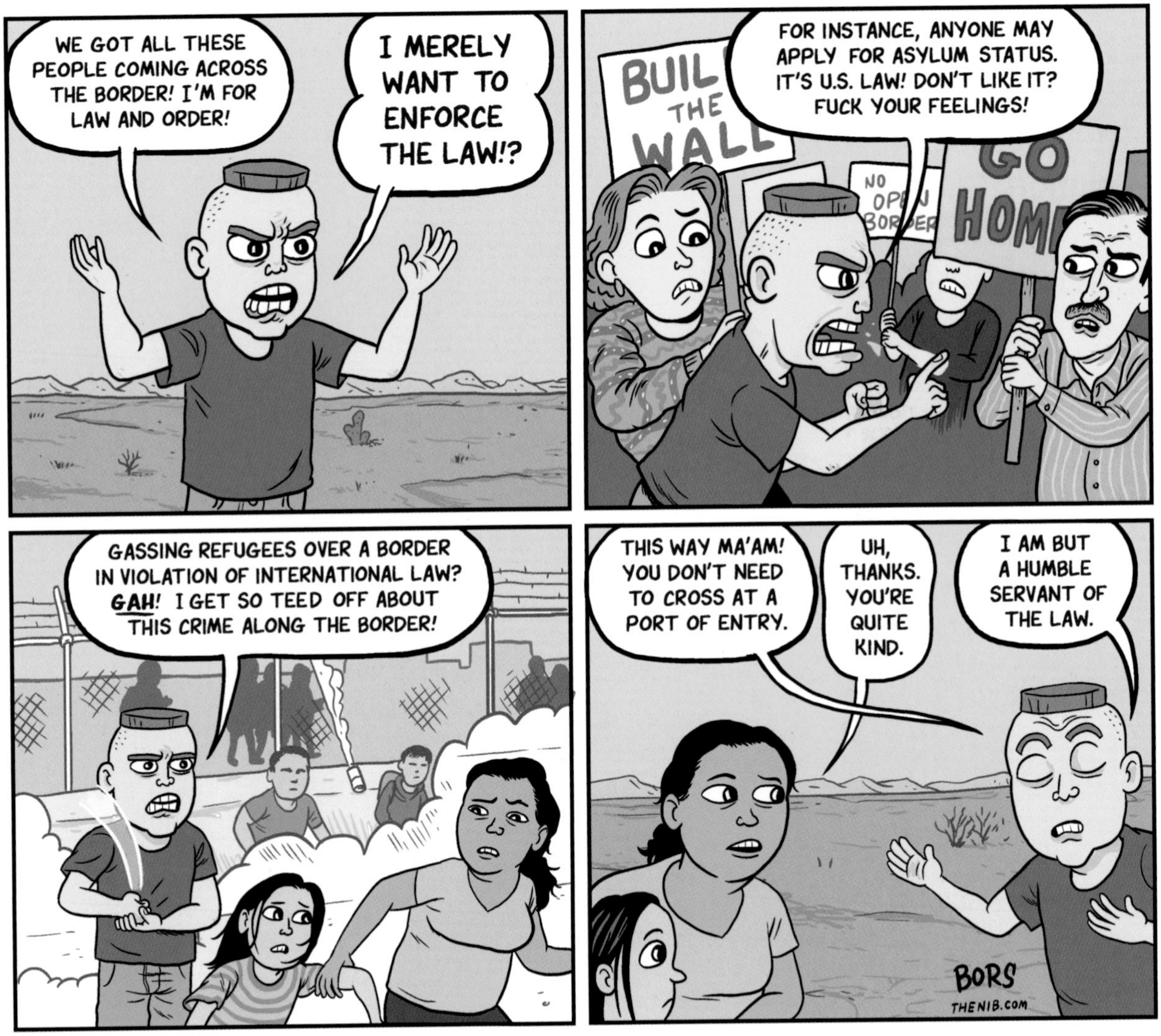
WE GOT ALL THESE PEOPLE COMING ACROSS THE BORDER! I'M FOR LAW AND ORDER!
I MERELY WANT TO ENFORCE THE LAW!?
BUIL THE WALL
FOR INSTANCE, ANYONE MAY APPLY FOR ASYLUM STATUS. IT'S U.S. LAW! DON'T LIKE IT? FUCK YOUR FEELINGS!
NO OPEN BORDER
GO HOM
GASSING REFUGEES OVER A BORDER IN VIOLATION OF INTERNATIONAL LAW? GAH! I GET SO TEED OFF ABOUT THIS CRIME ALONG THE BORDER!
THIS WAY MA'AM! YOU DON'T NEED TO CROSS AT A PORT OF ENTRY.
UH, THANKS. YOU'RE QUITE KIND.
I AM BUT A HUMBLE SERVANT OF THE LAW.
BORS
THENIB.COM

When Trump declared, "I am the law and order candidate" he meant more "Sundown town" than "Universal Declaration of Human Rights."

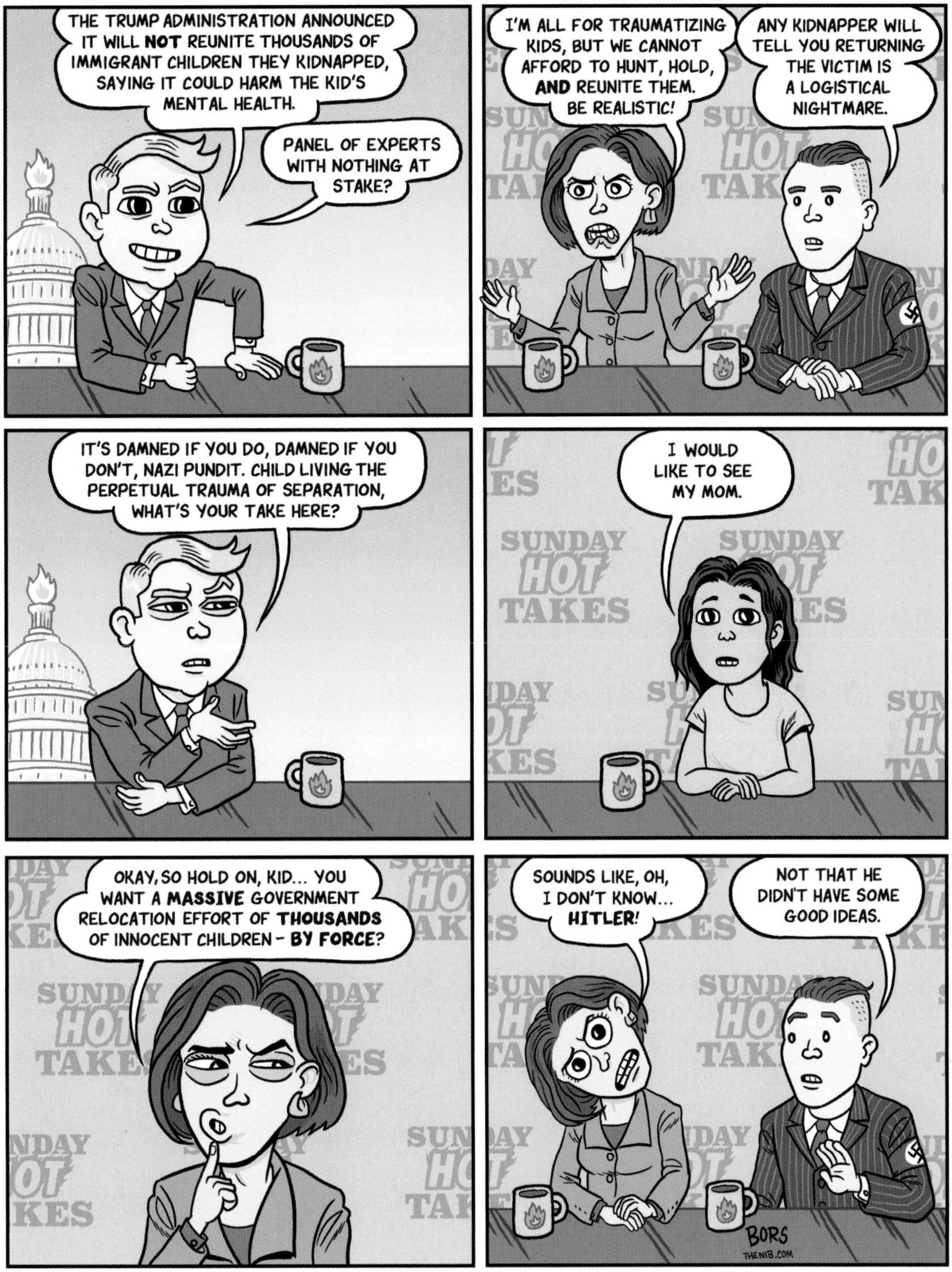
THE TRUMP ADMINISTRATION ANNOUNCED IT WILL NOT REUNITE THOUSANDS OF IMMIGRANT CHILDREN THEY KIDNAPPED, SAYING IT COULD HARM THE KID'S MENTAL HEALTH.
PANEL OF EXPERTS WITH NOTHING AT STAKE?
I'M ALL FOR TRAUMATIZING KIDS, BUT WE CANNOT AFFORD TO HUNT, HOLD, AND REUNITE THEM. BE REALISTIC!
ANY KIDNAPPER WILL TELL YOU RETURNING THE VICTIM IS A LOGISTICAL NIGHTMARE.
SUNDAY HOT TAKES
IT'S DAMNED IF YOU DO, DAMNED IF YOU DON'T, NAZI PUNDIT. CHILD LIVING THE PERPETUAL TRAUMA OF SEPARATION, WHAT'S YOUR TAKE HERE?
I WOULD LIKE TO SEE MY MOM.
OKAY, SO HOLD ON, KID... YOU WANT A MASSIVE GOVERNMENT RELOCATION EFFORT OF THOUSANDS OF INNOCENT CHILDREN - BY FORCE?
SOUNDS LIKE, OH, I DON'T KNOW... HITLER!
NOT THAT HE DIDN'T HAVE SOME GOOD IDEAS.
BORS
THENIB.COM

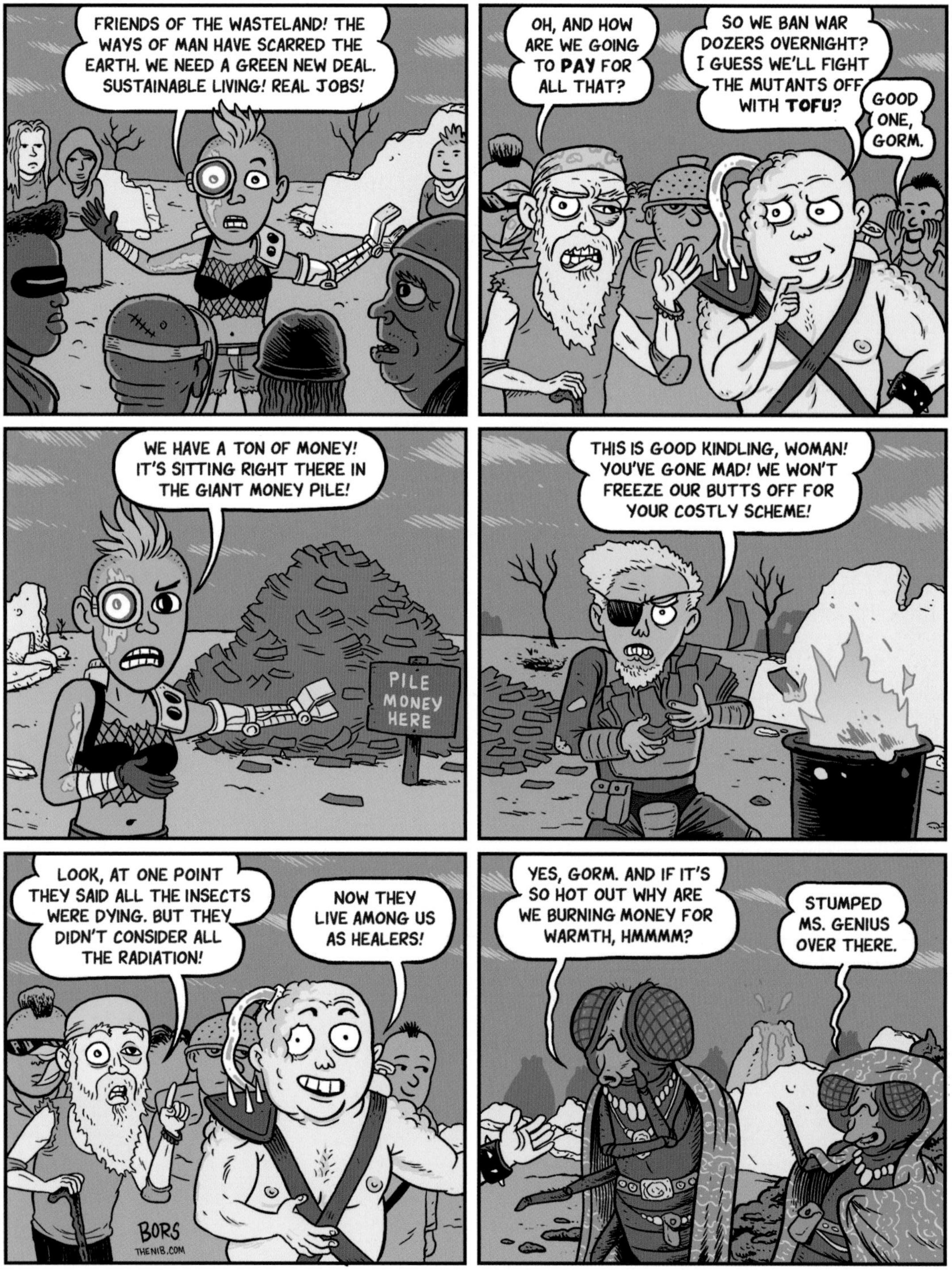
FRIENDS OF THE WASTELAND! THE WAYS OF MAN HAVE SCARRED THE EARTH. WE NEED A GREEN NEW DEAL. SUSTAINABLE LIVING! REAL JOBS!
OH, AND HOW ARE WE GOING TO PAY FOR ALL THAT?
SO WE BAN WAR DOZERS OVERNIGHT? I GUESS WE'LL FIGHT THE MUTANTS OFF WITH TOFU?
GOOD ONE, GORM.
WE HAVE A TON OF MONEY! IT'S SITTING RIGHT THERE IN THE GIANT MONEY PILE!
PILE MONEY HERE
THIS IS GOOD KINDLING, WOMAN! YOU'VE GONE MAD! WE WON'T FREEZE OUR BUTTS OFF FOR YOUR COSTLY SCHEME!
LOOK, AT ONE POINT THEY SAID ALL THE INSECTS WERE DYING. BUT THEY DIDN'T CONSIDER ALL THE RADIATION!
NOW THEY LIVE AMONG US AS HEALERS!
BORS
THENIB.COM
YES, GORM. AND IF IT'S SO HOT OUT WHY ARE WE BURNING MONEY FOR WARMTH, HMMMM?
STUMPED MS. GENIUS OVER THERE.

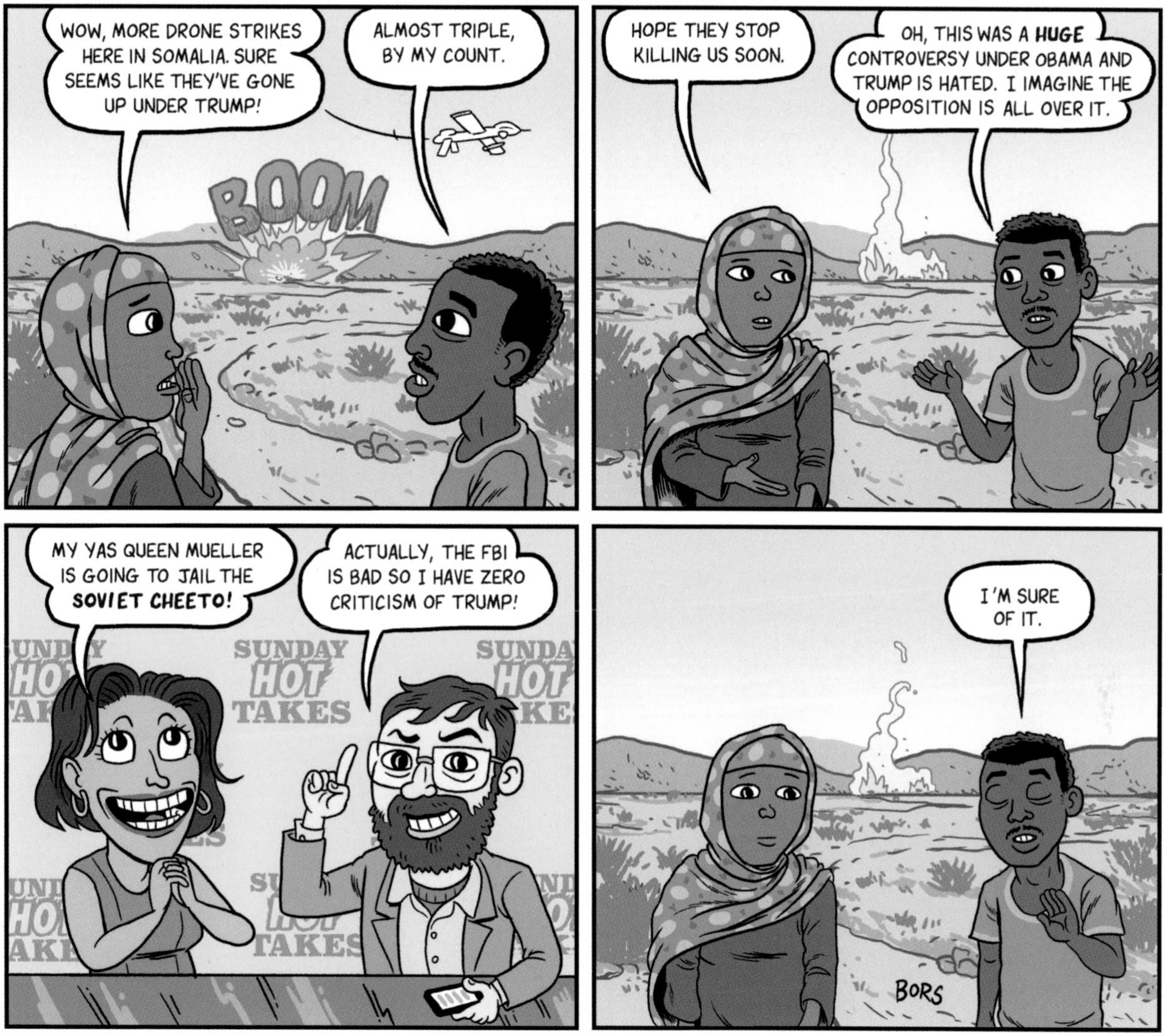
WOW, MORE DRONE STRIKES HERE IN SOMALIA. SURE SEEMS LIKE THEY'VE GONE UP UNDER TRUMP!
ALMOST TRIPLE, BY MY COUNT.
BOOM
HOPE THEY STOP KILLING US SOON.
OH, THIS WAS A **HUGE** CONTROVERSY UNDER OBAMA AND TRUMP IS HATED. I IMAGINE THE OPPOSITION IS ALL OVER IT.
MY YAS QUEEN MUELLER IS GOING TO JAIL THE **SOVIET CHEETO!**
ACTUALLY, THE FBI IS BAD SO I HAVE ZERO CRITICISM OF TRUMP!
SUNDAY HOT TAKES
I'M SURE OF IT.
BORS

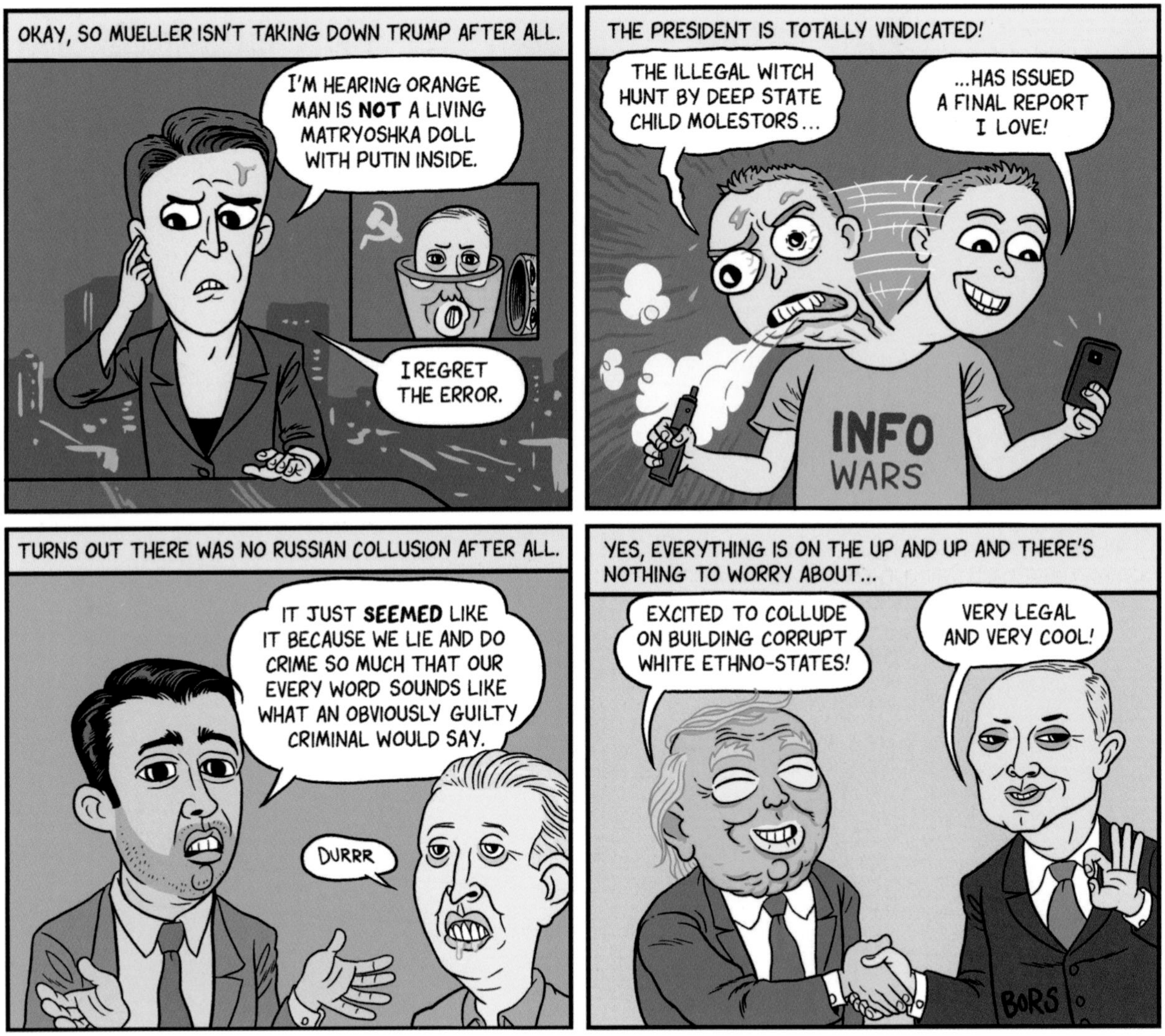
OKAY, SO MUELLER ISN'T TAKING DOWN TRUMP AFTER ALL.
I'M HEARING ORANGE MAN IS **NOT** A LIVING MATRYOSHKA DOLL WITH PUTIN INSIDE.
I REGRET THE ERROR.
THE PRESIDENT IS TOTALLY VINDICATED!
THE ILLEGAL WITCH HUNT BY DEEP STATE CHILD MOLESTORS...
...HAS ISSUED A FINAL REPORT I LOVE!
INFO WARS
TURNS OUT THERE WAS NO RUSSIAN COLLUSION AFTER ALL.
IT JUST **SEEMED** LIKE IT BECAUSE WE LIE AND DO CRIME SO MUCH THAT OUR EVERY WORD SOUNDS LIKE WHAT AN OBVIOUSLY GUILTY CRIMINAL WOULD SAY.
DURRR
YES, EVERYTHING IS ON THE UP AND UP AND THERE'S NOTHING TO WORRY ABOUT...
EXCITED TO COLLUDE ON BUILDING CORRUPT WHITE ETHNO-STATES!
VERY LEGAL AND VERY COOL!
BORS

Yet another in my popular series "everybody commenting on this news event is starting to annoy me."

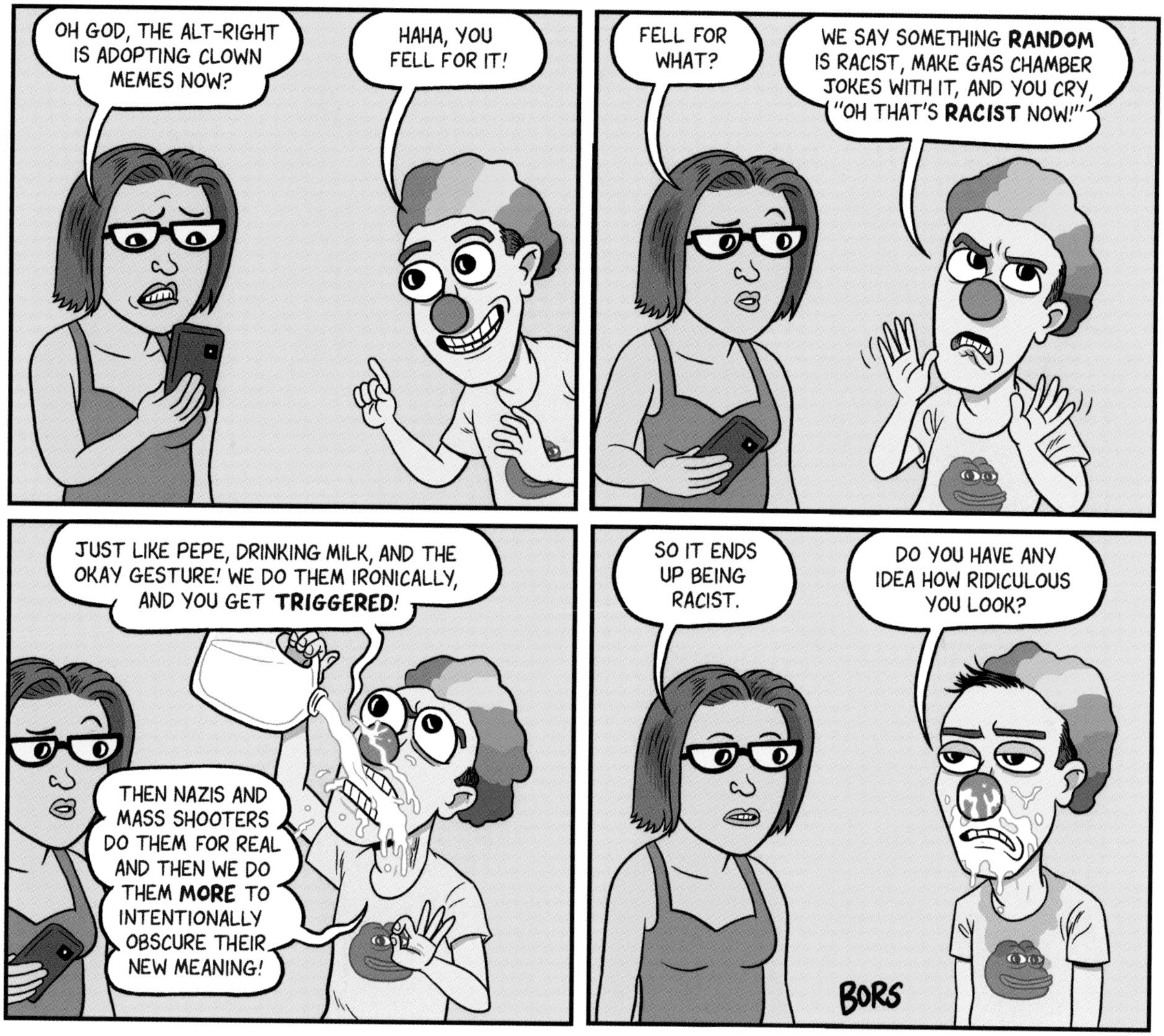
OH GOD, THE ALT-RIGHT IS ADOPTING CLOWN MEMES NOW?
HAHA, YOU FELL FOR IT!
FELL FOR WHAT?
WE SAY SOMETHING **RANDOM** IS RACIST, MAKE GAS CHAMBER JOKES WITH IT, AND YOU CRY, "OH THAT'S **RACIST** NOW!"
JUST LIKE PEPE, DRINKING MILK, AND THE OKAY GESTURE! WE DO THEM IRONICALLY, AND YOU GET **TRIGGERED**!
THEN NAZIS AND MASS SHOOTERS DO THEM FOR REAL AND THEN WE DO THEM **MORE** TO INTENTIONALLY OBSCURE THEIR NEW MEANING!
SO IT ENDS UP BEING RACIST.
DO YOU HAVE ANY IDEA HOW RIDICULOUS YOU LOOK?
BORS

Writer Jared Holt at Right Wing Watch noted in 2019 that a clown Pepe the Frog, known as "Honkler," was the next meme the right was trying to make happen. Indeed, directly after it was published a bunch of accounts attempted to troll me in the exact manner depicted in the comic, thus defeating me with logic and proving they aren't racist!

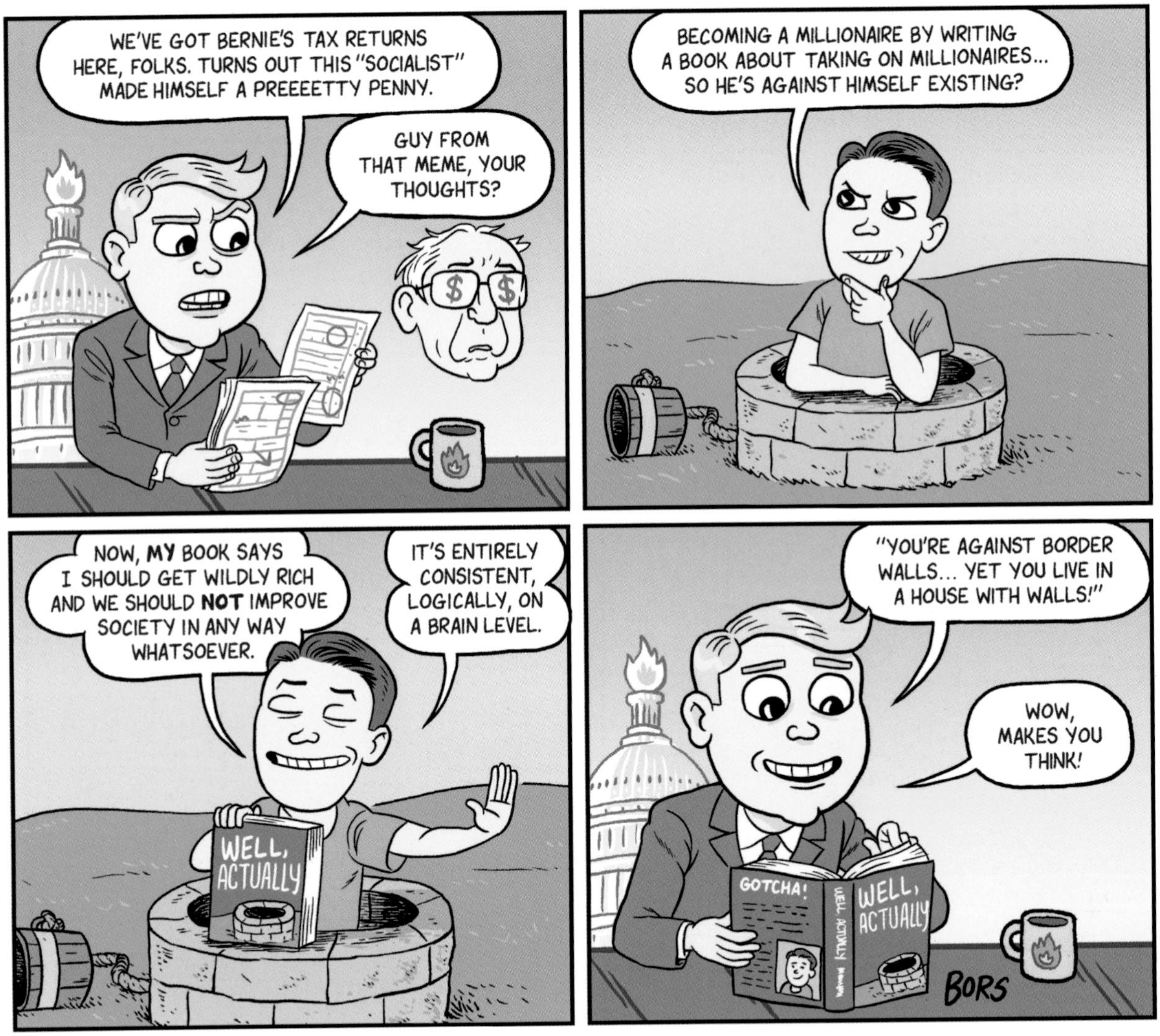

WE'VE GOT BERNIE'S TAX RETURNS HERE, FOLKS. TURNS OUT THIS "SOCIALIST" MADE HIMSELF A PREEEETTY PENNY.
GUY FROM THAT MEME, YOUR THOUGHTS?
BECOMING A MILLIONAIRE BY WRITING A BOOK ABOUT TAKING ON MILLIONAIRES... SO HE'S AGAINST HIMSELF EXISTING?
NOW, **MY** BOOK SAYS I SHOULD GET WILDLY RICH AND WE SHOULD **NOT** IMPROVE SOCIETY IN ANY WAY WHATSOEVER.
IT'S ENTIRELY CONSISTENT, LOGICALLY, ON A BRAIN LEVEL.
WELL, ACTUALLY
"YOU'RE AGAINST BORDER WALLS... YET YOU LIVE IN A HOUSE WITH WALLS!"
WOW, MAKES YOU THINK!
GOTCHA!
WELL, ACTUALLY
BORS

We're getting into a Mr. Gotcha Cinematic Universe now with a canonical timeline and as-yet-unexplained origin in the well.

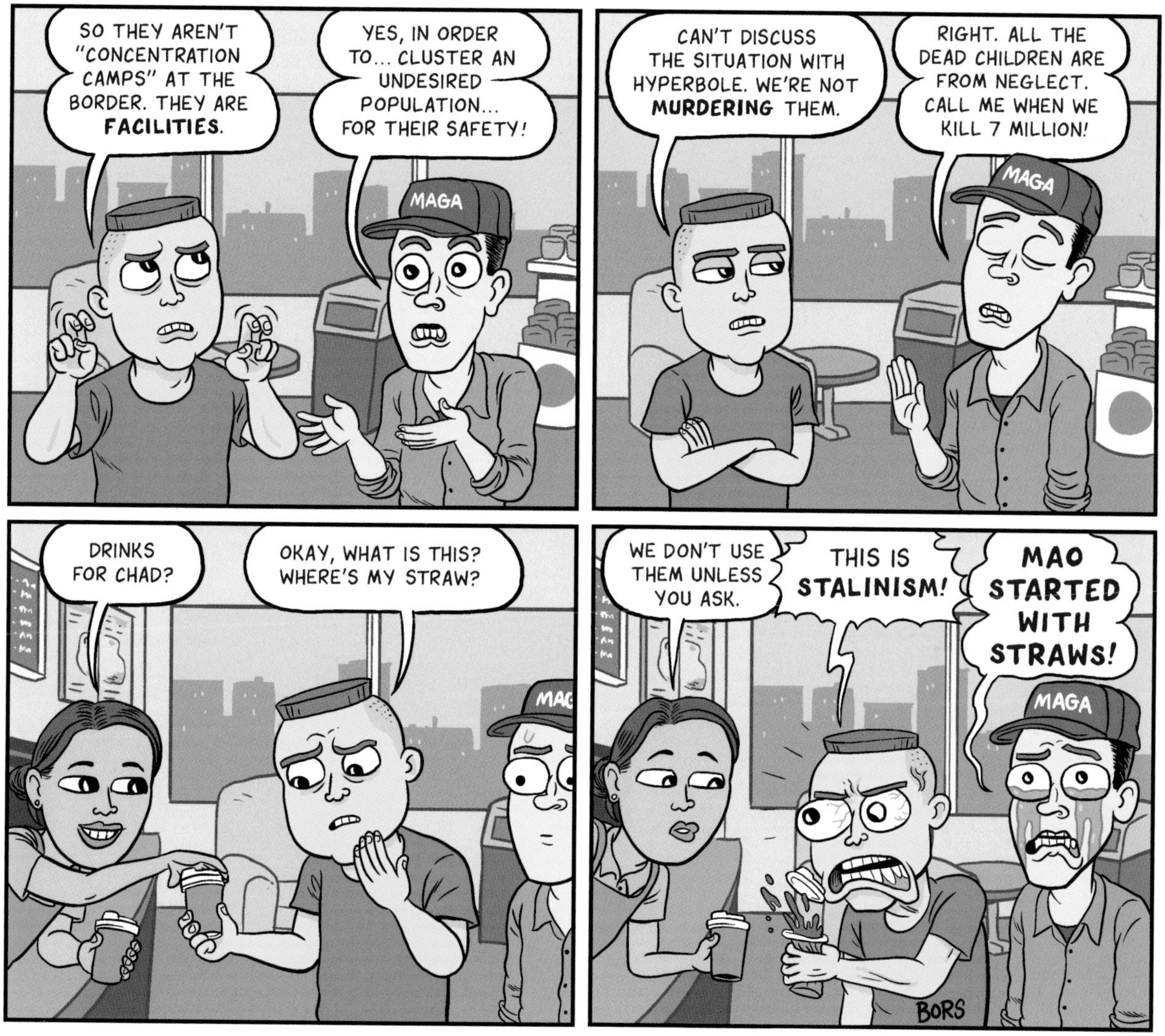

SO THEY AREN'T "CONCENTRATION CAMPS" AT THE BORDER. THEY ARE **FACILITIES**.
YES, IN ORDER TO... CLUSTER AN UNDESIRED POPULATION... FOR THEIR SAFETY!
MAGA
CAN'T DISCUSS THE SITUATION WITH HYPERBOLE. WE'RE NOT **MURDERING** THEM.
RIGHT. ALL THE DEAD CHILDREN ARE FROM NEGLECT. CALL ME WHEN WE KILL 7 MILLION!
MAGA
DRINKS FOR CHAD?
OKAY, WHAT IS THIS? WHERE'S MY STRAW?
WE DON'T USE THEM UNLESS YOU ASK.
THIS IS **STALINISM!**
MAO STARTED WITH STRAWS!
MAGA
BORS

There's a special place in hell for the person who named the places where we house migrant children ripped from their parents as "tender age shelters."

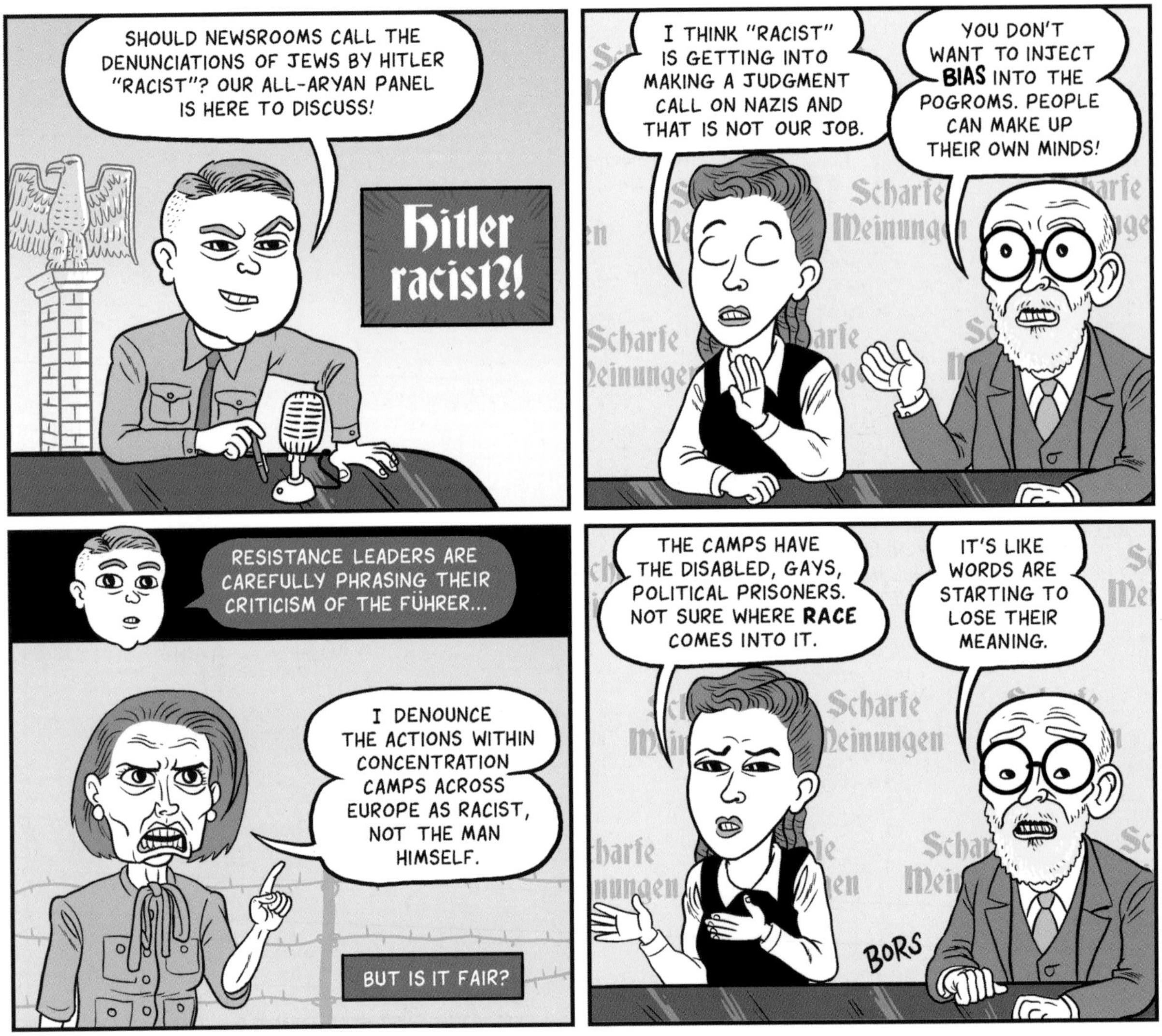
SHOULD NEWSROOMS CALL THE DENUNCIATIONS OF JEWS BY HITLER "RACIST"? OUR ALL-ARYAN PANEL IS HERE TO DISCUSS!
Hitler racist?!
I THINK "RACIST" IS GETTING INTO MAKING A JUDGMENT CALL ON NAZIS AND THAT IS NOT OUR JOB.
YOU DON'T WANT TO INJECT **BIAS** INTO THE POGROMS. PEOPLE CAN MAKE UP THEIR OWN MINDS!
Scharfe Meinungen
RESISTANCE LEADERS ARE CAREFULLY PHRASING THEIR CRITICISM OF THE FÜHRER...
I DENOUNCE THE ACTIONS WITHIN CONCENTRATION CAMPS ACROSS EUROPE AS RACIST, NOT THE MAN HIMSELF.
BUT IS IT FAIR?
THE CAMPS HAVE THE DISABLED, GAYS, POLITICAL PRISONERS. NOT SURE WHERE **RACE** COMES INTO IT.
IT'S LIKE WORDS ARE STARTING TO LOSE THEIR MEANING.
BORS

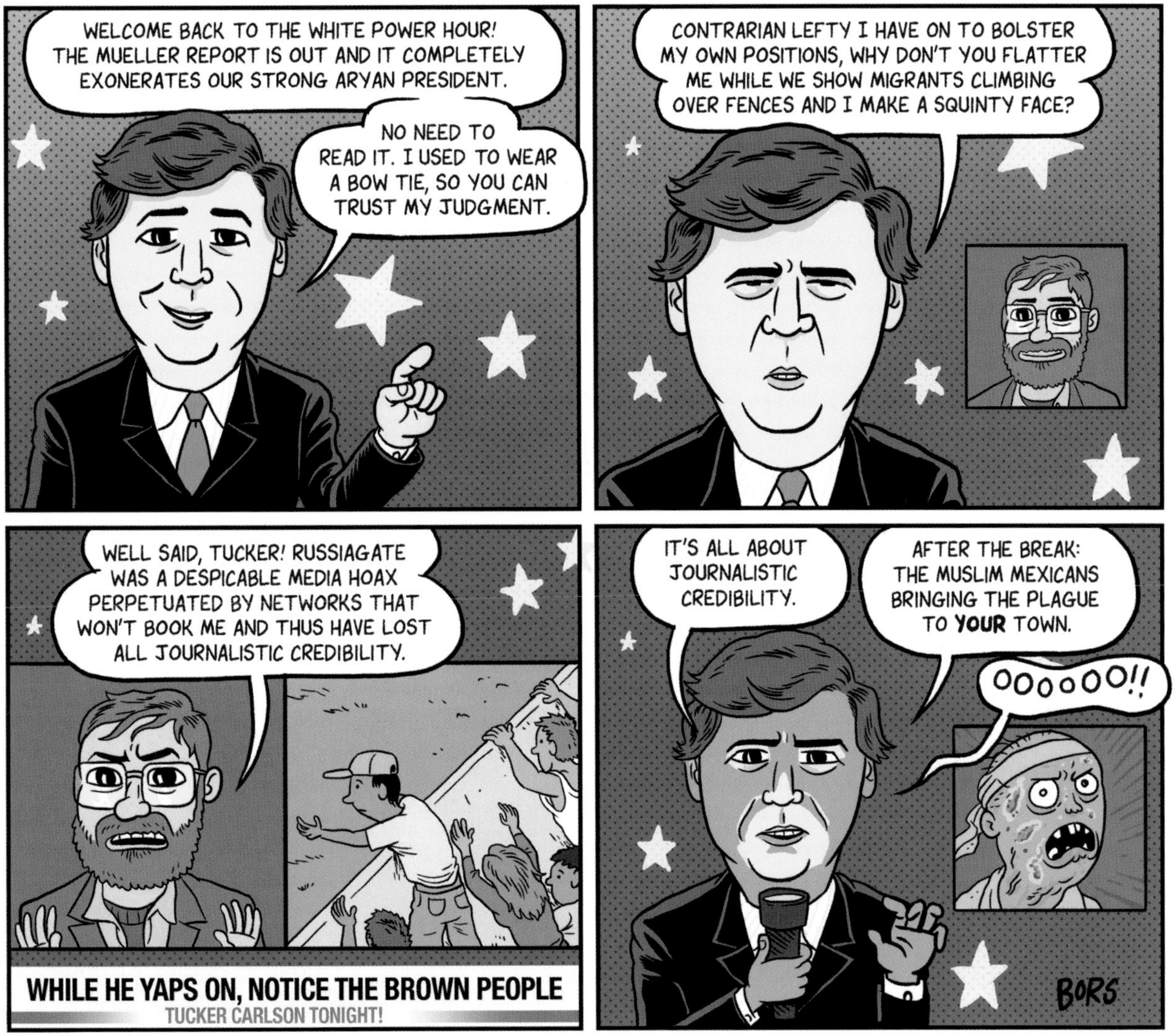
WELCOME BACK TO THE WHITE POWER HOUR! THE MUELLER REPORT IS OUT AND IT COMPLETELY EXONERATES OUR STRONG ARYAN PRESIDENT.
NO NEED TO READ IT. I USED TO WEAR A BOW TIE, SO YOU CAN TRUST MY JUDGMENT.
CONTRARIAN LEFTY I HAVE ON TO BOLSTER MY OWN POSITIONS, WHY DON'T YOU FLATTER ME WHILE WE SHOW MIGRANTS CLIMBING OVER FENCES AND I MAKE A SQUINTY FACE?
WELL SAID, TUCKER! RUSSIAGATE WAS A DESPICABLE MEDIA HOAX PERPETUATED BY NETWORKS THAT WON'T BOOK ME AND THUS HAVE LOST ALL JOURNALISTIC CREDIBILITY.
WHILE HE YAPS ON, NOTICE THE BROWN PEOPLE
TUCKER CARLSON TONIGHT!
IT'S ALL ABOUT JOURNALISTIC CREDIBILITY.
AFTER THE BREAK: THE MUSLIM MEXICANS BRINGING THE PLAGUE TO YOUR TOWN.
OOOOOO!!
BORS

In the Trump era, Fox News host Tucker Carlson has become the most eager to launder white nationalist talking points to his viewers, something that's earned him praise from neo-Nazi website Daily Stormer. The pundit depicted here is some bedraggled media loser called up when Tucker's boots need a tongue cleaning.

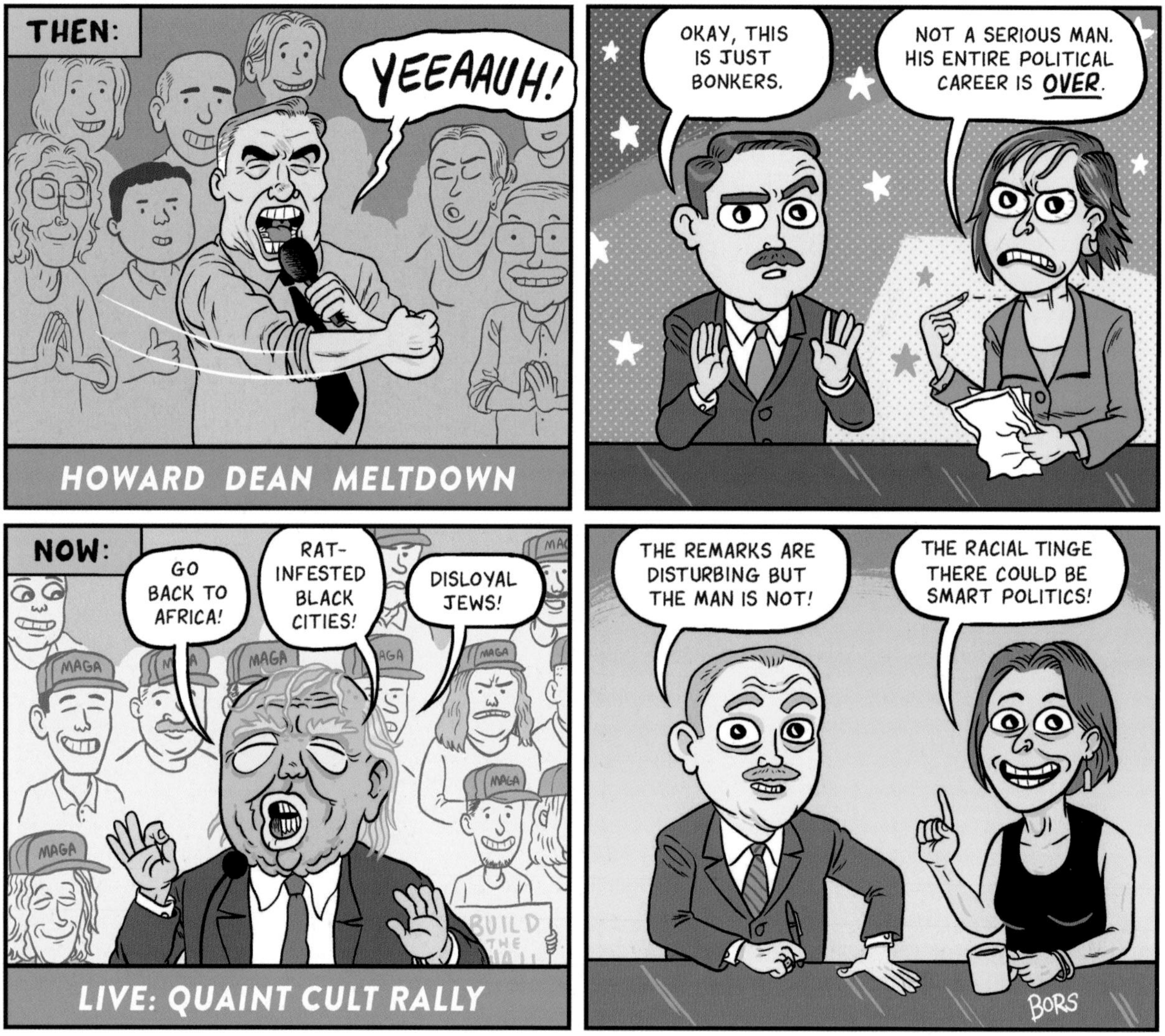
THEN:
YEEAAUH!
HOWARD DEAN MELTDOWN
OKAY, THIS IS JUST BONKERS.
NOT A SERIOUS MAN. HIS ENTIRE POLITICAL CAREER IS OVER.
NOW:
GO BACK TO AFRICA!
RAT-INFESTED BLACK CITIES!
DISLOYAL JEWS!
MAGA
LIVE: QUAINT CULT RALLY
THE REMARKS ARE DISTURBING BUT THE MAN IS NOT!
THE RACIAL TINGE THERE COULD BE SMART POLITICS!
BORS

One unfortunate result of being a political cartoonist is having nearly instant recall of every inane political scandal of the last 15 years. The infamous Howard Dean Scream of 2004 has a 4,200 word entry on his Wikipedia page, about 2,000 more than the section on Trump being accused of assault and rape by 22 women.

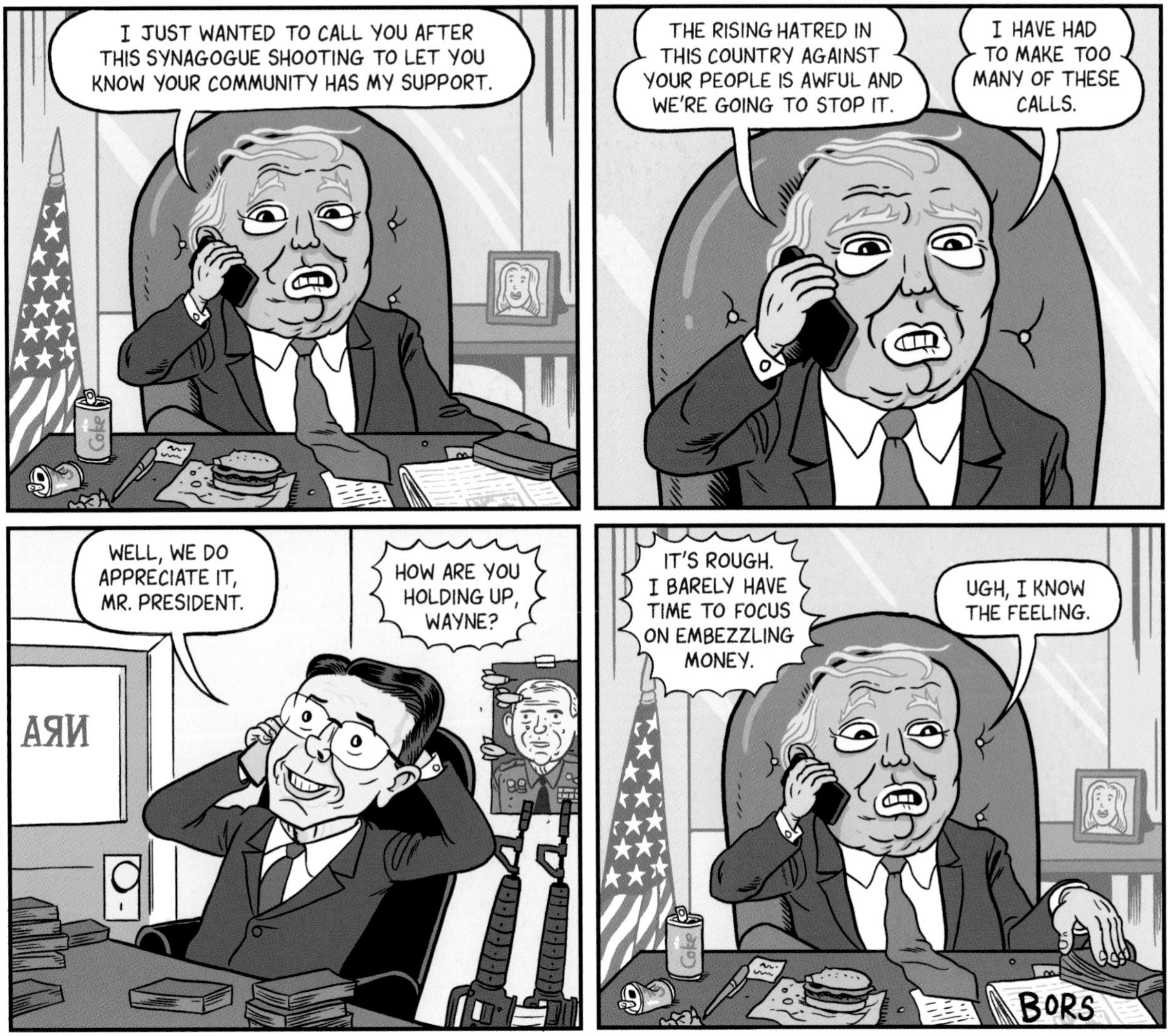
I JUST WANTED TO CALL YOU AFTER THIS SYNAGOGUE SHOOTING TO LET YOU KNOW YOUR COMMUNITY HAS MY SUPPORT.
THE RISING HATRED IN THIS COUNTRY AGAINST YOUR PEOPLE IS AWFUL AND WE'RE GOING TO STOP IT.
I HAVE HAD TO MAKE TOO MANY OF THESE CALLS.
WELL, WE DO APPRECIATE IT, MR. PRESIDENT.
HOW ARE YOU HOLDING UP, WAYNE?
NRA
IT'S ROUGH. I BARELY HAVE TIME TO FOCUS ON EMBEZZLING MONEY.
UGH, I KNOW THE FEELING.
BORS

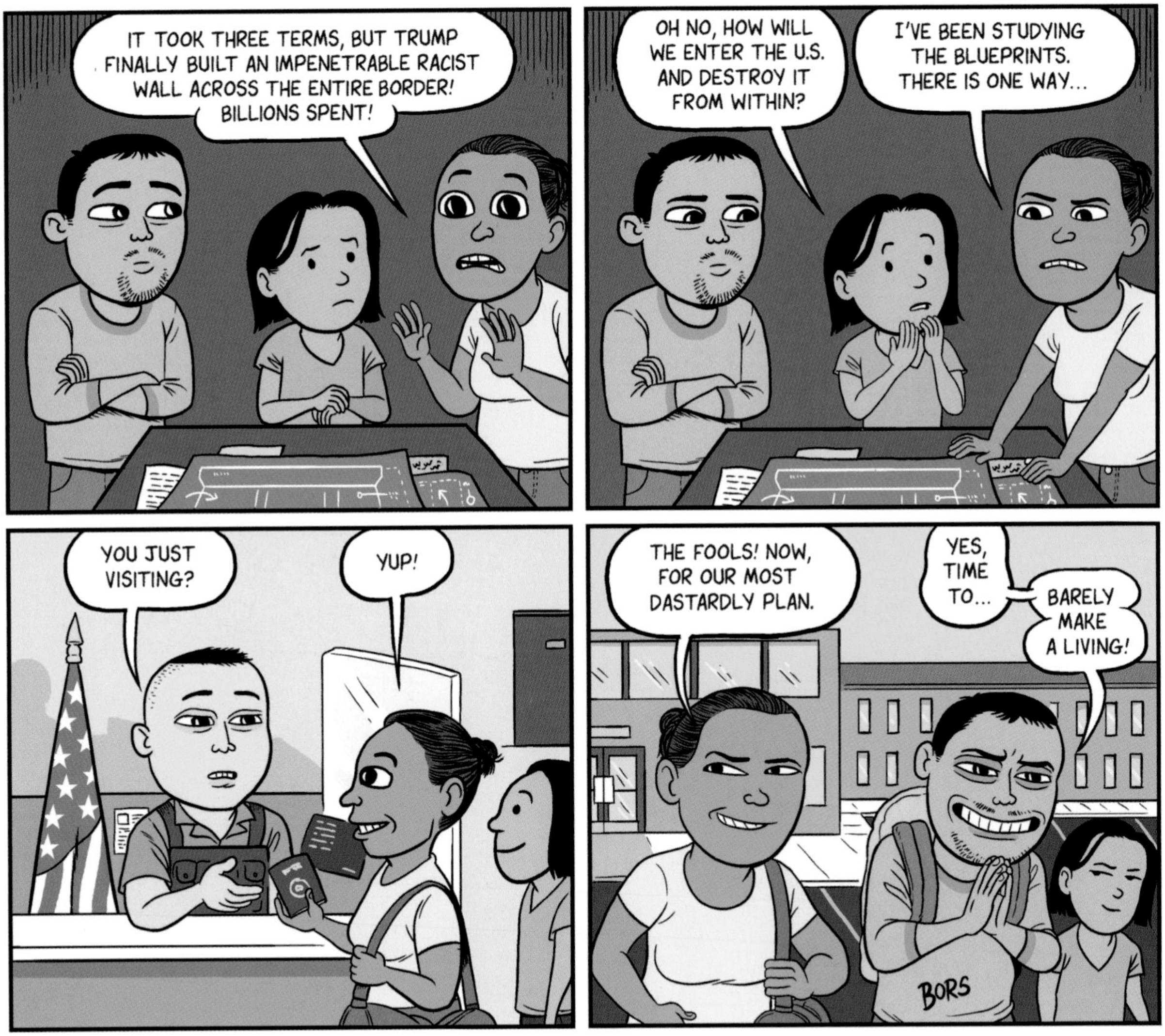
IT TOOK THREE TERMS, BUT TRUMP FINALLY BUILT AN IMPENETRABLE RACIST WALL ACROSS THE ENTIRE BORDER! BILLIONS SPENT!
OH NO, HOW WILL WE ENTER THE U.S. AND DESTROY IT FROM WITHIN?
I'VE BEEN STUDYING THE BLUEPRINTS. THERE IS ONE WAY...
YOU JUST VISITING?
YUP!
THE FOOLS! NOW, FOR OUR MOST DASTARDLY PLAN.
YES, TIME TO...
BARELY MAKE A LIVING!
BORS

Most people who reside here illegally simply come across our border through a port of entry, such as a thing called a road or an airport, along with thousands of other people who traverse between our borders daily. The wall would not even be very effective from the standpoint of being wildly racist.

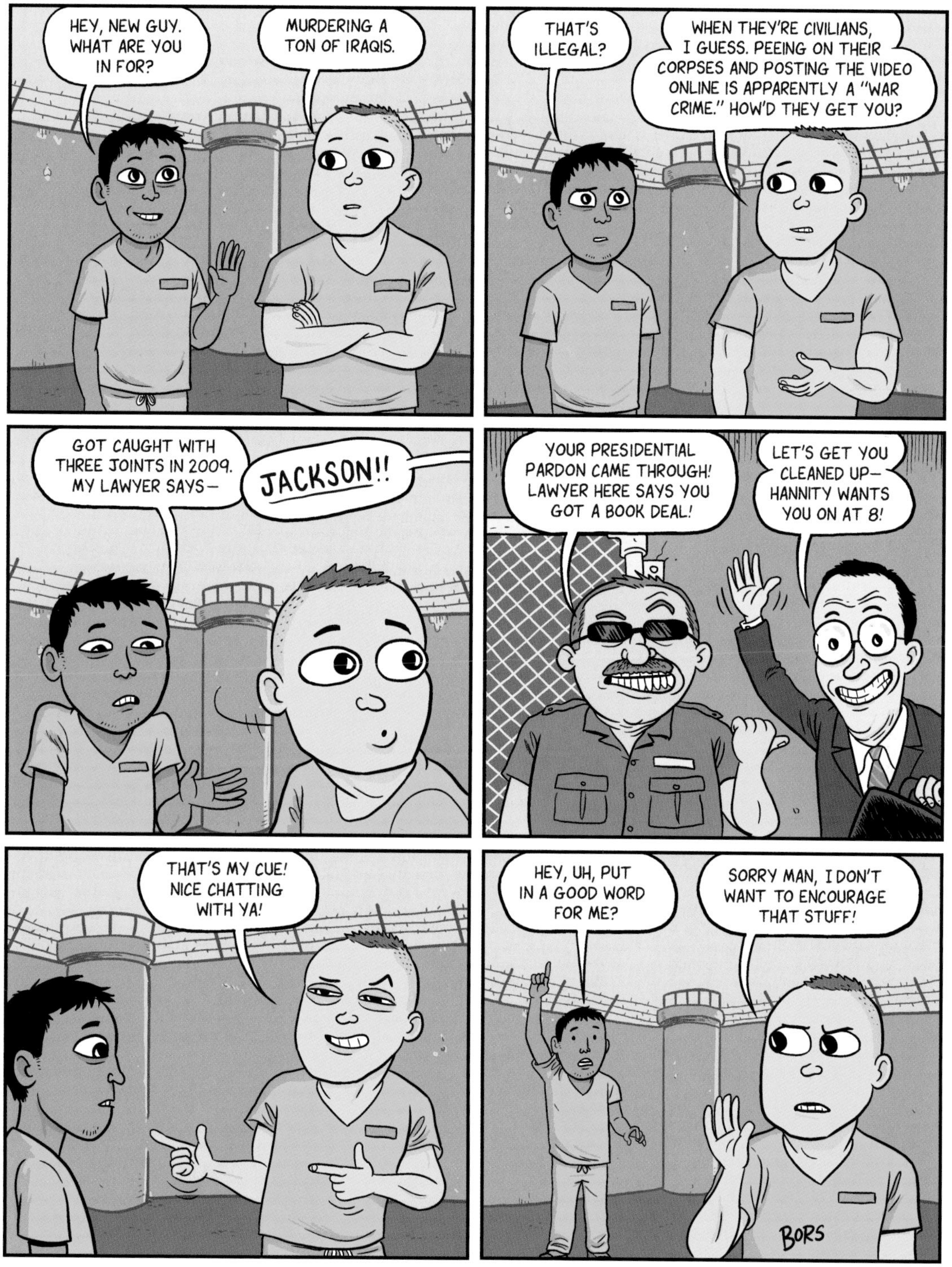
HEY, NEW GUY. WHAT ARE YOU IN FOR?
MURDERING A TON OF IRAQIS.
THAT'S ILLEGAL?
WHEN THEY'RE CIVILIANS, I GUESS. PEEING ON THEIR CORPSES AND POSTING THE VIDEO ONLINE IS APPARENTLY A "WAR CRIME." HOW'D THEY GET YOU?
GOT CAUGHT WITH THREE JOINTS IN 2009. MY LAWYER SAYS—
JACKSON!!
YOUR PRESIDENTIAL PARDON CAME THROUGH! LAWYER HERE SAYS YOU GOT A BOOK DEAL!
LET'S GET YOU CLEANED UP— HANNITY WANTS YOU ON AT 8!
THAT'S MY CUE! NICE CHATTING WITH YA!
HEY, UH, PUT IN A GOOD WORD FOR ME?
SORRY MAN, I DON'T WANT TO ENCOURAGE THAT STUFF!
BORS

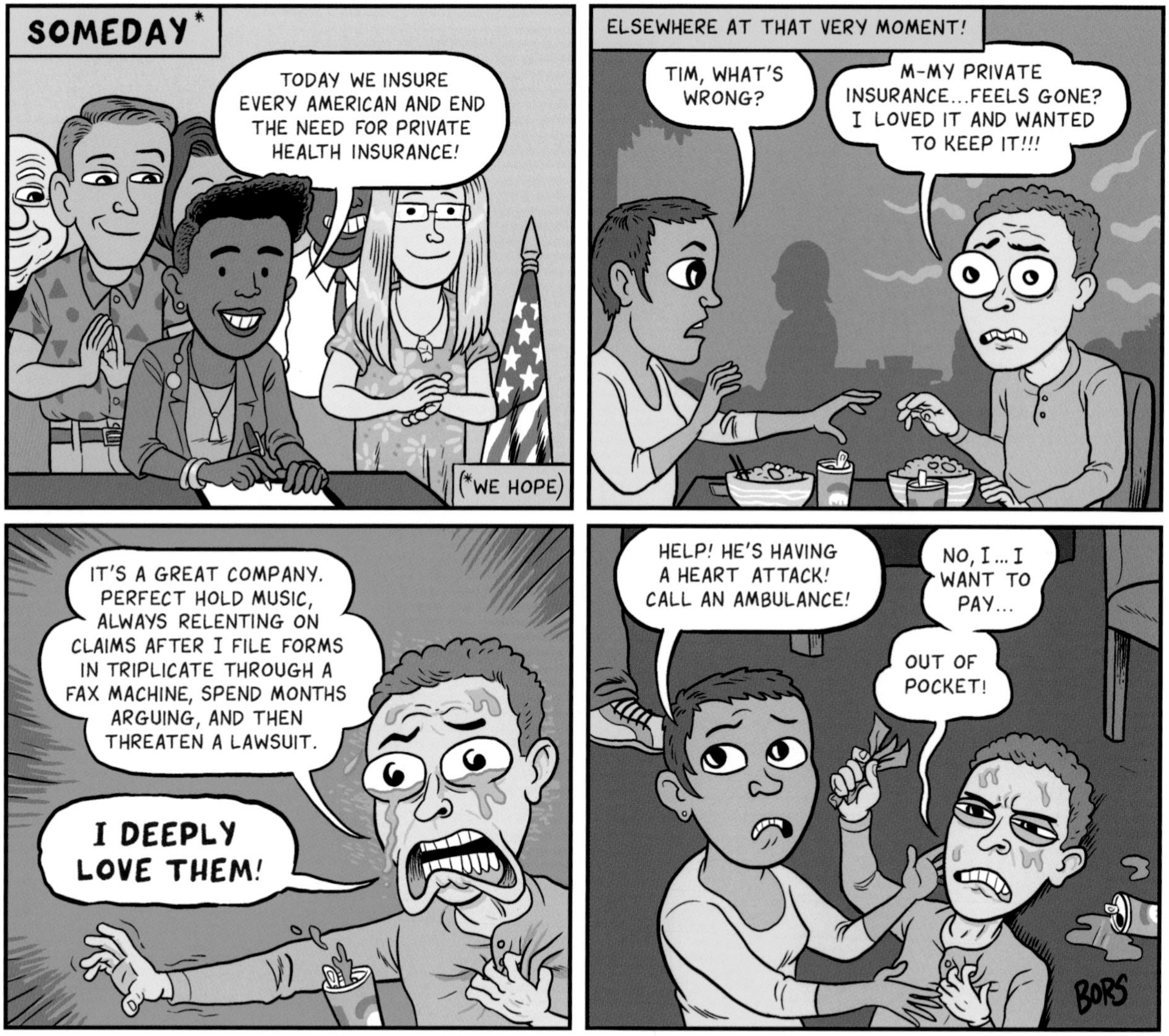
SOMEDAY*
TODAY WE INSURE EVERY AMERICAN AND END THE NEED FOR PRIVATE HEALTH INSURANCE!
(*WE HOPE)
ELSEWHERE AT THAT VERY MOMENT!
TIM, WHAT'S WRONG?
M-MY PRIVATE INSURANCE...FEELS GONE? I LOVED IT AND WANTED TO KEEP IT!!!
IT'S A GREAT COMPANY. PERFECT HOLD MUSIC, ALWAYS RELENTING ON CLAIMS AFTER I FILE FORMS IN TRIPLICATE THROUGH A FAX MACHINE, SPEND MONTHS ARGUING, AND THEN THREATEN A LAWSUIT.
I DEEPLY LOVE THEM!
HELP! HE'S HAVING A HEART ATTACK! CALL AN AMBULANCE!
NO, I... I WANT TO PAY...
OUT OF POCKET!
BORS

The mythological man who loved his health insurance and wanted to keep it. I've certainly liked "having" insurance before, but can't say there's ever been any love for the companies who have denied my claims. Having been laid off three times in my life, I've found no matter how much you like it your employer can actually decide that you aren't getting it anymore. Good thing there's no solution to this problem other countries have adopted.

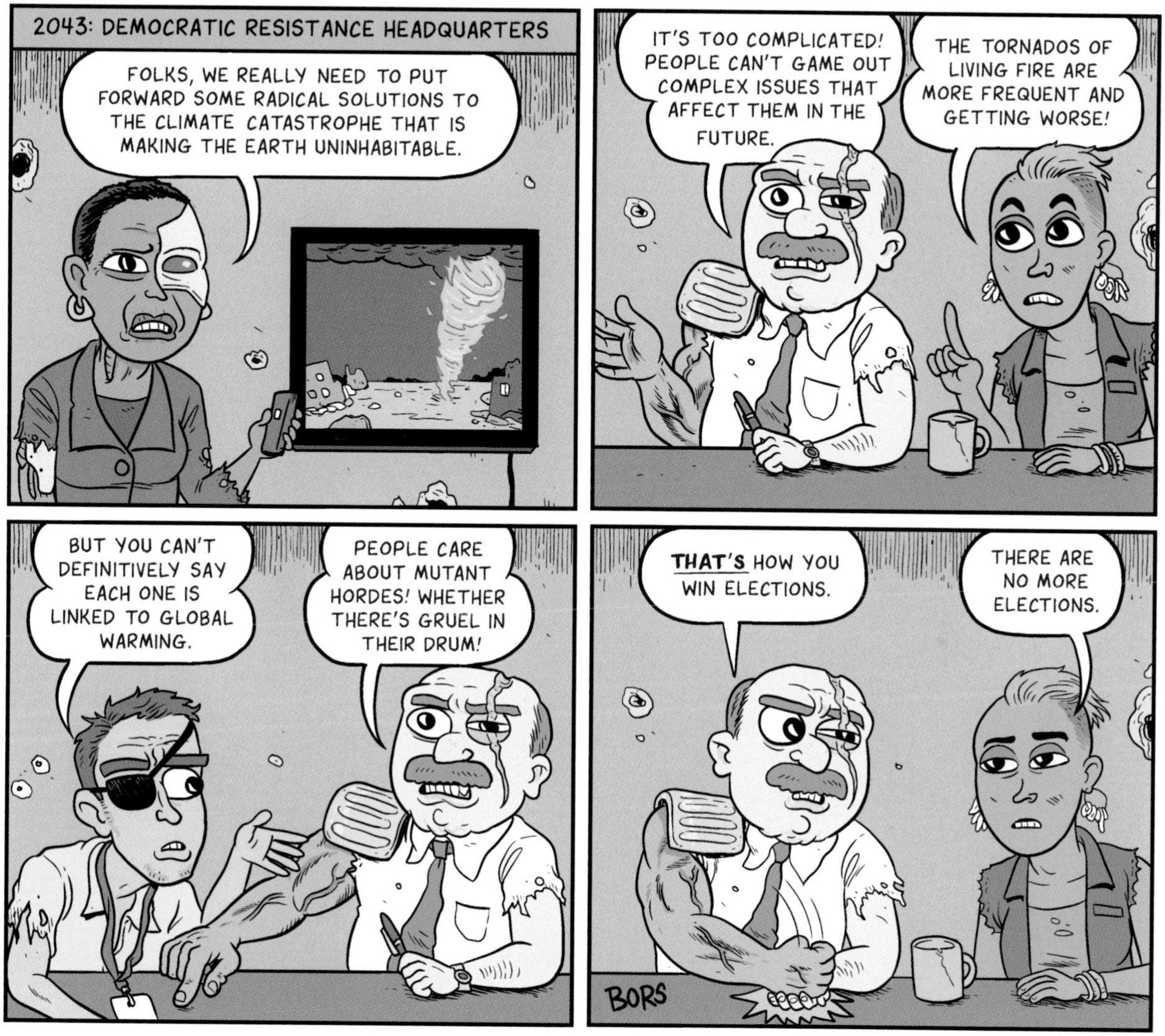
2043: DEMOCRATIC RESISTANCE HEADQUARTERS
FOLKS, WE REALLY NEED TO PUT FORWARD SOME RADICAL SOLUTIONS TO THE CLIMATE CATASTROPHE THAT IS MAKING THE EARTH UNINHABITABLE.
IT'S TOO COMPLICATED! PEOPLE CAN'T GAME OUT COMPLEX ISSUES THAT AFFECT THEM IN THE FUTURE.
THE TORNADOS OF LIVING FIRE ARE MORE FREQUENT AND GETTING WORSE!
BUT YOU CAN'T DEFINITIVELY SAY EACH ONE IS LINKED TO GLOBAL WARMING.
PEOPLE CARE ABOUT MUTANT HORDES! WHETHER THERE'S GRUEL IN THEIR DRUM!
THAT'S HOW YOU WIN ELECTIONS.
THERE ARE NO MORE ELECTIONS.
BORS

Eventually it became easier for me than not to process news events and commentary through The Wasteland. We all cope in different ways.

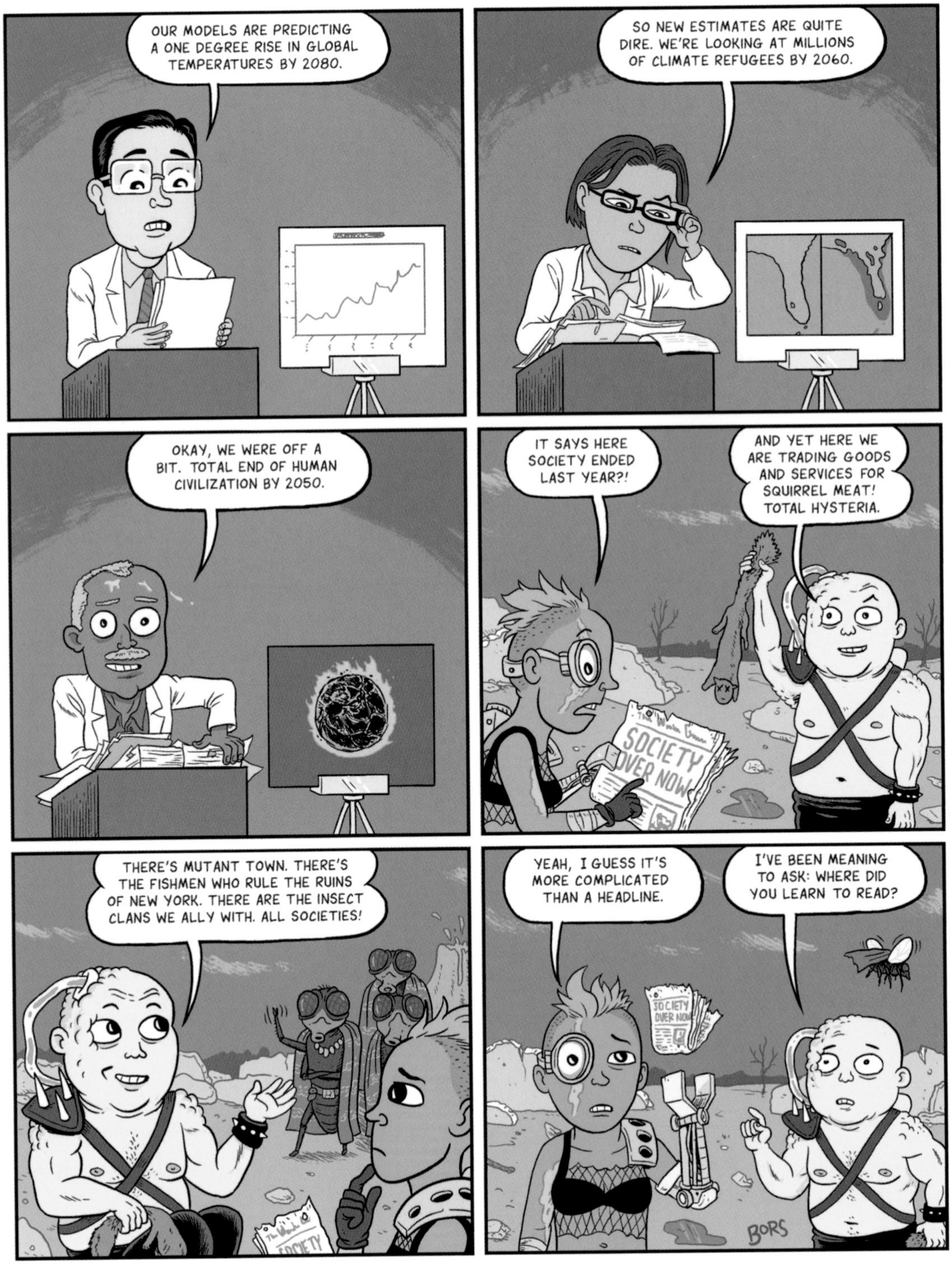
OUR MODELS ARE PREDICTING A ONE DEGREE RISE IN GLOBAL TEMPERATURES BY 2080.
SO NEW ESTIMATES ARE QUITE DIRE. WE'RE LOOKING AT MILLIONS OF CLIMATE REFUGEES BY 2060.
OKAY, WE WERE OFF A BIT. TOTAL END OF HUMAN CIVILIZATION BY 2050.
IT SAYS HERE SOCIETY ENDED LAST YEAR?!
SOCIETY OVER NOW
AND YET HERE WE ARE TRADING GOODS AND SERVICES FOR SQUIRREL MEAT! TOTAL HYSTERIA.
THERE'S MUTANT TOWN. THERE'S THE FISHMEN WHO RULE THE RUINS OF NEW YORK. THERE ARE THE INSECT CLANS WE ALLY WITH. ALL SOCIETIES!
YEAH, I GUESS IT'S MORE COMPLICATED THAN A HEADLINE.
SOCIETY OVER NOW
I'VE BEEN MEANING TO ASK: WHERE DID YOU LEARN TO READ?
BORS

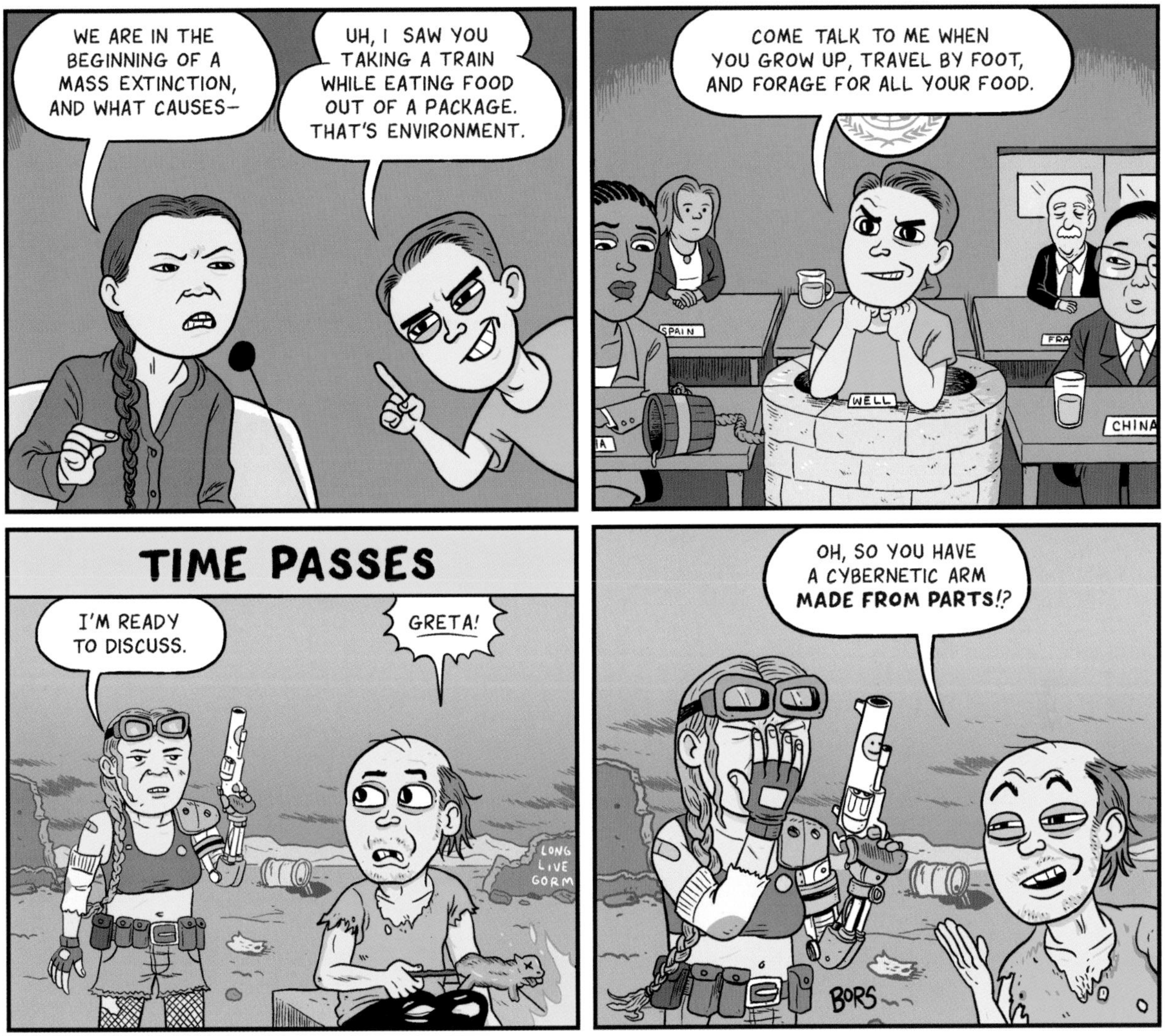
WE ARE IN THE BEGINNING OF A MASS EXTINCTION, AND WHAT CAUSES—
UH, I SAW YOU TAKING A TRAIN WHILE EATING FOOD OUT OF A PACKAGE. THAT'S ENVIRONMENT.
COME TALK TO ME WHEN YOU GROW UP, TRAVEL BY FOOT, AND FORAGE FOR ALL YOUR FOOD.
SPAIN
WELL
CHINA
TIME PASSES
I'M READY TO DISCUSS.
GRETA!
LONG LIVE GORM
OH, SO YOU HAVE A CYBERNETIC ARM **MADE FROM PARTS!?**
BORS

A then-16-year-old Greta Thunberg was spotted eating food from a package on board a train, thus disproving her argument that the planet is warming at an alarming rate.

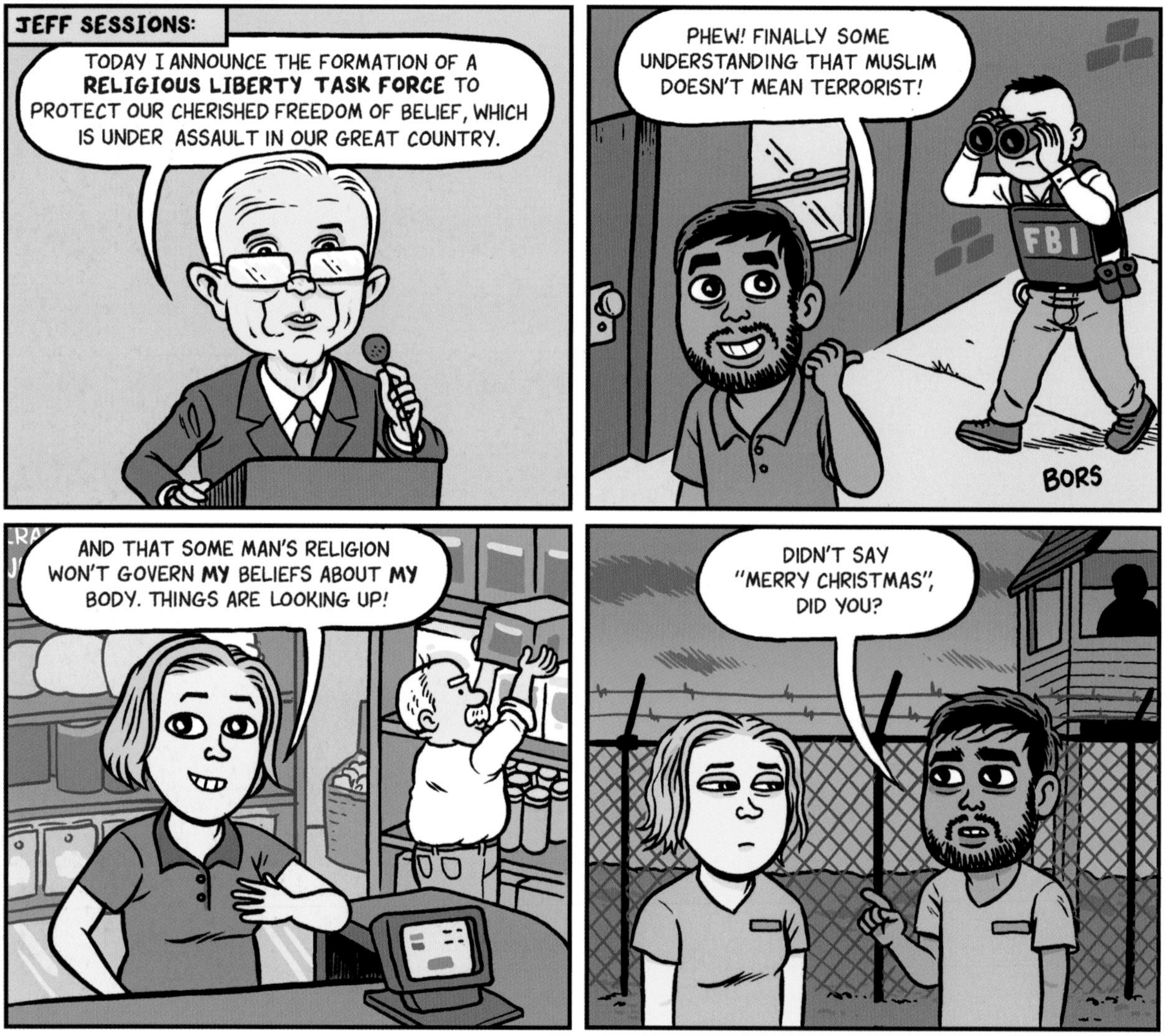
JEFF SESSIONS:
TODAY I ANNOUNCE THE FORMATION OF A **RELIGIOUS LIBERTY TASK FORCE** TO PROTECT OUR CHERISHED FREEDOM OF BELIEF, WHICH IS UNDER ASSAULT IN OUR GREAT COUNTRY.
PHEW! FINALLY SOME UNDERSTANDING THAT MUSLIM DOESN'T MEAN TERRORIST!
FBI
BORS
AND THAT SOME MAN'S RELIGION WON'T GOVERN **MY** BELIEFS ABOUT **MY** BODY. THINGS ARE LOOKING UP!
DIDN'T SAY "MERRY CHRISTMAS", DID YOU?

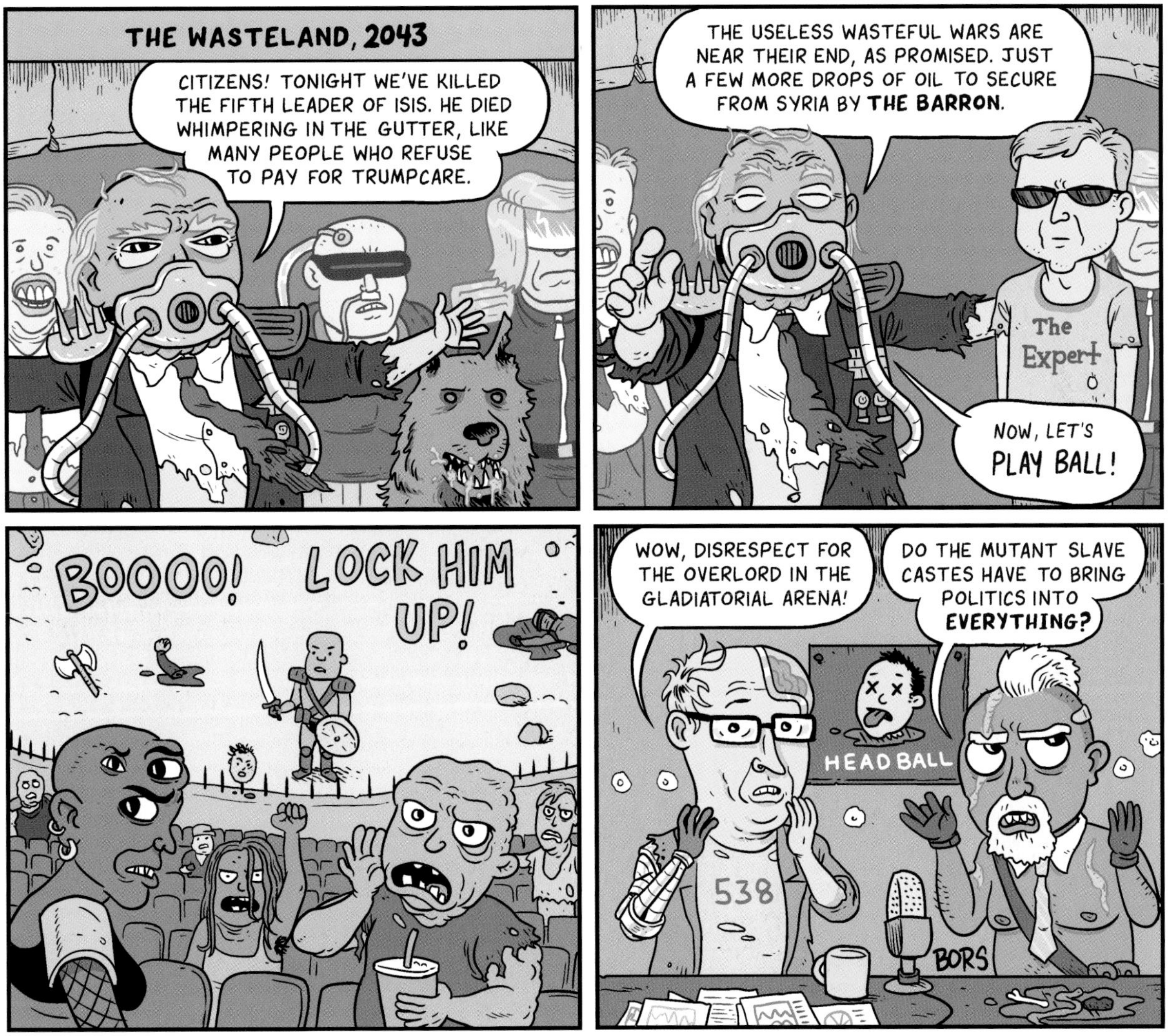

THE WASTELAND, 2043
CITIZENS! TONIGHT WE'VE KILLED THE FIFTH LEADER OF ISIS. HE DIED WHIMPERING IN THE GUTTER, LIKE MANY PEOPLE WHO REFUSE TO PAY FOR TRUMPCARE.
THE USELESS WASTEFUL WARS ARE NEAR THEIR END, AS PROMISED. JUST A FEW MORE DROPS OF OIL TO SECURE FROM SYRIA BY THE BARRON.
The Expert
NOW, LET'S PLAY BALL!
BOOOO!
LOCK HIM UP!
WOW, DISRESPECT FOR THE OVERLORD IN THE GLADIATORIAL ARENA!
DO THE MUTANT SLAVE CASTES HAVE TO BRING POLITICS INTO EVERYTHING?
HEAD BALL
538
BORS

The belligerent racist and (alleged) rapist president looting the country for personal gain while caging children was booed in a baseball stadium, prompting discussion of how respect for the office has eroded enough to cause concern.

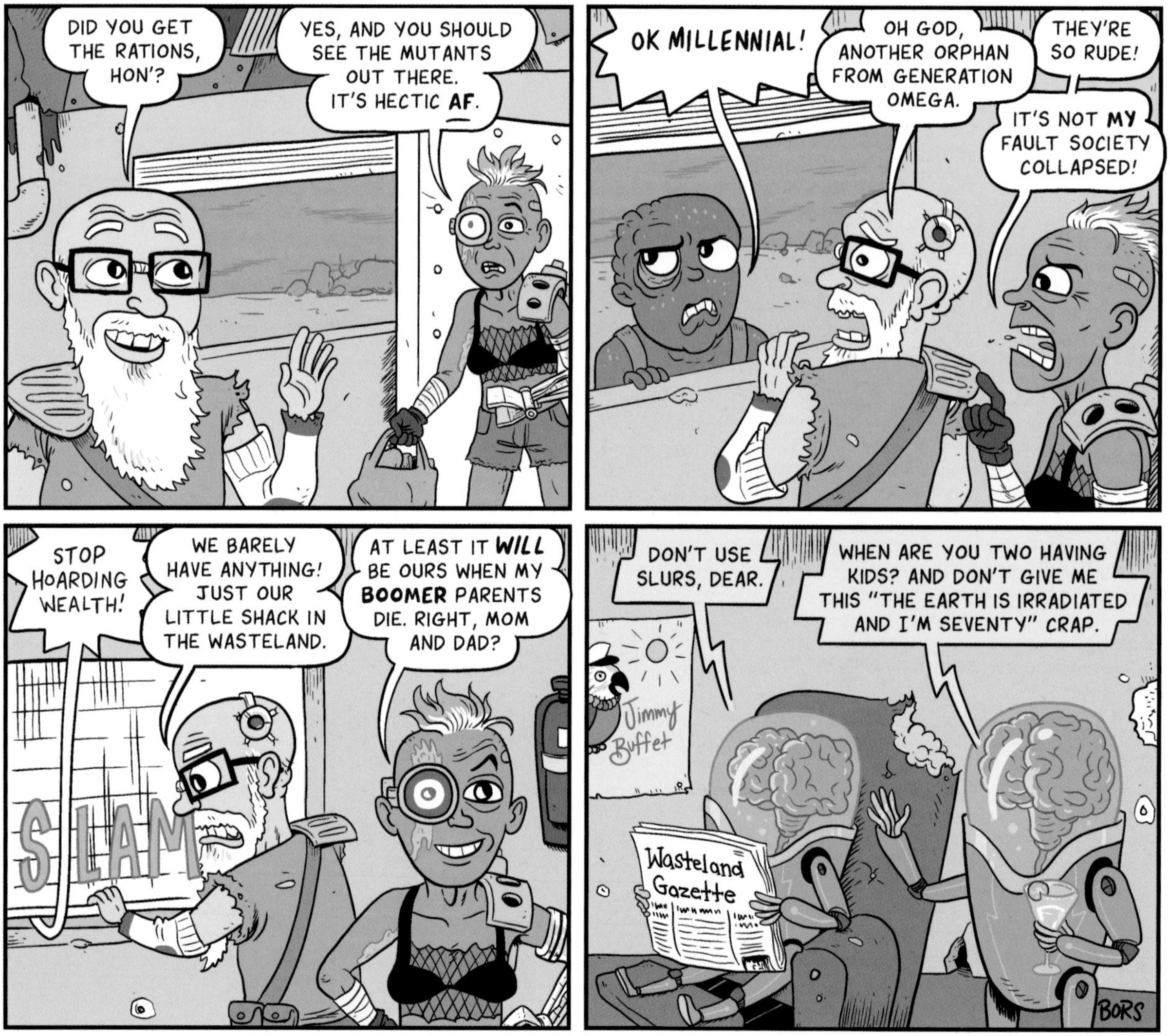
DID YOU GET THE RATIONS, HON'?
YES, AND YOU SHOULD SEE THE MUTANTS OUT THERE. IT'S HECTIC AF.
OK MILLENNIAL!
OH GOD, ANOTHER ORPHAN FROM GENERATION OMEGA.
THEY'RE SO RUDE!
IT'S NOT MY FAULT SOCIETY COLLAPSED!
STOP HOARDING WEALTH!
WE BARELY HAVE ANYTHING! JUST OUR LITTLE SHACK IN THE WASTELAND.
AT LEAST IT WILL BE OURS WHEN MY BOOMER PARENTS DIE. RIGHT, MOM AND DAD?
SLAM
DON'T USE SLURS, DEAR.
WHEN ARE YOU TWO HAVING KIDS? AND DON'T GIVE ME THIS "THE EARTH IS IRRADIATED AND I'M SEVENTY" CRAP.
Jimmy Buffet
Wasteland Gazette
BORS

WHO KILLED JEFFREY EPSTEIN?

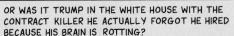

NO FUCKING CLUE

MAYBE IT WAS THE CLINTONS ON THE PRIVATE ISLAND WITH THE SPIRIT COOKING DAGGER?

WE WERE CHILLIN' IN CEDAR RAPIDS AT THE TIME.

CHECK THE FLIGHT LOGS!

OR WAS IT TRUMP IN THE WHITE HOUSE WITH THE CONTRACT KILLER HE ACTUALLY FORGOT HE HIRED BECAUSE HIS BRAIN IS ROTTING?

CLINTON BODY COUNT! CLINTON CRIME FAMILY!

DO I GOTTA SUE YOU FOR THIS PAYMENT?

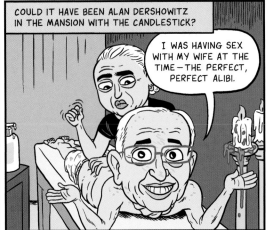

COULD IT HAVE BEEN ALAN DERSHOWITZ IN THE MANSION WITH THE CANDLESTICK?

I WAS HAVING SEX WITH MY WIFE AT THE TIME—THE PERFECT, PERFECT ALIBI.

MAYBE IT WAS THE GOVERNMENT HEADS, PRINCES, CELEBRITIES, AND GLOBAL FINANCIERS ON THE LOLITA EXPRESS WITH THE BLACK BOOK?

WELL, WE'RE ALL BREATHING A LOT EASIER THESE DAYS.

OR WAS IT THE OVERWORKED GUARDS IN THE UNDERSTAFFED PRISON WITH THE BRUTAL SYSTEM THAT KILLS COUNTLESS PEOPLE THROUGH MALICE, NEGLIGENCE, AND INCOMPETENCE EVERY YEAR?

SOUNDS A LITTLE FAR-FETCHED TO ME

I GUESS WE'LL NEVER KNOW!

BORS

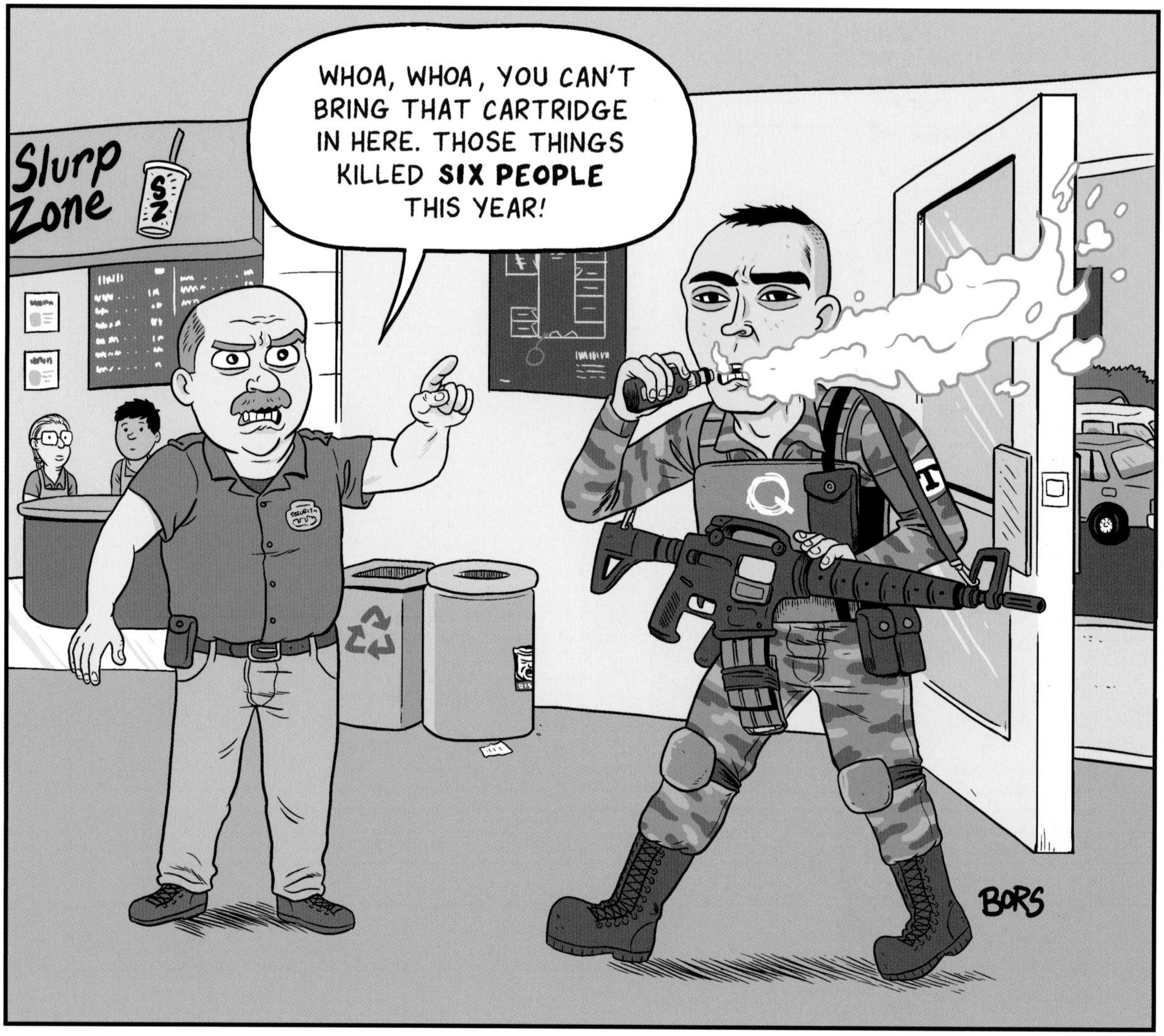
WHOA, WHOA, YOU CAN'T BRING THAT CARTRIDGE IN HERE. THOSE THINGS KILLED **SIX PEOPLE** THIS YEAR!
Slurp Zone
BORS

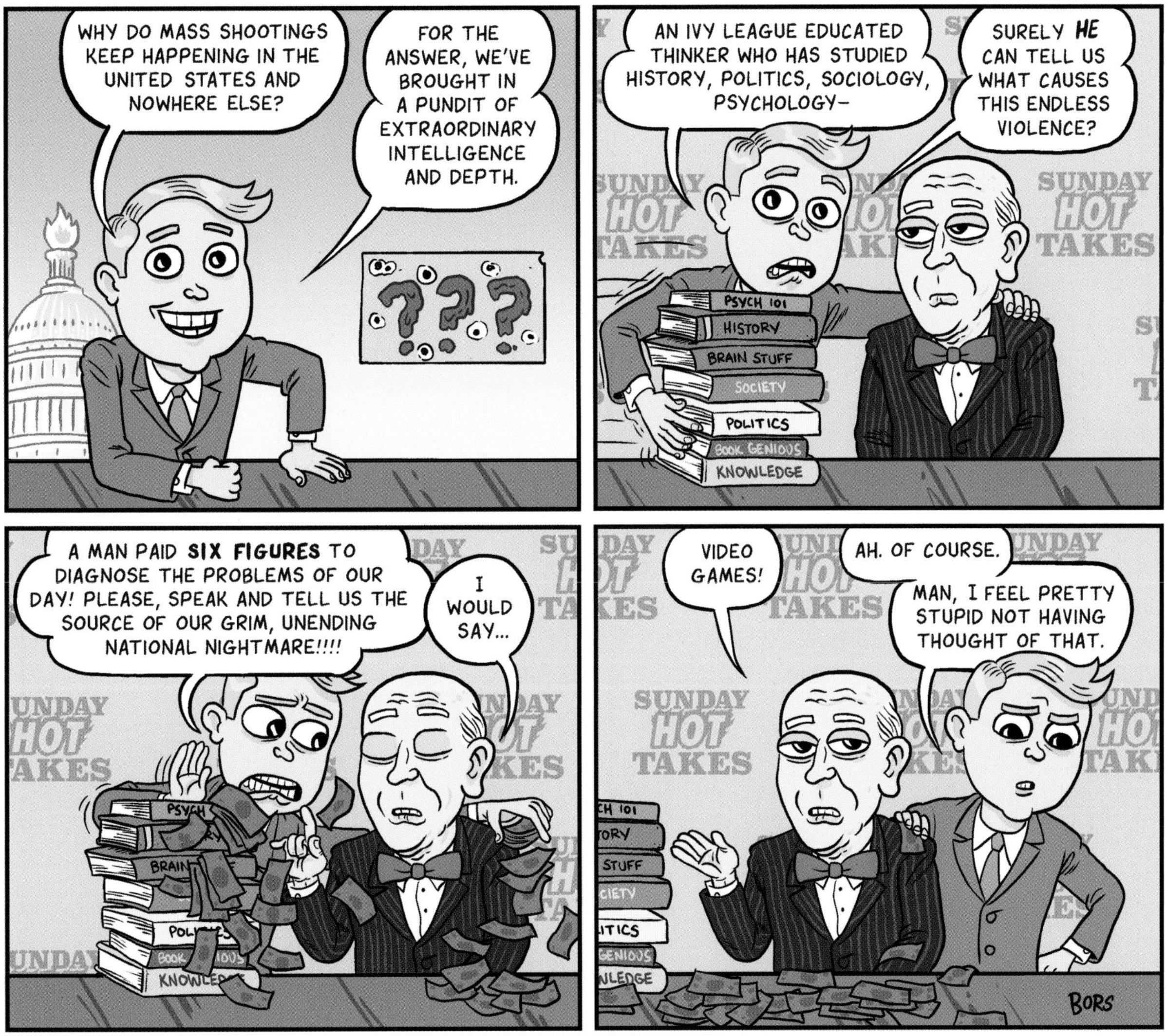
WHY DO MASS SHOOTINGS KEEP HAPPENING IN THE UNITED STATES AND NOWHERE ELSE?
FOR THE ANSWER, WE'VE BROUGHT IN A PUNDIT OF EXTRAORDINARY INTELLIGENCE AND DEPTH.
AN IVY LEAGUE EDUCATED THINKER WHO HAS STUDIED HISTORY, POLITICS, SOCIOLOGY, PSYCHOLOGY–
SURELY HE CAN TELL US WHAT CAUSES THIS ENDLESS VIOLENCE?
SUNDAY HOT TAKES
PSYCH 101
HISTORY
BRAIN STUFF
SOCIETY
POLITICS
BOOK GENIOUS
KNOWLEDGE
A MAN PAID SIX FIGURES TO DIAGNOSE THE PROBLEMS OF OUR DAY! PLEASE, SPEAK AND TELL US THE SOURCE OF OUR GRIM, UNENDING NATIONAL NIGHTMARE!!!!
I WOULD SAY...
VIDEO GAMES!
AH. OF COURSE.
MAN, I FEEL PRETTY STUPID NOT HAVING THOUGHT OF THAT.
BORS

I was in high school during the 1999 Columbine shooting that kicked off the modern era of mass shootings. 20 years later the NRA and their well-paid thought-leader allies are still pushing Mortal Kombat and Marilyn Manson as the true culprits.

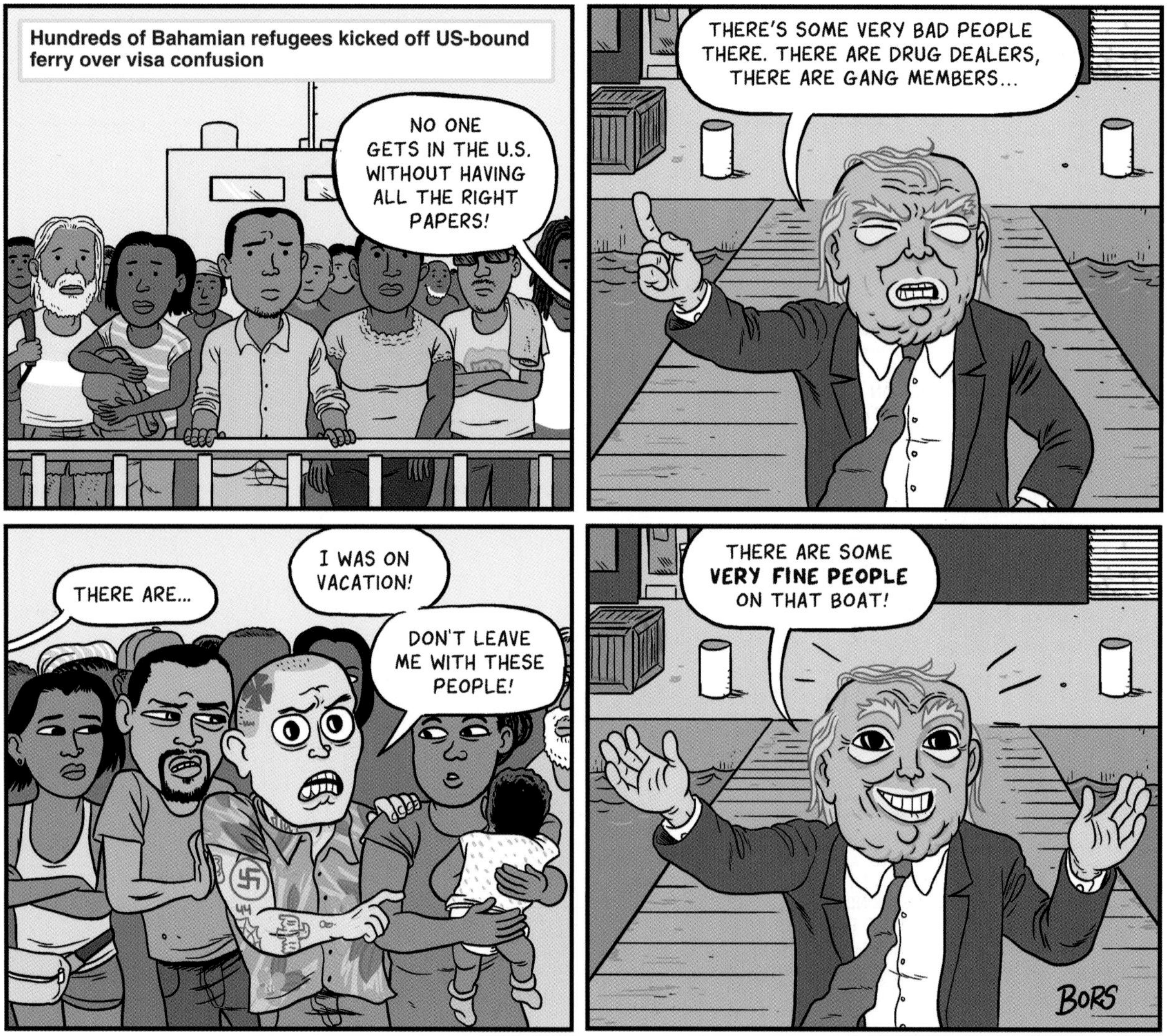
Hundreds of Bahamian refugees kicked off US-bound ferry over visa confusion
NO ONE GETS IN THE U.S. WITHOUT HAVING ALL THE RIGHT PAPERS!
THERE'S SOME VERY BAD PEOPLE THERE. THERE ARE DRUG DEALERS, THERE ARE GANG MEMBERS...
THERE ARE...
I WAS ON VACATION!
DON'T LEAVE ME WITH THESE PEOPLE!
THERE ARE SOME **VERY FINE PEOPLE** ON THAT BOAT!
BORS

When Hurricane Dorian decimated the Bahamas, leaving tens of thousands homeless, refugees were turned away at our shores for having not prepared proper U.S. Visas before having their lives destroyed. Trump cited an insidious plot of unnamed bad dudes to once again sneak into our country.

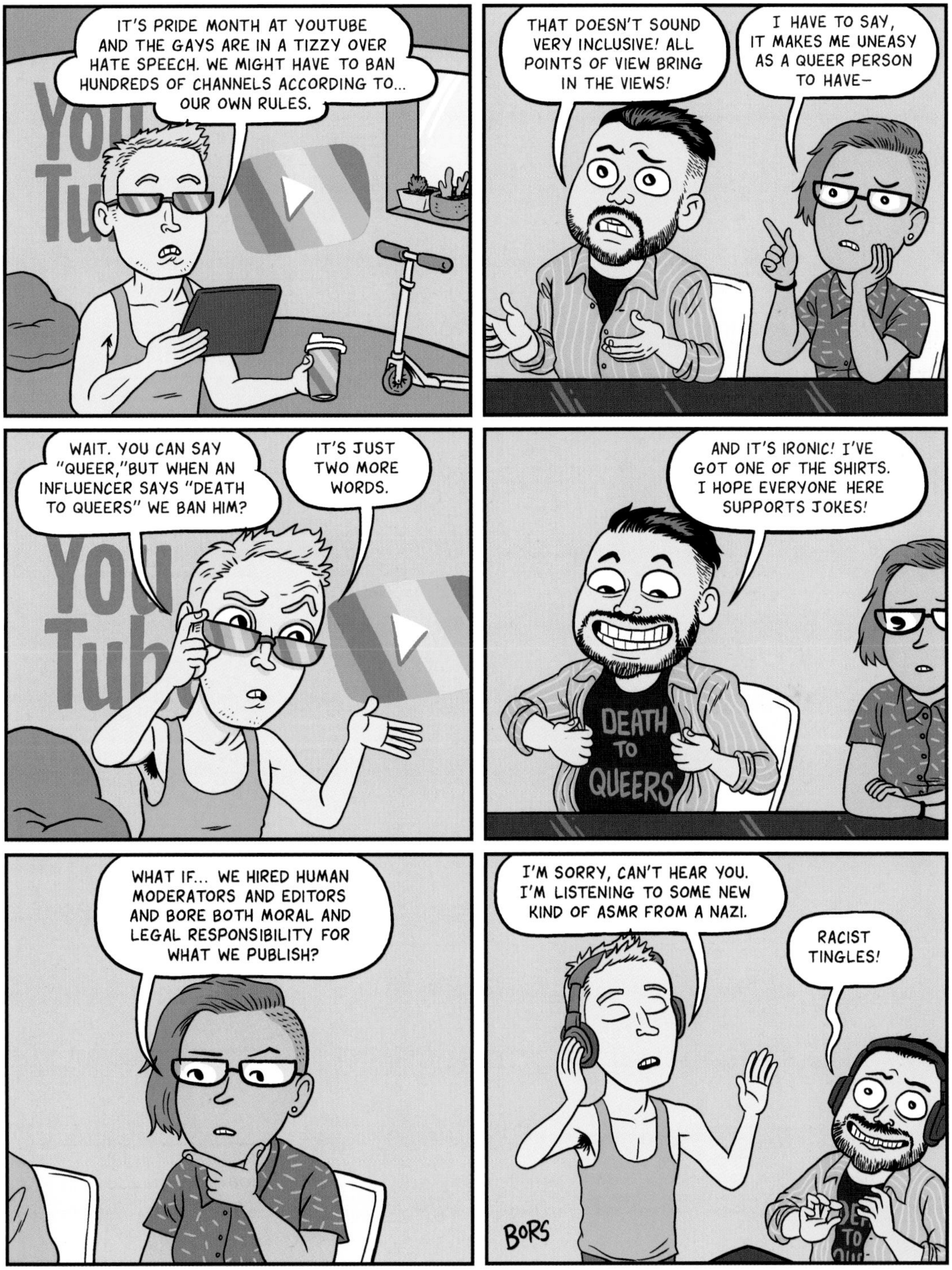

IT'S PRIDE MONTH AT YOUTUBE AND THE GAYS ARE IN A TIZZY OVER HATE SPEECH. WE MIGHT HAVE TO BAN HUNDREDS OF CHANNELS ACCORDING TO... OUR OWN RULES.
THAT DOESN'T SOUND VERY INCLUSIVE! ALL POINTS OF VIEW BRING IN THE VIEWS!
I HAVE TO SAY, IT MAKES ME UNEASY AS A QUEER PERSON TO HAVE–
WAIT. YOU CAN SAY "QUEER," BUT WHEN AN INFLUENCER SAYS "DEATH TO QUEERS" WE BAN HIM?
IT'S JUST TWO MORE WORDS.
AND IT'S IRONIC! I'VE GOT ONE OF THE SHIRTS. I HOPE EVERYONE HERE SUPPORTS JOKES!
DEATH TO QUEERS
WHAT IF... WE HIRED HUMAN MODERATORS AND EDITORS AND BORE BOTH MORAL AND LEGAL RESPONSIBILITY FOR WHAT WE PUBLISH?
I'M SORRY, CAN'T HEAR YOU. I'M LISTENING TO SOME NEW KIND OF ASMR FROM A NAZI.
RACIST TINGLES!
BORS

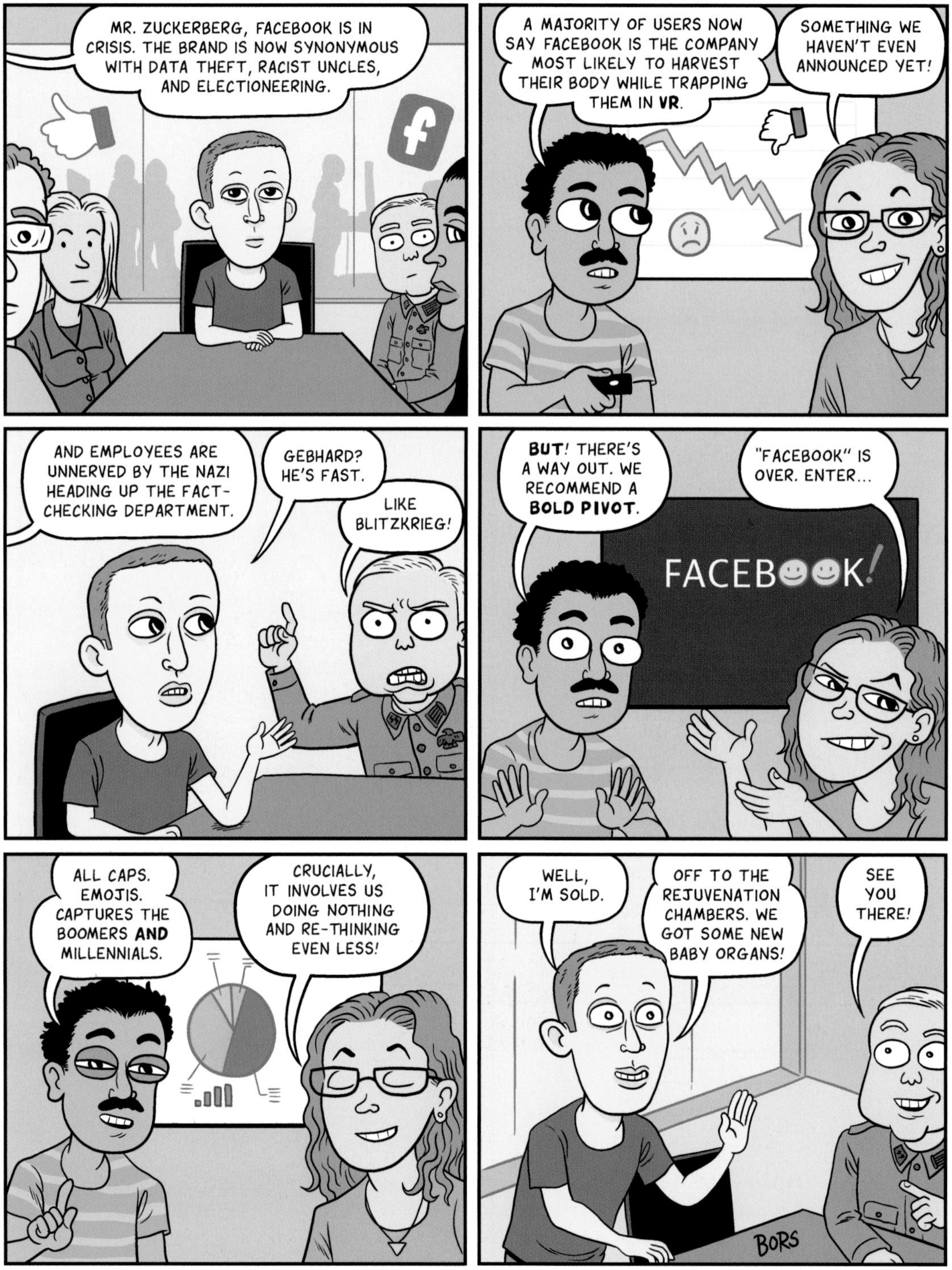
MR. ZUCKERBERG, FACEBOOK IS IN CRISIS. THE BRAND IS NOW SYNONYMOUS WITH DATA THEFT, RACIST UNCLES, AND ELECTIONEERING.
A MAJORITY OF USERS NOW SAY FACEBOOK IS THE COMPANY MOST LIKELY TO HARVEST THEIR BODY WHILE TRAPPING THEM IN **VR**.
SOMETHING WE HAVEN'T EVEN ANNOUNCED YET!
AND EMPLOYEES ARE UNNERVED BY THE NAZI HEADING UP THE FACT-CHECKING DEPARTMENT.
GEBHARD? HE'S FAST.
LIKE BLITZKRIEG!
BUT! THERE'S A WAY OUT. WE RECOMMEND A **BOLD PIVOT**.
"FACEBOOK" IS OVER. ENTER...
FACEBOOK!
ALL CAPS. EMOJIS. CAPTURES THE BOOMERS **AND** MILLENNIALS.
CRUCIALLY, IT INVOLVES US DOING NOTHING AND RE-THINKING EVEN LESS!
WELL, I'M SOLD.
OFF TO THE REJUVENATION CHAMBERS. WE GOT SOME NEW BABY ORGANS!
SEE YOU THERE!
BORS

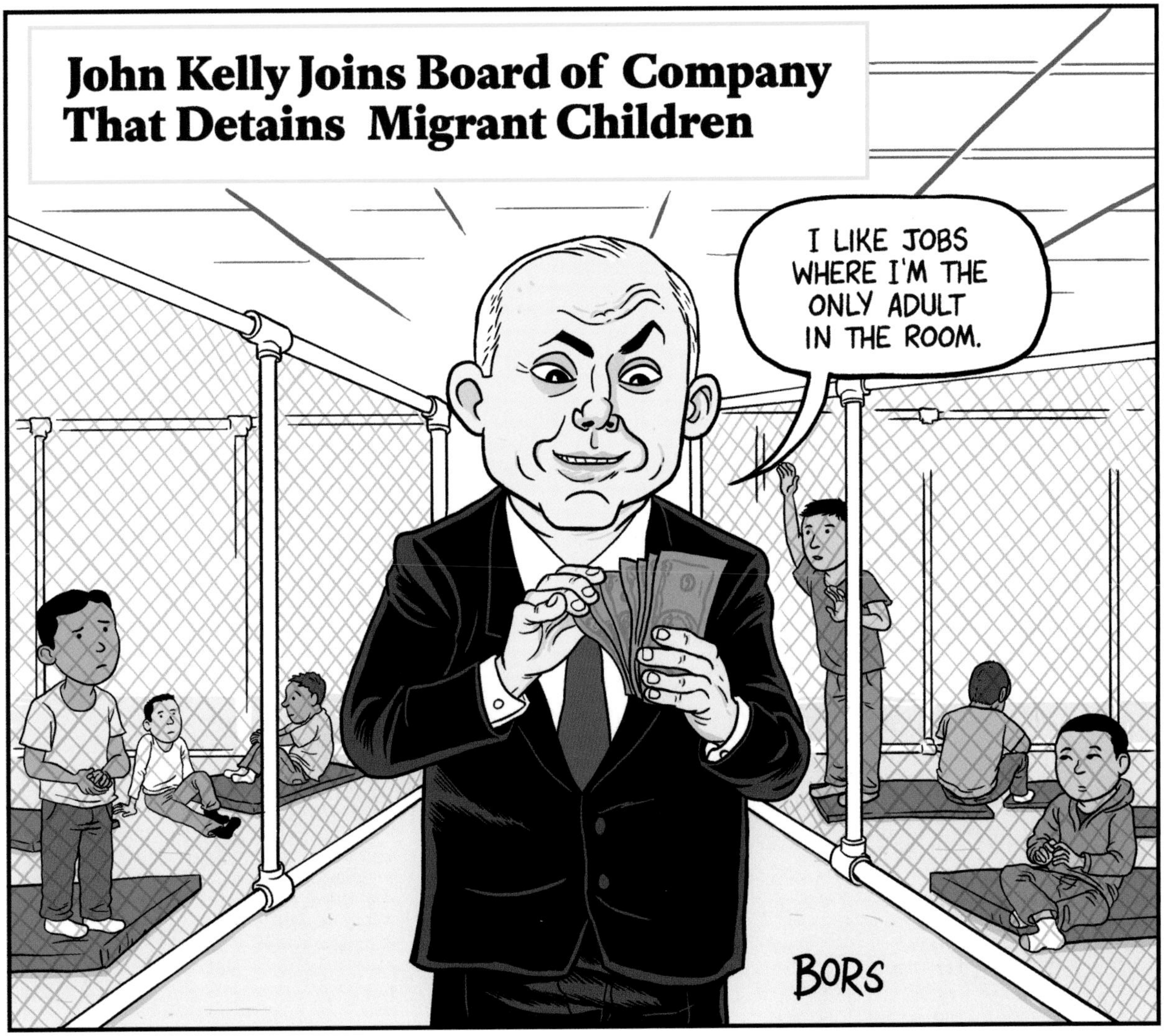
John Kelly Joins Board of Company That Detains Migrant Children
I LIKE JOBS WHERE I'M THE ONLY ADULT IN THE ROOM.
BORS

John Kelly is probably one of the worst Trump administration officials who ever lived. Hailed by the press as bringing order and gravitas to a dysfunctional White House, Kelly helped it operate more effectively and implement its most heinous policy, child separation, which he personally defended. "[The] children will be taken care of," he argued. "Put into foster care or whatever."

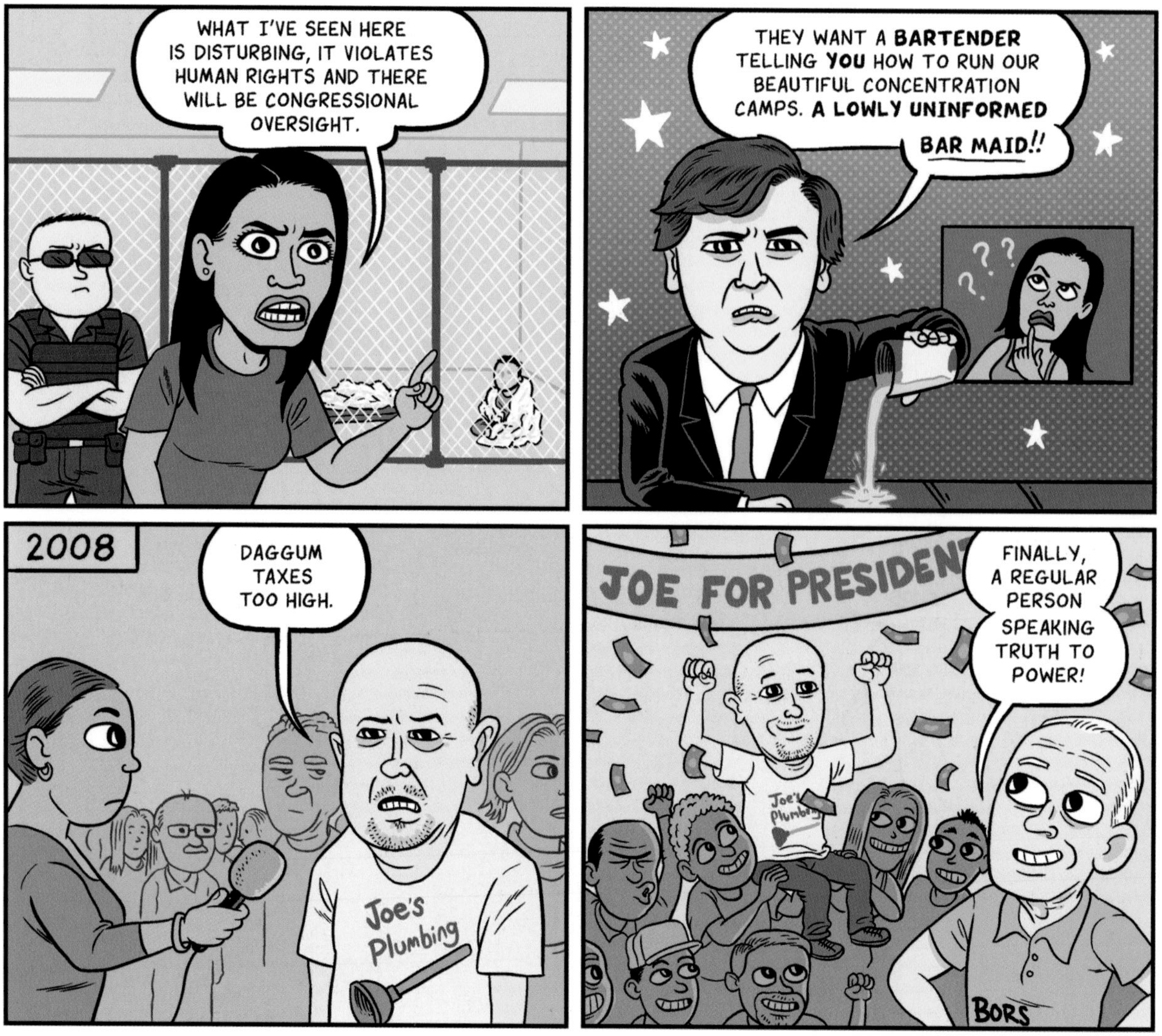
WHAT I'VE SEEN HERE IS DISTURBING, IT VIOLATES HUMAN RIGHTS AND THERE WILL BE CONGRESSIONAL OVERSIGHT.
THEY WANT A BARTENDER TELLING YOU HOW TO RUN OUR BEAUTIFUL CONCENTRATION CAMPS. A LOWLY UNINFORMED
BAR MAID!!
??
2008
DAGGUM TAXES TOO HIGH.
Joe's Plumbing
JOE FOR PRESIDENT
FINALLY, A REGULAR PERSON SPEAKING TRUTH TO POWER!
Joe's Plumbing
BORS

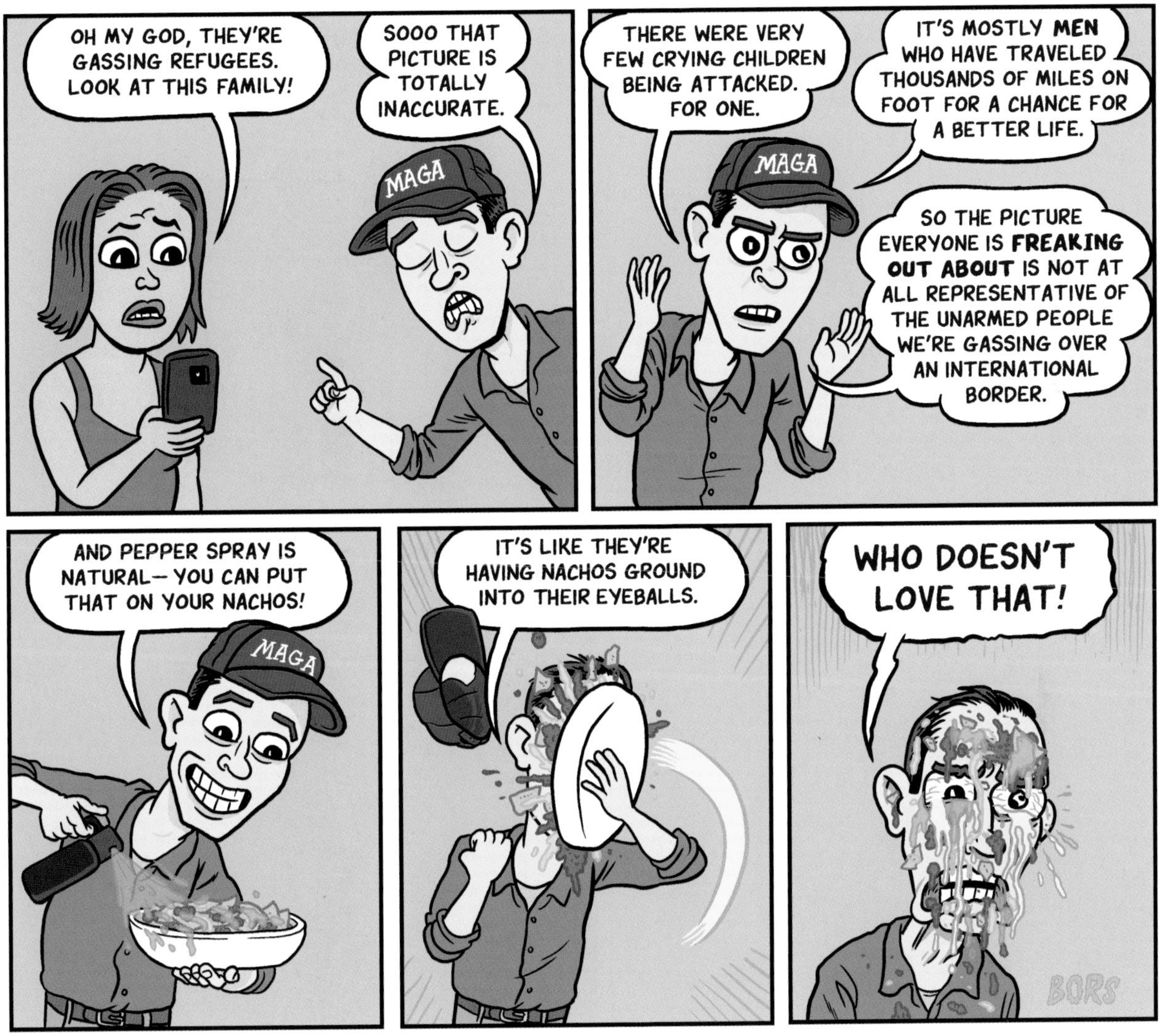
OH MY GOD, THEY'RE GASSING REFUGEES. LOOK AT THIS FAMILY!
SOOO THAT PICTURE IS TOTALLY INACCURATE.
MAGA
THERE WERE VERY FEW CRYING CHILDREN BEING ATTACKED. FOR ONE.
IT'S MOSTLY **MEN** WHO HAVE TRAVELED THOUSANDS OF MILES ON FOOT FOR A CHANCE FOR A BETTER LIFE.
MAGA
SO THE PICTURE EVERYONE IS **FREAKING OUT ABOUT** IS NOT AT ALL REPRESENTATIVE OF THE UNARMED PEOPLE WE'RE GASSING OVER AN INTERNATIONAL BORDER.
AND PEPPER SPRAY IS NATURAL— YOU CAN PUT THAT ON YOUR NACHOS!
MAGA
IT'S LIKE THEY'RE HAVING NACHOS GROUND INTO THEIR EYEBALLS.
WHO DOESN'T LOVE THAT!
BORS

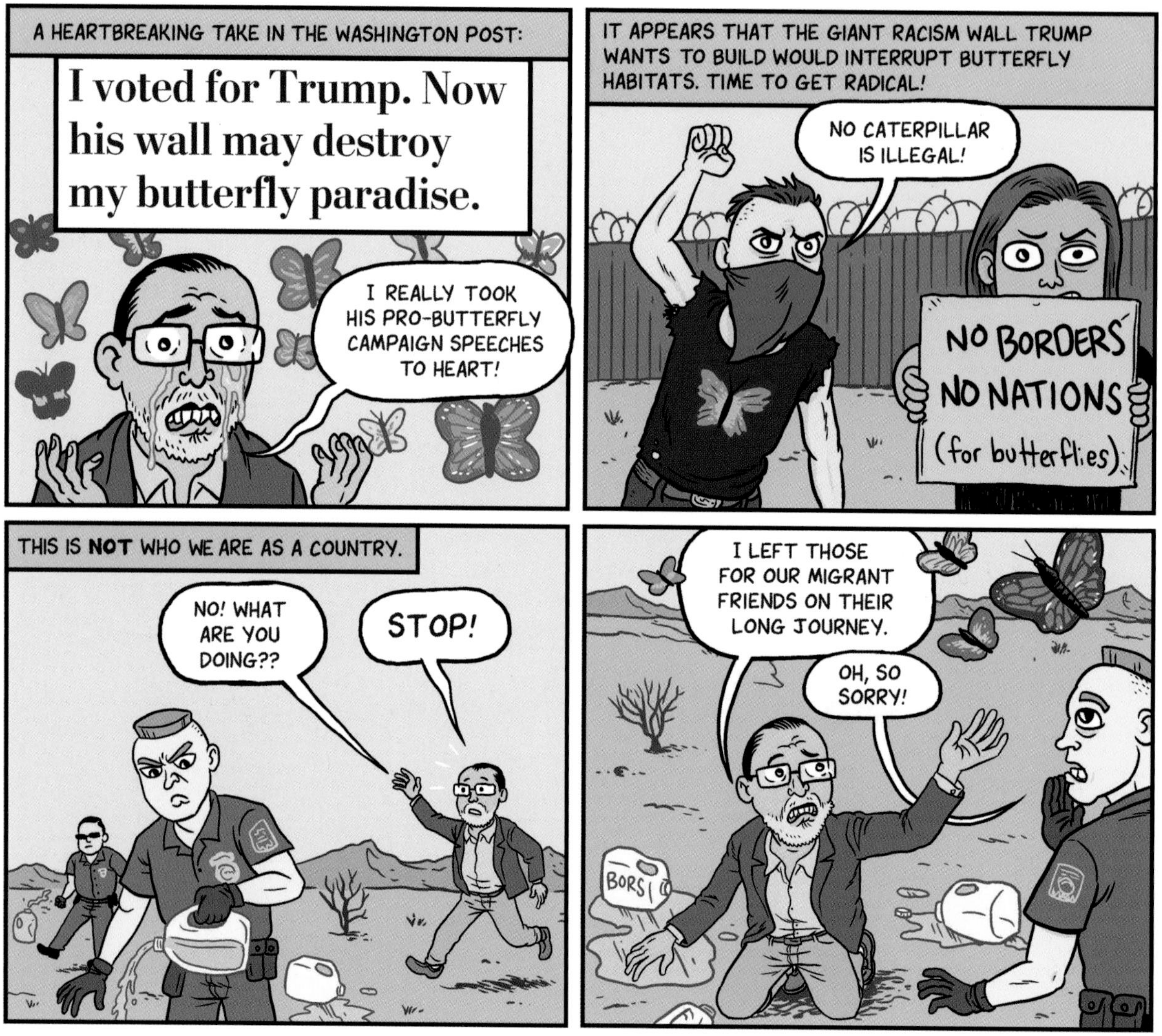
A HEARTBREAKING TAKE IN THE WASHINGTON POST:
I voted for Trump. Now his wall may destroy my butterfly paradise.
I REALLY TOOK HIS PRO-BUTTERFLY CAMPAIGN SPEECHES TO HEART!
IT APPEARS THAT THE GIANT RACISM WALL TRUMP WANTS TO BUILD WOULD INTERRUPT BUTTERFLY HABITATS. TIME TO GET RADICAL!
NO CATERPILLAR IS ILLEGAL!
NO BORDERS NO NATIONS (for butterflies)
THIS IS NOT WHO WE ARE AS A COUNTRY.
NO! WHAT ARE YOU DOING??
STOP!
I LEFT THOSE FOR OUR MIGRANT FRIENDS ON THEIR LONG JOURNEY.
OH, SO SORRY!
BORS

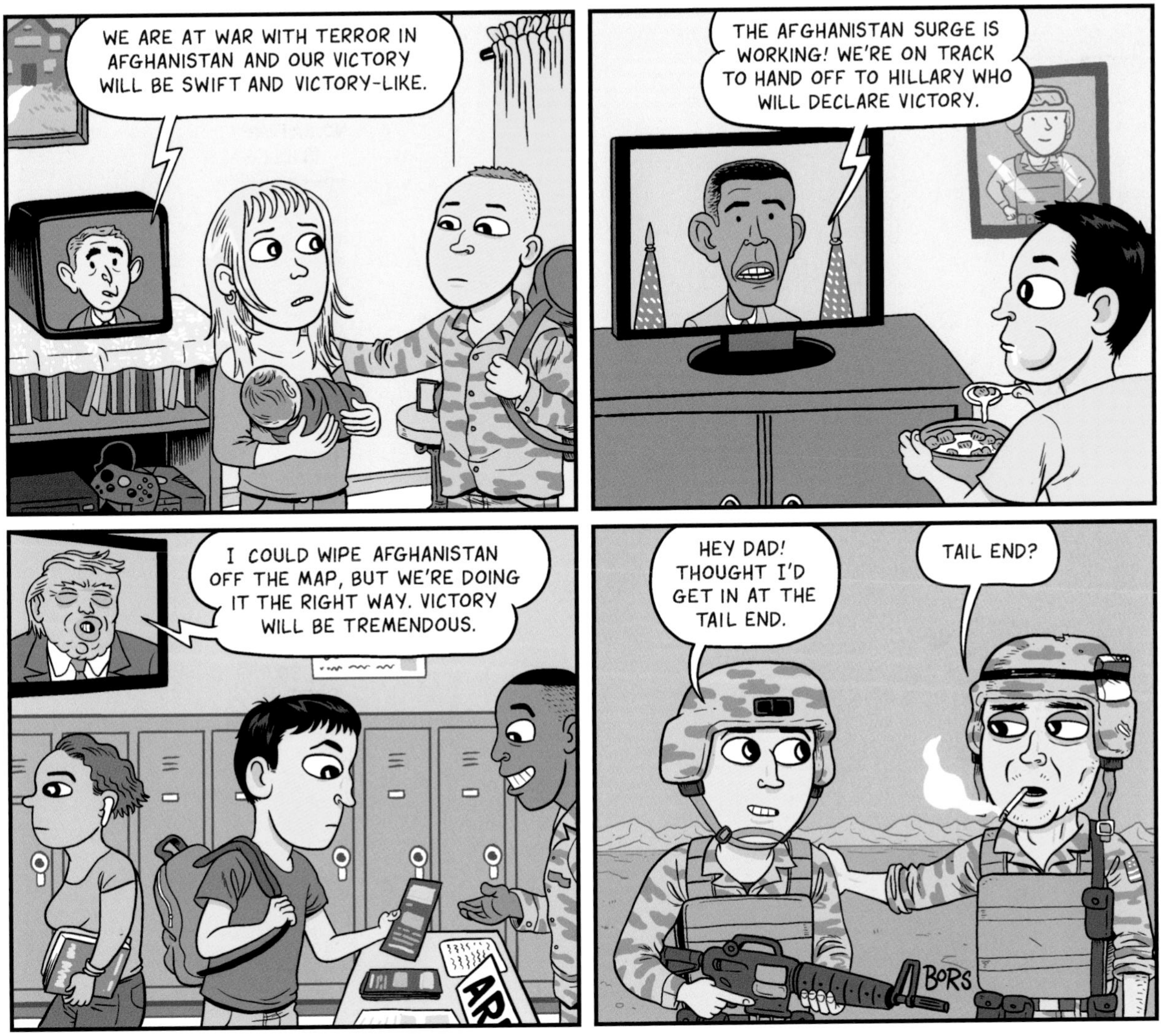
WE ARE AT WAR WITH TERROR IN AFGHANISTAN AND OUR VICTORY WILL BE SWIFT AND VICTORY-LIKE.
THE AFGHANISTAN SURGE IS WORKING! WE'RE ON TRACK TO HAND OFF TO HILLARY WHO WILL DECLARE VICTORY.
I COULD WIPE AFGHANISTAN OFF THE MAP, BUT WE'RE DOING IT THE RIGHT WAY. VICTORY WILL BE TREMENDOUS.
HEY DAD! THOUGHT I'D GET IN AT THE TAIL END.
TAIL END?
BORS

In late 2019, The Washington Post *published documents that showed three administrations over nearly 20 years routinely lied to the American people about the war in Afghanistan, privately believed it unwinnable, and manipulated data to indicate progress when there was none. I assume that in whatever year you are reading this, no one was punished for this and we are still there.*

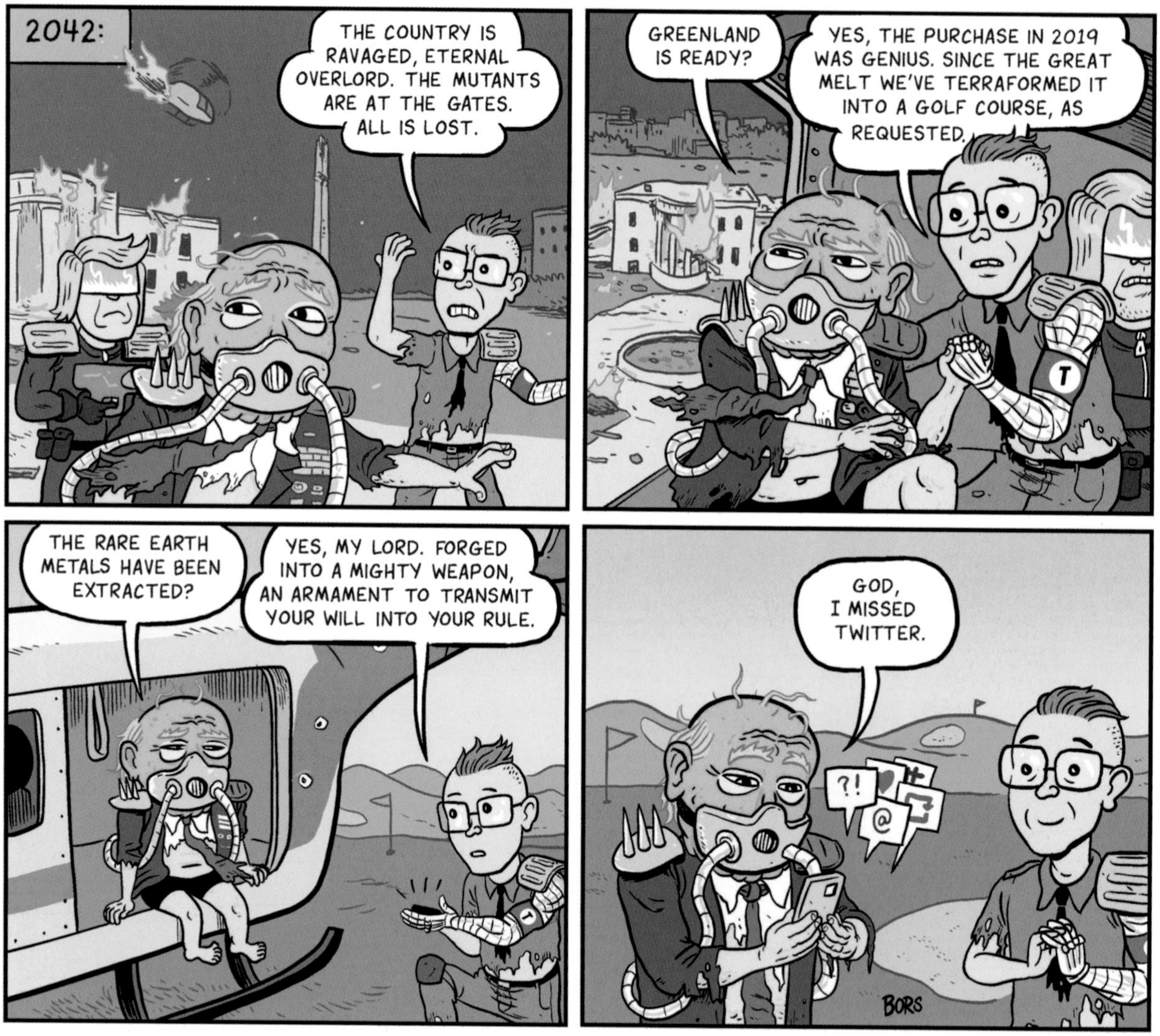
2042:
THE COUNTRY IS RAVAGED, ETERNAL OVERLORD. THE MUTANTS ARE AT THE GATES. ALL IS LOST.
GREENLAND IS READY?
YES, THE PURCHASE IN 2019 WAS GENIUS. SINCE THE GREAT MELT WE'VE TERRAFORMED IT INTO A GOLF COURSE, AS REQUESTED.
THE RARE EARTH METALS HAVE BEEN EXTRACTED?
YES, MY LORD. FORGED INTO A MIGHTY WEAPON, AN ARMAMENT TO TRANSMIT YOUR WILL INTO YOUR RULE.
GOD, I MISSED TWITTER.
?!
@
BORS

Trump just randomly insisted he was buying Greenland at one point.

Biography

Photo: Kathleen Marie Barnett

Matt Bors is an editor and cartoonist based in Portland, Oregon. His work has appeared in *The Nation*, *The Guardian*, *The Village Voice*, and dozens of other print and web publications, many now defunct due to the vagaries of the market. He was a 2012 Pulitzer Prize Finalist and Herblock Prize winner for his political cartoons, which were collected in the book *Life Begins at Incorporation*. He also drew the graphic novel *War Is Boring* with author David Axe. In 2013 he founded The Nib, a publication for political and non-fiction cartooning that has expanded into an award-winning print magazine.

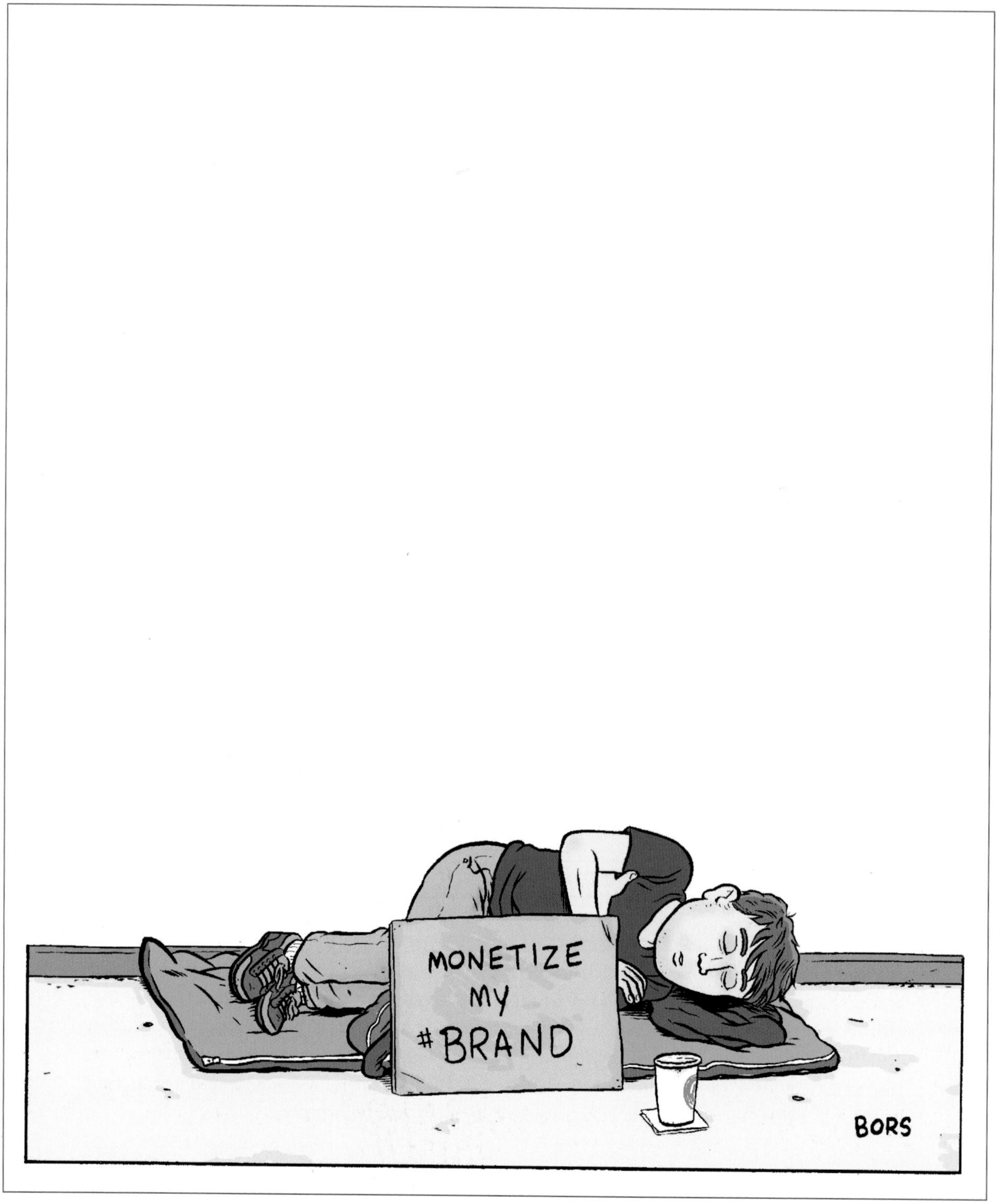
MONETIZE
MY
#BRAND
BORS